SEARCHING FOR TILLY

SEARCHING
FOR TILLY

Susan Sallis

BANTAM PRESS

LONDON · TORONTO · SYDNEY · AUCKLAND · JOHANNESBURG

TRANSWORLD PUBLISHERS
61–63 Uxbridge Road, London W5 5SA
a division of The Random House Group Ltd
www.booksattransworld.co.uk

First published in Great Britain
in 2007 by Bantam Press
a division of Transworld Publishers

A CIP catalogue record for this book
is available from the British Library.

ISBN 9780593058541

Addresses for Random House Group Ltd companies outside the UK
can be found at: www.randomhouse.co.uk
The Random House Group Ltd Reg. No. 954009

The Random House Group Ltd makes every effort to ensure that the papers
used in its books are made from trees that have been legally sourced from
well-managed and credibly certified forests. Our paper procurement
policy can be found at: www.randomhouse.co.uk/paper.htm

Typeset in 12/14pt New Baskerville by
Kestrel Data, Exeter, Devon.

Printed and bound in the UK by
CPI Mackays, Chatham ME5 8TD

2 4 6 8 10 9 7 5 3 1

In memory of my mother-in-law, Jane,
who walked from Brighton to Cheltenham with
her mother and sister in the 1890s

One

Tilly was the dreamer in the Quince family. Her mother insisted that one of her 'spells' always came on when there was work to do but her father understood they were triggered by some special sight. ''Tis awe and wonder, Bessie,' he would tell his wife. 'Awe and wonder at God's work. Don't stop our girl from that.'

'She dun't get no spell when she's in chapel!' Bessie would protest.

'Sometimes she do. And 'tis something no one else do get, my love. This be pure worship.' He wanted to tell her that the difference between his middle child and his wife was the same difference as that between Mary and Martha. But he did not. Bessie could be sharp at times. Instead he inclined his head towards the garden, full of fat winter cabbage at the time. 'See out there, my lovely Bessie. What do you see?'

'I see our winter dinners. I see rain what will be turning to snow before long. I see a lot of mud which will be trod into my kitchen, prob'ly by Tilly 'erself—'

'An' what d'you suppose Tilly do see?' He was grinning at her, turning her so that her back was to the fire, lifting her draggled skirt to warm her bare calves. She could feel herself going soft against him.

'God's green cushions a-watered by 'is blessed tears . . .' She started to laugh and he kissed her and then nuzzled his face into her neck. She let it go, loving it in one way, frightened of it in another.

7

'With my body I thee worship . . .' he whispered into her ear as he undid the rope that kirtled her sacking apron around her waist. She let it fall but held his hand still. 'No more children, John Quince. You did promise me. No more children.'

'No more children, wife. I did promise you.' He could have been murmuring anything, she knew that and began to struggle. 'I love you, Bessie Quince. I love you with my heart and my soul and my body . . . my hands and arms and eyes and mouth . . .' He did. And she was no match for him. She wept for love of him. She could not find words like he could, but she could cry tears and she could return his kisses and make it easy for him.

They heard Tilly scraping her boots at the back door and John Quince lifted his Bessie and carried her into the wash house and put his back to the door while he went on kissing her.

'My apron—' she gasped, still turned to melting butter by this man of hers who was sometimes a stranger.

For some reason this made him laugh and he let her go so that she stumbled back against the copper set in its brick furnace. The dolly went flying and Tilly's voice called anxiously, 'Ma, be 'ee all right?'

''Course I be all right.' Bessie did not mean to sound so irritable; Alice would not worry if she thought her mother was scalded to death in the wash house and as for Billy Boy – still her baby at six years old – he would squawk the place about their ears but make no enquiry. It was dreaming Tilly who would want to know what she was doing in the wash room when it weren't a Monday and why her sacking apron was thrown so carelessly on the hearth.

Sure enough Tilly raised her voice again. 'Ma, your apron be a'most in the fire! And why you doing washing today?'

Bessie jerked open the door and went into the kitchen. 'The wise don't never ask why's,' she snapped as she snatched back her apron and kirtled it too tightly, so that she could barely breathe. 'Get that kettle pushed into the

8

coals, my girl. Your pa is home early from the pit and will want a wash down.'

Tilly's face cleared. 'Ah. I see. Where is he?'

'In the wash house, where does 'ee think? Leave 'im be for five minutes.'

But Tilly pushed at the kettle inexpertly and went straight to the door.

'Pa, did you see the rainbow?' she called through it. 'It were different today. It had a green in it. And a red, 'cept that Mr Tompkins did call it magenta. In't that nice, Pa? Magenta. I do like that word.'

He was still laughing. Bessie could have murdered him but she could not help her mouth curving into a smile. Her body felt blessed by his hands and she was different herself; special. Worshipped. He had said worshipped. She was worshipped. Her smile grew. God was worshipped. Was she God? She clapped her hand over her mouth in terror. Such a thought was blasphemy and would be punished. God knew every thought in her head however much she tried to obliterate them.

John Quince, her husband, spluttered through the wash-house door, 'If we should 'ave another girl, our Tilly, would you like to call her that name – whatever you did say . . . Maggie what?'

Tilly knew well when her father was teasing her and she started to splutter too. Bessie thought irritably that they sounded identical and frivolous. The minister at Bethesda down Trevose way had condemned frivolity. 'A frivolous woman is as hollow as a sounding cymbal!' he had declared. He had not mentioned a frivolous man.

Tilly held her side. 'Magenta, Pa! Madge Enta.'

'Right. Madge Enta it shall be!' pronounced John Quince magisterially.

And Bessie had known right then that she was in fact pregnant and it would be another girl. Tears of sheer terror flooded her eyes. Another birth, more pain, more sickening weakness just when there was extra work to be done, less money; worse than any of those was the fear

9

of another death. There had been two dead babies before Alice and another two before Billy Boy came along and clung tenaciously to life. Eighteen years of marriage, seven children and only three to show for it. And now . . . what?

Tilly was there by her side. 'Ma, what is it? Is it a pain? Why's you crying?'

She pushed her aside. 'I heard Billy Boy. I'll go up and fetch him. Put a pinch more tea in the pot and top it up. I'll be down directly.'

But of course John Quince, who had ears like jug handles when needed, was out of the wash house like a long dog, no shirt, braces over his copper-red shoulders, sweeping her up in his arms and climbing the loft ladder as if she weighed a farthing. He lifted the trap with the top of his head, pushed her through and slid after her, then called down to Tilly to watch for her sister and give her some hot tea as soon as she came through the door. Then he closed the trap and cradled Bessie's head and started the kissing again. But it took him a long time to kiss away her tears.

Alice Quince was thirteen – fourteen come Easter – and was a balmaid down at Wheal Three Legs on the Trevose road. The maids worked at the mine entrance, sorting, washing, spotting the red copper in the rock. Alice had not reached that stage of expertise yet and she was a run-for-your-money girl, kilting her skirt and splashing through the mud to the wagons and back again, paid a shilling a day – which was better than Wheal Trevithick – and sharing her pasty with the ponies or one of the snotty-nosed urchins who ran around their mothers' heels begging for food. She was Bessie's favourite girl – obviously Billy Boy superseded both of them but that was how it should be. Alice was pretty and practical too. Her five shillings each week made a difference to the family's comfort. Bessie herself worked the morning shift, splitting the ore with an enormous hammer and revealing the copper. Alice cooked up the

10

oats and added bee sugar and milk, made certain Tilly had her school slate and a cob of bread for midday, flannelled Billy Boy's face and hands, secured the fireguard and set him down to play till his mother came home. If her father was on a later shift she would get him up before she went too. She was a good girl; you could rely on Alice. Not a bit like Tilly.

The morning after the incident in the wash house, when it seemed as if the whole world was drowning in rain, Tilly and Alice set forth before Bessie got home. They wore enormous sou'westers which almost covered their shoulders; their shawls were crossed over their shirts and the ends pinned at the back of their waists; and rickety boots gleaned from the miners' relief fund chafed their bare feet. Three yards from the cottage door their skirt hems were soggy with water. Their father called, 'Lift your skirts, my maids! You be getting soaked!' But their hands were tucked well inside their shawls and they pretended not to hear.

The cliff path was treacherous with liquid mud which ran from every adit that Wheal Three Legs possessed.

'I wouldn't want to be down there today.' Tilly shuddered. 'All the walls a-running and cold like a grave.'

''Tisn't like that,' Alice said comfortingly. ''Tis the dryest place you could find on a day like this. And it will be warm. The walls is sweating, you see.'

'You never been down,' Tilly objected.

'Pa told me. Often. We must never worry about him. He said he felt like a rabbit in a burrow. 'Specially in bad weather.'

'Did he really say that?' Tilly was entranced. She could see it in her head, the men fitting into the shaft, eyes bright, noses sensitive to the slightest smell, ears attuned to the sounds of the earth. 'Mother earth,' she murmured into the brim of her sou'wester.

Alice gave a small laugh. 'You talking about Ma? Reckon you're right, our Tilly. Ma can be kind an' 'ard too when she 'as to be. I'd know that,' she commented without any

11

kind of criticism. She knew she was her mother's favourite, but she never used that knowledge. She was certain that Tilly was unaware of it and she did all she could to hide it from the younger girl. She said now, soberly, 'She 'asn't been the same since Billy Boy.'

Tilly looked up and a drop of rain fell on her nose. 'He isn't no trouble. And she loves him very much.'

Alice looked back. 'You've got a dewdrop, our Tilly. Get your rag and wipe it off.' But she herself stopped, fished out the rag that was pinned to Tilly's bodice and wiped the rain away. She put her face as close to her sister's as the sou'wester brims allowed and said quietly, 'Too many babies, our Till. Just you remember that when you've grown.'

Tilly looked surprised. 'There's only us three. Mrs Baker at the Miner's Lamp has got fourteen and another one on the way!'

'Who told you that?'

'Iris Stevens. Her ma is the midwife down at Tregeagle.'

'Yes . . .' Alice thought a moment then added, 'Mrs Baker is a different kettle of fish. She's strong as a horse. Ma isn't like that. Anyway she's had seven babies, our Tilly. I've told you that before. The others died.'

That set Tilly off on one of her 'rambles'. She wanted to know what their names were, boy or girl, fair or dark . . . 'I can't believe that we've got four brothers. Or sisters. Or two of each. Or one sister and three brothers. Or—'

'Don't go on so, Tilly. And don't say anything to Ma about it. It hurts her.'

Tilly was silent then said, 'She told you?'

'Yes. But I'm the eldest and I helped her with Billy Boy.' Alice spoke shortly. She had been seven years old and absolutely terrified. She thought she might manage better now but she was very sure that she would never have any babies herself.

The girls separated at the school and Alice pulled her hat right down over her face and went back along the cliff path alone to the mine. Tilly stood on the bottom rung of the school gate and let Jacko Miles swing her into the yard. Raindrops flew off the back of her hat and there were screams and giggles and then the school bell clanged from the porch and they shuffled into lines; one for the little children and one for the senior. Tilly had been in the seniors for a whole year now and took her place next to Philip Radjel, who should have been down the mine, as he was almost thirteen; but he had a weak chest and the mine captain said it wasn't worth taking him on for the time he had left. So Mr Tompkins, the schoolmaster, let him stay at school and used him to keep the garden tidy at the schoolhouse, and wash the floor when anyone vomited or – and this was Philip's favourite thing – help Miss Casson with the little ones. He had told Tilly that he wanted to be a teacher when he was old enough. Tilly had said nothing. She knew he would be an angel.

They filed in; Tilly hung her shawl and sou'wester on a hook labelled with a yellow and orange crayoned quince, coloured on her first day at school five years before. She had been one of the first to use the fat wax pencils sent by Sir Geoffrey Bassett, who had been anxious for the Reverend Carridon to approve his second marriage before his first wife was actually dead. The Reverend came to school once a week to conduct an orthodox service and had graciously demonstrated to the children the various colours. Purple, crimson, yellow and orange; blue, green and – excitingly – black. But no gold, which was the colour of quinces. So he had suggested streaks of yellow and orange. And there they were. She had loved the Reverend Carridon from that day and vowed she would be buried in the churchyard at Tregeagle.

They stood behind their long desks and waited in silence for Mr Tompkins to walk in from his study and take over from Miss Casson who stood before them, smiling slightly at Philip Radjel, then straightening her face in case Jacko Miles thought the smile was for him. Mr Tompkins had told her on numerous occasions not to 'encourage' Jacko Miles.

The hymn that morning was 'Eternal Father strong to save', which Tilly found frightening. The sea was frightening. Even in the summer she saw its glitter as menacing. And God's arm did not calm the restless wave however much they prayed and sang about it. But the tune was good and Miss Casson managed the harmonium extremely well. The big clock on the wall above Mr Tompkins's raised desk showed that it was nine thirty. Pa's shift started at ten o'clock and he was always early. He would be standing by the engine house talking to Dick Stevens. She smiled to herself.

They prayed – standing up because Mr Tompkins couldn't bear the fuss made by twenty-four children getting down on their knees – for fishermen, farmers and miners. The miners came last, Tilly noticed. Then they said Our Father, then Mr Tompkins and Miss Casson went halfway down the room and dragged across the screen which divided the juniors from the seniors, and the day began.

It was mid-morning and Tilly's stomach was rumbling, and her thoughts were concentrating on the bread cob in her pocket and completely by-passing the long-division sum on her slate. She would have put her hand down and tried to pinch off a corner of the bread except that when she had done so before, Mr Tompkins had known instantly what was going on and had taken away the cob so that she went hungry until she got home. Even so her hand went into her pocket without any conscious command from her and, as if on a clockwork neck, Mr Tompkins's head swivelled in her direction. And then it happened: God did intervene. The earth moved; the school moved; the dividing screen jumped up and hit the ceiling, and plaster snowed upon the children.

Jacko Miles yelled, 'Earthquake!' and from next door Philip Radjel could be heard saying, 'It's all right, Miss Casson . . .' and then the sound came to them: overpoweringly loud, yet somehow muffled, an explosion.

They all knew what it was. They stood stock still, glued to their benches, staring at Mr Tompkins; from next door the little ones could be heard starting to cry. The sound had barely died away when the hooter sounded. Above that, above the sound of the rain, someone screamed. Tilly knew it was her scream when Jacko Miles took her hand and held it tightly.

Mr Tompkins strode down their half of the room and took hold of the screen, pushing it back on his own, having to shove hard when it got stuck. When they could all see each other, he picked up one of the weeping eight-year-old girls and carried her back to his desk. Her legs were bound with rags and they dripped miserably on to the floor; she had wetted herself. He sat her on his desk and encircled her with a protective arm.

'Children, listen to me. Stop crying, Carrie. I want you to listen to what I have to say.'

He waited, and gradually Carrie stopped crying and the other children watched him with terrible apprehension.

He said, 'There's been some kind of accident. That is why the hooter is sounding. It must be at Wheal Three Legs. Some of you have fathers in that mine. You will be anxious about them. I want you to go home in an orderly fashion. You will go quietly and fetch your outdoor things, put them on in here and walk home – do not run. If anybody needs me, I shall be in the schoolhouse and Miss Casson will stay in the school itself. You will know where to find us.' He looked around. 'I don't doubt that God will spare all the miners whatever has happened. But your families will need you now.'

He glanced at Miss Casson and she took over the exodus, helped by Philip Radjel. Jacko Miles was at the gate, tugging it open, swinging on it so that it crashed against the school wall. The children poured out. Tilly took to the cliff path, holding in her mind the picture of her father, safe in his burrow like a rabbit. The rain hit her hard. It came from the sea, beneath which the long arm of Three Legs cautiously explored for the precious red copper. She must not imagine that.

She was almost home when a second tremor hit the soles

of her feet and convulsed her legs and body. And then the crunch of another explosion. She stopped in her tracks and turned to face the sea. 'You can't have him!' she shouted. 'You've got to save him . . . save him . . . please save him!'

Something happened. She did not at first know what it was. And then she looked down at her shawl and saw the flakes of snow settling in the folds.

That day the Armistice was signed.

Two

The three women were sitting in the old parlour of Widdowe's Cottage with the French doors wide open to the garden sloping down towards the sea. It was too hot for comfort; the coastal footpath ran past the end of the garden and the head of the occasional walker moved slowly and carefully along the top of the escallonia hedge. None of the walkers glanced their way: their sights were set on the cove below, with its incoming tide and towering rocks offering some shade. The three women looked their way now and then but without much interest.

Of the three, Jenna was obviously the youngest. With her brown hair carelessly looped into a rubber band at the back of her head, she could have passed for eighteen – until the sun caught the planes of her face and revealed the skin, stretched so tightly over her bones that it showed too much of her skull. Her brown eyes had been moving slowly between her mother and her aunt, not always seeing them. But now her aunt was speaking and Jenna stared at her with disbelief.

Jenna's mother, Caroline, was fifty-two and could easily have been her older sister. Her brown hair was threaded with grey but well cut in an ear-length bob and her eyes saw most things but gave nothing away. At that moment she too stared incredulously.

Laura, on the other hand, twelve years her senior, looked older than sixty-four. She was clearly an outdoors woman: her hands were rough with gardening, her face

17

burned by the sun. Her short straight hair was white and nearly unkempt. She had been blonde and beautiful and her eyes still reminded the others of her old self. They were startlingly violet-coloured, large and full of dreams. She had just announced that they were going to start knitting squares for Oxfam. It was 9 August – 'one of the dog days' as she had pointed out – and they had to do something.

'We could sunbathe,' Caroline protested, but without enthusiasm.

'I mean, we have to *do* something,' Laura emphasized.

'But knitting?' Jenna's inward stare focused in astonishment. 'We don't *like* knitting. Do we?'

'What *do* we like?' Laura returned the look with interest.

Jenna said nothing and seemed to be drifting back to her thoughts. Caroline said, 'Well . . . we could try a three-handed reading group. Perhaps.'

Laura beamed. 'That's excellent, darling. We'll do that too. And we'll sunbathe too, Caro. And we'll cook.'

Caroline said with just a touch of sarcasm, 'Why don't you draw up a timetable, Laura?'

Laura continued to smile. 'I will. We don't have to stick to it of course, but it would help.' She glanced at Jenna meaningfully. 'We have to make new lives. And if we don't organize ourselves we might go right off the rails. Which would be a pity.'

Caroline followed her sister-in-law's gaze and, after a second, nodded.

'We can try.' She managed a wry smile. 'But honestly, Laura . . . knitting.'

Laura nodded too, a congratulatory nod. 'I know. But I was in Oxfam yesterday. D'you remember Madge Appleton, lived next door to Geoff and me when we came to Cornwall first? She works there on Mondays and she rushed out to ask how we were. And she was knitting – yes, even as she rushed out!'

Caroline laughed; Jenna appeared not to hear. Laura went on, 'They need blanket squares. I bought wool and

18

needles and jotted down the instructions and . . . here we are!'

Jenna surfaced and smiled briefly. 'How long will it take?'

'To knit a square? The rate we shall go, probably a week.' Laura smiled at her niece but Jenna's brown eyes widened and her face stretched so that it looked as if it might split.

'I don't think I could bear that.'

Caroline said swiftly, 'Take a turn round the garden, Jen. Laura and I noticed a handsome toad under one of the stones on the gravel patch. See if he's still there.'

Jenna made for the wide-open French doors. As she moved out of earshot, Caroline turned towards her brother's widow and said in a low voice, 'Darling, I know your intentions but you're going too fast. The accident happened two months ago. Jeremy was killed – she lost her *husband*, Laura. You and I know about being widowed. She was sitting next to him in the car, they skidded on that oil patch, went into the crash barrier, she had some bruises. Don't you think she may well be wishing . . .' She stopped because Laura's gasp was a small scream.

'Of course I know what she is wishing, Caro! Of *course* . . . You probably wished it when Steve was killed. When Geoff was dying I wanted to go with him . . . I know I did. But life has to go on, darling – we know that too. And you told me it was Jen herself who wanted to come down here until she was fit for work again.'

Caroline patted her sister-in-law's arm. 'It was, Laura.' She made a small face. 'That was probably because un-diluted mum all the time was a bit too much for her!' She tried to laugh. 'And I'm the first to agree with you about life going on, even when it's the last thing we want.' She drew a deep breath, then expelled it with another forced laugh. 'But blanket squares? You want us to take up knitting blanket squares? You can see she's not up to it.'

Laura looked up from her lap where several balls of wool

nestled expectantly. Her eyes were wide. She had actually cast on some stitches and managed two or three rows.

'Oh Caro, I'm so sorry! You always tell me I blunder in where angels fear to tread. It's just that I want so much to rescue her from that awful place she's in, when her eyes go like a seal's with a caul of total misery over them. I wanted to do something.'

Caroline put an impulsive hand over the knitting. 'Dearest Laura. Geoff's been dead for . . . how long?'

'Fifteen years and eight and a half months,' Laura said promptly.

Caroline swallowed; it came out so pat . . . fifteen years, eight and a half months . . . a generation ago, an age to most people, obviously not to Laura.

'Can you remember anything from the first four months?'

Laura blinked. 'I try not to remember. It's all a bit of a fog.'

'Yes. It was the same for me when Steve was killed.' Caroline sighed. 'You have to fumble about a bit, don't you? And that feeling of being alone—'

'Jen's not alone, Caro. She's got you.' She paused and added in a smaller voice, '. . . and me, for what that's worth.'

'She knows that, of course she does. You've always been another mother to her, Laura. Better than me at times.' She shook her head wryly when Laura protested. 'It's true, my dear. She often resents me, I can feel it. If I told her that I know what she is going through, she would hate me for it – my grief is nothing like her grief. I accept that. But if you said it to her, Laura, it would be different.' Again she shook her head as Laura protested vigorously. 'Look, it doesn't matter, my dear. I know that you are important to her – all right, both of us are important to her . . . that hasn't changed. It's everything else that has changed. She needs us. But we still cannot share her grief. It's personal. It's private. She's *got* to be alone with it. You can see how she shuts herself off – the seal's caul as you so aptly put it.'

She removed her hand and put it carefully on to the arm of her chair. 'You were the same,' she went on in a new, matter-of-fact voice. 'Coming down here all on your own. Wouldn't let Steve and me visit you.' She shook her head at the protests. 'All right. You couldn't stop us when we turned up but you never let us stay a night. You never let Steve help you with the repairs—'

'Geoff and I had started them. Don't you see, I was doing it for Geoff?'

'Pointing? Reroofing?'

'Mr Jempson helped with both those projects.'

'We never saw him. All we saw was you up a ladder. Iron hoops on the one which went over the roof ridge. Those sort of bungee-rope things holding the other in place!'

'They were his ladders. He secured them like that. And I was still in my forties, remember! Anyway, that's not the point – you've already made that.' Her eyes were full of tears and she said, angry with herself, 'I must give Jen more space. I must stop finding jobs for her.' She looked at the wool again with disgust. 'I must drop the knitting business.'

She pulled her needles out of their stitches. Caroline gave a little scream and leaned forward to prevent her from unpicking the small piece of work.

'No! Laura, you are still so incredibly impulsive! Of course you must not stop knitting! And I'll definitely join you. Let's make that timetable and carry it through! Not for Jen – for us – you and me! We need it. And she will, too, when she gets through some of this fog! And if she sees us placidly knitting—'

'I can't do it all day, for God's sake!' wailed Laura, watching Caroline wriggle the stitches back on to a needle. 'I hate knitting, actually!'

'We'll do it for an hour a day,' Caroline said soothingly. 'Can you manage that?'

'I suppose so.' Laura accepted the repaired square reluctantly. 'I can't think what possessed me to imagine this could help poor Jen.'

'It will. Eventually.' Caroline took a ball of wool from her sister-in-law's lap, and needles from the coffee table, and began to cast on stitches expertly. After a moment, Laura stabbed her needle through a stitch and wound the wool around it fiercely. Caroline said, 'We're doing this for us at the moment, Laura. And if it works for us then Jen will see that and might – just might – join us.'

Laura glanced at her sister-in-law and sighed. She was so like Geoff at times. This, nearly always, was an enormous comfort, but then, quite suddenly, it would twist Laura's gut so that she had to move away. This was such a moment. The way Caroline had taken her silly, impulsive idea and made of it something so sensible, just as Geoff had always done . . . it was heartbreaking. Laura stood up, pocketed her ball of wool and, still knitting, went to the window.

'She's looking for that toad at the bottom of the garden. Poor Jen. Oh Caro . . . poor, poor Jen.'

'Yes.' Caroline's voice was infinitely sad, then she added briskly, 'But she could be so much worse off, darling. She could be on the breadline. She could be completely alone. Whereas she has a good job which they are holding for her indefinitely. And she has her Aunt Laura who has made a life for herself in this rather lonely corner of Cornwall . . .' She laughed as Laura began to refute this. 'And of course, she has her poor old mum!'

'Poor old mum, indeed! You look like sisters and you know it—'

'And part of this knitting deal is that we do it sitting down and relaxing as much as we possibly can, Laura. You can never manage longer than ten minutes in a chair. No wonder you sleep badly. Come on. Sit down until it's time for tea.'

Laura tried to laugh but it was difficult when Caroline was using the same words Geoff had so often used: *sit down, my beautiful girl . . . no wonder you're so skinny.* She sat down so she was still able to see through the window, and tried to project her thoughts into Jenna's. Jeremy and Jenna. The names had sounded like a music-hall double act, even

22

more so when Jeremy had fondly contracted them into Jen and Jem. 'Sounds racy, doesn't it?' he had said. 'And we're such conformists, Jen negotiating insurance deals with building consortiums, me a very junior architect with one of those consortiums.' They had met at a conference centre on the south coast where they had come together because their youth separated them from the others. Throughout their five-year marriage they had stayed that way, shiningly young with their destinies intertwined for ever and ever and ever . . . And here was Jen now, half of the act, Jen without Jem, another widow to swell the ranks at Widdowe's Cottage. Except that it was no longer singular; they should rename it 'Three Widdowes' Cottage'. Her difficult laugh became a sudden sob.

Caroline's response was instant. 'Look. You've come through your grieving, Laura. I've come through mine. Jen will come through hers, eventually.'

Laura knitted furiously, carelessly. 'It's so unfair, Caro! I was forty-eight! I'd had over twenty-five years with Geoff! You were younger! And Jen younger still! Too young . . . too bloody young!'

'Darling, you're messing that up completely! Give it to me . . . just lean back. Breathe gently. Try to let it go . . . down through your body. Out through the soles of your feet. You remember.' She was smiling; she was repeating Laura's own words to her when Steve had died. But actually, Caroline had never wept.

She went on speaking, gently and calmly, even as she reknitted Laura's royal blue square. 'Nobody is too young for anything. You know that. And in a way, Jen is lucky to have known Jeremy at all! They were like Romeo and Juliet, probably a true match made in heaven . . . born for each other . . . all the things most people dream of but realistically know will not happen.' She paused and then added as an afterthought: 'The same applies to you and Geoff, darling. It was different for me.' She finished a row and changed needles to start on the next. 'As you know, Steve had left me – I know we don't talk about it, Laura, but now and then . . .' She was knitting very fast. 'I felt the most enormous regret. There would not be another chance to make it work . . . it was another opportunity I'd let slip by.' She laughed. 'Did you know I was going to take dear Ma on holiday just before she died?' She started another line. 'Yes, I was going to drive her down here to see you and Geoff and what you were doing with her old home. Steve was on one of his cruises in charge of the leisure activities, Jenna had mumps and by the time she was better and Steve was back home, my mother was in hospital with pneumonia.' She turned the knitting again. 'Jenna was fourteen when Steve left us, sixteen when he was killed. She always blamed me.' Caroline spoke levelly and without emotion.

Laura made a sound of protest and forgot her measured breathing. She said, 'You've always put up such a front, Caro! Have you never spoken of this to Jen?'

'Of course not.' Caroline managed a laugh. 'I'm all right. I really am. What about you?' She handed back the battered knitting and resumed her own.

Laura said, 'You've nearly finished this one! Oh Caro, I'm fine. You just said it, didn't you? Jen and Jeremy made for each other. Geoff Miller and Laura Wheatley . . . likewise.' She put the knitting down and fumbled for a handkerchief. 'I was – am – so lucky, my dear. Don't take any notice of me sniffing away madly! We're so different yet so similar. You show one side of the coin – always a calm and cheerful face. I show the other. Geoff said I should have been on the stage!' She laughed.

Caroline nodded. 'That's a nice thought. Two sides of one coin. I like that.' She said, 'Don't forget I was brought up by Tilly Miller, née Quince, who always maintained it was as easy to be cheerful as it was to be sad!' She laughed. 'Let me do the supper tonight. I'll make a salad and scrape some of those potatoes you dug yesterday. We'll hard-boil eggs and dig into the cheese. Too hot for anything else.' She smiled sideways at her sister-in-law. 'D'you know, when Geoff brought you home to meet Ma I was five and so jealous I could not even look at you. And now, here I am trying to say the sort of things Geoff would have said . . . trying to make you sit still for just an hour.' She stopped smiling and concentrated on her needles. 'I love you, Laura. But there's a tiny bit of me that is still jealous!'

If she had wanted to shock Laura out of her sudden spat of grief, she certainly succeeded. Laura's violet eyes opened wide.

'Jealous? Of me?'

'Well, of course. Geoff was like a father to me. He must have been almost twenty-five when I was born. He would come home from his school and give me all the time I demanded – apparently I was very demanding. I had him all through the school holidays. He taught me to read and write and do up my shoes. And then you did a stint helping out with everything at his school and . . . suddenly there you were. And it was so obvious he could see no one else but you.'

'But I knew about you – I knew how you felt about Geoff. And I knew how he felt about you. I respected that, Caro. Didn't you know that?'

'Of course. That's why I loved you too. But – but – your *generosity*, yes, that's what it was. Generosity. It was almost too much . . .' She finished a row and turned the knitting around. 'Perhaps I don't mean that I was jealous. Perhaps I mean that I've always known you were a better person than me. I didn't deserve Geoff's love. You did.'

Laura put down her knitting and blew her nose and said something about rubbish. Then stood up. 'I'll do the supper. I absolutely refuse to cry again. You're good at knitting and I'm not. I've always been good at talking things out . . . now you're doing that better than me, too!'

Caroline looked up, surprised, then smiled. 'All right. I accept all that. And I can certainly knit better than you – look at this! But it's your idea and it's a brilliant one. About time we did something for charity. Go and do the meal and I'll pick up your dropped stitches and set you right again. Go on – shoo!'

Laura went, thankfully. The kitchen was her domain. It smelled of the bunches of sage and rosemary tied to the old beams, drying to the crispness needed for 'rubbing down'. Soon she would be bringing in the onions and their pungent smell would override the subtler ones. She stood on the coconut matting, which made the uneven slates less perilous, and held on to the edge of the table, inhaling the familiarity of the space, fighting for that precious calm which Caroline had talked about. She closed her eyes and imagined it flooding her being. She wanted it so desperately. Too desperately.

Jenna's voice spoke from the open back door. 'I can't see any toads. And actually . . .' She came to the table. 'I'm frightened of them anyway. Perhaps my mother doesn't know that.'

She tried to make it sound funny, then saw the tears trickling from her aunt's closed eyes. She enfolded her. They wept together.

Three

August eventually lapsed into September. Burning-brass-hot days when Laura felt nothing happened. Jenna had moved out of her flat in London in June, two weeks after Jeremy's funeral, and Caroline had brought her here on the train. Laura had met them at Penzance and driven them to Widdowe's Cottage, almost rejoicing because she was so certain this was the right thing to do. Caroline would nurse her daughter back to life and Laura would prepare wonderful meals and let the cliffs and the sea work their healing powers just as they had for her all those years ago and then, ten years back, for Caroline. It was never going to 'get better' of course. That had been rammed home to her on the day of the knitting. There would always be scars, but . . . but . . .

The fact was, Jenna's flood of tears on that day – the day of the knitting – had not helped her. She still wandered around, doing what she was told, drifting into semi-consciousness, eating Laura's carefully prepared meals without appreciation; without even identifying them. Locked away somewhere with her grief.

Caroline tried to compensate.

'Laura, my dear, these courgettes – I've always thought courgettes were tasteless and mushy but these are heavenly. Don't tell me. Coated in egg – and then breadcrumbed? And of course, the fresh herbs . . . simply delicious!' And Jenna, recalled to herself, might echo a murmured 'delicious' or simply smile at her aunt.

Then, as the sun mellowed and the dews soaked the parched grass, Jenna's wanderings took her further afield. She had taken the route to Tregeagle along the cliff path with Laura but had turned back quite soon. She went to the cove and swam. She had gone the other way towards the old mine workings and then up on to the road where there was a cluster of shops and a pub called the Miner's Lamp. Then, for two days, she did not tell Laura or Caroline where she was going; it became another secret, locked away with everything else.

Early in the second week of September she announced after breakfast that she would have a walk. Laura said nothing. Caroline said, 'Which way will you go? If you go towards the mine you could go up to that one-stop shop and get some bread.'

'I thought of going the other way,' Jenna said.

'Oh. Thanks,' Caroline came back.

Laura, just as quickly, intervened. 'I plan to take the car into Penzance tomorrow, Caro. Why don't we all go and stock up and look round the shops?'

They stood at the back door and watched Jenna walk down the garden and through the azaleas and on to the cliff. The sea, no longer blindingly bright, moved lazily below.

Laura said sadly, 'She still can't really *see* anything, can she? That's what's so awful about it. She's cut off from everything that could give her life meaning. Even the soaking wet grass – she didn't notice it!'

Caroline watched as her daughter's head moved along the cliff path, only just visible above the high ferns. 'She's noticing something. I don't know what it is. She knew which way she was going, for instance.'

Laura said nothing; she had thought Jenna was simply being contrary.

Caroline sighed sharply and turned to go into the house again. 'It's cooking morning, isn't it?' She managed a glint of a smile at Laura. 'I must be getting into the swing of things – didn't even have to consult the timetable!'

28

Laura stayed where she was, looking across the ferns.

'Listen. This is the first day of autumn – yes, I know it's too soon and all that. But it's cool enough so that I can do some proper gardening. I want to get the bean sticks out and put away and lay the beans to rest.'

'Darling, I'll do most things for you but I cannot dig or weed,' Caroline protested.

'Of course you can't! That's why – if I want my garden to survive – I wouldn't dream of asking you!' Laura turned and laughed with a feeling of sudden release. She hated the slight conflicts between the three of them; it was nothing, of course, small undercurrents . . . that was all. 'But I think you should be outside too, and I wondered about your sketch book.'

'I didn't pack it,' Caroline said immediately.

'No, I thought you might not have done. Geoff's is in the writing desk. Second drawer down.'

Caroline held the back of a dining chair and stood very still. 'Geoff's?'

'Surely you knew he painted? Only when we came down here, of course – no time otherwise. He'd make sketches and work on them at home. Oils. He liked slapping them on to canvas as thickly as he could!' She started down the path to the shed. 'I'll do an hour, then make coffee.'

Caroline stayed where she was, watching. She was beginning to feel that this gathering of the three of them at Treleg was a mistake. Laura was too emotional and imagined she understood Jenna better than anyone. It was ridiculous. One minute she was insisting on her wretched timetable, which Jenna almost always ignored, the next she was closeted with Jenna, encouraging her into the sheer self-indulgence of tears. Caroline knew that if she'd stayed at Jenna's flat in London, she could have invited Jenna's old college friends to visit and got her back to work before Christmas. But Jenna herself had suggested Laura's cottage – the only wish she had been able to voice.

Caroline nibbled her lip, remembering too that it had been she herself who had told Laura to give Jenna time for grief. And never once in Jenna's twenty-six years had Caroline ever said, 'She's my daughter and I know her better than you do.' And now here was Laura underlining the fact that she had known Geoff was an artist. And Caroline, his beloved little sister, had not. She took a deep breath, acknowledging to herself that she was being unfair and petty and totally unreasonable.

And then she went into the parlour and opened the second drawer of the desk and there was an enormous manilla envelope printed in Laura's large square letters GEOFF'S SKETCH BOOK. She took it out – it was heavy – and put it on the coffee table and then slid off the envelope and was confronted with Geoff's work. Fifteen years, eight and a half months since he could have touched the book, let alone worked in it. She knelt down and began to turn the pages.

Laura stuck the fork into the ground and began to twist out the bean sticks. She bound them in bundles of six, which was the heaviest she could handle. She had done four wigwams of sticks this year and they had yielded splendidly. She thought she would do wigwams next year, too. It made picking that much easier.

She lugged the bundles, four of them, into the shed and stacked them at the back. She would need to sort everything out to make room for the deckchairs that had been left out most of the summer. She stood, looking around, wondering how the spaces left by the garden furniture had somehow filled themselves in the last two months. She loved the smell of the shed, its clutter, its complete absence of organization. Flower pots were stacked everywhere, seed packets, bulbs, wire netting, strange fleece material to protect exotic plants from the frost, the mower and its miles of cable, a rack of tools – the shears had opened wide and looked predatory – the rake and spade that had been there when they bought the place. She had invested in a sort of corkscrew designed to extract weeds but she had never used it, as the hoe was easier to manage. And there it hung, its extra-long handle almost touching the wooden floor, its two heads looking right and left, the two-pronged side protruding like snail's eyes, the other a conventional pusher and puller. She reached out and touched things because Geoff had touched them and that comforted her. Then she took down the spade. She would cover the old bean vines, then go in and make coffee, because obviously Caroline did not intend to do any sketching.

She stepped out of the shed and glanced back at the house and there was Caroline sitting on an old kitchen chair, eyes down on a large sketch book.

Laura shouldered the spade and walked on down the garden.

Jenna knew only too well that she was missing out on the sensual delights of this first autumnal day. She had chosen to accept Laura's invitation to live at the cottage because she had assumed the smells, the sights and the sheer exhilaration which she associated with Widdowe's Cottage would help her to bear the dreadful loss of Jeremy . . . even to forget it . . . even to forget *him* for a blessed while. It hadn't worked, of course; she was shocked at herself for thinking it would. As if she would want to forget what had happened . . . as if she would want – ever, ever, ever – to forget Jeremy! She wanted her grief, she needed it now. Grief was her life and she embraced it, hugged it to her so that she would not fully see, hear, smell, taste, anything else at all. And she had gone into Tregeagle Church, not to find solace, but to emphasize that grief, to make it the tearing, aggressive emotion it had been. And she went back. She went back yesterday and she was going back today. Because it was working. Because she had found something that made the grief . . . precious.

It had been a surprise to find the church unlocked and she had assumed it was occupied by cleaners or flower arrangers. Not so. It had been completely and wonderfully empty. It had also been uncleaned and . . . dead. Not a single flower, not a gleam of brass. The sun had struck colours from the few stained-glass windows but she had barely seen them through the all-pervading mustiness. The thick smell of dust had been everywhere. She had trailed through the pews, glanced at the pulpit, walked right up to the altar, fingered the cloth, stared at the crucifix and then up at the east window; and been reminded of Miss Havisham's time-capsuled house in *Great Expectations*. This was what she wanted. For time to stay still so that it could not put a space between herself and Jeremy. She had felt something inside her sigh and relax.

She had turned and gone through the Lady Chapel and into the vestry, and found a cupboard full of vases, some stained teacups and saucers, piles of tattered prayer books. She had walked back into the nave and out through the door, then circled the whole church, threading her way through tombstones and long grasses, a standpipe with a watering can beneath it. The weather had been hotter that day and the whole place had shimmered. It was dead yet it was visible . . . she had stood still by the lychgate and willed Jeremy to appear; dead but visible. There had been a recent film, she had forgotten its name. The dead husband in the film had come back to comfort his wife. She had willed Jeremy to do the same . . . willed him until she was exhausted. Nothing had happened.

'You're just . . . dead,' she had said aloud, almost angrily. Nothing had happened after all. An empty, dust-filled church, a long-ago graveyard. They all amounted to nothing. She had turned back to go home, determined not to come this way again.

But she had come the day after. Yesterday. The deadness had brought her. She had wanted to be dead, atrophied at the lychgate or in front of the altar. She had considered suicide and knew with a basic sanity that she could not do that to her mother or her aunt. But this kind of death was different; the church was there, but dead. And that was how she was.

She had repeated the circuit she had done the day

before and then gone inside and sat in one of the pews. And after a while she had felt a kind of numbness; all feelings and emotions had gone away. She had supposed she could have moved but she had made no attempt to move, not even her eyes. She had become part of the church. There, but dead. She had been conscious of breathing very shallowly and she had sensed that her heart had slowed right down. She had sat and sat and felt nothing.

And then an enormous involuntary breath had come upon her; it had been there, in front of her face, waiting. She had opened her mouth and drawn it into her lungs, and then continued to breathe slowly but deeply. She had felt her toes in her soaking wet tennis shoes; the tips of her fingers had tingled. She had waited and registered herself rising back to full life; coming up slowly but surely as if through water, breaking the surface very gently. And being. Being her physical self again.

There was disappointment but it had not been devastating this time. She had discovered something. She could do it again. For a space of time she had been anaesthetized from pain.

She had moved her arm and checked her watch. It had been an hour. Just over an hour, actually. She had stayed where she was, breathing, moving her legs, rubbing her jeans with the palms of her hands, being conscious of herself over and over again. After a time – allotted, she was sure of that – she had known she could stand. So she had stood and then moved slowly to the altar and stared around her, frowning. Already the certainty of what had happened had begun to elude her. Had she been resting? Or had something enormous happened . . . had she had some kind of out-of-body experience – the sort she was always reading about in the Sunday papers?

She had gone into the vestry and rummaged in more cupboards. There was an urn and in the tiny robing room there were candlesticks and an enormous Bible; and a locked cupboard above a desk. She had left the church and stood again by the lychgate, looking. Something was happening. She had had no idea what it could be. Perhaps she was closer to Jeremy here than anywhere else? Perhaps this was a way of summoning him?

She had put her hand to her heart and found it beating hard; slowly but hard. And then she had gone home.

After breakfast the next day, she put everything away meticulously; her aunt had shown where she kept jams and marmalade, the butter compartment in the fridge, the carefully sectioned cutlery drawer. Laura had said, 'Anyone can wash up, darling. It's more important to put things away where we can all find them.' And Jenna had understood that her aunt was forestalling any possible criticism from Mum. She also knew that although Laura accepted her walks without question, her mother . . . suspected something.

The dew was extra heavy and by the time Jenna reached the church on the cliff her jeans were soaked to the knees. The path veered inland just here and she supposed went on past the church and eventually into the village of Tregeagle itself. She stood at the junction and stared along the cliff side. It would have been possible to continue walking by the sea; she knew that the coastal path went right along here to Land's End. Why had she taken this turning two days before? Had it been some kind of divine providence? The path that led past the church was a tunnel of hazels. She could have been looking for shade; it was still very hot.

She crouched now. The hazel tunnel was heavy with dew and would have rained on her had she knocked the low branches. When she came to the lychgate the church looked different: the granite gave off a pink, mellow glow where before she had seen only its hardness. She had not noticed the weathervane yesterday; today it glinted, and as she looked up it swung to point due south. She had felt no breeze until then. She began to measure her breathing; it was fast. Was this the day she was to see Jeremy? Was it? Could it actually happen?

She almost ran to the door, looking for other differences which she might construe as some kind of evidence. She stood at the back of the nave, staring. The light was orange instead of red, blue instead of purple. It lay across the pews when before it had lit only the dusty floor. She glanced at her watch and found she was much earlier than yesterday and the day before. And the light was softer today; Laura had called it autumnal. Even so . . .

She sat in the same pew, put her hands in her lap, her feet together, dropped her head, began to measure her breaths. Slow, slower. Then less air, and less again. Very shallow now. Her blood pressure was dropping. She was within reach of the nothingness. Within reach of the place where Jeremy would be waiting.

A voice, gentle, precise consonants, spoke. It said, 'Are you all right?'

It wasn't Jeremy's voice so she kept her eyes closed. It was someone who had come for her. She said on a brief outward breath, 'Yes.'

There was a long pause while she waited. Then the voice said, 'All right. I will leave you for a while, but I am within call.'

And then there was silence. And in that silence, confident that this was the right time, she entered nothingness.

The next minute it was as if the church itself was caving in. The voice – the same but very loud now – was saying, 'Come on! You are not going to die in my church! Come back this minute— d'you hear me? Come *on*!'

A hand gripped her ponytail and held her head up, another patted her face – slapped her face almost – and the voice blared in her ears like a klaxon and echoed around the ancient pillars and beneath the pews, skidded up to the altar and back again via the pulpit.

The strange thing was she couldn't 'come back' because she hadn't got to where she was going, and she fought the hands and the voice although she knew it was useless. And then, of all dreadful things, she was sick. She tried to warn the hands but the voice got in the way, so she flung herself forward until her head met the coarse cloth of a pair of jeans and she was sick all down them.

The klaxon cut off quite suddenly and the hands went to her shoulders and held her while she retched repeatedly and then groaned.

'That's better. Let it all come up. You really will feel better.' One of the hands disappeared and then came back with a handkerchief and mopped her up.

'There's water in the vestry. We'll get cleaned up in a minute. First of all . . . what are you on?'

She looked up blearily. It was a man, not old, not young, black curls needing cutting, black eyes too, a snub nose, a long mouth and round chin. He wore a sweatshirt and stained jeans – stained by her, she supposed dimly.

'On?' she repeated.

'What drug?'

'I have something called marzipan – a name like that – to help me sleep. But it doesn't work.' She felt really ill and wanted her mother.

He grinned suddenly and his long mouth split his face into two separate halves.

'I wouldn't have thought it would,' he said. 'Sorry. We get a lot of addicts in here. They come to Cornwall, sleep rough and then get ill and have to find shelter. I leave the church open for them.'

'I see. It's so dusty. I thought it might not be a church any longer.'

He sat by her. The smell of her own vomit was choking. It overlaid the soft dead smell of dust and mustiness. She thought that she mustn't cry; the one thing she must not do was to cry.

He said, 'It's not actually decommissioned. We use it at Christmas, Easter, Harvest . . . that sort of thing.' He looked at her. 'What is your name?'

'Jenna.'

'Have you come far? You need food, I expect.'

She shuddered at the thought. 'I've come from Widdowe's Cottage. I'm staying with my aunt. Laura Miller.'

36

'Ah. The Quince place. I haven't actually met Mrs Miller. I'm newish.' There was a silence; he seemed comfortable with it, Jenna was not. She battled with tears and felt her insides crumpling helplessly.

He said, 'I'm the rector. The church is cutting down on us so I have five parishes in my benefice. That's why Tregeagle Church isn't used most of the year.'

For some reason she was appalled that he was a church-man; as if she had been caught practising demonic rites in a holy place. At least she forgot her imminent watery collapse.

'I – I was just sitting. Absorbing . . . the atmosphere.'

'Of course. And you've walked . . . what . . . three miles? You need to drink. You are probably dehydrated after throwing up.'

She half laughed; his frankness was refreshing.

'I haven't apologized. Your clothes . . . my clothes . . .'

'Tell you what.' He stood up and waited for her to do the same. 'Let's see if there's any tea in the cupboard. I can drink it black, can you? Then we could swim in Tregeagle Cove. I've been here two years and haven't tried it.' He looked at her. 'Stand for a few minutes, then come on into the vestry. I'll have a forage.'

She did as he said; she was still bewildered by her sudden emergence from the nothingness of waiting, the shame of the vomiting, and this man . . . who had interrupted . . . whatever it was, and had no idea of the enormity of what he had done.

After perhaps a whole minute she walked steadily up the aisle and cut in front of the pulpit to the vestry. He greeted her with a smile. There were cups on the table and the sound of singing water somewhere.

'You've been here before,' he said.

'Yes. Twice. Look, I don't want any tea and I'd better get back to the cottage. Forgive me, I don't mean to be churlish but—'

'That's perfectly all right. But I think I might know what you've been looking for here. And I thought we might look together.'

37

She stared at him, brown eyes enormous. His smile widened.

'It's all right. Lots of people come looking, you know. And when you said you were at Widdowe's Cottage, I remembered it was named for a widow called Quince and the name rang a bell. I was just going to unlock the cupboard and look it up for you. Hang on a minute.'

He disappeared into the tiny back room and she could hear him fiddling with a key. At the same time there was a loud click from a very modern electric kettle next to the sink. Next to the kettle was a teapot. She went to it and automatically put some boiling water into it, swilled it round and tipped it into the sink. Then she opened a tin nearby and discovered it full of teabags. She put two into the pot, switched on the kettle again and made tea.

He came through and laid a black-bound book on the table.

'This shouldn't be here. I've got the others at Penburra Church. All the information is in London now, of course, and the Truro Cathedral archives. But people still come to us to look at the parish records.' He was opening pages as he spoke. 'Your family name is Quince, isn't it?'

'Yes. My grandmother was a Quince. But nothing will be in there. They were all Methodists.' She brought the teapot to the table and poured two cups.

He smiled appreciatively. 'Don't worry, those teabags are fresh. Our churchwardens have started preparations for Harvest Festival with the main thing – teabags.' He laughed. 'The "holy dusters" will probably be starting next. As soon as they've got time the sound of vacuum cleaners will be heard in all the land!'

She felt only dismay. It had been so secret, so private.

'How long will they be?'

'Well, they have to be finished for Harvest Festival next Sunday.'

Her heart sank. She picked up a cup and sipped so that her expression did not show.

He said, 'Look at the colours here.' He picked up his

own cup and looked into it. 'Translucence. Beautiful. Like a stained-glass window. And you rarely see tea-coloured windows.' He glanced at her for an answering smile which did not come. 'Let's have a look at this book anyway. It might not matter that your grandmother was a "Methody". Sometimes the children were christened in the traditional church. Hedging all possible bets!' Still no smile. He turned the pages gently, they seemed powdery. 'Let's see. Reckoning on thirty years a generation that would mean perhaps ninety years . . . the early part of the century . . . have to go to the one beyond that, perhaps . . .' He was murmuring as he carefully folded back pages. Then there was a small whoop. 'Here we are. Quince. Mathilda Jane. 9 March. In the year of our Lord nineteen hundred and seven. Female. Infant. Three weeks. They christened them very young – mortality rates pretty high then in Cornwall.' He looked up. 'Does that mean anything to you?'

Jenna looked at him and said slowly, 'My nanna was called Tilly.'

'And when was she born?'

'About then, I suppose.'

The rector was far more excited than Jenna herself. 'That's the one then!' He grinned at her. 'Let's go back a bit. See if there are any more Quinces.' He turned some pages and then stopped. 'Ah. John Quince.' He darted an upward glance at her. 'It's a death. Do you want to know about it?' She nodded and he said, 'John Quince. Born eighteen seventy-five. Died nineteen eighteen.' He looked up again. 'He was forty-three. Your grandmother – Tilly – was eleven. Not very old to be orphaned.'

'She and her mother and my uncle and my mother . . . they lived in the Cotswolds. A village called Childswickham. Great-grandmother made gloves. Kid gloves. Until her eyes gave out.'

She sipped more tea and let the steam blur her vision. Another widow. Was the whole family to end up with women only? She said, 'Of course she was dead by the time I came along. My mother was upset by the fact that her grandmother never saw me. But she had Geoff with her for some time.' Her tone was politely conversational. She wanted him to close the book now; it was unbearable.

He was thoroughly caught up. 'That accounts for the fact that neither Tilly's marriage . . .' he turned pages, 'nor her death is recorded here. Those things are in another church, another place.' He picked up his tea absent-mindedly as he went on turning the pages at random. He sipped and then said, 'There are two other christenings recorded here for Quince, one before Mathilda and one after. William . . . does that ring a bell?' He looked up at Jenna expecting similar interest and immediately checked himself. 'Oh. I'm sorry, Jenna. Forgive me. This is a real intrusion.' He closed the book and took his tea in both hands. 'I get carried away like this, you know. People . . . people fascinate me.' He gave a wry smile. 'I suppose . . . I just love them. The good, the bad, the in-different.' His smile became a self-mocking laugh. 'That's what I'm supposed to do. And I do it. I love them.'

She said nothing; the caul was across her eyes. He said conversationally, 'This tea would be better with milk, but will you have another cup?'

She blinked. 'No. I must go home. My mother said something about needing bread.' She took her cup to the sink and rinsed it beneath the mottled tap. He watched her, frowning slightly, then brought his own cup to be washed.

'All right. I'll walk you up to the coastal path again and perhaps we can wash ourselves off in a pool.'

'No!' She moved quickly to the door into the church. 'I'm all right. I'm sorry about messing up your jeans . . . I think it was the shock of you being there. I came before, you see. A couple of times. And no one was here.'

He said, 'Wait. I'll unbolt this outside door and you can go that way . . .' but she had gone.

She walked back to the cottage and then kept going and struck up to the pub and the shop. The bread was stacked just inside the door, pre-packed and sliced, the kind Laura did not like; but there was no other sort. She bought a thick-sliced loaf and wandered back. Her mother and aunt were in the garden bending over a book, both smiling. They looked up in unison as she came past the flattened bean patch. Whatever had been between them was gone; they were happy together and happy to see her. She registered this picture and it made her . . . comfortable.

She smiled back and said out of the blue, 'Did we have a Quince relative called William? There's an entry in the parish register – that name.'

Both women looked completely blank. Laura said, 'What date? Was it a christening? I thought they were all Methodists.'

'I don't know the date,' Jenna confessed. 'He was looking at pages in the early 1900s.'

Her mother said sharply, 'He?'

'The vicar. No, rector.' She was already regretting the impulse that had brought it up. 'He thought I was one of those people looking for their family. He found Nanna, then he was all fired up and got a bit carried away. I left.'

'Nanna?' Her mother looked like a drama queen and put her hand to her throat. 'How could Nanna's death be registered down here?'

Jenna sighed. 'It was her birth, not her death.'

'Oh my God. I – I'd like to see it. D'you think he – the vicar chap – would let me see it?'

Jenna did not answer. Laura put an arm around Caroline's shoulders. 'Of course he would, Caro.' She smiled up at Jenna. 'How fascinating, darling. You've had quite a morning – and you fetched bread, too. Well done!'

'But Laura . . .' Caroline twisted her head to look at her sister-in-law. 'Ma. An entry for Ma down here.'

'But you knew they all lived here, Caro. You look as if you've seen a ghost!'

'I knew with my head.' She gave a little laugh. 'I know a lot of things with my head, Laura. This is something

41

else. Ma . . . it's as if she might still be here. My mother, Laura.'

'Darling, I know. You and Geoff . . . so close to her.'

Caroline smiled blindly up at her daughter. 'Jen, perhaps . . . tomorrow . . . you could take me to see this man.'

'I'd rather not, Mum. I made a bit of a twit of myself.' She pointed to her jeans. 'I was sick.' She tried to make it sound funny. 'He got more of it than I did. I really don't want to go back to the church or to see him!'

They were both concerned. They ushered her indoors and she had to drink more tea and have a cheese sandwich. 'It must have been the sun . . . though it's not so hot today as it has been . . . I'll make some soup for tonight. Those courgettes . . . they settle the stomach wonderfully.'

She watched them as they moved around the kitchen. For the first time since Jeremy's death she felt part of something again.

Laura selected a courgette the size of a marrow from the vegetable basket and began to scrub it. 'You know,' she said over her shoulder, 'Grandma Bessie was the last tenant of this cottage. Her husband was killed in the mine disaster and she had to move out and the cottage was then called Widdowe's Cottage.'

Caroline, who had been putting away Geoff's sketch book, came in and said, 'How on earth do you know all this?'

'Geoff told me. I don't know how he knew. Perhaps he talked to Tilly about it . . . or even Bessie herself. He could remember her. I suppose Bessie married again and they left Cornwall. The other mining cottages fell into disrepair and were bulldozed away, but Geoff managed to get this one and we started to do it up . . . well, you know all that.'

'Yes.'

There was something in Caroline's voice. Jenna recognized it. She sounded . . . lost.

Jenna stood up. 'Listen. While Laura is doing the soup, let's do some knitting, Mum. Come on.'

She stood up and went into the parlour. Just for a moment she thought resentfully of the vicar. Just for a moment she longed for that nothingness that could have led her straight into Jeremy's arms. Then she lifted the knitting bags from behind one of the chairs and placed them on the coffee table.

Four

September 1999

Caroline cried off the trip to Penzance. She told Laura that she wanted to finish the sketch she had started yesterday. That was enough for Laura; she would not allow her smile to show but Caroline saw it at the back of her intense, violet eyes. Normally it would irritate her; she would see it as self-congratulatory . . . Laura having a breakthrough with Caroline as well as with Jenna . . . Caroline cut the thought off quickly. Laura was never smug. Caroline knew she must not project her own weaknesses on her sister-in-law.

Jenna said, 'You're not coming, Mum? I thought you'd be keen to look round the shops. You're into things like retail therapy.' She laughed. It was a proper laugh and Caroline realized with a little shock that she was being affectionately teased. That hadn't happened for a long time.

'Oh, I am!' She smiled back. 'In fact, here, I've written you a cheque. Have a crazy spend and then tell me honestly if it worked.'

Jenna took the cheque but the moment had passed and she said sadly and honestly, 'It may well work, but only for a time, Mum. But thanks, anyway.'

Laura got in before Caroline could. 'Darling, don't you see that tiny little pieces of time are worthwhile. They can be stretched out bit by bit into longer pieces . . .' She too laughed, at herself. 'You know what I mean.'

Caroline had been about to point out the same thing but more concisely. Jenna nodded and that satisfied Laura. It

44

did not satisfy Caroline. There was something about Jenna . . . something that had happened at that church. The vicar man?

She ushered them out to the garage and waved them goodbye. Then she got out one of the picnic tables and a chair, fetched Geoff's sketch book and some HB pencils and placed them on the table. She glanced at her watch. Nine thirty. She could not rely on them staying out longer than three hours; Jenna would tire easily and if the town was crowded she would want to fight her way out of it. Also – Caroline buttoned her cardigan – the weather was definitely chillier; there was a sort of mist lying heavily on the sea, masking the horizon.

She tramped along the footpath, following the headland, then began the descent into the steep combe which led to Tregeagle. She had never actually walked the cliff path this far before; in the days of Geoff – so long ago now – they had all walked the other way towards the Miner's Lamp and a drink before bedtime. She had not reckoned on this steep descent which would mean an equally steep climb the other side.

There were stepping stones across a narrow but rushing stream and she negotiated them with difficulty. Why on earth hadn't Jenna mentioned this tricky terrain? And the colour of the fern, deep red, climbing the next headland? She sighed, remembering that Jenna would not have noticed any of it. Then she took off her cardigan and tied it around her waist; not halfway up yet and she was desperately hot.

She almost missed the turning to the church. The trees were thick and unkempt and made an unwelcoming tunnel; she hesitated. At some point she would have to turn off the cliff path and, looking up at Tregeagle Head, there was not another footpath in sight. So she crouched and entered the tunnel.

It was not long, which was a good job as woody off-shoots kept snagging her hair and the back of her shirt. She emerged into a proper path, the ferns only just held back by chain-link fencing, the path disappearing around a corner but obviously heading for the road. On her right the little church of Tregeagle huddled in a dell which was itself dotted with leaning gravestones. There was a roofed lychgate dissected by a stone coffin-rest; she sat on it thankfully and surveyed the front of the church and its graveyard with interest.

The mist had collected in the small depression and the stubby tower was barely visible. Caroline stood up and unwound her cardigan and put it back on. Then she combed her hair with her fingers, smoothed it into its usual ear-length bob and walked slowly towards the church door. She did not consider herself particularly sensitive but there was something about this place that was indefinable; and Caroline preferred to define things. Even grief.

There were gates across the porch and they were very visibly padlocked. She jiggled the chain and nothing clicked or moved. So this had not been the way Jenna had come in. She stood there for a while peering into the gloomy interior, then turned and began to circle the church. The vestry door was tucked away behind watering cans and dustbins which she negotiated gingerly. For some reason she did not want to make a noise; it seemed to be a secret place. The door handle was an iron ring and she lifted it and turned it gently but firmly. The door was bolted from inside; it jarred slightly against her hand. She released the handle and swore softly. The whole expedition had been ridiculous, she had known that from the outset. But she had wanted so much, so very much, to see her mother's name in the register. She could have wept with childish and angry disappointment.

She turned away from the door, negotiated the dustbins again and sat on a low headstone beyond a sheltering buttress. She felt so strange, unable to collect her thoughts and wishes and disappointments. Everything, every last little thing about her life – about herself – was somehow unsatisfactory. She had the company of Laura and Jenna. Jenna was consumed with grief, Laura full of anxiety and

46

sympathy, trying to find practical ways of dealing with the grief even though she knew that it was next to impossible. And Caroline; beautiful, practical, talented Caroline was . . . what? Certainly not consumed with her own grief, nor Laura's abysmal grief for her daughter. She knew that Jenna would survive and would want to survive. She had herself said that Jen and Jem had been a match made in heaven but there were other kinds of love and Jenna might be lucky enough . . . Oh God. She was back where she started . . . another kind of love.

She rested her forehead on her hand with some force, physically driving out that particular thought, and then straightened convulsively as a faint but definite sound came from inside the church. A laugh. She had heard a laugh. She stood up and listened until her head sang. It did not come again. But it had happened, she was not one to imagine things. Someone inside the church had laughed. A female laugh.

After a period of intense listening she began to traipse back through the dew-wet weeds to the front porch again. Thank God Laura wasn't with her; she would have sworn it was Ma. She would have been breathless, awestruck. She dramatized every last little thing; Geoff had loved her for it – 'living life way past the full' he had said once. Caroline found it irritating; at times embarrassing. There was an element of that in Jenna's grieving . . . it couldn't come from Laura, there were no blood ties there.

She reached the gated porch again and held the rails to peer inside. And she saw it. The most ordinary and un-dramatic evidence possible. An umbrella. Propped against the stone benches which ran either side of the porch. Buttoned closed but there in case the mist turned to rain. Someone was inside the church.

She let her breath go in a gigantic exhalation of relief. Honestly! Had she really thought . . . of course she had not. It would mean she believed in ghosts, which was laughable. So . . . she laughed.

There was a sort of waiting silence. As if someone had

heard her and was curious. She shook her head and called loudly, 'Is there anyone there?' Nothing happened so she repeated the words twice. And then one of the double doors inside the church opened and a head came round.

'Is that you, Edna? I thought you were never coming . . . Lost your key again?'

A woman in a pinafore emerged, took something from the stone bench and came to the gates. It was a key. She was about to fit it into the padlock when she realized her mistake.

'Oh. It's not Edna! Sorry, I thought you were someone else. Can I help?' But she made no further attempt to unlock the gate.

Caroline gave a reassuring smile. 'I'm staying with my sister-in-law at Widdowe's Cottage and my daughter discovered that my mother was christened here. I hoped to see the entry.'

'Oh.' The other woman peered. 'Yes, I've heard you're there. Heard about your daughter too. So sad, my dear. So sad.' She unlocked the gate and ushered Caroline through. 'I can't help you with the entry, though. The rector's took the register down to Penburra Church. But come and sit a bit and get the feel of the place.' She went ahead, talking over her shoulder. 'You know I'm quite glad to find you, my 'ansome. Once or twice I thought I could hear things . . . The church is only used three or four times a year and the rector won't have it locked, so we gets . . . well, vagrants I s'ppose is the right word. An' as Christians we should give 'em a roof and a seat to sit on, I s'ppose. But if they're on drugs, you never know.' She smiled briefly to take the sting out of her words just in case Caroline might have connections with that kind of world. Then she added, 'I s'ppose.'

'So that's how she got in.' Caroline explained briefly about Jenna. 'And the vicar was here too. I rather thought most churches were locked these days, so I wasn't surprised to find I couldn't get in.'

The woman stopped several rows from the chancel steps.

'I'm a bit nervous, see,' she said apologetically. 'Always lock myself in.' She rubbed the back of a pew with a very bright yellow duster. 'Look. I done down to here. Shocking state, don't know where all the dust do come from. But these are clean if you want to sit awhile. I got to get on, especially if Edna isn't coming. Gen'lly the two of us do it, you see. Can't think what's happened to Edna.' She smiled brightly. 'I'm Etta Tompkins by the way. Church cleaner by profession I s'ppose.' She giggled. 'They call us the two eehs – Etta and Edna!' She laughed. It was definitely the laugh Caroline had heard before, and she echoed it gladly.

'I won't sit down. But I'd like to walk around a bit if you don't mind. And then if your friend hasn't turned up perhaps I could give you a hand?'

Etta was almost overcome. 'The Lord has sent you, I s'ppose,' she said. 'Tell you what. If you scurridge around in the vestry you'll find teabags and cups. I've brought milk – it's standing in the sink – you could make us a cup of tea if you would. Water and electric is both switched on.'

Caroline was delighted. She followed Etta's pointing finger and skirted the side chapel to the door at the back of the church. This was where Jenna must have come. This was the place for parish records even if they weren't here any more.

The vestry was not as big as Laura's front parlour; the middle of the floor was covered by a threadbare carpet and the edges showed wide floorboards thick with dust. Cupboards lined the walls; Caroline could imagine them full of moth-eaten cassocks, old candlesticks, piles of tattered prayer books. One side of the room was taken up by a cooker, a Belgian sink and more cupboards, doubtless full of cracked and stained cups and saucers. There were no windows. It was downright unhygienic. Caroline imagined Jenna in here, she would not have noticed the dirt. She would have felt that here time had stood still. It came to Caroline in a flash: here, Jenna had imagined that Jeremy was still alive – or at least some kind of presence. Caroline blinked and shook herself, found the electric kettle and set to.

Etta came through ten minutes later and the two women sat in the ill-lit room and drank tea and Etta s'pposed what on earth could have happened to Edna, while Caroline nudged her around to remembering the time when Tregeagle had been a thriving copper-mining village.

'I suppose—' Caroline wondered if Etta's catchphrase was in fact catching. 'I suppose that Treleg is a shortened version of Tregeagle?' She topped up Etta's cup and threw the dregs of her own tea down the sink.

Etta laughed. 'Oh no, my 'ansome, not at all. It means three legs. 'Cos Treleg Mine was once called Wheal Three Legs and was separate from Tregeagle village entirely. Tregeagle was 'ere long before the mine. It were a fishing village. We haven't got a harbour but we got the creek d'you see. That was what started the fishing I s'ppose.'

'Why Three Legs?' Caroline rinsed her cup. She looked hesitantly at the others balanced precariously in the open cupboard and put them in the sink.

'It was owned by a man called Sir Geoffrey Bassett. A big family in Cornwall, owned half the land round here. And he had a wooden leg, lost it in the wars, I s'ppose. Any rate, he grew another. So he was Geoffrey Three Legs and he called his mine Wheal Three Legs, you see.' She laughed with Caroline. 'I know. It's an unlikely story. But that was how it went.'

'And the cottage? My sister-in-law's cottage?'

'That's one of the mine cottages. There was a whole terrace of 'em built by the mine captain for miners they brought over from Wheal Grace. They all fell into rack and ruin and Mrs Miller's man bought Widdowe's Cottage.'

Caroline felt a small shock at hearing Geoff described as Laura's 'man'. She said quickly, 'Geoff Miller was my brother.'

Etta was surprised. 'My patience! There was a lot of years between you, then. Surely he'd be nigh on eighty now? And you can't be more 'n fifty?'

'There were over twenty years between us,' Caroline said,

deftly avoiding giving her own age. 'I think my mother must have been a genuine child bride!'

'Ah. That's why you want to see the parish records.' Etta stood up reluctantly and picked up her duster. 'Well, the rector will be only too glad to go through them with you. He might be young but he's keen. I got to give 'im that.'

Caroline finished washing the contents of the cupboard and left them draining. 'I'll put them back before we leave,' she said. 'The tea towels don't look very clean.'

'No they won't be. Queenie Maybrick does the washing.' Etta led the way back into the nave and handed Caroline some dusters and spray polish. 'This is good of you. I'd've been here all day I s'ppose. That Edna . . . Anyway, it's just the south side now. If you can manage that while I get on with the altar . . .'

'Of course.' Caroline was delighted to have something definite to do while she thought about what Etta had said. It was beginning to make a pattern but a few pieces seemed not to fit. She rubbed one end of the pew to shining darkness then sat on it to do the other end.

She had lived all her life knowing that she and Geoff had been born at the beginning and end of her mother's child-bearing years. But there had never been details; that was how it was, fixed and immutable. Tilly had never volunteered any background information. It occurred to her now that there must have been information, quite a lot of information. The death certificate, the wedding and birth certificates. They were needed for all kinds of things, she knew that very well from her own experience after Steve's death. Of course, Geoff had dealt with everything after Tilly died. He had said, 'Don't worry, Sis. I'll take care of all the business.' And she had been only too glad, grateful beyond words, beyond questions. Her world had caved in when her mother died. She had known always that her mother was her best friend, that she would never ever have anyone like her. In her head she had called her Tilly . . . never to her face. Just thinking about her now, in this place, where apparently she had been christened, made

Caroline's breath catch in her throat. She stopped polishing and held herself still. She thought consciously, my mother . . . my mother was here. And then – and this was totally unconscious and came with her next breath: she might still be here.

Etta's voice echoed eerily around the nave, 'How we doin', my 'ansome? I swept the floors, no point doing any more to them for just one service.' She walked up the central aisle and looked at Caroline. 'Reckon we'll call it a day. If we start on the brasses that will be wrong – Queenie does the laundry and the brasses – she gets funny if anyone tries to help.' She peered. 'You look a bit pale. Come 'ome with me if you like. Catch the bus back to Treleg.'

Caroline pulled herself together. 'It's all right. Rather a nice walk. The others won't be back from shopping yet.'

But when they got outside the mist had rolled in damply and Etta declared the cliff path unsafe. 'Barely see your 'and in front of your face, let alone the edge of that path. Why they can't afford a fence 'ere and there, beats me. Come on. We can't go wrong through the nut grove.' She led the way on through the tunnel of branches and they emerged on to a country lane. The mist was turning into rain. A row of telegraph poles disappeared into it; behind them were houses and then a farm. Caroline felt a kind of regret. Everyday life was claiming her; she could feel it. She was cold, colder than the weather warranted. Back there in the church she had been close to finding . . . something.

Etta made her another cup of tea and then phoned her friend, Edna. She replaced the receiver and looked at Caroline, wide-eyed.

'Guess what? Edna started out all right, remembered her key and the little brush she'd use on the squiddly bits of the pulpit. She reckoned it was ten o'clock when she left her cottage. Mist came down when she got to the lane . . . slipped in some cow-muck and did in her ankle!' She sighed, exasperated. 'She says she's sprained it but she don't know what the word means. She'll make the most of it. No more help with the cleaning, I'll bet you a brass farthing!'

Caroline wanted to laugh and knew she must not. She finished her tea quickly and stood up. Etta lent her an umbrella and told her where the bus stop was. 'Any chance of seeing you next Sunday at the Harvest Festival, my dear? You could drive along and leave the car outside the cottage . . . walk down with me if you're a bit shy.'

Caroline said, 'I might. I just might. But anyway I'll see you before then to return the brolly. Thank you so much. For everything.'

She wanted suddenly to be by herself. She needed to think. There was so much to think about. Enormous possibilities, just out of her reach. She stood under the inadequate bus shelter, watching the rain drift across the road. Eventually, the bus came and she was welcomed aboard by the driver before she remembered she had no money. It didn't matter. 'Give it me next time,' he said. 'No inspectors on this route.'

What with that and the borrowed umbrella she felt like a charity case and sat there, smiling slightly, thinking of how Tilly would have reacted: walked to Treleg, probably. The bus turned inland along the edge of Tregeagle combe and followed the creek; she could see masts emerging from the mist, and when the bus pulled up for more passengers the lonely clank of halyards cut through the idling engine-sounds. They then diverted to two hamlets of half a dozen houses each before regaining the main road. She stood up and made for the door and saw that the car was back in the drive; it was after all nearly three o'clock.

She was still thanking the driver and suggesting times for paying her fare when Laura and Jenna came flying out of the front door; they both looked bedraggled and wet. She felt her face tighten with anxiety and ran to meet them. Surely there couldn't be another death? What on earth had happened?

The bus pulled away; they met at the gate and spoke in unison.

'Are you all right? What's happened?'

'Where have you been?'

Laura's arms were tight around her; Jen put a hand on her back. 'Where have you been?' Jen said again.

Caroline tried to laugh through Laura's stranglehold. 'I've been to Tregeagle Church – didn't think you would be home yet – what's happened?'

Jenna was silent, her hand dropped away. Laura relaxed slightly. She looked at Caroline and tried to laugh as well. 'Nothing. We got stacks of groceries. And I made Jenna buy a new top and some pyjamas. We've only just got home. Your sketches . . . ruined by the rain . . . back door unlocked . . . definitely thought the worst!' She forced the laugh again and moved back. 'Sorry, darling. You've had a walk, got caught in the rain and got the bus back home.'

Caroline pushed the gate wide and went round to the back of the house. The sketch book was a soggy mess . . . Geoff's precious sketch book which Laura had kept safe for fifteen years. Oh God, Oh *God*! And the unlocked door – anyone could have got in. It wasn't like her, she was so methodical. What had she been thinking?

Jenna said tightly behind her, 'What were you thinking, Mum? That book was Geoff's. Surely you knew that?'

She swung round. 'Darling, it was so warm when I left . . . Laura, what can I say? I am so terribly sorry. It wasn't a spur of the moment thing, I intended to walk to the church . . . when Jen said about Tilly's name in the register . . . Oh God, I am so sorry, so very sorry.'

Laura smiled without a trace of anger or resentment. 'For goodness' sake, Caro. You are safe. That is what matters. We can dry the book.' She gathered them both together. 'Let's go and eat. That's what we need. Food. Drink. And by the feel of your hands, Caro, warmth!'

Jenna said stiffly, 'I'll light the fire in the parlour.'

'Good idea. We can have a tray of tea in there while the casserole warms through.'

Caroline stayed in the kitchen with Laura and laid the tea tray. Even that seemed difficult; she couldn't find a small jug for the milk and knocked the spoon on the edge of the caddy, scattering loose tea everywhere.

'Laura, I don't know what to say. I was so curious . . . so set on the idea . . . and Geoff's book is ruined. And I didn't see the entry in the end!'

'The book is a book. You are you. Come on. Let's go into the parlour and you can tell us all about it.'

'There's nothing to tell,' Caroline said miserably. And really . . . there wasn't.

Five

They all went to the Harvest Festival together the next
Sunday. It was an act of forgiveness and solidarity. As
Laura said, 'Please, please, *please* let's forget Geoff's sketch
book and concentrate on being together again.'

Jenna said defensively, 'It's not that. I don't want to go to
that church again.' But it wasn't true. What she really
meant was she didn't want to go to the church when there
were other people inside it. She wanted to think of it again
as her precious secret, the secret Jeremy had given to her
and where he was waiting for her.

The whole experience – she supposed she could
legitimately call it an out-of-body experience – was not easy
to hold and retain any longer. It was moving away from
her, becoming an isolated memory, a shining light in her
subconscious mind rather than a part of her being. She
knew now that she should never have told the others about
the church and the records at all; and that she should
have guessed that her mother had declined the shopping
trip to Penzance because she wanted to see the church
for herself. When Jenna had blurted out – fairly light-
heartedly – that she had found a church with a parish
register that mentioned a William Quince, Caroline
had quickly become alert. She had been shocked to
hear that her own mother's name was in the records.
There had been no sense of mystery, no wonder at the
amazing discovery. Simply an avid curiosity. And then had
come that familiar expression, tightening her face for a

moment . . . hard to put a name to it but Jenna chose to call it speculative. It had twitched and pursed her mouth when Jenna spoke of the new young rector. Surely, surely she could not have imagined for one moment that he had been a part of the Tregeagle experience? A spurt of pure anger surged through Jenna at the thought that her mother might already be matchmaking, however tentatively.

And then – and *then*, Caroline's disappearance and dramatic reappearance after she and Laura had discovered the abandoned and soggy sketch book and had been on the point of calling the coastguard to search the cliffs. It was so typical of Caroline McEvoy. Basically she was selfish. As simple as that.

Jenna knew that she was being unfair. She knew that sometimes she used her mother as a scapegoat – not even that, as a sounding board for her own anger and frustration. She stopped thinking of her as 'Mum' and called her Caroline McEvoy. It had been Caroline McEvoy who had left her husband and deprived Jenna of a dearly loved father. Even when Jenna discovered that Steve was living with a rich widow who financed his expensive habits, she still maintained that it was six of one and half a dozen of another.

She remembered Jeremy's surprise when she had told him. 'But darling Jen! He married your mother thinking she had prospects and when he discovered she hadn't, he went off with Widow Twankey. I don't quite see . . .'

'She never really loved him.'

'Surely the boot was on the other foot?'

'Jem, you are so open and honest. You never hold anything back. My Aunt Laura is a bit like that. Mum is different. She pretends a lot of the time. She pretended that Daddy's . . . departure . . . didn't worry her two hoots . . . maybe it didn't . . . in fact I'm sure it didn't. And after Nanna died she sold the cottage immediately and bought into Beddoes the auctioneers . . .' She sighed. 'You only see the very tip of the iceberg with my mother. And actually the iceberg thing is very apt. There is something chilly about her.'

He had looked hurt. 'Stop it, Jen! You sound . . . not like Jen at all.'

She had been horrified and had apologized immediately. 'I'm sorry, Jem. So sorry. Perhaps I'm terribly envious of the way Mum copes! I don't, you see. I can't cope with the awful things that happen . . . Nanna dying and Daddy going . . . Mum just keeps right on. I'm sorry. I'm often horrid like this – can you just stop me immediately?' She was very serious but he laughed.

'You cope, darling. Just in a different way, that's all.'

'But you will understand? You will help me?'

And he was suddenly serious, too. 'I will always help you, Jen. Always.'

As that thought became conscious, her eyes filled with tears. Because of course, that's why he had led her to Tregeagle Church. That's why he was there for her. Always. And that was why she must go to the Harvest Festival and let her mother and Laura see where . . . *it* . . . had happened.

Laura was not keen on going to the Harvest Festival because, in all the years she had lived in Widdowe's Cottage, she had kept herself very much to herself and people had accepted that without question. There were one or two who helped her to maintain the house. And for a time she had gone to art classes in Penzance in a desperate bid to paint as Geoff had done. But she had no real skills in that direction and had given the classes up during a particularly wet winter. The artist who ran them still brought a few painters out to the cottage each summer to try their hands at seascapes. Laura enjoyed making an old-fashioned tea for them – she called it her Sunday school treat – and she saw one or two of them each summer and corresponded at Christmas. But she was not a member of any community and preferred it that way. And a visit to church at an important festival time would be tantamount to making a public appearance and would probably open the floodgates. Caroline already knew one member of the congregation – they had got on like a house on fire, apparently – and there would be others who would want to be introduced and encourage her – all three of them – to come to church regularly. And she did not want that. After all, Caroline and Jenna would eventually leave the cottage; Jenna had a job with a big insurance firm which they were holding for her, and Caroline had always worked for a local auctioneer in the Cotswolds and had bought a partnership when her mother died. And when the two of them had gone, Laura was assuming her life would go back to how it had been before Jeremy's death, regulated by the seasons and the tide times and the weather. So close to Geoff that sometimes she knew if she looked round quickly he would be there.

But Caroline was keen to go to this Harvest Festival; she had obviously found something at Tregeagle Church that intrigued her. And Jenna . . . well, it had been Jenna's discovery. The first sign of life she had shown since the funeral. And Laura saw the festival as an opportunity to come together. Having the effect she had hoped the knitting would! She could not hold back from that.

Caroline herself was not entirely certain of her feelings. She was never ever certain of her feelings, so that did not surprise her. But there was something about that church. Tilly, her adored mother, might have gone there; might have knelt in those pews and prayed for rain or sunshine or forgiveness. She had always been one for forgiveness. Tilly Quince, then Tilly Miles, then Tilly Miller. She had forgiven the whole world. Even God or fate or what Steve had called 'the big dealer in the sky', the one with all the cards and most of them marked. Caroline had never once heard her mother complain about her lot. When she cuddled Caroline and said as so many mothers have said, 'I am the luckiest woman in the world', she had meant it. She was lucky to have had Geoff so early in her life, lucky to have had Caroline so late. Two good husbands, a very special mother, and other shadowy relatives Caroline never knew in the flesh. Never much money but so much happiness . . . the cottage near Childswickham in the Cotswolds where she had sewn kid gloves and made Cornish pasties for Geoff and her first husband. The grief of losing that husband . . . but the joy of keeping Geoff through the war. Meeting her second husband and losing him but having Caroline. And enough money . . . just enough money . . . to live comfortably in Withy Cottage and take up sewing again.

Caroline had often wondered about her father. There had once been money in the family – and then there was very little. She dimly remembered a big house and a nursemaid. Had he been a gambler like Steve? Had she inherited her mother's predilection for marrying the wrong man? There was – she saw now – a mystery surrounding Tilly. She had spoken of her life in sudden spurts which never seemed to connect properly. And Geoff had known about it; he must have known about it; Tilly could only have been about fifteen when she had him, and in a sense they had grown up together. Geoff. Geoff was the mystery, too. As always she felt the tremor in her hands and heart at the thought of Geoff. She was no longer insanely jealous of Laura, but . . . there was another mystery. How the hell had Laura lived almost sixteen years of her life without Geoff?

She needed to see those parish records.

So they went to church on that Sunday in September. They took a wicker basket laden with traditional vegetables: tomatoes, another giant courgette, potatoes and leafy summer cabbage tucked in with long-eared cos lettuce. A second basket contained more practical gifts: tins of peas and beans, corned beef and ham, packets of soup-mix and dried apricots. They drove inland to skirt the combe, passing the Miner's Lamp, then the scattered detritus from the old mine and the eight-till-late shop (which was also a post office). Caroline was driving and swung on to the main road behind a tractor with a tut of impatience.

'He'll be turning off at Court Farm,' Laura reassured her. 'They have to work every day, remember.'

Caroline said musingly, 'Court Farm. Is there a Court to go with it?'

'Yes. It's a hostel now – a youth hostel. I believe Geoff's grandmother worked at the Court for a time.'

'My grandmother, too,' Caroline reminded her.

'Yes. Yes, of course.'

'Perhaps . . . as she grew older . . . Nanna worked there too.' She glanced in the mirror at Jenna. 'They started work at a very young age then, didn't they, Jen?'

'I'm not sure when "then" was, Mum. Compulsory education must have put an end to the ten-year-old balmaidens. Domestic work may well have been fitted around school. I don't know.'

Caroline could have reminded Jenna that she ought to know: her dissertation had been about the working conditions of British women in the early part of the twentieth century, but the tractor turned off then and she sped on towards the turning to Tregeagle. Laura did not have to point it out: 'Right. Just past that bus shelter – can you see it?' Ever since returning Etta's umbrella, Caroline had started to feel that she knew the area almost as well as the Cotswolds villages where she had so often valued the contents of big houses – and small finds in cottage attics. She had learned about the Cotswolds from her mother, and she was learning about this small corner of Cornwall from her mother, too. It was in her bones.

She slowed right down as she ran past the terraced cottages, getting the feel of the place again. It had been so wet before, the mist dissolving into heavy rain by the time they had reached Etta's place. Now the sun was back, without any real warmth at this time of day, but lighting the roofs and trees, glinting off the rocks which thrust themselves between the terraces as if claiming their primeval rights. The road ran parallel to the creek at first but then cut into the bank above it. The sound of water was lost but the road suddenly turned left and ran steeply down towards a cluster of masts below them. A sign said, 'To the ferry'. To their right another one proclaimed 'To the church and cliff walk'.

Laura said, 'No wonder they are abandoning this church. The ferry has been closed for donkey's years and most of the village is on the other bank anyway – they must all use Penburra Church, or even Treleg. That young rector you met must have his work cut out trying to keep everything going.'

Jenna made no comment. She should not have come, she knew that much. All the mystery had been stripped from the experience of last Monday. She should have stayed at home and cooked lunch or something. Better still, she should never have spoken of the church and the 'young rector'. Words did not work any more. Only for mundane communication . . . like now. She cut across Caroline's description of the mud last Tuesday and said abruptly, 'My God. This is so tame and touristy. Let's go home.'

But of course that was no good. Laura looked as if she had been stabbed in the heart. Jenna said quickly, 'Sorry. It looks so different from this side.' Caroline parked the car next to two others and they got out, gathered up the two baskets, smoothed their clothes self-consciously and started up the footpath. Jenna followed the other two, drearily compliant now, wondering why on earth they hadn't walked along the cliff path which was three miles instead of ten, then felt the weight of the basket on her arm and tried not to think any more. Just do. Just follow her mother's sandalled heels as the path reared towards the top of the cliffs and disassociate all of this with what had happened on Monday.

Laura had not been to this church for over eighteen years. She and Geoff had come once or twice – they were not great churchgoers – but in those days it had been High Anglican which had not suited Geoff. 'I'm probably still

Cornish Methody,' he had said, smiling. 'Tilly was C of E. In her time down here there was a wonderful bloke in charge. And her father had been Anglican – she adored her father. But Bessie – my grandmother – was Methodist. I probably get it from her.'

When they first bought the cottage and started to rebuild it, they had gone to church as if to establish their rights to the place. 'Foreigners' were not always acceptable and Geoff had let it be known that Widdowe's Cottage had been his family home. So they had gone to Tregeagle Church, they had enjoyed an evening drink at the Miner's Lamp and they had explored the remains of Treleg Mine. Perhaps that was why her need for privacy had been respected later. Everyone knew about her already. She was not really a foreigner at all.

She led the way up the path to the lychgate almost without thinking. She told herself that this visit had nothing to do with her personally; she was doing it in an effort to heal the cracks between mother and daughter. She had been aghast at Jenna's reaction to Caroline's reappearance last Tuesday; the sketch book had been like the bursting of a boil. Since then the acrimony had been tangible and although Caroline pretended she did not notice it, Laura knew she was putting up a front. And it was not really to do with the sketch book; it was something deeper; something to do with the church. And that meant nothing to Laura . . . except that the last time she had been here was with Geoff. She edged past the coffin-rest and walked up the path. The doors were open wide and a dozen or so people were already in their pews. A verger was holding service books and smiling.

Caroline waited for Jenna on the steps and they both presented their baskets. Laura had gone ahead and was sitting in a long empty pew. Hardly anyone was there. Caroline felt a nervous thump in her chest; the last time she and Jenna had been to church together was for Jeremy's funeral . . . They shouldn't be doing this, it was a really bad idea. And then Etta surged down the aisle, smiling hugely, beckoning them to come forward and put their offerings with the others, then – incredibly – hugging Caroline as if she were a proper friend. Caroline smiled over her shoulder, holding the plump arms, delighted that she had recognized Etta in her Sunday finery and, indeed, that Etta had recognized her. Someone was at the lectern marking readings in the Bible with leather bookmarks. He looked up, smiling at Etta and Caroline. Caroline realized it was the 'young rector' and that he was pleased to see such demonstrations of affection in his church. But he was not smiling at Etta after all. He left the lectern and moved towards them and then to Caroline's left. He was doing his bit – welcoming someone else into the fold. It was Jenna.

The three of them sat like stone in the long pew which Caroline had polished. Etta disappeared, then reappeared in the choir stalls, her flowered nylon dress covered with a royal blue surplice and her hat replaced with a matching mortar board. Everyone sang 'We plough the fields and scatter' while the choir processed from the vestry right through the church and then back up the centre aisle. Another handful of people came in miming apologies for being late and the verger scurried furtively about with service sheets and books for them. The young rector let his gaze wander over the scanty congregation, smiled happily and said, 'Welcome, all of you, to this special service of Harvest Festival. We are licensed to open this ancient church of Tregeagle three times a year and this is one of them. I would like to thank everyone for their wonderful gifts. They will be distributed later among the housebound and to the nursing homes. The tinned goods are traditionally sent to a charity in Penzance – known as Centrifugal Force – which runs a drop-in centre for the homeless.' He paused and seemed to come to rest within himself. 'God be with you,' he said.

'And also with you,' the congregation intoned.

The service was under way, the dialogue between priest and people picked up and laid down with reverent familiarity. The three women followed in the service books, gradually relaxing, emotions laid aside as the readings led into the Gospel and the Litany gave way to spontaneous intercession and then the sermon.

Jenna appeared to lose interest as they settled themselves back on to their polished bench; she sat very still, her eyes seeing nothing, her breathing shallow. Laura, sitting on one side of her, was very conscious that Jenna was somewhere else. Elsewhere. She wondered whether this was one of those things that happened at big religious rallies and Jenna was listening to . . . what? A calling? When her breathing stopped for long periods, Laura became anxious and put her hand on her niece's leg. Nothing happened and Laura leaned forward slightly and tried to get Caroline's attention. But then Jenna took a long and trembling breath, closed her eyes and put her own hand on top of Laura's.

Caroline was unaware of the other two. As the young rector spoke of the mustard seed and the vineyard and the Old Testament famines and brought them all together into contemporary experience of the rich West and the starving Third World, she was aware only of this place, this building. A building soon to be left behind. Hearts had been broken and maybe mended here; babies christened, weddings celebrated, funerals wept through, and they were all going. She thanked God that Geoff had not been christened, married or buried here. But her mother? Tilly? Tilly had seldom spoken of Tregeagle. She had already left all those memories . . . maybe right here in the church. In which case, they were still here and there must be – *must* be – a way to access them. Just as computers stored things which could be accessed, then so must places. She tried to empty her mind completely and leave space for Tilly.

The sermon must have been coming to an end – she heard quite clearly when the rector spoke of the starvation within our midst and knew he was talking about the drop-in centre – when she was conscious of warmth. It was not a cold day but the church buried in its dell was unheated, probably damp, and when she had held Etta's lovely plump arms they had been cold. Now there was warmth coming from somewhere; inside her own body? She waited.

'We all feel a sense of frustration at how little we can influence world affairs. The secret is to look around us and do what we can for each other.' The rector paused and looked around the sparse congregation; he was smiling. Caroline knew well it was a professional pause, a professional smile, but found herself responding to it. The warmth spread through her body. She met his eyes and felt her face lift. He focused on her. 'Friends and families often repel any offers of help. The days of taking soup to the poor are gone.' His smile was personal, as if he had known Tilly Quince . . . as if he were actually talking to Tilly Quince. 'I would like to think that some of you might go to CF and meet the helpers there . . .' He saw the question in her eyes and said, 'CF is the short way of saying Centrifugal Force. A good name for them but rather cumbersome.' He looked behind him at the choir. 'The keenest of carers need caring for themselves.'

Caroline was transfixed. Her mother had been a natural carer, but who had cared for her when her two husbands died? Certainly not her only daughter. And it was too late now.

After the Eucharist there was coffee served in the church because the vestry was a glorious muddle of disrobing choristers. Etta arrived with a tray and a small girl carrying a plate of biscuits. Laura was introduced. Jenna had gone to a side chapel and was sitting staring at a small statue of the madonna and child. The women chatted pleasantly and were presently joined by the rector, who asked to be called John and then asked after Jenna.

'I saw she was with you. I expect she told you that she was taken ill right here in the nave just a few days ago?'

'Ill? Well, she told us she was sick. But by the time she got back home she was all right.' Caroline looked at Laura. 'Did she say anything more to you?'

'No. But . . . just now, during the service, she was so still . . . I thought she might be going to faint.'

'I thought she was on drugs!' The rector – John – laughed. 'It was quite a shock when she . . . anyway, has she left? She might like to pop into the rectory some time. I have a bit more information for her, actually.'

'About my mother? Tilly Quince?' Caro felt her eyes stretch wide. 'I wanted to talk to you about it too. Etta tells me that the parish records are held at Penburra Church and I wondered whether I could call there and see them myself. I am trying to piece together bits of my mother's life and why she moved – she and her mother – from Cornwall to the Cotswolds.'

Laura looked surprised. 'Darling, I could have told you that. There was no mystery about it. There was no work after the mine disaster and her mother's brother had a farm labourer's cottage and offered a home.'

'But she had a home – the cottage. Besides, you said Bessie worked up at the Court after the mine closed . . . it doesn't add up, Laura. Who told you that?'

'Well, Geoff, of course.'

Caroline stared at her speechlessly. The rector said, 'You would be most welcome to see the records, Mrs McEvoy. My number is on the top of the pew sheet. Do telephone and let us make a time.' Caroline transferred her gaze to him. Her eyes were almost black. He took her hand. 'I shall look forward to it.'

He slipped along the next pew and made for the Lady Chapel.

Caroline whispered, 'Why didn't you tell me?'

Laura said, 'I thought you knew. It was common knowledge . . . I thought everyone knew.' She was stammering. Caroline's mask had slipped and Laura could see raw pain in her dilated eyes. Laura said, 'Widdowe's Cottage belonged to the mine. They had to leave. I told you. The alternative was the workhouse.'

'My mother . . . the workhouse . . .' With a gigantic effort Caroline swallowed and turned to the back of the

67

church. Etta surged forward to take their empty cups.

'So nice that you came. My friend, you remember, the one who fell in the mud and did her ankle? She's in Truro hospital. So if you need a part-time job . . .' She laughed to show she wasn't serious. 'There's a team of us does Penburra and Tregeagle and Treleg. We calls ourselves the "holy dusters". Always room for another.'

They made their way into the churchyard; people spoke to them; they lingered on the footpath waiting for Jenna.

Laura said, 'Are you all right now?'

Caroline nodded and managed a smile. 'I felt odd in there. At first it was quite marvellous. As if I was in touch with Ma and everything was going to be all right and tight and tickety-boo—' She laughed at herself. 'And then I knew I hadn't been in touch at all. My mother and grandmother had not led a halcyon existence down here. Ma had lost a father she loved dearly. And poor Bessie had lost her husband and then her home. And the workhouse . . . the very word smacks of Victorianism at its worst.' She smiled again, a wry smile at her own romanticism. 'But I'm all right now. It's over after all. The past is the past.'

Laura said, 'The past is important, Caro, don't dismiss it lightly. It shapes all of us. D'you think that's why Jen nearly fainted today?'

'Because of Tilly and Bessie? No, I don't think so. I think Jen's past is entirely concerned with Jem. For some reason she feels close to him in that church.'

Laura sighed. Caroline was back to being so thoroughly realistic it was off-putting. She sat on the coffin-rest. 'Here she comes now. I shall be glad to get back in the car. It's been quite . . . tiring.'

Jenna joined them and they trooped back through the tunnel of trees to the tiny car park. One of the cars had gone, just theirs – and presumably the rector's – was left. They settled themselves in silently. Caroline eyed her daughter in the rear-view mirror. 'Well?' she said.

Jenna smiled. 'He didn't have any more information that might interest you, Mum,' she said. 'Just that someone called Edith Miles had died in 1918. Consumption, apparently.'

'Miles . . . that was the name of my mother's first husband.' Caroline frowned. 'I don't know anything about him. Except that he was Geoff's father, of course. I suppose Edith Miles might have been Geoff's grandmother . . . Tilly's mother-in-law? Was that why the rector told you about that particular entry?'

'Maybe. We didn't talk much. We're supposed to call him John. Anyway, if Geoff's father was called Miles, why was he Geoff Miller?'

Both women started to answer at the same time. Laura said, 'You tell her, Caro.' And Caroline said, 'Typical Geoff. He had his name changed to Miller. So that he and I would be a proper brother and sister. He used to joke about it and say it was such a small alteration we must be three-quarters related anyway.'

Jenna said, 'He was . . . lovely. How did you bear it, Laura?'

'Just as your mother bears it and you bear it. And, it would seem, Tilly Quince bore it twice over. And before her—'

'Stop! stop!' But Jenna was laughing, actually laughing. 'Don't let's be sad. It's going to be a lovely day. Let's take a picnic down to the beach and have a swim.' She leaned forward and put her hands on the shoulders in front of her. 'It was a good idea to go to the Harvest Festival. Reminded us that we've still got stuff to celebrate.'

Laura turned and smiled and Caroline did the same into the mirror.

Six

September 1999

Jenna said, 'You go alone, Mum. I'm not really interested in family trees.'

Caroline frowned. 'It's not quite like that, Jen. Besides, I rather think he is expecting you.'

Jenna looked up sharply from casting off her tenth knitted square. 'What are you getting at, Mum?'

Caroline was suddenly and unusually flustered. 'Nothing. It was just that he invited you. And then you invited me. As a matter of fact he suggested I telephone him for an appointment. Nothing was said about tea. I feel a little bit . . . awkward.'

Jenna shrugged, cut off the wool and threaded it through the last stitch.

'Sorry. I suppose I'm tender in that direction. He was nice enough to let me be sick all over him . . .' She smiled and the other two laughed, delighted that she had made another joke. Laura wondered briefly whether that was the second or third joke since their arrival at Penzance in June.

Jenna's brown eyes became serious as she put the finished square with the others. 'Listen, what I really want from him is a key to Tregeagle Church. I want to be able to walk along that cliff top and let myself in. It's OK, I'm not being morbid. But there is something there. You both felt it, didn't you?'

Caroline nodded instantly. Laura thinned her lips as if considering the question, but gave no answer. After all, she felt Geoff's presence in so many places; certainly he had

70

been there on Sunday in the ancient church but he was always in the potting shed. The important thing was that the three of them were back to being . . . friends.

'If I could do that on a daily basis I think I might . . . manage. Somehow.' Jenna picked up the finished square again and pulled it this way and that.

'You wouldn't want anyone with you?' Caroline asked tentatively. She had hoped to go back alone and sit quietly, thinking of her mother and all that must have happened here.

'No.' Jenna looked at her mother's chestnut-brown head bent over the fast-moving knitting needles and noticed the grey. 'You'd like to do the same, wouldn't you? D'you feel Nanna close by?'

'I – I don't think quite like that. But she spoke so highly of the church and I tried to imagine her there. I would love to see her name in an official record – actually *see* it. She was buried in Cheltenham and I often go to the cemetery there just to read the inscription on the gravestone!' She laughed at herself. 'And now . . . to think she was christened at Tregeagle is so good. A proper beginning and a proper end.' She glanced up. 'What do you think, Laura? Do you think I'm mad? You're so quiet today.'

'Actually, I feel really peaceful.' Laura smiled at them in turn. 'We've reached some kind of plateau, my dears. I was on edge during the service on Sunday but then, afterwards, I felt as if we'd all been through something and got somewhere.' Her smile widened into a laugh. 'I don't know what and I don't know where – crazy isn't it? D'you know, a long time ago, just after Geoff died, I overheard someone in the shop refer to me as that woman with the hair – Loony Laura. It really shocked me and I went to the hairdressers in Penzance and had something done with my hair. And I felt then I'd got somewhere.'

Jenna stopped pulling her knitted square into an oblong and hugged her aunt. 'I hate that . . . talking about you . . . calling you names!'

Laura patted the hand on her shoulder. 'It didn't bother

me in that way, Jen. Geoff called me loony. I'm happy with that.' She smiled upward. 'Listen, why don't we do this sensibly for once? You both go for tea with the rector. Jen collects her keys and goes to the church. You stay and look at the records, Caro. And after that you work out who goes for a quiet prayer and who doesn't.'

'A prayer? I didn't say a prayer and I don't expect Mum did, did you, darling?'

Laura laughed again. 'You were in a state of prayer the whole time, Jen. I was sitting next to you and I can vouch for that!'

Caroline just smiled and shook her head helplessly but then said, 'I'll add to your suggestion, Laura. We go as a threesome. I'd like you to be there. You might know stuff about the family that I don't.'

Laura instinctively knew this was difficult ground. 'Not very likely, Caro. But if it will help of course I'll come. We could take a cake or something. Poor man, little did he know he would get the whole trio!'

The Reverend John Canniston had applied for the living of Penburra without much hope. He was forty-two and had come to the church only ten years previously from an inner-city school in Birmingham. He had thought of it as an escape from the sheer drudgery of trying to hold the interest of forty teenagers who only wanted to get out of the classroom and into what they termed 'real life'. It was only two or three years after they had done so that they realized the value of 'old Canny's' teaching. Some of them looked him up and asked for advice. He discovered that pastoral care was his forte and applied to the diocesan training adviser – and also, there were family reasons why he felt he had a calling. Four years later he found himself curate in an enormous Victorian church assisting a charismatic evangelistic vicar and ministering to a small but fervent congregation. Still in Birmingham.

Tregeagle had come out of the blue. He had talked to the bishop about it and was gently encouraged to apply.

When the interviews came up he had discovered he was one of only two applicants. The other one had withdrawn his application when he discovered he was expected to administer several parishes. The Reverend John Canniston took up residence in the new rectory in August 1997 and was inducted into his three churches a month later. It didn't create much of a splash anywhere. That bit of the north Cornwall coast was not known for tourists and those that came were fishermen and walkers; if they were also churchgoers at home they were not when they were on holiday. Penburra yielded a congregation of nineteen, Tregeagle eight and the red-brick edifice at Treleg – built at the same time as Truro Cathedral – managed over thirty souls. During gentle teatime visits, the new vicar discovered that the church members went to church for a variety of reasons: Etta Tompkins had declared frankly with a laugh, 'I like seeing folks, hearing their news, vicar. I like getting a bit of polish on the pews too – the brasses 'd be even better but Queenie Maybrick dun't let no one touch 'em 'cept herself. One day . . .' John had thrown back his head and laughed. 'Sounds like the opening of an Agatha Christie murder, Mrs Tompkins!' And Etta had laughed, too, and told him to call her Etta.

Some had told him how they loved the music. 'When do you get a chance to sing else?' Eddie Murt had sucked his gums thoughtfully. 'In an open boat I reckon. But since I gave that up the best place is a church. Takes the voice and rolls it round the tower and it comes back better 'n what it started if you gets my meaning, Rev.'

'I get it, Eddie,' John had said.

Nobody had mentioned God until he spoke to the shared organist, who was named, unforgettably, Martin Madrigal.

'Something to do with the gloriousness of everything.' Embarrassment had stiffened the seventy-year-old neck muscles. 'Makes a kind of tunnel.'

John had waited then repeated, 'Tunnel?'

'The music and the people and everything. A connecting

tunnel. To . . . well, to God.' He looked reproving. 'You shouldn't have to ask that, John. You should know it already.'

'I think I did. But I needed you to voice it for me.'

It might have been about then when John began to suspect that he loved them all. The Tompkinses and the Stevenses and the Madrigals and the Murts and now, perhaps, the three women he bracketed together as the widows.

They stood at his door looking sheepish; the older one carrying a cake tin, the middle one very practically clutching an umbrella and the young one still with that distracted air which had led him to assume she was a drug user. He remembered her name.

'Jenna. I thought you might have forgotten.'

'Yes. We're late. We went to the Tregeagle side of the combe and then had to come back to the main road and down this side.'

The smart one with the umbrella said, 'If only the ferry still worked we could have . . . but . . .'

The older one, Laura Miller, who never came to church and was always out when he called on her, said, 'We brought you a cake.' She smiled and her face was transformed; she had been beautiful. 'We couldn't believe this was the rectory. Two cottages knocked into each other?'

He had to smile back, though three of them were a bit much; he remembered inviting Jenna, not the others. Why was the Anglican Church so full of women?

'Absolutely.' He ushered them in. 'This hall is the whole ground floor of the first cottage and is intended for meetings – large gatherings generally. Coats and umbrellas go here where the old staircase was . . .' The middle one did not relinquish her umbrella. They exclaimed and murmured their way around . . . the fireplace must have been a range . . . inglenooks still there . . . The two younger women were so alike, brown-haired, brown-eyed. The youngest one wore jeans and a light blue sweater and managed to look underdressed and somehow ragged. Her

74

mother wore grey slacks and a russet sweater and looked as if she had just stepped out of a bandbox.

The older one was holding out her hand and saying, 'How rude – it's just so interesting to me because of Widdowe's Cottage. I'm Laura Miller and this is my sister, Caroline McEvoy, and niece, Jenna Adams.' She was also wearing trousers but was bunched into some kind of jacket. Holding herself together. Whereas Jenna was letting herself fall apart.

Confused by his own thoughts, he said, 'I'm John Canniston. And let's go through to my living quarters where there are some armchairs . . . Come this way through the kitchen which runs along the back of both cottages . . . Yes, it's marvellous, isn't it . . . deep freeze . . . cupboards . . . washing machine.' He glanced at Jenna and smiled. 'I make full use of that.'

The mother was babbling about it being convenient and what a view of the garden and Jenna said, 'I don't think I apologized – it was an awful thing to happen and I've never done it before – can't think—'

'Please. It was a very special introduction.'

He sensed her withdrawal and opened the door into his sitting room. 'The old kitchen is my study,' he explained. 'And of course, as you see, the kitchen is a dining room as well.' He smiled at Laura, who seemed the only one at ease. 'Do you want to put your cake on the table, Mrs Miller?'

'Yes.' She gave that smile again. Her eyes were amazing; he'd heard of violet eyes but never actually seen them before. She said, 'How practical of the church to set you up here. You can walk to Penburra, and Treleg is . . . how far? A mile?'

'About that.' He indicated the armchairs. 'There were, of course, two rectories. One for Penburra and Tregeagle and the other for Treleg. They were both built for large families and the hunting type of vicar. This suits me very much better.' He smiled at Laura and turned to Jenna. 'Are you staying down here for long? We could go in to

75

visit the church archives in Truro and do a proper search if you had time. The Methodists use the facility. In fact all the denominations—'

Jenna interrupted quickly. 'Actually, it's my mother who is interested in the family tree. I was hoping very much you would let me borrow the keys of Tregeagle Church for a while. I would appreciate the opportunity to go there by myself.'

He said nothing about private prayer; he remembered only too well that this girl had deliberately slowed her breathing to the point of unconsciousness.

'Of course. But I would prefer you not to be by yourself. I am free tomorrow morning. Or perhaps your mother would like to—'

Jenna said, 'I'm not going to clear off with the silver, you know. Surely you understand the need for solitude? I need to be by myself.'

Caroline said swiftly, 'We think that Nanna – my mother – might have used the church occasionally. It seems . . . appropriate . . . in the circumstances.'

Jenna said brutally, 'The circumstances being grieving widowhood.'

John was embarrassed. 'That is why I thought that to be alone and in such a place was not a good idea. Unless you wanted to pray.'

Jenna leapt at it. 'Of course I want to pray. Of course I do. Ask Laura – didn't you tell me I was in a constant state of prayer during the Harvest service?'

'Yes. I did.' Laura looked again at the priest; he was young, probably very early forties. What was his name? 'Is it such an unreasonable request . . . John?' She beamed her smile at him. 'Bessie's first husband was called John. John Quince. I know it's a much-used name but it strikes me as more than coincidence.'

Caroline, confused, said, 'I forgot for a moment that Grandma Bessie was not always married to Jimmy Oates!'

Laura laughed, pleased that the conversation had veered right away from poor Jenna, who was silent and flushed with frustration. 'Yet you know very well that the family name is Quince! You just haven't thought about it, Caro. There are no mysterious secrets.'

'Not mysterious maybe, but secrets nonetheless.' Caroline turned to the rector. 'Jen is right. I would love to know more. May I take up your offer of a visit to Truro?'

He looked at her; she was the least interesting of the three women, but as he met her eyes, brown like her daughter's yet quite different – clear as milkless tea – he changed his mind abruptly. She spoke of secrets . . . she was secretive herself, yet for a moment the clarity of her eyes opened a door for him. She was telling him something and he did not know what it was.

He said – what else could he say? – 'Of course. It would be great. Tomorrow? Saturday will be busy. But Monday is my day off . . .'

'Tomorrow will be fine.'

She turned towards Laura Miller and he waited for her to suggest they go together. But then she didn't. There was an awkward silence and he turned again to Jenna. 'Listen. Sorry I was churlish about Tregeagle. Of course you can take the keys. There are two sets, anyway. As you know I normally leave the outer gate unlocked but it is locked at present and the wardens would prefer it that way.'

Her face lit up; she took hold of the chair arms ready to leap to her feet.

'Thank you so much. Please don't worry – I am most particular about locking up properly and everything.' She looked at her mother and aunt. 'Don't wait for me. I'll walk home along the cliff path.'

He said, 'Now? Do you want to go now?'

Laura said, 'Surely tomorrow, darling—'

Caroline said, 'You can't go now. You'll have to walk up to the main road and then all the way back down the other bank! It will be dark before you get home and that path is not safe!'

Jenna looked blank with disappointment and then, quite suddenly, surrendered to common sense. 'Sorry, everyone.

Look, I'm up. Shall I put the kettle on? You were going to give us tea, weren't you? I noticed the tray was all ready on the table. Only two cups, though. Where shall I find more?'

Laura laughed and John Canniston joined her, then stood up and led the way back into the kitchen. Jenna followed. Laura looked at Caroline, hoping to be the first to say something about the significance of their departure, but Caroline did not return her look. Instead she was staring at her hands as if she had never seen them before.

Jenna left early the next morning, her hands in her pockets in case the keys to the church should leap out of their own accord. Caroline watched her, frowning slightly. Her fall of chestnut-brown hair was not as smooth as usual, and as she looked at Jenna she raked it back behind her ears. From just inside the kitchen Laura called, 'Take the car, Caro. I'm going to be gardening today.'

'I'm not leaving you here without transport.' Caroline turned and came indoors. 'And it's too cold for gardening.'

'Just the weather for a bonfire. That's the best of having no neighbours. I can have a bonfire whenever I like.'

'Well anyway . . . I'm not going. I'm interested, not obsessed. Archives . . . dust . . . boredom . . .' She sat down at the kitchen table. 'No. I decided last night I wouldn't go. Waste of time.'

'Is there any other way you want to use your time?' Laura put a mug of coffee in front of her and sat with her own. 'Go for me, Caro. I'd like to know more about your family. Your mother had two marriages, so did her mother. And there's this William. What happened to him?'

'Oh come off it. It doesn't matter to you.'

Laura was shocked. 'Caro! How can you say that? I had no family. And now, there are no children. Geoff was my family and he gave me his.'

'Sorry. Sorry, love. It's just that . . . I don't want to go. There's something about that young man . . . He looked into my head yesterday. I didn't like it.'

Laura opened her eyes teasingly. 'What secrets have you got, Caro McEvoy?'

Caroline looked up and her eyes were as clear as they had been yesterday. Quite suddenly, she broke down.

'You know. Probably you've always known. And you were so kind – generous – you have never said anything. Oh Laura, I'm sorry. I couldn't help myself and I can't now.'

Laura put down her mug and tried to hold the shaking shoulders. 'I don't know what you're talking about. For goodness' sake, Caro—'

Caroline wailed, 'You must know I never loved Steve. Not properly. Not like you loved Geoff and like Jen loved Jem.'

'There are different kinds of—'

'Of course there are! I know that! I was in love with someone but there could never be anything . . . I met Steve and he was fun and he told me I was fun and he made me pregnant so . . . I married him.'

'Right.' Laura tried to keep her voice steady. Geoff had suspected something of this sort. 'Perhaps it wasn't too dreadful then, when he left . . .'

'No. It wasn't. Funnily enough it was worse than I expected when he was killed. I thought that if I'd tried a bit harder we might have made something of it. But it was too late.' She made a moaning sound and then looked up. 'I was in love with Geoff, Laura. I thought you knew. I was in love with my brother.'

It was as if she wanted some kind of punishment. She sat there, tears pouring down her face, waiting for . . . what? Laura to scream or hit her or tell her to get out of the house?

Laura said, 'Your half-brother, darling.'

'Nevertheless.'

There was a long pause. Laura started to fiddle with the mustard pot. She thought with the top of her head that perhaps she had always known Caroline was far too possessive of her brother. Deeper down, she just felt terribly sorry for her.

Caroline started to say something and Laura left the mustard pot and put a hand on hers. 'Listen. There's nothing to be done about it now. As for that young priest seeing anything in your head – well, we both saw he only had eyes for Jen. Poor thing, he's on a losing wicket there. So . . . go and wash your face, comb your hair and drive over to the rectory. Who knows? You might find something that will take your mind off this. Just as Jen might find peace at that crumbling old church.' She stood up. 'Come on, Caro. We're all walking tightropes and you've had the guts to jump off yours. Stroll around a bit and enjoy terra firma. Go on.'

Caroline was about to shake her head when a car horn sounded from the front of the house. The two women peered through the window. An ancient Morris Minor was parked at the gate and the young rector was waving through its window.

Laura shooed Caroline up the stairs and went to speak to him. She had the feeling Caroline's apparent frankness was deceptive. Why had she chosen that moment to confess her feelings for Geoff? Maybe it was because she wanted to cover up something else.

Seven

Caroline had imagined a morning of intense embarrassment. Her mediocre degree in sociology had got her a job
with an old-established firm of auctioneers in Cheltenham
who were branching out from cattle and into property,
and there she had learned what Jenna had always called
'trivvitalk'. 'Start with the weather and finish up with the
customer's aches and pains.'

Jenna said, not always kindly, that Caroline could have
taken her Master's in trivvitalk.

Unfortunately, John Canniston had jumped several
social hurdles and already knew far too much about the
three women to be fobbed off with weather, arthritis or any
other kind of trivvitalk. Caroline huddled into the small
bucket seat next to him and started to tell him that she
would not take up much of his time, and he actually
laughed.

'I mean it,' she said, not with cool assurance but with a
kind of bleat in her voice.

There was a pause while he negotiated the left-hand turn
on to the main road. The engine roared. 'Sorry, I have to
keep the revs up otherwise she dies on me. And as for
taking up my time, I'm afraid the boot is on the other foot.
I intend to take up quite a lot of yours.' He glanced at her,
his face one enormous grin. She avoided his eyes. After a
second's hesitation he looked back at the road. It had once
been the north coast's main road to Land's End, but that
was in the days of horse traffic. It was narrow and winding,

81

and in places the isolated farms encroached on it so that he had to press a warning honk before negotiating them. The Minor's horn was raucous.

'Sounds like a squawking hen,' he commented the first time.

'Yes,' she said and cleared her throat, wondering what on earth was the matter with her. Laura had managed to make her enormous confession sound almost normal, as if all small sisters fell in love with their adult brothers. But it hadn't been normal. Laura hadn't taken in its enormity at all. She hadn't realized that all her life Caroline had been looking for a love like that. And never found it. And if it hadn't been for this young man at her side seeing into her eyes and knowing that there *was* a dreadful secret, she would never have said a word to Laura.

To her horror she felt angry tears in her throat. She cleared it again.

John Canniston said, 'We're right above the sea – it's rather misty but can you see it? Twist around a little – you can do that in these seats – and you'll get a glimpse of Pendeen Watch.'

She twisted and couldn't see a thing. 'Oh yes,' she said throatily.

'And somewhere down there is where Lawrence stayed with his wife Frieda during the First World War.' She murmured something which she hoped sounded in-terested. 'D. H. Lawrence, you know,' he enlarged. 'They had to leave because of the violent anti-German feeling at the time.'

'How awful.'

Her voice sounded normal and she thought he relaxed. 'Yes.' He negotiated the outskirts of St Ives and Hayle and reached the A30 trunk road. Lorries, cars, vans roared past them; the Morris chugged on unconcerned.

He broke the silence at last. 'I know Maisie is practically in her dotage but she's very reliable. Please don't be nervous.'

For a moment she was completely lost, then she noticed

him patting the steering wheel reassuringly and she almost laughed. Maisie. The Morris Minor. He wasn't psychoanalysing her, the long silences were simply to do with coaxing his precious antique through the traffic; he hadn't seen into her head at all, she was still safe. She spoke almost liltingly.

'I think she's beautiful. She doesn't make me nervous, not a bit. It's just that . . . it's much colder today, isn't it? I'm afraid summer must have well and truly come to an end.' Trivvitalk. Start with the weather. And he must have been glad, too, because he started to tell her how sorry he was for the itinerant field workers.

'Such a romantic idea in the summer. Rather like the hop-pickers in Kent. A cheap summer holiday. And then winter comes and whatever they say about our mild climate, we still get frosts.'

The weather lasted until they turned off for the city, then he said, 'I hope you won't mind. I'll take you into the centre and introduce you to the archivist – get you started, as it were. Then I have to see the archdeacon about a new appointment. I'll probably be a couple of hours. Will that be long enough?'

She felt intense relief. If there were any secrets to be found today she would find them on her own. 'Of course,' she said enthusiastically.

He eased Maisie down the steep street towards the cathedral precinct. He needed to increase the revs considerably as he looked for a parking space on the enormous cobbled apron and several heads turned enquiringly. But the school holidays were over and the small city was not crowded. Eventually he parked in a space marked 'cathedral staff only'. He switched off and turned to Caroline.

'I am staff. Just for a few hours, surely?'

Was he asking her for reassurance? She felt her usual confidence return with a rush. 'Hang on. This usually does the trick.' She rummaged in her capacious bag and came up with a disabled parking card which one of her clients had left in her car about a year ago. He was shocked.

'I couldn't possibly! Unless it's for you . . . but surely . . .'

She was going to laugh at him and tell him that the holder of this particular card was doubtless now dead. But then she didn't.

'Actually,' she said very seriously, 'I don't mention it, of course. I have a prosthetic foot. Don't even need a stick, as you see, but I do tend to tire quite suddenly.'

He did not know what to say. Half of him knew very well it was a sick joke; the other half was not quite certain. She watched him wrestle with this dilemma while she set the cardboard digits to two hours and sat the card on the dashboard. Then she opened the car door, swung out her legs, and stood up in one fluid movement. And still he said nothing, but got out himself and stood hesitantly, key in hand, looking at her across the roof of the car. She would have liked to meet his eyes and challenge him to believe or disbelieve, but she did not dare do that in case yesterday afternoon's incident was repeated. She rummaged in her bag again and came up with some kid gloves which she drew on, by which time he had joined her and held out his arm – which she ignored.

She shouldered her bag and they started across the precinct and down the wide road towards the river and Lemon Quay. There was plenty of traffic and the gutters were small troughs lined with paving, and bridged here and there; quite difficult for a woman with an artificial foot. Caroline had seen the same wide gutters full of water like mountain streams in Cotswold villages and they did not bother her; she practically leapt across them. She had a sudden recollection of coming here with Laura and Geoff when Jenna was about ten . . . swinging Jenna over the small rivulets, pointing out the Corn Exchange . . . The tears threatened again.

He grabbed her just in time. 'Steady the Buffs!' He smiled at himself. 'You don't have to show me how independent you are, Caro. It's just round here. That narrow

84

building with the oriel window . . . can you see? Just one more river to cross and . . . we're there!'

She wanted to tell him what a condescending, pious, unbearable young upstart he was. She managed to smile bravely instead; she was, after all, leading him right up the garden path and he was going to realize later what an absolute fool she had made of him. So she let him help her up some stairs and into an office where they were expected, apparently, by a Charles Cledra. Older, spectacles on the end of his nose, a habit of chewing the inside of his mouth judiciously while he considered each word he uttered.

Caroline realized she was in a really bad mood and she would have to do something about it, otherwise the whole expedition would be a total waste of time. She forced herself to listen avidly to what the Cledra man was saying. It was all about the importance of archives, not merely for family interest, as in her case, but for legal matters, historical perspectives, and to forecast future trends and patterns of behaviour. Apparently sociologists used the archives extensively; social services found them immensely useful; probation officers queued up to discover the fore-bears of their clients. 'Fascinating,' she breathed, never taking her eyes off the flashing spectacles.

'Obviously . . .' he must have chewed an enormous ulcer in his cheek by now '. . . we have the largest collection of photographs held anywhere in the county. Editions of the *Cornish Herald* going back over a hundred years. Copies of birth, marriage and death certificates . . .'

Thankfully, John Canniston said firmly, 'Shall we start with those, Charles? I have to be in the cathedral office in ten minutes and I would like to see Mrs McEvoy installed in a seat.'

'Certainly, certainly. Here we are. They are photocopies, obviously. Even so, the greatest care should be taken . . .'

'Are you comfortable there, Caro? Enough light? I suggest you let Charles bring you the back copies of the newspapers afterwards. Not as daunting as it sounds – they

85

were very thin in the old days.' He leaned down so that she was forced to meet his eyes. 'I'll be back as soon as I can.' His voice was lowered. 'Don't worry, Charles will leave you alone. Will you be all right?'

How long since anyone had asked her that? Steve never had and Jenna thought she was the strongest, toughest woman in the world. Laura was thinking it all the time but knew she must not voice her anxiety in case it became a burden. But Tilly . . . Tilly had always said, 'Are you sure you're all right? You are all right, aren't you, my chick?' She had wanted reassurance and had always got it. 'Of course I'm all right, Ma . . . never better . . .'

She said now, 'Will you get into trouble about the parking permit thing? It's not in my name.'

'I suspected as much.'

'I've got both my own feet, too.'

'Yes. I know.'

'I'm sorry. It seemed funny. I'm so sorry.'

He kept looking at her and then he said quietly, 'You are the most honest human being I have met.' He straightened and turned to Charles Cledra. 'I expect you will be making coffee soon. I think Mrs McEvoy would enjoy that.'

He glanced at her, grinned and was gone.

Her bad mood went with him but a kind of all-embracing misery took its place. She was still staring at the file of photocopies when Charles Cledra appeared with coffee and a solitary digestive biscuit.

'You can scroll through the microfiche of course. Bring up the names you want to see and go straight there.'

She forced a smile. 'The trouble is, I want to see them in print. On paper. The real thing, you know. And there are other things I'd like to see as well.' She drank some coffee, which was really good. Her smile widened at him. 'Unfortunately I won't know what they are until I see them. I'm sorry, Mr Cledra. I'm not a lawyer or a social worker. I suppose I'm a sentimentalist. I want to get in touch with my roots.'

He sat down and sipped his coffee like a Victorian lady. She thought he might be trying to avoid the hot liquid getting in touch with his mouth ulcer. He tipped his head back and she saw, with a sinking heart, that he was about to pontificate again.

'There are times in life when we need to do that. We are uncertain, lonely and frightened. We feel the need to know that our forebears, who have always seemed so strong and inviolable, dealt with the same difficulties. And came through them.' He sipped again and stared at the ceiling. 'It often means that those around us are not helping us – no fault of theirs. We tend to push people away at times.' He stood up. 'John Canniston is a good man. A very good man. You can trust a man like that.'

Without another word he turned and walked away. And she stared after him over the rim of her cup and wondered what was happening. And then turned to the first of the box files.

She had brought a reporter's notebook and, with her usual efficiency, wrote down everything she thought might be of interest. Surprisingly, the first Quince she came to was in 1912. William John Quince. The mysterious William. Born to Elizabeth Alice and John Geoffrey Quince at 3, Miners' Cottages, Wheal Three Legs, Cornwall. She wrote it down and sat back for a moment. William had been christened at Tregeagle Church but there had been no funeral recorded. She moved across to the death certificates and leafed through them. There was the death of her grandfather, John Quince. 'Killed in a mining accident at Wheal Three Legs on 11 November 1918.' Jenna had already discovered that from the rector but the sight of the certificate, so official and impersonal, made Caroline tighten her hold on her pen. She drew a breath, entered it into her notebook and went on looking for William John Quince. Nothing. She wrote in her book: 'Could still be alive. Would now be eighty-seven.'

She went back to the birth certificates and suddenly there was Tilly, her dear Tilly. Mathilda Jane. Born to Elizabeth

Alice Quince and John Quince of 3, Miners' Cottages . . .
Caroline leaned close and looked at the stark copy in front
of her. The original ink had been sharpened to a stark black
by the photocopier but the copperplate seemed to bridge
the years: 1907. Caroline realized with a shock that she had
never known her mother's actual age. She too could still be
alive. Lots of people lived until their nineties these days. She
must have been only seventy when she died. Caroline
straightened, closed her eyes and breathed deeply. Her
mother must have been forty when she had Caroline. That
was all right, lots of women had babies 'on the change'. But
Geoff was twenty-five years older. . . why hadn't she done
this sum before? Tilly must have been as young as fifteen
when she had Geoff. Unless . . . unless Geoff had lied about
his age. And why would he have done that? Maybe to join
the RAF at the beginning of the war? She squeezed her
eyes in a frown. It had to be something like that. Tilly a
frightened fifteen-year-old mother? It was something she
had never imagined..

A voice said from behind her, 'Would you like another
coffee, Mrs McEvoy?'

'No!' She cleared her throat, opened her eyes. 'No thank
you, Mr Cledra.'

She heard him close his office door. It might have had a
glass window in it; she would not turn round to look. She
breathed again and relaxed her shoulders, made some
notes in her book and turned over more certificates. She
would think about Geoff's age later . . . Laura. Laura would
know. Of course. She turned the laminated leaves carefully,
slotting them down firmly on to the clip, barely registering
them. And then another Quince grabbed her attention.
After two years' gap there was another Quince, another
stranger. Alice May was born in 1905 to Elizabeth Alice
and John Quince of 3, Miners' Cottages . . . She entered
it beneath William and Mathilda, frowning again. Why
hadn't any of them known about William John and Alice
May? She shifted to the file of death certificates. Again,
there was nothing.

She did some more sums; Alice May would now be in her mid-nineties. Not very likely. But possible. She riffled backwards and found no more Quince babies, then came forward again and studied the ones she had found, looked for others. Elizabeth and John had been married in 1900 and Alice May had been born five years later. No babies in all that time? Had John been in the Great War? Surely not if he had been killed in the mine disaster. And the fact that there were no death certificates for Bessie, Alice, Tilly and William must mean they all went to live in the Cotswolds. She would have to look in the records there. Or maybe in London.

She closed the box files carefully and stood up. Cledra appeared as if by magic, opened and closed them again with a decisive snap, then indicated the files of newspapers on the shelves at the other side of the room.

'I take it you know the approximate dates you are looking for?' He glanced at her notebook. 'Ah, the 1918 mine disaster. Terrible thing. On Armistice Day, you know. My father was born that day. They called him Armistice.'

He smiled and she managed a smile in return. Armistice Cledra. Quite a mouthful. Her smile widened. She said, 'It could be around then. I really don't know. It seems my mother had a sister and a brother. She never mentioned them, and their death certificates are not here. But then, neither is hers. They probably all moved away together. The simple explanations are the usual ones.'

'Of course.' He pulled out a heavy file and opened it up on the shelf under the window. Past his head and below she could see the quay and a young couple walking towards the floating restaurant. The boy held the girl closely to his side; her hand was in his back pocket. It struck her forcibly that they were in love in the way Jen and Jem had been in love. Separately they were ordinary people; together they shone.

Cledra said, 'This issue was published after the mine disaster. Looks as if the news was all about the wayward children's home . . . Of course the papers were tiny compared with today's. And after the war, news was a bit thin on the ground. We should go back a year, perhaps.'

She glanced at the banner headlines: 'Young Boy Absconds from Home for Wayward Children'. She blinked and looked back at the window; the young couple had disappeared.

She said, 'I may as well start from here, Mr Cledra. I can work backwards and forwards. Honestly, I can manage.' She sat on the stool he pulled up and put her palms on the plasticized copies. She felt quite suddenly as if her heart might break for Jenna. Physically it was an impossibility, yet the pain of grief tightened her chest to the point of suffocation. She squeezed her eyes tightly again and opened them on to the view of Lemon Quay. The young couple were there again, standing by the gangplank of the restaurant, looking closely at some sort of notice. The menu. They were reading the menu. She felt her face relax; there was the answer and she was the one who had always known it. Life goes on.

She turned to the newspaper beneath her palms and read those headlines again. Had Tilly read them when they had been freshly printed? Would she have been interested? Probably not. She would have known no one in a home for wayward children. It sounded a fairly normal occurrence too. The local inspector and chairman of the board of governors had asked for a more sympathetic approach. 'These children need loving carers, not wardens,' he had said during his Sunday sermon. Caroline blinked and went back through the print more carefully. The chairman of the governors was the vicar at St Andrew's Church, Tregeagle.

She paused. Tilly had always spoken highly of the church. 'The rector, he were a good man. A saint,' she had said. For a long time when she was small Caroline had thought her mother had said 'the wrecker' and she had imagined a pirate with a soft heart. A Long John Silver made good. This . . . this may well have been the same man. A connection with her mother.

She read on and then turned to the file and went quickly through another half a dozen copies. It made depressing reading. Life in Cornwall must have been very hard after the end of the war; as late as 1921 there were still casualties being reported. And lists of emigrants too. Young boys birched for petty theft. Fishing boats lost in heavy seas . . . A Mr Philip Miles drowned off Pendeen in the winter of 1921–2. Miles had been the name of her mother's first husband, but he had died in the Second World War . . . She started to turn to the next paper and then saw a report of yet another escape attempt from the orphanage or whatever it was. This one was more successful.

The authorities are becoming anxious for the latest missing boy from the Wayward House. Our informant tells us that he is in fact mentally retarded and in need of constant attention. He answers to the name of Billy Boy and should be approached with caution.

Caroline read it carefully. Then shook her head and went on to the next issue.

Behind her John Canniston's voice – unmistakable with its slight Birmingham twang – said, 'Any luck?'

She turned and looked up at him, and for a moment her defences were forgotten. She said, 'I thought you'd be ages yet!'

He was suddenly rigidly aware of her. 'Is that good or bad?'

And she said instantly, 'Good. Of course.' Then realized what he meant and turned back to the papers. 'I've found stuff. Whether it's good or bad I don't know. I need to think.'

'Sorry. I didn't mean to interrupt. Take your time.'

'No, I think I've got something to think about. I'll just make a note about this children's home . . . Laura has never mentioned it.'

'It was closed down. It's now a hotel. They moved to a place in Penzance in the early thirties.'

She scribbled and then said, 'You've learned a lot in a short time. Didn't you say you were new here?'

'Well, yes. But . . . I had previous connections. And it so happens that the CF group took this place over last year.' He paused. 'I was rather hoping to get you and your daughter interested in them. That's what I meant when I said I intended to use up a lot of your time. I planned to go home via Penzance and show you the place.'

She looked up, puzzled for a moment, and then remembered that CF stood for Centrifugal Force, which was the drop-in centre he had spoken of in his sermon. She smiled spontaneously because while she had played such a cruel trick on him, he had partially turned the tables by planning to co-opt her into his pet charity. He met her tea-brown eyes and blinked, then looked away, and she thought, surprised, that neither of them could sustain much in the way of proper communication.

'I'd be delighted,' she said much too effusively, and closed her notebook, capped her pen and reached for her bag.

Charles Cledra was hovering, waiting to put away the newspapers.

'Hello, Charles. This looks like a bit of a cover-up, wouldn't you say?' John Canniston indicated a short article inside the last paper. 'Looks as though the mine owner was attacked by some disgruntled worker . . . What date is this . . . 1922? The mine was still closed then?'

Charles Cledra nodded. 'It never reopened. There was a lot of unrest. Miners emigrated or went to other mines. It could well have been one of them.' He looked over John Canniston's shoulder. 'And he must have got away with it. There was still a gibbet at Penburra in those days. No mention of a hanging.'

John Canniston read aloud. 'Sir Geoffrey Bassett has recovered well from his injuries and wishes to put the attack behind him.'

Cledra said, 'You're right. He was embarrassed. Maybe ashamed of himself.'

They said their farewells and Caroline thanked Cledra profusely. 'Any time . . . any time, my dear.'

John led her towards the floating restaurant. 'He's smitten.' And before she could respond he added, 'Let's have some lunch and if you don't want to go to the CF centre we can go straight home.'

They were too late for lunch but there was tea and toast. And the young couple were sitting by the saloon windows. She sat where she could see them and said, 'Actually, I would like to go to the CF centre. We're trying to organize our lives back at Widdowe's Cottage. Laura has got us knitting squares for Oxfam. And I am supposed to be taking up sketching. And Jen – who is the champion knitter, incidentally – has suddenly acquired this interest in our family, though she won't admit to it. I rather think a stint or two in your centre might be a good thing.'

'It's not mine, Caro. But I have to admit help is badly needed. The people who drop in have given up on the drug programmes offered at their local health centres. They want a cup of coffee or a Coke, a sandwich and possibly lockable toilets where they can administer the next fix.' His voice was level and expressionless, which made his words sound brutal.

She replied similarly. 'In other words, it's not a pleasant afternoon where do-gooders get together in order to feel good themselves?'

He gave a wry grin. 'Sorry. But I wouldn't want you to put the centre in the same bracket as knitting squares.'

She sighed and nodded. 'OK. Eat up your toast and let's go. You can't help being like you are, John Canniston. Our lives are very different, I know that. But we are not quite as idiotic as you seem to think.'

Surprisingly he started to laugh. She said curtly, 'That wasn't meant to be funny.'

And he controlled the laugh and said, 'No. Sorry. It's just that when I told you how honest you were, I didn't take into account that your honesty would – obviously – include me!'

She shrugged. 'I know nothing about your life but I imagine it has been difficult and still is. But – well, I also realize that the thought of three widows sharing their lives sounds almost cosy. I assure you, it is not.'

'No.' He was serious now. She thanked God that he was not also oozily sympathetic. He took a bite of toast and said through it, 'Can you see that young couple on the other side of the saloon? Would it be unbearably presumptuous of me to imagine that they remind you of your daughter and son-in-law?'

She felt her eyes stretch wide with shock. Was he some kind of mind-reader?

'As a matter of fact . . .' she began and then stopped because the cursed tears were there again.

He said swiftly, 'You don't want that toast, do you? Let's go.'

Eight

When Jenna left the church at midday she paused at the gates which screened the porch and then suddenly fitted the key into the lock and secured them. John Canniston had said she could leave them open for any other callers, but that would mean that next time she came she would have to search the place before she could be certain of having it to herself. She knew now that solitude was what was needed. She'd had complete solitude today and nothing had happened; she was disappointed but by no means devastated. She knew it could not happen by an act of will on her part because everything had to be right. She could now arrange for the solitude – she clutched the precious key like a talisman – but there were obviously other conditions of which she knew nothing. She must not panic . . . she must take it in stages. The first time it had happened conditions had been accidentally perfect. All she had to do was replicate them and, if she took everything slowly and carefully, it would happen again. She was still unbearably excited, so churned up at the prospect of finding Jeremy . . . maybe she needed to be totally calm. She had to bring herself down to the complete emptiness she had felt that precious day . . . interrupted by the maddeningly irreverent rector.

She actually smiled at the thought. It didn't matter any more; the poor man had given her the key, that was what mattered. She could come here every day and very gradually reach that place of nothingness, that void, where she would find Jeremy.

She put the key into the pocket of her jeans and began to wander around the churchyard, trying to decipher the names on some of the headstones, feeling nothing of the angry frustration she so often did these days when she stepped away just a little from her grief. She was relaxed yet still excited. It was as if she and Jeremy had arranged a meeting, just as they had done in the old days. When he had finished one of his pasteboard models he had usually managed to smuggle her in when the offices were empty. 'Until the client says yea or nay, it's a deadly secret,' he had explained to her. 'I'm not saying I'd get the order of the boot, but it would definitely mean a black mark.' She had thought it was ridiculous. 'A cardboard model!' she had expostulated. And he had smiled and said, 'Wait till you see it.'

She had been seriously amazed. The model had been to scale and so much more accessible than the accompanying computer image. She had no longer teased him about his work; she had never ever told him again that he was reliving his schoolboy days when he and his beloved father had made models of Spitfires and Hurricanes. She had watched him assembling the last part; he still used old-fashioned implements – compasses, protractors, a guillotine, a Stanley knife – besides the computer which he constantly referred to. She had said, 'You're not just a mathematician, a technician. You're a craftsman, Jem. A wonderful old-fashioned craftsman. I love that. I love it!' He had glanced up and sideways and grinned at her. 'What you are saying is that you love me with all my faults. That's the way we love each other, Jen. It's special.'

She had known that he was referring to her hang-up over her mother. When he had straightened from the work table, she had put her forehead against his and felt for the small indentation in the nape of his neck. It was what they did when there were no words left.

And then there had been the millennium project. An art

gallery. It hadn't sounded much when compared with the Dome and the enormous London Eye. But she had known it was special; she had sensed Jeremy's excitement.

'I want you to see my model,' she recalled him saying to her when he had finished working on the plans one of the architects had made. 'It's going to be very twenty-first century – solar power for a start – completely self-sufficient energy-wise. Japanese influence . . . movable walls and so forth. If I can make sure the showroom is going to be empty at lunch time next week, I'll give you a quick ring and you can dash round.' His grin had become rueful. 'That new girl in recep. told me the other day that we were the most important people in the building. She is the first person enquirers speak to and my models are the first time they know what their building is going to look like!' He had laughed at her indignant expression and added, 'Actually, Jen, I'm nervous about this. If they like the model and go through to the next stage – money – and we get the job, it will put Thaxted and Matthews into world class.'

She remembered the excitement of waiting for his call. The clients had been due to view the model and computer printouts at the end of the week, and until then the whole project was 'under wraps' as Jeremy put it. She had been going to get a preview of the new millennium art space.

Now, two and a half years later, she sat on the edge of one of the graves and looked up at the sky and let the memories flow around her and become part of the present. The weather was overcast but not yet threatening rain. She could not see the sea; the cliff reared up behind the church, protecting it from the worst of the south-westerlies. She looked forward to walking back along the cliff path and watching the white horses which would be coming in now with the high tide. She frowned, bewildered. It was the first time she had really noticed what the sky was doing, what the sea might be doing. And as that registered, so she found herself wondering how her mother was getting along with the rector. Poor Mum, she hadn't wanted to go in the end. Nothing to do with searching the archives; she hadn't wanted to be with poor old John Canniston. Perhaps nobody did. She herself certainly hadn't wanted to be. Poor man. Except that he was alive . . . She closed her eyes and fought the rush of bitterness that so often engulfed her when she saw men, so much lesser men than Jeremy, walking around, being alive.

Gradually that too drained away and there were her memories waiting for her . . . and she was back to the day when Jeremy had telephoned her office and said, 'As soon as you can, Jen. The place is empty for an hour.'

She had abruptly changed her lunch hour to start immediately and rushed down to the foyer and the revolving doors and . . . yes, a cruising taxi. It must have been summer because she had had no topcoat over her suit jacket, and the long chiffon scarf binding her slim neck like a choker had lain on the lapels quiescently, not a breeze to disturb it. She was remembering properly now: the smell of exhaust and dust and then the burgeoning foliage around Russell Square. She had paid off the taxi and run between the Georgian façades to the back of the square where a row of coach houses had been converted into the offices of Thaxted and Matthews. And outside the dark green front door had stood Jeremy.

She had stopped running and held herself still, hanging on to one of the railings at her side. He had been expecting her to use the bus and to arrive on the other side of the road, so his back was to her. He had a good back, wide shoulders and narrow hips. He had left his suit jacket inside and taken off his tie and she had been able to see the back of his neck above the collar of his white shirt and his neat buttocks beneath the grey flannel trousers. He looked so wonderfully *familiar*. For some reason this thought had made her eyes fill with tears. They filled again now, remembering what had happened next.

He felt her eyes on him and turned to face her. He had smiled but not moved. They had simply stood where they were, looking at each other, assimilating each other,

98

making the space between them full of the two people at either end. She had seen a conventional young man of the nineties, formal yet, at that moment, informal too. Fairer than she was herself, but not much, with grey eyes that could be penetrating, a short nose and a wide mouth which revealed his teeth often – 'buck-toothed' he called himself – and a chin that was determined or stubborn as the case might be. Jenna was tall and he only just topped her; she made a great thing of looking down on him when she wore heels. Once when they had gone old-time dancing, he had asked her to take them off so that he could lead properly, then refused to return them. 'You always become a dominatrix in heels,' he had told her calmly as he had gone to check them into the cloakroom.

Remembering this little incident took its toll. She tilted her face again to the sky and forced another smile and quite suddenly tears poured down her face and melted the smile. He was gone. That was the end of it. The only way to find him was to simulate death herself . . . She knew in her heart that slowing her breath and her pulse as she had done that day, was a way of pushing herself into death. Was she in fact trying to commit suicide in this little church where it seemed her grandmother and great-grandmother had worshipped?

She was shocked out of her tears, out of her sentimental memories. She stood up, tensing her muscles hard, fists clenched against self-revulsion. She gasped in air hard and fast as if trying to make up for her recent slow and shallow respiration. She deliberately recalled that although Jeremy's cardboard model had looked superb and she had lifted the roof lids and peered inside and . . . *played* with it . . . Thaxted and Matthews had not secured the job, and the art gallery was at this precise moment being built from a rival design. She found she was breathing normally and her legs were uncramping. She forced herself to walk along a little path beside the vestry door; she slipped the band from her ponytail and shook her hair free. She tried to think of Laura and how she had worked and worked; she wondered whether she should go back to the office and do the same . . . or at the very least help Laura with the gardening . . . maybe get to know her mother properly and understand her. Maybe.

The path became steep; there were no more headstones, just outcrops of natural rock. Sand oozed between the dead stalks of thrift and the bent hazel trees began again, thick and matted against the prevailing winds. She clambered up, hoping to find a short cut on to the cliff path, but the sand did not provide a footing and she slid back down and ended up almost spreadeagled on the bank. She got her breath again – how conscious she was of the whole breathing thing now – and saw how thin the sandy soil was just here. Sharp flint-like strata showed through where she had scraped it away; she should be able to get a grip on the rock and crawl to the top. She reached up and grabbed a bunch of dead stalks and pulled. They held long enough for her to find another ledge with her left foot and push herself up eighteen inches towards the trees. She lunged upwards and grabbed one of the branches, hauled herself up again and stuck her foot where the thrift was still holding. With a small sense of triumph she sat side-saddle on the root of the hazel and looked back down the length of the churchyard to the lychgate. Beyond and below she knew the little village of Tregeagle was going about its business and below that again the estuary of the River Geagle joined the sea. She hooked her right arm around the hazel and leaned down to press the thrift back into place, and it was then she found the tin.

The drop-in centre was situated in Market Jew Street and a long time ago had been the official residence of the portreeve. The guardians of Wayward House had acquired it in 1930 and had removed the porticoed entrance which fronted the pavement, and on the new cement facing had imprinted the words Wayward House. On one side of this door was a wide shop window incorporating a separate entrance, and on the other were the original sash windows through which could be seen chairs and tables, a dart-board, table skittles. The door was open and the clatter of crockery could be heard.

John nodded his head in that direction. 'Kitchen at the end of the hall. Lead the way.'

The kitchen was basic: a big gas cooker with six burners and a plate rack above it; a deep sink; lots of stainless steel. Three people were busy there and John introduced her briefly.

'Caroline McEvoy. Staying at Widdowe's Cottage along by Treleg. Denise is doing hot drinks and sandwiches this week, Caro. Mike and Gill are what we call "listening ears".' He grinned. 'I can see they are hoping you are a new recruit.' He turned to the others. 'Caro and her daughter are staying with Mrs Miller for a while. Conva-lescing in a way.'

Caroline smiled and said nothing. After all, he had to introduce her and how else could he have done it . . . she wants to look round the place but she's no intention of helping in any way whatsoever?

Everyone was very nice, smiling and nodding and then turning to the rector to report a new arrival or a broken chair . . . even just a soiled blanket. And then she realized exactly what a soiled blanket might mean.

'We run the shop to finance the centre,' John explained to her when he had the chance. 'Charity shops are very popular down here and we do quite a trade. I collect a lot of fairly decent stuff down our end of the county, bring it in once a month. People like the shop – even the other shopkeepers say it brings in the customers – but nobody likes the drop-in centre.'

'It gets rowdy sometimes,' Mike said. 'Especially when the pharmacist calls.'

Gill was arranging buttered buns on a tray. She said, 'Some of our callers are on a methadone programme and can get their weekly supply from here. The others don't always agree with that.' The three of them exchanged wry smiles.

'Caro, listen.' John seemed to think she needed some kind of help. 'I must spend about fifteen minutes here. Why don't you go and have a look around the shop? It closes at four thirty, that gives you half an hour.'

Caroline glanced at her watch and saw it was teatime. She was amazed; the time had gone so quickly. And she was obviously suddenly rather a spare part – John had sounded almost condescending when he suggested the shop. She was not interested in the shop; she wanted to do something to prove herself. The two hours in the archive centre had not really produced anything much. She wanted to be able to tell Laura something she did not already know about the Quinces. She wanted to eradicate the awful scene this morning when she had confessed her horrible incestuous secret – which Laura had so indulgently dismissed.

She reached for the tray of buns. 'Let me take these round for you, Gill. Then you can have a meeting here with John. No, honestly, I'll be all right. I'm used to people, wayward or not!'

Gill continued to protest but John said, 'She'll be all right, Gill—' and Caroline was off down the hall and into the sitting room just hearing his final words – 'she's a woman of the world' – and wondering how he could possibly know that.

The sitting room was not welcoming. The floor was covered in vinyl tiles which were scuffed and broken here and there, the chairs were metal-framed slung with canvas, the tables cracked Formica. In the fireplace, the wreck of some other piece of furniture had been packed halfway up the chimney. Six men sat around wrapped in their own worlds: two of them were looking at newspapers, three were watching motor racing on the television, sound turned right down, the sixth was staring out of the window, rocking slightly and singing. Caroline thought it was no wonder they had done their best to run away back in the 1920s.

She said brightly, 'Tea is on its way. I'll leave these here, shall I?'

Nobody gave any indication of having heard her, so she put the tray on the nearest table and went back for the teas. A metal catering trolley had appeared in the hall containing a giant teapot, a kettle and half a dozen mugs; no milk, no sugar. She wheeled it in, lifted the teapot in two hands and began to pour. Milk had been added directly to the tea; she wondered whether sugar was there too. She added water from the kettle and went on pouring, then discovered there were actually seven mugs. One for her? She hesitated, then picked up two mugs and sat by the man who was singing. She held one of the mugs so that he could see it and began to sip at her own. She had almost finished hers before he focused on the mug. He stopped singing. Then looked at her. Then he stopped rocking and became tensely motionless. She was conscious that the room was still, too; nobody looked across at them but everyone was waiting to see what would happen next. She wondered what on earth she could have said or done to gain such attention. Was the singer going to have a fit? Or yell at her? Or perhaps even attack her? She held the mug of tea very steady. Nothing happened.

She counted to ten inside her head, making up her mind that she would then stand up, replace the tea on the trolley and leave the room. Instead, she said clearly, 'Come on, my handsome. I'm halfway through mine and you haven't even started.'

There was another long pause; it became very important to her that her companion should drink his tea. She said, 'Take it', and held the cup closer.

He did nothing. Then a newspaper rustled behind her and someone stood up and came over. 'He can't hold the mug, missis. Look at 'is hands.'

She looked down and saw the hands twisted with arthritis. She made a small distressed sound. What a fool she was, as if it was some competition to get at least one man to drink the tea!

The mug was taken gently from her and held to the singer's lips. He sipped very carefully, then sipped again.

103

The tea was no longer hot. He drank while the other man tipped the mug to the right angle. Caro could have wept.

'Thank you so much. That was very kind of you.'

One by one the other men came to the metal trolley and took their tea. Caroline stood up and stacked the mugs. Her face was hot with embarrassment and she did not know what to say. She paused by the door and looked back; they were all watching the television now, even the singer. She cleared her throat.

'Good afternoon,' she said politely.

The man who had held the mug for the singer looked round and grinned. 'You're posh, aren't you?' he said. 'Come again, why don't you? Bring some biscuits.' He laughed suddenly. 'No, bring some cucumber sandwiches!' And he laughed again at his own joke.

At last they were in the car and chugging back to the A30 and then across country to the old Land's End road.

John said, 'Was it worth it?'

'Yes. Thank you for taking me to look at the county archives. And to the centre.'

'I know it's a bit of a one-horse show but it's well used. Especially as the weather gets colder.'

'I'm sure it is.' She wound down the window. 'One of the men – perfectly polite – told me I was posh. I don't understand it. I'm wearing trousers and tee shirt. How can that be posh?'

He laughed. 'Oh Caro! You've no idea, have you? You could be wearing a dustbin liner and still look good.' He glanced at her and away. 'You're well groomed in an era of untidiness. That's all it is. Don't change. You make me feel good.'

She was intensely embarrassed and did not know why. She had always taken pains with her outward appearance because she had known that the inside was pretty awful, but today she had wanted to be accepted at John Canniston's centre . . . she had wanted to be 'one of them'.

104

She changed the subject abruptly. 'That chap who was singing all the time . . . what do you know about him?'

'Only that he sings all the time. Don't forget I only discovered the centre when I was reading up about the original Wayward House – I haven't been here long enough to know the regulars.'

'You know he's a regular, though?'

'He's always there when I pop in with stuff for the shop. In fact, I think he sleeps there. They've got a couple of beds upstairs for emergencies. It's just so terribly difficult to get volunteers to cover twenty-four hours.'

She blew a sigh of resignation. 'All right. I'll do one day a week while I'm down here. And I expect Laura will join me. We're trying to work out a routine, and it will probably fit in well.'

He glanced again at her and his face was open and happy. 'Oh Caro, thank you! I was hoping so much you would.'

She wanted to tell him to guard against such obvious pleasure, not to show his vulnerability. She said brusquely, 'You've dropped enough hints, for goodness sake!'

'I know. And I thought the prosthetic foot might well put the mockers on the whole idea!' He was laughing and, after a moment's hesitation, she laughed too. Then tried to apologize again and he stopped her.

'You had to retaliate in some way. I can't help being a bit like a vicar at times.' He grinned at her. 'It took me down a peg very neatly. Actually that was when I fell in love with you.'

She knew he was joking but she was aghast. She had no idea why she was aghast. She said quickly, 'Stop joking just a minute and tell me one thing about the singer. He was singing a phrase from one song over and over again and I sort of know it. Do you?'

She held her breath. He was silent while they turned right to negotiate the lane to Treleg and Widdowe's Cottage. Then he said, 'Can you sing it for me?'

She had no idea whether her voice would work but she

had always been able to recall a tune and after another moment she produced the phrase. 'Lala la la la la laaah, lalala, lalala.' Then giggled. 'Sorry, that's hopeless.'

'No. I think I know it.' And he sang in a clear tenor, 'Where have you been all the day, Billy Boy, Billy Boy?'

She was delighted and determined to show it to the exclusion of everything else. She clapped her hands.

'That's it! That is definitely it!'

She grabbed her handbag and swung her legs out of the car. 'Listen, don't come in, it's quite late. Will Wednesdays be all right? I can drive in – park at the top of the Causeway. Will you let them know?'

But she could not stop him from leaping out and taking her hand.

'You've got to watch that foot,' he said. She did not smile. He leaned forward and pecked her cheek. 'Thank you, Caro. Thank you.'

He got back into the Morris and started a noisy three-point turn. And she opened the gate and ran up the path. He had been joking; it was the sort of thing Jenna used to say . . . 'In love' meant nothing any more, you could be in love with a restaurant or Buckingham Palace and he – *he* – could be in love with all his parishioners – and probably was.

Jenna and Laura were working in the garden. 'Ideal weather for gardening!' Laura called without stopping. They were digging, laying soil over the remains of the kidney beans. Caroline stood by them telling them about Wayward House and the man who sang 'Billy Boy'. Jenna looked up, momentarily surprised. Laura said, as if congratulating her, 'You're involved, Caro! Listen to you, you are thoroughly involved!'

And, as she had still been thinking about John Canniston, she said scornfully, 'What absolute rubbish, Laura! Of course I'm not involved.'

Then she went indoors to start on their evening meal and realized Laura hadn't meant anything like a romantic attachment. And anyway Caroline had only ever been totally romantically involved with one person, and that was her brother.

She switched on the kettle and went into the bathroom to swill her hot face. Laura was right in the other way; she could not stop thinking about Wayward House.

Nine

A week went by and it was the first day of October, with a wind coming off the sea that smelled of winter. Laura had gone to church the previous Sunday. She had not been very keen and had thought either Caroline or Jenna might have accompanied her. Eventually, when it became clear that neither of them intended to go, she could not bear to hurt the nice newish vicar and had gone alone. Caroline had been so adamant that Laura suspected the trip to the archive centre had not gone well, and she did not pile on the pressure – as Jenna put it. Jenna herself had simply explained for the umpteenth time that she did not like the church when it had people in it. 'But the people *are* the church,' Laura had protested. 'Anyway, it won't be Tregeagle.' Jenna had said nothing. She had not told either of them about the tin. Caroline had been almost as reticent about her investigations at the archive centre and had been busy rationalizing the whole peculiar day. She could not speak objectively about her findings; or about her feelings. So much of that last Friday in September had been about feelings: feelings about that dratted song, feelings about William John and Alice May, even Charles Cledra with his embarrassed kindness. Most of all, feelings about that earnest young priest.

So she dealt in facts. Laura helped with rationalizing. She maintained that the fact that there were no death certificates for Alice May and William John was because they had left Cornwall with Bessie and Tilly. Laura was absolutely certain that if they had been alive in Geoff's time, he would have known.

'Why did they leave at that point? That's what puzzles me,' she admitted. 'I'm fairly certain that Bessie worked at the Court so she was earning a living. And domestic service usually meant extra food, too. There seems to have been no reason to leave.'

Caroline nodded. 'They left four years after the mine disaster. They hadn't got over it, of course, but they were making new lives . . . unless Grandma Bessie was going to the rescue of Uncle Lemuel. He was her brother and lived alone. No children.' She looked up from her reporter's notebook. 'That's probably what it was, you know. There's no mystery about it.' She had been at pains to be very normal with Laura; neither of them had mentioned her confession since. She would have gone to church with her except she could not face John Canniston again – not yet, anyway.

Jenna came to look over her shoulder and Caroline flipped over the page. 'The mystery is that no one has ever mentioned Alice May and William John,' she went on smoothly. 'Did they disgrace themselves in some way?' She glanced up at Jenna. 'Your great-grandmother could be very unforgiving at times. But if they went up to Childswickham all together then surely someone would have known of them?' She put a line under William's name, then turned the page again to where she had made some notes about the CF group. At the top she had written 'Where have you been all the day, Billy Boy, Billy Boy?'

Jenna said, 'What on earth is that?'

'An old song apparently. One of the people at the drop-in centre was singing it on Friday.'

'Oh . . . I can't think what possessed you to volunteer to help there next Wednesday.'

'It's just that the building itself was used by the Wayward House people from 1930 to . . . I don't know, not long ago, when orphanages gave way to fostering. I think – I only think – that I remember my mother mentioning

109

Wayward House. She might have worked there for a time. I'd like to find out more about it.' Caroline gave a small apologetic smile. 'Besides, they need help. *And* I can take my knitting!'

How could she possibly explain that if anyone but John Canniston had asked her to do a stint at such a run-down place she would have refused? It would mean admitting that she owed John Canniston a favour, and that might well have led on to telling them about the prosthetic foot . . . and that would have given away even more of her feelings.

Laura had enjoyed the morning service very much and wondered why she had held out so firmly against going to church and meeting people. She was surprised when John Canniston shook her hand in the porch and said how delighted he was that she would be doing a turn at the centre. 'Caro wasn't sure about how Jenna would feel. But apparently you got her interested in knitting squares for Oxfam, so perhaps she will follow in your footsteps and come to Penzance with you and her mother.' He beamed. 'Meanwhile it is so good to see you here. I have called once or twice when I've been in the Treleg area but unfortunately you have always been out.'

Laura thought it possible that she had seen him driving to the gate and had escaped upstairs to the bathroom. She felt dreadful. 'I do apologize. I could have been at the bottom of the garden. You can't hear the bell from there.'

'It's tricky when you live alone,' he agreed. 'I'll telephone next time.'

'Great.' After all the poor young man had put up with all three of them arriving on his doorstep the previous week. Probably that was why Caroline had included Jenna and herself in her offer of help. Laura smiled to herself; Caroline was somehow . . . unbuttoning. It was the sudden admission last Friday just before John Canniston had arrived in his little Morris car . . . She had always known that Caroline had been close to Geoff, had loved him dearly. But *in* love with him? She had to smile because

Geoff himself had shaken his head over Caroline when she had married Steve McEvoy. 'My baby sister hasn't fallen in love yet,' he had said sadly. 'And when she does . . . I think it will be rather like you and me, darling. Meanwhile let's hope something comes of this marriage.'

And it had, in a way, because of Jenna. But perhaps it had been during that marriage that Caroline had decided she was *in* love with her half-brother.

Laura moved on down the path thinking her thoughts, and was soon joined by Etta Tompkins who enquired kindly after Caroline and Jenna.

'So strange and so very sad that the cottage was named for a widow all those years ago and now . . .' Etta checked herself and changed the subject with forced cheerfulness. 'My husband's grandfather lived at Treleg. He was headmaster of the school there. Prob'ly knew the first widow . . . a Mrs Quince – your husband's grandmother prob'ly. He was actually teaching on the day of the mine disaster when I believe she lost her husband.'

Laura was surprised and pleased by this small coincidence. She could not wait to get back home and tell the other two the latest piece of the jigsaw. Then she wondered why Geoff had not tried to trace his maternal relatives. Probably Tilly had filled him in on the details and told him that they were all dead. Mother and son had been so close . . .

'What's happened to the school now?' Jenna asked.

'It's been converted into a rather interesting house. An artist called Roland lives there through the winter and lets it to visitors during the summer.'

Jenna pursed her lips and thought about producing the tin, but then Laura made a joke about Caroline volunteering all three of them to help out at the centre and she said shortly that she wasn't interested. She had not been back to the church since the Friday before, when she had discovered the tin; she needed to think it through.

So Laura and Caroline drove into Penzance the next

Wednesday and did the best they could. Caroline cut cucumber sandwiches, and Laura helped one of the men to fill in a form about his benefit money. Then they both loaded up the trolley and Caroline made the tea and sat with the arthritic man again, hoping he would talk. Once or twice while she was working in the kitchen she heard him singing but when she took his tea to him he was completely silent. She held his cup when the tea had cooled and asked him his name. He looked at her as if trying to make up his mind, then shook his head.

John Canniston did not appear. During the afternoon the ladies from the shop took it in turns to come round for a cup of tea and a chat. They closed at four thirty and at five a voice called from the open front door. 'Who's on tonight, then?' and Charles Cledra walked down the hall into the kitchen. Laura was helping Caroline with the washing-up and was introduced. Laura smiled at him and he smiled back. He was surprised and amused to find Caroline there. 'John Canniston does not waste much time,' he commented. 'Was it only last Friday that he was going to bring you here to look around?' She nodded and he sucked at his cheek. 'I told you he was a good man – in more ways than one! He persuaded me to help out, too. I sleep over sometimes if the beds are being used.' He sucked in both cheeks while Caroline murmured something appreciative, then he said deprecatingly, 'I don't actually do anything. Just keep an eye on the place. Insurance regulations, you know.' He went to a clipboard and glanced at a list. 'Looks as if Bill Legge is still here. I'd better go and fetch my toothbrush. He always sleeps over.' He smiled again.

Caroline thought what a very suitable companion he might make for Laura – nothing more, just a companion. And Laura noted him chewing his cheek as he glanced at Caroline and wondered whether they had struck up any kind of friendship in Truro last Friday. How nice – how very nice – that would be. Caroline living in Truro, only an hour's drive from Treleg. Then she laughed at herself and her galloping imagination, and Charles Cledra smiled back warmly and assured her that he lived in Penzance, just around the corner, in fact, and it would take him five minutes to fetch a toothbrush. And she laughed again because Penzance was even closer to Treleg than Truro!

Caroline gave him tea and asked tentatively whether Bill Legge was the one who loved to sing.

Charles nodded. 'Before the arthritis got to him, he was a busker. He collected stories and songs locally and made a living. One of these free-for-all types – never applied for any help, couldn't stand a regular job. He picked cabbages one winter but he was always drifting off in search of some apocryphal yarn – so interested in the past he couldn't be bothered to live in the present. And as for the future . . . well, it didn't exist till it happened.' He chewed for a moment then added shyly, 'I've got some of his stories on tape. When he could still talk I got him to tell me some of them.'

Caroline said, 'Is there anything about that song he is always singing? It's well known.'

'Billy Boy? Funny, John Canniston was asking me about that. Gave me a ring only yesterday. I ran the tapes while I was mounting a new contribution – a pre-war map showing how much land the Bassetts controlled. A great deal of it has gone now, in fact the estate is close to bankruptcy – sorry, that's another story. No, there were no clues about the song. He did not sing that particular song at all so I couldn't help. Pity. John seems to have become very interested in what happened at Treleg just after the mine disaster. Must keep my ears open.'

Caroline nodded and swallowed at the same time. John Canniston had been much too interested in her family affairs ever since he had first met Jenna.

Laura smiled and said conversationally, 'My husband's family name was Miles. He changed it to Miller when his mother remarried. He tried to find out whether there were any Mileses left in the area but he never had any luck. If you come across anything, I would be interested.'

'By all means. Only too pleased . . .' Charles Cledra stopped chewing and looked much more than pleased. Caroline remembered guiltily that Philip Miles was one of the names in her reporter's notebook.

Charles dashed off to get his toothbrush and Laura went to bring the car around from the Causeway car park. She was worried about Jenna being alone when it got dark. Caroline left out the coffee jar and a clean cup and put the milk away in the fridge, then she went into the sitting room to tell everyone that they were going to lock up. Bill Legge was staying, also the man who had held his cup for him and asked her to bring cucumber sandwiches.

He said now, 'I was joking, you know, missis! But I enjoyed them sandwiches, made me feel like I should be watching some cricket again.'

'You like cricket?'

The man called Bill Legge was rocking in time to his song.

'Used to play. County side. Bill used to come and watch sometimes.' He leaned over the swaying figure. 'Didn't you, Bill, eh? Used to come and watch Shanks play cricket.'

The man called Bill Legge stopped swaying and nodded once.

Shanks – if that was his name – looked up at Caroline. 'Bill picked strawberries in the summer, cabbages in the winter. Kept body and soul together while he wrote his book. *Cornish Customs*. He was going to call it *Cornish Customs*. It went right back to the smuggling days – play on the word "customs", d'you see? Cos it were mainly about local customs, how people were.' He looked at the bent head. 'Never finished it, did you, Bill?' Bill shook his head. 'He was born the year Wayward House moved here. He can tell some tales about that place. Most of 'em he's made up himself. But it shows the kind of place it was. Awful.' He leaned down. 'What was that one about someone else called Bill? Murdered one of the Bassetts and jumped off a cliff and drownded 'isself? What was that one, Bill?'

But Bill had shot his bolt. He began to rock again and

Shanks gave up. He moved back to the table and said furtively, 'I'm expecting a friend with a package for me. If you're still here, missis, bring it in, will you?'

'We're leaving as soon as Mr Cledra gets back, I'm afraid.' Caroline could guess what was in the package.

Shanks blustered, 'Listen, it's not what you think – I'm on the methadone programme. Gets my dose brought in of a Thursday morning. That's why I'm staying tonight.'

Caroline gave him the sort of smile she gave when a client was outbid at an auction. 'That's all right, then,' she said. 'Perhaps I'll see you next week? And Mr Legge too?'

Shanks said, 'Who knows? Reckon Bill and me might take to the road again. Eh Bill? Eh?'

And Bill Legge suddenly, shockingly, sang as clear as any bell, 'And me Nancy tickled me fancy. Oh me charming Billy Boy.'

Ten

It was getting towards the end of October, half-term for many schools in the country, so there were other cliff walkers with their backpacks or their dogs or their maps which never seemed to tally with their actual positions on the coastline. At the end of half-term the clocks would go back and it would be dark by five o'clock and Laura and Caroline would worry even more about Jenna being out there on her own. Worse still, maybe not on her own.

Jenna herself had a sense of things coming to an end. She went to the church each day but had not contacted Jeremy yet and the frissons of anticipation which had buoyed her these past three weeks were giving way to desperation. She knew that was counter-productive too; any sense of panic or even hurry interfered with the enormous act of will which could send her into . . . what was it? A void? Oblivion? Or peace? She shivered slightly whenever she tried to define her precious 'experience'. Sometimes she deliberately touched the tin which she kept in the pocket of her jeans; as if it were a talisman of some kind.

She found herself hurrying the last mile home; it was Wednesday and she would have the cottage to herself for another couple of hours; she planned to grab a towel and her costume and go down to Treleg Cove where the old mine adits still dribbled red copper water and turned the sea pink. She would have a dip, let the cold shock her into the present day, give her an appetite for once, so that she

116

could go back to the cottage and start preparing the evening meal.

She actually had her hand on the latch of the garden gate when she saw the figure sitting in the garden. It was John Canniston. The ubiquitous newish vicar. He was wearing jeans and a tee shirt, no sign of a clerical collar. She breathed the most unpleasant word she could think of and withdrew herself behind the escallonia. Had he seen her? Dammit, he knew Mum and Laura would be in Penzance at his dratted Centrifugal Force place; it was their third or fourth Wednesday there and they were obsessed with it . . . some chap called Bill Legge who had not spoken for ages and now was uttering the odd word . . . the archive chap who slept over on Wednesday nights and chewed his face off from the inside . . . someone called Gill and someone else called Denise and a bloke with the unlikely name of Shanks who had played cricket and liked cucumber sandwiches . . . Jenna tried to be interested and had obviously taken in more than she had realized. But it was so . . . She couldn't think of a word to describe it and then came up with *parochial*!

Laura, dear, beautiful Laura, who had lived here in a kind of glorious isolation since Geoff's death, was attending church each Sunday, doing good works in Penzance on Wednesdays and, apparently, going to look at newspaper cuttings in Truro. And Mum, who had always kept real emotions at arm's length, got tears in her eyes every time she mentioned Bill Legge. She'd be moving down here permanently and joining the Women's Institute; she was already knitting like a fiend, it would be jam-making next. Jenna bit her lip guiltily. She still had not shown either Laura or her mother that blasted tin. The one thing that had interested her when they had talked about the centre had been the song. The other was the fact that John Canniston never turned up on Wednesdays. Probably Mother's Union day or something.

But now he was here and waiting for them and he would have a long time to wait because she had no intention of welcoming him indoors and making him tea and listening to him talking about Great-grandmother and balmaidens and the old orphanage-cum-reformatory. And again she felt guilty because it was three or four weeks since they had seen him at the cottage. Laura saw him at church but he had not visited them at all.

She peered through the wodge of hedge; she could not see him but he could not see her either, otherwise the sort of bloke he was – tramping in where angels feared to tread et cetera – he would be wandering down the garden with that soppy grin all over his face, amazed that she was still going to the church every day and probably thinking he'd got a convert on his hands. She did not know what to do; he might have already left, though wouldn't she have heard the rumble of his car starting up – Maisie Morris or whatever he called her?

She made up her mind suddenly. She would stand up and walk right past the gate and go on down to Treleg Cove as she had planned to do. It did not matter about the costume and towel, no one used the cove for swimming, especially in late October.

And it worked. She was abreast of the gate, then walking – striding – past the slate floor of the demolished cottages, then the escallonia again and the sudden dip in the path which led past the ruined engine house of Treleg Mine to the cove with its random rocks and bank of shingle.

The tide was out, leaving a strip of sand for soft entry into the sea. She clambered over the rocks and down on to the edge of the shingle, stripped off her trainers and jeans, rolled them inside the sweater she had tied around her waist, and as she paddled into the sea took out the rubber band fastening her hair and made her ponytail into a tight topknot. And then she leaned gently forward and let the water gather her into itself. It was icy. A wave went over her head. She gasped and then laughed and frog-legged herself past the line of surf where she could ride the swell. She felt her anger and frustration float away from her; suddenly, unbidden, she could visualize Jeremy beside her, turning his head to grin at her as they went feet first over a mounting wave. This was not in a place of nothingness, where the old Jeremy and the old Jenna were gone and a new being created . . . perhaps. This was the real sea, icily cold, and it was the Jeremy who was inside her all the time, the Jeremy who could still laugh, the Jeremy who had the little indentation in his neck so familiar to her fingers. She had called him out of her memory four weeks ago, the day she had found the tin buried under the thrift roots. It had hurt, but everything hurt now and at least he had been there. And he could be there at any time, he was there, in her head . . . Oh God, was this the answer? Was this what people meant when they said that they always had their memories? So trite, so obvious. But maybe much more realistic than what she had been looking for . . . Maybe the whole church thing had been a kind of . . . a kind of trick.

And it was then, as she lay on her back knowing that Jeremy was there, that she heard someone screaming. She tore her eyes away from that dear figure and trod water, lifting herself up to search the sea for the source of the scream.

She saw someone, knee-deep on the shoreline, waving hands, yelling frantically. She was not surprised to see it was the rector. He had interrupted her before when she was almost with Jeremy. Then, he had thought she had overdosed on something and was about to die. She supposed with a kind of humorous resignation that he was under the impression she was now intending to drown herself.

She swam back, catching a wave and body-surfing the last twenty yards on to the edge of the shingle. He waded towards her and held out a hand as she scrambled to her feet.

'Jenna. I'm so sorry. I was a bit . . . anxious.'

She looked at him, wiped the sea from her face. 'Ruined another pair of jeans, I see,' she remarked, po-faced.

'Oh . . . dear. The same jeans, actually.'

She began to walk gingerly over the pebbles to where she had left her own jeans and trainers.

'Tell you what,' she said over her shoulder. 'When I actually do intend to commit suicide, I'll give you a ring. All right?'

'Jenna, I'm sorry. It wasn't that. I saw your clothes there and knew if you were intending . . . anything . . . you would hardly have bothered to undress. But I saw you sailing over an enormous wave and thought you had someone with you so—'

'Someone with me?' she echoed, turning as she tugged the sweater over her soaking tee shirt. 'Someone *with* me?'

'I know. I'm going crazy. The waves create shadows and I was worried you'd gone to help someone.'

She turned back and shook out her jeans. She reversed the usual process of taking shallow breaths and drew in air until her lungs felt ready to burst. What was happening? What was actually *happening*?

He waited while she tugged her shoes over wet feet then said, 'I've been waiting for you, Jenna. I knew that Laura and Caro would be at the centre. I need to talk to you alone. Shall we go back to the cottage? I imagine you need a hot shower.'

She did not know what to say. If it weren't that he had, or might have – seen Jeremy . . . *seen Jeremy* . . . she knew she would have made an excuse at this point.

She said hesitantly, 'OK.' She began to tramp back up the steep footpath and halfway up turned and said, 'Listen. I am glad you saw . . . what you saw . . . and of course you need to talk about it, but I don't want to go into it too much. In case it spoils anything. Do you understand?'

'Of course. Of course.' He sounded embarrassed. 'But I do need some reassurance, Jenna. And you are the only one who can give it. The three of you are so close and you will know how the others feel about it.'

She tramped on, frowning, not knowing what to make of that. Once in the house, she switched on the kettle and put milk and two mugs on the table.

'I won't be long. Make the tea and help yourself to cake and stuff.'

She wasn't long. She felt the need to know what he was talking about. Did he think she told Mum and Laura what was happening, or rather what was not happening in the church? She switched the shower to hot and shook her hair free of the rubber band and soaped herself vigorously, then towelled herself and wrapped Caroline's bathrobe around the prevailing dampness. She took another towel downstairs and rubbed at her hair while she watched him make the pot of tea. Neither of them spoke. Conversation, even Caroline's trivvitalk, was somehow beyond the pale; Jenna was conscious that each of them was weighing up the other.

He hadn't found anything to eat so she put the old biscuit tin on the table and cut two wedges of Laura's cake; she was suddenly hungry after four fruitless hours in the church and the icy swim afterwards. She waited for him to ask her who had been in the sea with her. He was finding it difficult. At last, sated with cake and tea, she said, 'You go first.'

He stared down at his untouched plate. 'I haven't seen her since 24 September. I expect you know that.'

She frowned. 'Sorry. Who are we talking about?'

He looked up, startled. 'Your mother, of course. Who did you think?'

She could have laughed with relief. Any explanations of Jeremy's presence with her in the sea would have been just awful. He must have seen just a shadow in the arm of the wave. That was all right.

She said, 'She's OK, John. Did you worry? You really are good and kind – Laura is always telling me you are good and kind!' She laughed but he did not join her. She went on reassuringly, 'She is going to the CF place. I thought you knew that – I thought you went there yourself, actually.'

'I do. But I haven't been there on Wednesdays since – since Caro started.'

She frowned slightly. 'Well, that's OK. She hasn't mentioned it. I assume they thought you were busy doing the vicar bit.' No smile. She ploughed on. 'Laura sees you on Sundays so she knows you're OK, too. What's the problem – am I missing something here?'

His eyes went back to his untouched cake. 'I think you are. Sorry. I imagined you chatting about it. Women are supposed to be able to talk to each other about everything.'

'We don't. Not often anyway. Not about things that matter. Especially my mother.'

'I know she is very reserved.'

'You can say that again!' She waited for him to repeat his last words and when he didn't she added, 'You're the same, I gather?'

'Not a bit of it! I'm a blabbermouth.' He made a real effort to laugh and then said all in one word, 'Whatyouseeiswhatyouget.' There was a pause. He cleared his throat. 'I think I might have done it this time, too. If you don't know what I'm talking about then it probably means neither did she. Which is fine.'

'You'd better tell me, hadn't you? Otherwise I might let this rather odd conversation be known during one of the typical woman-to-woman chatter sessions you mentioned.'

His smile became more genuine. 'Well, if I tell you, you must promise—' He paused when she said dismissively, 'Yes, yes . . .' then went on, hesitantly at first, talking about how kind her mother had been to help Etta Tompkins with the cleaning and how she had 'lit up the church' with her presence at the Harvest Festival. Then he blurted, 'I'm in love with Caro. It sort of hit me that day, 24 September, when we went to Truro. She started off by teasing me and then she felt guilty and she sort of . . . let me in. When I say it hit me, that's what I mean. Right between the eyes. I knew there would never be anyone else. And I told her. And then I knew she didn't feel the same and I tried to recover myself, and I didn't know what to do. So I kept away.'

By the end of this he had slowed again and his gaze had

dropped to the cake, still untouched on his plate. Jenna said nothing. She was totally shocked. She clutched the bathrobe across her throat and stared at him incredulously. He was talking about her mother.

After a while he said miserably, 'How could I have thought . . . She did not even notice. She would surely have said something to you and Laura. What a fool I am! When you go back it will get better, of course. But now . . . even though I don't actually see her, the air is full of her. I go into the centre every Thursday because I know she was there the day before. I talk to Billy Legge because I know she was talking to him. She is so beautiful, so perfectly imperfect, so human. And I get this feeling – ' he laughed apologetically – 'that she has been waiting for me all her life.' He looked up and met Jenna's enormous brown eyes and checked himself. 'Jenna, I'm sorry. This must be such a shock for you on top of everything else.'

She said, 'She adored my father. It went wrong, I know that, but . . .' She too stopped herself. Then said icily, 'How old are you?'

He said, 'Forty-two. I'll be forty-three—'

'She is fifty-two. When you are her age she will be – she will be – in her mid-sixties!'

'Jenna, do you think I haven't worked that out for myself? I am just so thankful that somehow our times on this earth did not miss each other completely! She is still here and I am here too. That is enough for me.'

'But not for her!' Jenna did not know why she was so angry.

He nodded sadly. 'You're right, of course. It's just as well she has no idea at all how I feel.' He looked again at his plate and stood up. 'Listen, I won't stop now. I don't want to risk running into her.' He scraped back his chair and made for the back door. She noticed he was still dripping water from his sodden jeans. 'I dare say she will be going back to Gloucestershire soon. And will you return to London as well?'

'Of course. That's where I work and where we lived.'

He opened the door and started down the garden. It was overcast now and chilly.

She raised her voice. 'I might look for a smaller place nearer the office. My mother moved when my father was killed. It's probably a good thing to do.' She wanted to ram home the fact that they both had lives to lead; that her mother had led hers without him for the last fifty-two years. He crouched slightly as if she had hit him, so he had got the message. She closed the door with a click and pressed herself against it. She could see him through the window. He hadn't brought his Maisie Morris; he kept going, through the gate and turned left along the footpath that led to her church. His church. He was a vicar for goodness' sake. How on earth could he fall in love with a woman who hardly ever entered a church and had steeled herself against her own feelings so strongly she had probably strangled them all by now?

Jenna went upstairs and put on her pyjamas and dressing gown. She plugged in the hairdryer and hung her head down to blow her hair dry, then felt horribly giddy and sat on the edge of her bed. She began to cry.

Laura and Caroline arrived home later than usual. It was dark and the headlights shone through the windows into a dark house. Caroline shot out of the car and was in through the front door before Laura could open the driver's side. She tore through to the kitchen just as Jenna switched on the light.

'God!' Caroline looked angry. 'I thought you must have fallen off the cliff or something!' She managed a crooked smile. 'Sorry. What on earth are you doing sitting here in the dark – and in your night clothes!'

'I'm all right. I've put some chicken to braise in the oven. It was warm sitting by it . . . must have drifted off or something.' Jenna opened the oven door and peered inside. 'Roast veg. Everything is ready. You must be starving.'

Caroline surveyed the table: a basket of bread, the dark blue napkins. 'We are, actually. This is great.' She called down the hall. 'Come and see this, Laura. She's fine. Dropped off in front of the cooker.' Laura came in, smiling even more than usual. They both exclaimed with pleasure.

'You look different, darling.' Caroline put her head on one side and looked from the table to her daughter. 'Flushed. Lively. Have you had a good day?'

Jenna turned her mouth down, considering. 'Yes and no. I got home earlyish and had a swim in my tee shirt and pants. So then I rushed in to have a shower and put my pyjamas on . . . It seems ages ago.'

Laura and Caroline exchanged quick glances; they were used to a Jenna who lived half in another world. They drifted off to wash their hands, then settled around the table while Jenna put the casserole dish in the centre flanked by a big tin of roast red and green peppers, onions, new potatoes, globe artichokes and carrots. 'A meal fit for a king,' Laura murmured tritely.

Caroline laughed. 'We've got loads to tell you, darling. That's why we're late. Charles arrived to do the sleep-over as usual and had photocopied lots of stuff from the old newspapers at his office. I'd already come across odds and ends that time I went there.'

'24 September,' Jenna supplied.

Caroline was surprised. 'Fancy you remembering the date! But yes, I think it was then. I jotted things down, then forgot them. They did not seem relevant to us at all. But he followed up a couple of things and we've fitted together some bits and pieces from later editions and have come up with something that just might be relevant to your grandmother. And great-grandmother, of course.'

Jenna felt herself relax a little. Her mother was so wrapped up in this business of searching the family background; that was what was animating her. Nothing to do with being in love with a man ten years her junior. Jenna served the food, smiling now, recalling wryly the angry energy which had spurred her into mopping the kitchen floor, preparing the casserole, putting her wet clothes into the washing machine, and sitting in the dark kitchen fulminating pointlessly – very far from sleeping.

At last Laura sighed, replete, and said, 'Geoff couldn't have known that he had an uncle and an aunt, you know. Unless . . .'

Caroline said, 'Unless what, Laura?'

'Unless he was protecting someone.'

'Who, for goodness' sake?'

'Well, there aren't many people to choose from.' Laura frowned slightly, thinking back. She did not like the idea that Geoff had had secrets from her. 'Tilly. Or maybe Jacko – it could have been Jacko, his father.'

'It could have been you, Laura,' Caroline said quietly.

Laura shook her head. 'I honestly don't think so.' Her frown deepened. 'Unless he thought I might have let it go further.' She looked at the other two as if discovering something they did not know. 'I'm a fairly open person,' she said.

Even Jenna smiled and Caroline laughed freely. 'I think we both know that, darling.'

Jenna said, 'It could have been you, Mum. Uncle Geoff was very protective. You've said yourself he was a father figure in your life.'

Caroline coloured slightly but Laura said, 'I hadn't thought of you, Caro. But yes. Especially after what you told me.'

Caroline said quickly, 'Anyway, never mind that now. Tell Jenna what we have concocted from Charles's trawl!'

Laura looked across the table at her niece. 'Only some of it is a concoction, Jen. The actual newspaper reports are about a boy who escaped from Wayward House, which seventy-odd years ago was up by Court Farm. It seems this Wayward House took in boys who had stolen stuff, petty pilferers perhaps, troublesome boys generally. The policy at that time was towards making a real effort to rehabilitate young wrongdoers and get them back into the community. A big step from sending them off to Australia or birching them.' Her beautiful eyes clouded for a moment.

Caroline put in, 'There was one dormitory of five boys who had learning difficulties. Probably Down's syndrome . . . brain damage of some kind. They were sent to work on the farm, no attempt made at education.'

Laura nodded. 'It was one of them who escaped. He must have gone straight to the Court. Remember the Bassett family still lived there. At the time the squire was also the owner of Treleg Mine, this cottage and the others that were still here. He was a director of the Great Western Railway Company, which was busy opening up Cornwall for tourism. He was a big man. Very powerful. His name . . .' she paused for effect '. . . was Sir Geoffrey Bassett. Our Geoff must have been named for him.'

Jenna noticed with a pang of love that Laura referred to Uncle Geoff as 'theirs' rather than 'hers'. The thought flashed into her head that Jeremy also belonged to all of them. It was a good thought.

'Anyway,' Caroline said, 'this boy, he's not named in the newspaper reports – at least, we can't find a name anywhere – his goal was this powerful man.'

'We forgot to mention,' Laura said, 'that Sir Geoffrey Bassett had a wooden leg. He must also have had part of his real leg because he was known as Geoffrey Three Legs.'

Caroline looked at Jenna. 'Did I tell you that the day I went to Tregeagle Church, Etta Tompkins, the cleaner, told me that the mine was called Wheal Three Legs?'

Jenna was confused. 'I can't remember, Mum. But . . . why did Billy want to see old man Bassett?'

Both women almost shrieked, 'Billy? Why did you just call the boy Billy?'

'Well, the William John who was born in 1912 – Mum had it in her reporter's notebook – aren't you trying to tie him in with Sir Geoffrey Bassett?'

They were silent, astonished. Laura said, 'Well, yes. But we've got nothing to go on except intuition, which you must have, too.'

Jenna said, 'For goodness' sake, do you know any more? Did he find old Three Legs himself?'

Laura said, 'Oh yes. He found him. He tried to kill him. With his own wooden leg.' Her eyes unfocused slowly as she recreated the scene for herself. 'He must have taken off his leg. Perhaps he always did that as the evening came on. The stump must have ached unbearably. He unstrapped it and put it against his chair. The boy came through the long windows. They were never locked, of course. It was early April. The lawns running down to the ha-ha were probably covered in primroses. He came from there, clambering up the wall and simply walking through the flowers, opening the casement, stepping inside . . .' She came to herself with a little laugh. 'He picked up the leg and belaboured Sir Geoffrey. That's what it said in the report, "belaboured" him. He was only ten. No way could he have killed anyone. But that was what he was accused of – being a murderer.' She smiled ruefully at Jenna. 'He was never seen again.'

'The thing is, Jen,' Caroline said in her sensible voice, 'William John Quince's birth certificate says he was born in 1912. This happened in 1922 when he would have been ten. And it was 1922 when your grandmother and her mother left Cornwall. Did they have William John with them? Were they running from the law? Or was William John nothing to do with the boy who belaboured Sir Geoffrey Bassett?'

Jenna looked at her mother and felt tears pressing behind her face, tears that had nothing to do with Jeremy. She said, 'William John was the boy. He was the one who escaped from Wayward House and wanted to kill old Three Legs. He had learning difficulties. He did not go to Gloucestershire with Nanna and Great-grandmother. He died here, where he belonged.' She saw their astonishment and their fear too. They thought she was going mad, they thought she had been sitting in that church having hallucinations or visitations.

She stood up. 'Wait here.'

She went upstairs and fetched the tin from her bed, where she had left it when she took her clothes downstairs to the washer. She put it on the table next to the empty casserole. It was a small tin with a hinged lid. On the top words had been painted in flowing letters; they were eroded by rain but it was possible to decipher that the tin had once contained Doctor Zephaniah's cough lozenges. Jenna opened it and removed a piece of paper and smoothed it out on the table, then sat back. The other two women crowded over it. Laura said something about her glasses. Jenna said, 'Read it aloud, Mum.'

Caroline read slowly and carefully.

'This place should be held in memory of William John Quince, born 1912, died April 1922. He knew the important things in life. Right. Wrong. Who he loved and who loved him. He went into the sea because he was protecting the people he loved. He is now with God.'

She looked at Laura. She said, 'It seems to be signed by John.'

Laura spoke through tears. 'D'you mean our John? John Canniston?'

Jenna spoke quickly, 'It's actually Carridon. I looked at it very closely tonight. The Reverend John Geoffrey Carridon. He's on the list of incumbents just inside the door of the church. He was there from 1908 until 1923.' She cleared her throat. 'Turn the paper over, Mum.'

Caroline did so and uttered a little cry, then put her hands to her face.

Jenna said from memory,

'Where have you been all the day, Billy Boy, Billy Boy?
Where have you been all the day, my Billy Boy?
I've been walking all the day, with my charming Nancy
    Gray,
And me Nancy tickled me fancy. Oh my charming
    Billy Boy.'

They were a very long time sitting, talking about that early April night nearly eighty years ago, weeping for Billy and then for Bessie and Tilly, looking at the tin and the piece of paper, as if there were more secrets to find.

At last Jenna stood up and went to the kettle to make coffee. The other two watched her, only now recognizing the difference in her. Belatedly they asked when and how she had found the tin and she told them.

'It didn't seem to matter to me . . . It was the day you went to Truro, Mum. And when you came back with those notes, I nearly showed you but then – I can't remember why – I didn't want to stir it up. As if the past could become more important than my personal grief.' She shook her head as they both protested. 'Grief hems you in, makes you selfish. That's what it was. I'm really sorry.' She smiled at them as they continued to protest. 'Listen, you old biddies! It will happen again so save your breath to cool your broth!'

They all laughed. Laura looked at Caroline and knew it was the breakthrough they had both been working towards since the summer.

And then Jenna sobered and said, 'Two things. Why did Billy Boy try to kill old Three Legs? Was it because he had got Tilly into trouble? I suppose you realize, Mum, that Tilly must have been about fifteen when she had your brother?'

Caroline was silent for some time, then she said, 'And what was the other thing?'

'The other child you found at that archive place. Alice . . . what was her name? Older than Nanna. Alice something.'

'Alice May. Born at 3, Miners' Cottages, Wheal Three Legs, 1905.'

'Yes. No death certificate down here. No mention in the parish records. What the hell happened to Alice May?'

Eleven

October 1999

Jenna was against the whole idea.

'It's too late in the year. They went at the very beginning of the summer. And anyway, what's the point? We've found them, we know about dear Billy Boy – shouldn't we let them rest in peace now? In a strange sort of way I feel it's none of our business.'

Laura said in a low voice, 'There's still Alice.'

'You said yourself that this Cledra man was going to telephone his mate who used to be at Somerset House and ask about her death certificate.' Jenna looked from her mother to her aunt. They said nothing; they had already made up their minds. 'I can see you don't think there will be a death certificate.' She sighed. 'Mum. Laura. Those years after the First World War were messy to say the least. People disappeared. Billy, for instance. Why not Alice as well?'

Caroline said, 'We know about Billy now. And our knowing is important, Jen. People live on in memories.' She stopped speaking. She and Laura both knew that Jenna did not find memory sufficient.

But Jenna did not retreat into herself or go into the parlour to knit. Instead she nodded agreement and sighed a kind of resignation.

'Actually, I was thinking earlier that I should go back to work.'

'Really?' Caroline was instantly alert in the kind of way that often irritated Jenna and made her feel pushed into corners, forced to explain herself.

'We've been here over four months,' she pointed out.

'Has something happened, Jen?'

'No. And yes. And then no again.' Jenna grinned, acknowledging that she was being deliberately evasive.

Laura looked at the two mugs on the draining board. 'You've had a visitor,' she observed.

Jenna made a ticking sound of annoyance. She had prepared and cooked the casserole and vegetables, made coffee afterwards and found some chocolate mints to go with it, and still forgotten to wash up and put away the mugs.

'I have indeed, Mrs Sherlock Holmes,' she said. Then laughed. 'The vicar called.' She flicked a glance at her mother; there was no reaction. But then Caroline was adept at hiding her feelings, if indeed she had her full quota.

Laura said, 'Weren't you going to tell us? What on earth did he say?'

'Oh, the usual vicary sort of stuff.' Jenna laughed again. 'It was all a bit embarrassing, actually. He was walking along the cliff path past the cove, saw me swimming in my tee shirt and pants and came up with the idea I was trying to drown myself!' Both women gasped. Jenna opened her hands. 'He shouted and I swam back. I suppose he would have come after me. He was up to his knees in water as it was. So I brought him back and made tea.' She shook her head. 'He's a bit of a plonker, actually. But I guess he means well.'

Laura said quietly, 'I think he's a bit of a saint, Jen. He genuinely loves people. That's the second time he has rescued you, for instance.'

'Both times mistakenly, Laura!' Jenna protested. 'And I can assure you, that man is no saint!'

Caroline was alert again. 'What do you mean, Jen? Did he – I mean, did he?'

'Make advances?' Jenna thought back. 'It depends what you mean by advances, of course.' She laughed and then stopped. The meeting with John Canniston had not been

132

funny. She had thought at one time during the evening that it was absurd, ridiculous. But it hadn't been that either. The blasted man was so truthful, so sincere. And he had said he was deeply, madly, passionately in love with her mother! She said, 'Of course he didn't make advances. He waited while I had a hot – very hot – shower. During which time he made no attempt whatsoever to dry out his jeans. I had to mop up the floor after he'd gone.' Neither of them smiled at this and she sighed again and said, 'Listen, I promise you I was not going to drown myself. I feel more at peace than at any time since the accident. I have, as from now, officially given up my visits to Tregeagle Church. As Mum said, I've got my memories.'

Caroline's hand shot across the table and grabbed her as tears absolutely spouted from her eyes. Laura looked at them and said, 'Let's have some more coffee and finish up those mints. They're past their sell-by date I see.'

Jenna tried to choke out a laugh. 'And no one accuses you of trying to commit suicide, I notice!' She did not move away when Caroline scraped her chair back and came round the table to gather her up. 'Mum . . . Laura . . . I'm sorry I've been so . . . difficult . . .' She waited for their gabbling protests to subside. 'I'm still going to be the same. I'm never ever going to get used to being me again and not half of Jem and Jen. But I'm not going to die looking for Jeremy's ghost. I know I was the luckiest woman on earth to have been with him—' She suddenly remembered what John Canniston had said and she repeated his words. 'I am just so grateful that somehow our times on this earth did not miss each other completely. It might not have happened at all. But it did.'

Laura poured coffee and looked at the two people she loved most on this earth. They were intertwined into one being. She had never seen her sister-in-law weeping so unrestrainedly: huge, gulping sobs that she could not control, though she was very obviously trying to do so. She glanced at the kitchen clock; it was almost midnight. They had arrived back from Penzance very late, but they must

133

have been sitting around the table for well over two hours. Perhaps coffee was not such a good idea. She poured it anyhow. Gradually they settled down. Caroline took a huge shuddering breath and raised her head from Jenna's.

'I know this sounds crazy, but I'm . . . actually . . . happy,' she said, trying to compose her face into an ironic smile.

Jenna said, 'It sounds crazier still, but in a way, so am I.'

Laura ripped several sheets of kitchen paper from the roll above the sink and handed them across. Mother and daughter separated themselves and mopped at their faces, making snuffling apologies.

Laura said, 'If anyone dares to say they are sorry again I shall hit them with the dish mop!' She pushed their full coffee cups towards them. 'Come on, let's have this and go to bed. Any more discussion about our proposed pilgrimage can wait until the morning.'

'Pilgrimage?' Jenna sipped her coffee gratefully. 'You didn't call it a pilgrimage. I was thinking we were sort of tracking down poor old Bessie and Tilly. I felt we'd gone far enough with digging up the past. I felt it ended with Billy.'

Caroline let the steam from her mug soothe her sore eyes. She said, 'Perhaps you're right, Jen. Perhaps we're simply being curious now. Voyeurs.'

Jenna nodded. 'That's exactly what I meant, Mum. I think it might have been the reason I didn't immediately show you Billy's tin. The thought of someone discovering about my two so-called suicide attempts in eighty years' time doesn't exactly fill me with joy!'

They smiled at each other, easing the bitterness of the joke by being able to share it. At last.

And then Laura said quietly, 'I agree it would be a pilgrimage. But I'm afraid I am still curious. More than curious. I need to know, my dears. My memories of Geoff are – are – vital to me. And now I am wondering exactly what they amount to. You must have worked out, both of you, that Geoff was born when Tilly was only fifteen.

134

Fifteen.' She looked from one to the other. 'They always were more like brother and sister than mother and son.' She picked up her mug and drained it. 'I'm sorry. I really must try to find out more about it because of Geoff.' She put down her mug. Her face was set in lines of despair. 'Alice could have gone to Canada or Australia or she could be in an old people's home right now. He did not tell me . . . anything. Perhaps he was not the man I knew at all. And I couldn't bear that.'

She stood up and made for the hall. 'Forgive me, Jen . . . Caro. I thought I'd got my grief sorted out. And I was wrong.'

The next day, Thursday, Caroline announced that she was going to write everything down. 'I want to make sense of it. I know there are huge gaps but if we've got the salient facts we might be able to clothe them in some way.'

'Fictionalize it?' Jenna asked.

'No, of course not. But we've already got some idea of Tilly's character – pretty strong for a girl of fifteen – and from her we might pick up a lot about Alice and Bessie. Then we might be able to see what they would do . . .'

'We'll never find the exact route they took, Mum. They might have pawned things and got railway tickets right through to Gloucester or Stroud. Or they could have known someone who was going that way.' It sounded unutterably lame and negative too. Jenna said, 'I'll give you a hand. Won't take us long to write down those salient facts – I like that word, salient. Sounds as if we're making a war plan instead of a pilgrimage route.'

Laura was peering out of the window; it was raining. She said without enthusiasm, 'I'm almost certain they arrived October or November time. I remember Tilly telling me that Bessie made one pair of gloves each day and managed to complete the order in time for her first Christmas in the village.' She turned and looked at them with a kind of helplessness. 'Seventy pairs of kid gloves. And she'd never made a glove before then. The kid leather arrived in bundles and had to be stretched on a wooden hand-shape and sewn with tiny, tiny stitches. Most of the cottage workers wore strong glasses just like hers.'

Caroline was horrified, Jenna less so. She had studied the working conditions of women in the early part of the twentieth century; nothing surprised her.

Caroline said in a small voice, 'Why did she tell you things like that, Laura? She never told me.'

'She told you things she didn't tell me. She did not think that one day they might be important.' Laura smiled. 'We should write them all down too.' She went back to the window, wondering whether the rain was easing slightly. 'She needed to be strong for you anyway, darling. Believe it or not you were very shy as a child. Tilly and Geoff gave you complete security.'

'Mum? Shy? I. Do. Not. Believe. It!' But even as Jenna teased her mother, she wondered. Maybe the ice queen exterior had covered shyness and lack of self-confidence.

Caroline smiled. 'I don't know about the shyness. But certainly you three were always towers of strength.'

Laura said, 'Three? Jen wasn't born then.'

'No, but you were. You were always there for me, Laura. Why do you think I wanted to bring Jen down here after the accident?'

'We're still a family, after all.' Laura moved away from the window and said decisively, 'I'm going to the church. I'll take the car because the footpath will be impassable. You don't need it?'

'No. But why? Shall we come with you?'

'I'd prefer to be on my own, really. I want to see where the tin was buried. Give me a few pointers, Jen.'

Jenna looked anxious. 'It's all so steep and it will be muddy now.' Laura was already putting on her shoes so she described the place as best she could. 'Here. You'd better take the church keys. If it's pouring with rain you can go inside to shelter.'

'Thanks.' She opened the garage door and backed out the car, wound down the window and said, 'You do realize that if I've got that time-scale right, Geoff was born during the journey?' She did not wait for an answer.

They stood at the front door until the car disappeared. Caroline said, 'We've got to find out what happened on that journey. She's been knocked right back by all this.'

They drifted down into the kitchen again. 'Do you regret starting this whole search thing?' Jenna asked, automatically fetching coffee mugs.

'Not at the moment, no. I always wondered how Tilly felt about my birth so long after Geoff's. We talked about Jacko. Jacko Miles, her first husband, Geoff's father. Rarely about mine.' She smiled wryly. 'Maybe I'll go on and find out more about him.' She thought about it. 'Yes, I'll do that. After all, my mother married him, so he must have been a good chap.'

'Maybe you took after your father's side, Mum,' Jenna said. 'Lord – he was my grandfather. And I know less about him than you do!'

Caroline laughed. 'I never missed him, Jen. Tilly and Geoff and then Laura. They were enough for me.' She drew her notepad towards her. 'But I miss Tilly and Geoff. When I realized that Tilly had worshipped at that little church on the cliff . . . I wanted to move in there. I knew how you felt.'

'Oh Mum . . . I got there first.' Jenna flicked a look at her mother's downcast head and said, 'But then I opened other doors in a way, didn't I? John Canniston and the archive place. And then the Centrifugal doo-dah!'

'Yes.' Caroline did not look up. 'We probably wouldn't have stuck it except I knew darned well that the man who kept singing knew something. He doesn't know what it is himself. He's too young to have known Billy. Yet he knows of him somehow. He's always singing that song.'

'I think you would have stuck it.' Jenna drank her coffee and put the mug behind her on the draining board. She said deliberately, 'You're suddenly into good works, Mum. How many blanket squares have you knitted so far? It's since you met that vicar, isn't it?'

137

Caroline glanced up, surprised, then put down her pen and cradled her coffee cup consideringly. 'John? I haven't seen him since that day he took me to Truro. I made a bit of a fool of myself, actually. Embarrassed myself. I thought he was a pious so-and-so at first. People kept telling me how good he was – Charles Cledra for instance. And now Laura. And of course they're right. He is a genuinely good man and we're all suspicious of genuinely good men!' She laughed and went back to her notepad. 'Anyway, he's kept well away since then, even changed his day at the centre.'

Jenna bit her lip. 'He sees Laura at church so he knows we're OK.'

'And he came to see you yesterday.' Caroline did not look up.

'Hardly. He happened to see me in the cove—'

'I think, in different circumstances, he might feel drawn to you, love. I know you think that's unbearable but it will happen. You are beautiful and intelligent.'

Jenna said quietly, 'I am what Jeremy made me, Mum. And you're wrong about John Canniston. I think . . . there's someone else.'

'Really? Well, I'm not surprised. He's young, good-looking and single. And practically a saint!' Caroline managed a little smile. 'Now, stop talking about him and come and look at this. This column for dates, this one for happenings on those dates. We can do it other ways too, but this way we can cross-reference. I mean it's more than likely that Billy's escape from Wayward House, his attack on Geoffrey Bassett and his suicide all happened on the same day that Bessie, Alice and Tilly started their journey.'

Jenna sighed. She would probably never know whether her mother realized that John Canniston loved her; it did not really matter because Caroline, the woman, had hardly noticed him as a man. She sat down at the kitchen table and they began to assemble the very few things they knew about the Quince family.

*　　*　　*

Laura parked the car in the bay right next to the footpath and sat for a moment listening to the rain on the roof. She felt bereft again, this time bereft of her memories too. They were still there but somehow they were tarnished. Geoff had lived such a lot of his life when she met him first; he had told her about it very matter-of-factly. There were no mysteries. Tilly and Bessie had had to leave Cornwall after Tilly's father had been killed. There had been no mention of Billy or Alice. And when she thought about it, there had not been any mention of Jacko either. Yet Jacko and Geoff had both joined the Forces within a few months of each other. When Geoff had left school at fifteen he had been apprenticed as a mechanic because Jacko loved cars. Jacko had always been there. So why were there no stories about him travelling from Treleg to Childswickham all those years ago?

She knew she was being paranoid but since Jenna had produced that tin last night she had felt . . . odd. Peculiar. Shut out.

She shook her head irritably and got out into the rain, then reached back into the car for her trowel, which she pocketed. There was an umbrella in the boot but something contrary in her made her walk bare-headed up the footpath, face tilted upwards as if determined to get wet. She went through the lychgate and up the path then bypassed the double gates across the porch and made for the back of the church, the vestry door, the dustbins and the standpipe with its attendant watering can. Then she came to a halt at the base of the little path leading up beside the vestry. Water dripped from her short hair inside the collar of her mac and down her back and she shivered convulsively. She had to find the place. Billy had been Geoff's uncle, Tilly's brother, Bessie's only son. He deserved . . . something.

She clambered up the path slowly and at last saw what she was looking for: torn turves, a deep heel mark in the grass where Jenna had let herself back down, and a clump of dead thrift which she had tried to replant. Laura removed the trowel from her pocket and dug her first foothold. She stuck her toe into it, balanced herself shakily with her knee pressed into the softened earth, and dug the next. Just above the dead thrift was the springy root of a hazel where Jenna must have perched; she did likewise, hung on to the branch above her and looked down at the thrift. She saw not only the thrift but herself. She was plastered in mud from knee to toe. She stretched her arms in turn; they were the same. She said aloud and incredulously, 'What on earth am I doing – how will this help me or anyone else?' And she began to cry.

Caroline unearthed some courgette soup from the freezer, defrosted it and made some toast. It was one thirty and they had decided not to wait for Laura.

'I'm not worried about her,' Caroline maintained. 'She isn't accountable to us after all. It must irk her sometimes that we're here all the time messing up her life. She's making the most of doing something on her own.'

Jenna said, 'It's so cut off down there at the church. Only a few minutes from the top half of the village, but it could be miles. If she goes into the church I hope she locks herself in.'

'Is that what you've been doing?'

'Yes. So that I could have sole occupancy!' Jenna buttered toast. 'But John did say at one point that some of the down-and-outs sheltered there – he always used to leave it open for them.'

'Well, of course.'

'I locked it when I left.' Jenna opened her eyes wide at her mother. 'Well . . . I didn't want to find anyone already in there when I went the next day!'

Caroline said, 'Anyway, leave some of the soup for her. She probably won't be long.'

They had just finished their lunch when the front-door bell rang. Jenna got there first. It was a man she had never seen before. Caroline, halfway up the hall, said, 'Oh my God! Charles – has anything happened to Laura?'

140

Charles Cledra said, 'Not as far as we know. I've got John with me – just locking Maisie. I was hoping to see Laura. Is she driving? The rain is very wet!'

Caroline was suddenly nervous. She introduced Jenna and Charles and then backed down the hall and tried to shovel their soup bowls into the sink; spoons clattered on to the slate floor.

Jenna said, 'Let me, Mum. Sit down – er – gentlemen. Or would you prefer the parlour? It's full of knitting but the chairs are comfortable.'

'This is fine.' John spoke to Jenna but could not take his eyes from Caroline. 'We've interrupted your lunch.'

Caroline recovered. 'We'd finished. Do sit down, John. You're taking up so much space. Charles, sit here. I take it this is a social call?'

Charles chewed at his cheek while he waited for John to speak and when nothing interrupted the noise of Jenna washing-up, he said, 'Yes, in a way, but we've come because we've got some news for you. And we thought . . . well, we thought your daughter would be at Tregeagle.' He looked across Caroline's head at Jenna. He was quite hairy, she noticed; a bit of a teddy bear. 'I do hope this whole family tree thing isn't boring you, Miss – er – Mrs – er – Jenna?'

'Not at all.' Jenna dried her hands. 'Shall I put the kettle on? There's still some of Laura's fruit cake in the tin.' She smiled at Charles. 'I cut a piece yesterday for John but he left it. We might have better luck today.'

Charles looked perplexed. 'We hoped Laura would be here.' He looked around as if she might emerge from the pantry and she was his only hope of sane conversation.

Caroline said briskly, 'Yes. Put the kettle on, Jen. I'll cut the cake.' Charles began to protest at the trouble they were causing, and she said even more briskly, 'Actually, Jen and I would like some. It will round off our lunch very well.'

Jenna had a wild desire to laugh. Charles was chewing at his cheek frantically and John had transferred his gaze from her mother to the table while colour suffused his face.

She put mugs on the table with the salt-glaze jug and

141

sugar bowl, scooped some lingering breadcrumbs into her palm and sat down with much scraping of her chair. Caroline passed plates of fruit cake around, encompassing them all in what Jenna thought of as her hostess smile.

'Well,' she said, sitting down herself. 'Shall we begin? We're thinking of trying to retrace the journey the Quince women made up to Childswickham.'

The statement fell like a stone into the middle of the table. Jenna smiled at her mother. At this moment she realized she felt almost light-hearted. It was obvious that her mother did not reciprocate John Canniston's passionate feelings, but it would still be good to put a distance between them.

She said, 'I wasn't keen at first. It's such a leap into the dark. We don't know whether they went by train or carrier or . . . even walked!' She laughed at the thought. After all, her beloved Nanna had been pregnant at the time and it was over two hundred miles.

Charles Cledra released his cheek, cleared his throat and came out with 'Exactly!'

'But . . .' Jenna went on smoothly, 'Laura is keen. Very keen indeed. So I've come round to the idea.'

At last, at *last*, John Canniston spoke. He looked at Caroline and said, 'How do you feel about it?'

He did not use her name but she said, 'The same as Jenna. There are . . . certain things . . . we would like to know. For peace of mind.'

Charles Cledra started clearing his throat again and they all waited.

'Our news might help with that.' He glanced at John from beneath bushy brows, saw he was going to get no help there and went on. 'My bit – of news I mean – confirms a great deal of what we already know. I've been playing those tapes again. The ones I made of Bill Legge. The first time I played them I was looking for that song he sings and it wasn't there. This time I went over every word he'd said.' He sighed. It had obviously been a tedious task.

He went on ponderously, 'The old community who lived

at Wayward House told their stories. Most of them were what you would expect. They remembered the bad times and we have to assume there were no good times. Those stories went with them into the Penzance house and then gradually dissipated when such reform homes were closed. The stories that remained were embroidered into legends. They circulated among travellers and were nearly all about being lost, or lonely and homeless. Tales of despair. I would think that they will die completely with the next generation.' He waited, still looking at John. There was no response so he went on, his voice dropping, words slowing down.

'Just one of them was used to show that it is possible to . . . escape. It concerns a boy who was simple – that's the word used by Bill Legge. But this boy was also wise beyond his years. He was certain that the local squire had hurt his family. He ran away from Wayward House and went to find the squire. And he killed him. And then he walked across the moors to Penburra Cove and was taken into the sea by Neptune himself. There were trumpets sounding and a white horse.' He cleared his throat fiercely. 'It ties in with one of the newspaper headlines at the time. I think you saw it, did you not, Caro?'

Jenna said very clearly, 'Billy was not a murderer.'

Caroline said, 'He was ten years old, for goodness' sake!'

Charles Cledra tipped his chair back. 'We are assuming here that it is William Quince. But I must remind you that this is a story. Just a story.'

John said in a low voice, 'Parts of it coincide with recorded events. I have spoken to a member of the Bassett family. There is a record of an intruder entering the house in March 1922. It was a boy whose mother worked there.' He looked at Caroline. 'I think you told me your grandmother was there after the mine disaster?' She nodded. 'So it is my belief the intruder *was* Billy Boy.' Jenna noted that he used Billy's family name. 'They – the Bassetts – have suppressed whatever happened. They call it an "incident". But there was definitely no murder.'

143

'Of course not.' Caroline looked across the table. 'Jen, perhaps you had better show Charles and John what you discovered in Tregeagle churchyard.'

Jenna got up and took the tin from behind one of the teapots on the top shelf of the dresser. She gave it to Charles and he examined it with some interest.

'These cough lozenges were widely used in Cornwall at the time. But as their base was chloroform they were removed—'

Jenna said, 'Look inside.'

Charles unfolded the paper and read it aloud. It had more impact than ever; Jenna felt her eyes fill. It struck her that if there was an afterlife, Billy and Jeremy would now be together.

There was a silence. Charles looked at John, who was staring at the table again. 'I think it's your turn now, John,' Charles said very gently. 'You have to tell them. They deserve to know.' He looked at Caroline. 'John has known something of the Quince family all along. He has felt very diffident about sharing it. I think he feels you might find it intrusive.'

John stared at the table, his head so low that they could only see his dark curls. Jenna noted a lot of grey among the black. Yesterday he had seemed so young; much too young for her mother. Today she saw that he was not that young after all.

He said, 'My grandfather was rector here when the Quinces lived in Miners' Cottages. He left the church in 1923 and married the local schoolteacher, Helen Casson. She was pregnant by him and there was a great deal of bad feeling. They were both loved and respected and the locals felt they had been betrayed in some way. My grandfather changed their name slightly. From Carridon to Canniston – it incorporated his wife's name. Then the two of them opened a school in Worcestershire . . . I don't know why they went there.' He sighed deeply. 'The baby was a boy. My father. He was the happiest man I have ever known and his stories about his boyhood at the school . . . he

144

made it sound idyllic. He died ten years ago and that was when I decided to go into the Church. When this benefice became vacant, I couldn't believe it. I told the bishop why I wanted to come here and he could see my point immediately.' He looked up, straight at Caroline. 'I know you think I'm playing a part. In a way I am. I want to go on where Gramps left off. They loved him down here and he loved them.'

Caroline made no response. Her eyes were enormous and she tucked her fall of hair behind her ears and no longer looked sophisticated.

Charles coughed. 'John has been afraid that his interest in your background would seem to be mere curiosity.'

'Voyeurism?' Caroline asked suddenly.

'Well. Yes. Perhaps.' Charles tipped his chair again.

John said, 'That's why I backed away, Caro. Why I didn't say anything. It might have been better if I'd spoken of it immediately.'

'No.' Caroline was definite. 'Then I would have been put off.' She smiled suddenly. 'We wondered ourselves whether we should go on – whether our interest made us into voyeurs.' She turned her smile on Jenna. 'Isn't this completely amazing?' She looked back at John, drawing him into their family. 'Nanna spoke often of your grand-father. She always called him a saint. He was the reason she went to St Andrew's at Tregeagle. He spoke to her several times at school when she was helping Miss Casson with the little ones. She said Miss Casson was an angel. So your saintly grandfather married an angel!' She laughed, delighted, then said, 'And now we can find out from you which way they went. We'll be able to follow their route exactly!'

John, who had also started to look very pleased indeed, drooped slightly and said, 'Only up to a point. I rather gather that with the disgrace of the baby . . . I think Gramps was asked to leave. Defrocked. And he lost touch with the Quinces once he knew they were safely with Bessie's brother.'

145

'But the actual journey?'

'He put them on a train at Truro. The milk train. And Tilly wrote to say they were there safely. But that was the following Christmas. All I know is that Gramps went to Jacko Miles and told him everything and when Jacko's mother and uncle died Jacko left Treleg and was never seen again.'

Caroline said, 'He was seen again. Just in a different place.' She was still smiling. Jenna thought she looked like a girl. 'He was my mother's first husband. He was killed in the war but he was with them for almost twenty years. He must have caught up with them. Hopefully before Geoff was born.'

'But your brother's name was Miller, surely? The same as Laura's?'

'When my mother married my father, she became a Miller. And Geoff wanted us to be known as a family. So he changed his name. Like your grandfather.' Her smile beamed at John and there was nothing he could do but smile back at her.

The front door opened then closed, and Laura appeared in the kitchen door. She was covered in mud from head to toe. Charles exclaimed and half rose from his chair. But Jenna reached her first.

'Darling! What happened? Has there been an accident?'

Laura took in the assembled company and tried to laugh. 'I slipped down that bloody bank,' she said cheerfully. 'Went into the church to try to wash some of it off and just made it worse! Sorry, Charles. Sorry, John. I'll go and have a shower and change my clothes.'

Caroline said, 'Darling – amazing news. John's grandfather was the rector here at the time of the mine disaster and, as you know, my mother spoke of him often and he spoke to John about her, too! Isn't that the most incredible coincidence?'

Laura frowned, taking in this information. 'Yes. Yes, it is. Why didn't you say something before?' She did not sound pleased.

'I called on you three or four times and you were never at home, and I wondered whether you knew already and held something against my family.' He began to stammer apologies.

Caroline said, 'Laura, John was frightened he might hurt all of us in some way. It was a sensitive business and we still haven't really got to the bottom of it.'

'I'm sorry.' Laura turned her mud-streaked face from John to Charles and back again. 'Oh dear. What a muddle it all is. Perhaps we should let sleeping dogs lie.'

'Darling, the muddle is unravelling as easily as your knitting does!' Caroline laughed, trying to take away some of Laura's evident unhappiness. 'We now know for certain that Tilly had Geoff during the journey.'

John looked at her, surprised. 'Tilly? You've got it wrong, Caro. Tilly was only fifteen at the time. It was Alice who was pregnant. Charles and I assumed that was why Billy Boy attacked old Three Legs up at the Court! The dreadful, ironic thing was – it wasn't poor old Geoffrey Three Legs who made Alice pregnant. It was his godson.'

Laura stared at him for a long moment. Then put muddy hands to muddy face and began to cry.

Twelve

The next day Laura looked terrible. Her short hair would not sit close to her scalp and though Caroline sprayed on something called Holdhair, within half an hour it had bristled out with an indignant life of its own. Worse still, the skin below it on Laura's forehead showed an unpleasant purple blotch.

'It's just an allergic reaction to the hairspray,' Laura said, without much interest. 'I don't take kindly to anything like that.'

'Oh darling! I've done the wrong thing again! Why do I always do the wrong thing?'

Caroline did not look herself either. Laura's sudden appearance the day before, muddy and unkempt but apparently cheerful, and then definitely not cheerful, had shaken her. The tears had not lasted; Laura had turned and gone upstairs without a word and the two men, horrified, had stammered offers of help and then had been swept out unceremoniously by Jenna.

Laura had felt incapable of explanations after her shower and was just as monosyllabic the next day. At breakfast Jenna had said very decidedly, 'I'm going to put the tin back in the churchyard. All right? No one objects, I take it? And when I get back, we'll have lunch and we'll sort everything out.' She reached past the cereal box and grasped Laura's hand. 'We've totally disrupted your life, Laura. I think it's time we went. Think about it.'

They thought about it while they cleared the breakfast

things. But thought implied some kind of logic, and logic was no longer paramount. Caroline did not feel she wanted to leave Widdowe's Cottage but she did not know why. And Laura was suddenly frightened of being on her own again.

Caroline looked at her dearly loved sister-in-law and reminded herself that she was not a sister-in-law after all, then knew it did not make a scrap of difference. Laura had been her family for so long now . . . how could it make a difference? What concerned her was Laura's reaction to the news from Charles Cledra. She sat on her chair like a zombie, hair on end, the purple mark across her forehead slightly less livid, watching the rain blow across the garden from the south-west but not seeing it. Caroline remembered the way Jenna had been when she'd first arrived in Treleg. There had been no interest, no real interest, in anything around her.

She sighed, then said gently, 'Actually I think this antiseptic cream is helping. Let's try just a smidgeon more . . .' She applied another half-inch from the tube and was encouraged – when Laura made a sound of relief – to add, 'I really think we should leave all this family history now, darling. We've gone far enough. And at the end of the day, what does it matter?'

'It matters,' Laura said in a dull voice. 'It means that you and Geoff did not share mother or father. You were cousins.' She looked up, her violet eyes dark with misery. 'Think about that one, Caro!'

Caroline stared down into those eyes. They were so full of pain it was unbearable, and she sat down abruptly.

'Laura . . .' She swallowed convulsively. 'What do you mean?'

And Laura spoke again, her voice harsh, not Laura's voice at all.

'You have told me you were in love with the man you thought was your brother. If you had known he was your cousin, things might have been very different.'

Caroline clasped her hands very hard. She had thought

her confession had been dismissed because it was ludicrous; because Laura had always known that Geoff loved her. His relationship with Caroline had not mattered. He had always loved Laura best.

She stammered, 'It would have made no difference, Laura. Surely you know that?'

Laura blinked and shook her head as if physically emptying it of thoughts.

'How can I *know* anything any more, Caro? Geoff never lied to me . . . never. He told me we would be together again and I believed that above all things – that's why I never went to church. They – the whole of the rest of the world – were fallible. Not Geoff. Now I find that there is a whole hidden story. Still no lies, but an awful lot of secrets. And ultimately, Caro, secrets are lies!'

Caroline found she was having difficulty breathing. She gasped, 'He didn't know, Laura! He did not know!'

'Of course he knew. Why do you think he was always so protective of Tilly and then of you? Alice had died and Tilly had taken him on at the age of fifteen! He and she were so close . . .' Tears choked Laura's voice. There was a sobbing silence in the kitchen. Caroline could think of nothing to say. Put like that it was so obvious and accounted for Geoff's protective attitude to his 'baby sister'.

Laura said abruptly, 'I'm going into the garden. Don't come with me.' She stood up and made for the kitchen door. Caroline stood, too.

'Darling! Please! It's raining and you're not well!'

Laura opened the door. 'I'm going to the shed,' she said briefly, and closed the door after her. Caroline watched her go down the garden, not even bowed against the rain. She pressed her forehead against the glass and wept. And as Laura disappeared into the shed, there was a knock on the front door. Caroline knew who it would be. She pulled off a piece of kitchen roll, wiped her face, pushed her hair behind her ears and let them in.

*   *   *

The shed seemed to wrap Laura around with its smell, its roughness, its lack of any kind of triviality. Everything in here had a use, was important. She pulled out one of the folding canvas chairs, opened it up and sat down. She was below window level and could not see the rain or the house or anything except the interior of the shed. She held the arms of the chair and waited for some kind of comfort.

It did not come.

She then realized that the comfort the shed had always offered was Geoff's lingering presence. And that had gone. She looked around at the raffia bundle fraying from its hook and bought just a year ago in Penzance from one of the unromantic superstores now opened on the road to Marazion. Next to that were more chairs, bought from the same place. Some of the tools . . . yes, he had used those; and there was that rake and spade that had been hanging there when they bought the ruined cottage so long ago. She stared at them as if they might reduce the sheer awfulness of what was happening to her, and then shook her head. 'Things. Stuff. They don't matter any more.' She was speaking aloud and stopped, pressing her lips together and frowning. Was she losing her mind – after all this time of living alone, was she having some kind of breakdown? But no, she had always talked to herself, it didn't mean a thing. What meant something was that she was lost; all the familiar things around her had become unfamiliar. She leaned back and closed her eyes. She must wait. Be patient and wait. She would feel something other than pain . . . quite soon. It would be all right. It *would* be all right.

Caroline said firmly, 'Charles, I'm sorry, but you must give her some time. She needs to be alone and she's only just gone out there.'

Charles Cledra sat down again and stared at the ancient ridged grain of the kitchen table. He said miserably, 'I feel personally responsible for all this.'

John Canniston shook his head; as Charles sat down, he stood up and began to pace the width of the kitchen.

'I was the one who actually said that Alice was Geoff's mother. How could I have been so stupid?'

Charles said, 'It never occurred to either of us that you were thinking Tilly was the one who had the baby. And we were both horrified at Laura's reaction.' He glanced up. 'It does not seem to have shocked you, Caro.'

She spread her hands. 'In one way, it has. But of course, I still have Tilly for a mother.' She discovered something. 'That is what really matters to me.' She smiled at Charles. 'I should be as shocked as Laura that Geoff is not my brother. But the main thing is – must always be – that Tilly was my mother.'

'Right. I still cannot quite see why Laura is so completely devastated.'

Caroline said, 'John, please sit down. I need to get into the pantry and you're terribly in the way.'

'Sorry – sorry—' He sat down with a small crash and she put out a hand as if to save him and he grabbed it and hung on. 'You sit down too, Caro. You look exhausted.'

She did not want to sit down, but suddenly she did, and for a moment they held hands across the table – and then both withdrew.

Charles went on, 'What difference can it make to Laura that Geoff's mother was Alice and not Tilly?'

Caroline pushed her hair behind her ears and hung on to the ends as if pulling them out by the roots. She remembered what Laura had said, the pain in her eyes, and for the umpteenth time wished that blasted confession had never been made.

She said, 'Laura is terribly hurt by the fact that Geoff must have known all this from the day he met her. She cannot believe he would not have shared it with her. She said something quite shocking – she said that secrets are lies.'

Charles exploded. 'Rubbish! Can't she understand that it was not his secret to keep? It was Tilly's secret.'

Caroline looked at him. Over the past few weeks she and Laura had got to know this solitary, eccentric man fairly well. They knew that his nervous tics covered a sensitive and caring soul. Caroline was almost sure that the caring soul cared a lot for Laura.

She sighed. 'Perhaps you *should* go and talk to her in the shed, Charles. I could say that to her and it would not mean half so much as you saying it.'

Charles said hesitantly, 'I'm not sure. I stayed at the rectory last night and John and I talked a great deal about this. Probably too much. I think we all need a bit of time.' He looked around again. 'Is your daughter with her?'

'No. I told you, Laura needs to be alone.' Caroline sighed. 'Jenna has gone to bury that tin in the churchyard. She thinks we should go home. Leave Laura in peace.'

Charles said, 'In peace? Or simply alone?' At last he stood up. 'I'll ask her whether I can join her for five minutes. Excuse me.'

'Tell her I'm making fresh coffee,' Caroline said as he left. She stood up and went to the cooker, quite unable to stay at the table with John Canniston.

John ran a thumbnail down one of the table ridges and said, 'Do you agree with Jenna? Do you think you should go home?'

'I don't know any more.' She reached for mugs. 'I don't want to go, actually. But . . .' She turned and looked at him. 'You see, for years now I've thought I was in love with my own brother. And I told Laura that. She dismissed it – explained it away. At the time I was angry she would not take me seriously. But then, last night, when she discovered that my brother wasn't my brother, she must have started to take it much more seriously. She said as much just this morning. Just now. Before she went out into the rain.'

Caroline peered through the window. Laura had let Charles into the shed. She looked round at John. He had his head in his hands and she thought he was disgusted by what she had said. Then he removed his hands and looked at her. He was smiling.

153

'Oh Caro. D'you remember what I said to you that time in Truro? That you were the most honest human being I had ever met?' She had to smile back; she couldn't help herself. 'Do you go around telling everyone about this incestuous lust? Or is it just me?'

She said, 'Well, I told Laura. I never would tell Jenna and I never told my mother. My God – they'd both have had me committed!' She put the tray on the table, sat down and stared at him, still smiling. She said, 'Actually, I am not in the least honest about my feelings – and I gather that by honest you really mean open and frank. Most of the time I wear a mask. My mother always said it was just as easy to be happy as to be unhappy and I suppose when you keep making foolish mistakes in life, you tend to hide them anyway.' She spread her hands. 'I don't know why I tell you . . . things. It frightened me at first that you seemed to know them already. As if you could see into my head. Perhaps I thought there was no point in hiding much from you. Especially my prosthetic foot!' She laughed.

He said, 'Your ghastly joke was one thing. Your love for your brother is something else.'

'I told you about that so you would understand how Laura must feel now she knows that Geoff was not my brother and it was legally possible for . . . Oh, you know.' She gestured with her hands, helplessly. 'Not that it matters now because the moment I knew I had no brother – that was the moment I also knew that I had never really been in love with Geoff.'

'No?'

'No. He was everything to me when I was growing up. Brother, uncle, friend, father. So I suppose that was why I thought he was the love of my life.' She lifted her shoulders. 'I'm such a fool. I was jealous of Laura on one level, but I adored her on another. Nothing changed between Geoff and me. She never came between us. She was – is – always has been . . . wonderful.' Sudden tears filled her eyes. 'And now I've messed that up, too.' She dropped her head into her hands.

154

'No. It's finding out bits of the secret that is so awful for her. Wondering how much more there is to uncover.' He reached across the table and took her hands from her face. 'Listen, my love. That's why you have to go a bit further. Maybe try to follow their route to the Cotswolds. Or maybe find out something about the second marriage and your father.'

'I was only saying to Laura that I should do that.' She did not pull her hands away from his; she noted that he had called her his love.

He said slowly, 'Has Jenna said anything to you?'

'No . . . about what?'

'About my feelings for you.' His grip was hurting her fingers. 'Anyway, you must know. You cannot be in the same room with me and not know.'

'You've avoided me like the plague.' She made no attempt to move away.

He said, 'When I got you out of the car, when was it, four weeks ago now? I told you I loved you. I knew it was a mistake. I thought I had offended you. You're a working partner in a long-established firm of auctioneers and valuers, you're beautiful and sophisticated and I'm a country parson.' She said nothing. She could not see him now for the tears which ran down her face and dripped from the end of her nose. He began to massage her palms with his thumbs. It affected her breathing.

He said, 'Do you remember that young couple? We saw them in that floating restaurant place near the archive centre. They had eyes only for each other. They could not believe that in this endless universe of time and space they had found each other.'

She whispered, 'I remember.'

'They reminded you of Jenna and her young husband. But they made me think of my own luck. I was there. And you were there. It was – it was like a thunderbolt. I knew we were meant for each other.' He put one of her hands to his face and she felt his tears. 'At that moment, my love, I was so certain, so sure. I knew you would make the most wonderful wife for a priest – you could do all the things they're supposed to do – Charles has told me how hard you work at CF so it's no good you denying that. But there's so much more, Caro. You renew my faith every moment of every day. I only have to look at you to know the glory of God . . . Don't be embarrassed, Caro. I have to tell you this. I have to.'

'John . . .' She tried to focus on him. His black hair curling around his ears, his dark eyes . . . She said, 'I shall be fifty-three on my next birthday. You are still so young.'

He smiled. 'I'll be forty-three next month. You were ten – still a little girl – when I was born. And we've been catching up with each other ever since.'

'Perhaps if we'd met each other a few years ago . . . even just ten years ago. Women are having children later these days.' She released one hand and wiped the tears from his eyes and then from hers. 'You see, John, one of the reasons I know I could not have been in love with Geoff is because I am in love with you.'

He made a sound and started out of his chair. She stood with him and went into his arms. They held on to each other as if they might drown. She put a hand to his head and held it to hers. The thick mat of curls was strangely familiar; it was as if she already knew its dry springiness.

He whispered, 'Thank you, Caro. Thank you, my darling.'

He relaxed his hold slightly and she knew he was going to kiss her. She cleared her throat and said carefully, 'John, are you an only child?'

'What on earth – why would you want to know? Yes, I am.' He moved his head away from her hand so that he could see her face.

'And your father, too?'

'Yes.'

She said, 'Don't you see, my love? That man, who my dear ma said was a saint . . . started a line. It cannot end with you, John. That is why the difference in our ages is so important.' She moved her hand to his cheek and cupped it. 'Love doesn't stop with one person, John. There will be someone else for you—'

She stopped speaking as his mouth came down on hers with a sudden desperate fierceness that frightened her. She crashed into the table and it scraped hideously on the slate floor. He steadied them both and lifted his head to look at her. His eyes were black and so close she could almost see beyond them.

He gasped, 'Has there been anyone before for you? I know about your husband – I mean like this, like us. Tell me the truth. Has there – has there?'

She wept openly now. 'No. No one.'

He said, 'Nor for me. And never will be.'

She said, 'Oh John.'

He said, 'Caro. It's all right. We are the luckiest people in the world.'

And she reached across the tiny gap between them and kissed him.

Laura said, 'Charles, I know you mean well. And I thank you for your concern. But you cannot possibly begin to understand. I do not understand it myself.'

Charles Cledra made no attempt to gnaw the inside of his cheek. He had opened another folding chair when he had gone into the shed and he sat on it now facing Laura, their knees almost touching.

He said, 'It's very simple really, Laura. We all construct small worlds for ourselves in which we can live as comfortably as possible. We're not capable of taking in the universe and our places there, so it is very important to make our own space. Right?'

She said wearily, 'Right.'

He said, 'Every now and then that world is shattered, my dear. It was shattered for me when my wife died, and it was shattered for you when your husband died. Right?'

She sighed and looked at him with resignation. She had not known he had been married. 'Right, Charles.'

'So very slowly we reconstructed. Made something else. It

157

wasn't so good, but it was bearable. And with time it became more bearable. Right?'

'Oh Charles – please—'

'And now that's gone. And you're older than you were. You're tired. You don't want the horrendous struggle of making a new world. Especially as at the moment you feel that new world cannot contain any of your old memories. You believe them to be false memories. You feel cheated.'

'Charles, I cannot bear this. You are so kind. But—'

'I am trying to show you the problem. It's not a mess, not really. It's quite clear-cut. When you see it properly, then you can make plans for the future.'

'I don't think you quite realize—'

'Probably not. But having got this far . . . don't let's give up just yet. What do you say to looking at various possibilities?'

She shook her head, opened her mouth, then saw that he was chewing again.

'All right,' she said heavily.

He sat back, let his breath go, waited. She looked up. 'I thought you might have some suggestions,' she said.

'Well I have, but of course I can't just foist them on you. You must make them yourself.'

'I haven't got a solitary one, Charles. I thought you realized that.'

There was another pause. She closed her eyes and tried to visualize Geoff and found she could not. She made a sound like a sob.

He said quickly, 'I understand your niece wants to go back to work.' Her eyes opened wide. He went on, 'I suppose that would mean Caro would go as well. Would you welcome that?'

She thought for just a moment then said, 'No!'

'Why not?'

'I can't stay here on my own, Charles! I can't do it. Not any more. I was . . . in charge of myself before. The seasons, the garden, the sea, the tides . . . I don't know about them any more.'

158

'Well, that's one positive then. You want Caro and Jenna to stay.'

'It's too selfish. Especially in Jenna's case. She needs to get on with her life.'

'And Caro?'

'Not quite the same. Besides . . . now that she knows Geoff is not her brother she probably . . . possibly . . . needs me.'

'Excellent. You want Caro to stay, Caro needs to stay. We're getting somewhere.'

'It's not quite so cut and dried as you are assuming.'

Charles ignored the remark. 'So. Do you sit around – knit – go to the centre on Wednesdays, maybe oftener, and wait for another pattern to develop? Or do you do something?'

'What can we do?'

He paused, looked at her consideringly, then said slowly, 'You could try to trace the journey Bessie, Tilly and Alice made back in 1922.'

'No! I dare not risk uncovering any more lies.'

'There are no lies, Laura. Nobody has ever told you a lie.' He leaned forward and took her hands in his. 'You are doing your husband and your mother-in-law a grave injustice if you think like that.'

She snatched her hands back. 'She's not my mother-in-law!'

'Her sister died. She took on the child and she took on the role with all its responsibilities. D'you think she should have shirked that one?'

Laura sat there, her hair spiked wildly like a halo, the purple mark on her forehead still showing against the whiteness of her face.

She said, 'I lost my parents in the war. She was like a mother to me.'

'It seems she was good at that.'

'She wore draw-string skirts and bulged above and below them like a cottage loaf. Wholesome, good, sweet-smelling.' Laura's eyes overflowed. 'Why didn't Geoff tell me the truth, Charles? There was nothing to be ashamed of. Just the opposite.'

Charles smiled triumphantly. 'There you are, then! That's what you're looking for, dear girl. Geoff's reasons for hiding this enormous secret. There have to be reasons, and from what I hear of your husband they would be good ones. Don't you agree?'

She stared at him. Then she nodded dumbly.

Thirteen

Bessie always maintained that, left alone, they would have managed. The three women, Bessie herself, Alice and Tilly, drew together in their grief; they were within an inch of sharing each other's thoughts. Together they managed the house and the midden and Billy Boy's increasingly difficult ways. At last Bessie understood Tilly's affinity with the land and the sea and the burrows beneath; she drew comfort from Tilly's assurances that John had been snug in his burrow and could have felt no real horror at dying there – no more than if he had died above ground, as two of the balmaidens had done when they were lifted high and dashed against the rocks and lasted for two terrible, screaming days. Alice had seen that. Alice had knelt by them, holding them as best she could, praying aloud for God to open his gates and let them in.

It was harder for Bessie to share her own feelings. Her body cried out for its mate, her eyes longed to see him and peered into dark corners to find him, her nose constantly recognized the smell of him about the cottage, and her lips pined for the taste of him. She could not share that with her girls. But they could hear her talking to him when she thought she was alone. They knew that when she discarded her apron and went into the wash house, it was to weep for him. He had never hidden his physical love for her and they found nothing surprising in her stifled voice sobbing for him to hold her, begging forgiveness for brushing him away so often. 'I couldn't face another miscarriage, my

161

'ansome . . . and now, now 'tis going to 'appen without you. Everything is going to 'appen without you.'

An hour later when they were dishing up the broth for supper, Alice managed a wide smile as she said, 'Isn't it marvellous that Pa knows everything now. He sees everything and hears everything . . . he *knows* everything.'

Bessie looked at her sharply but made no reply. Tilly's eyes shone. 'I never thought we could be closer to him. But we are, aren't we?'

Billy Boy brought the palm of his hand smack down into his basin of broth and then screamed with the pain. All was commotion as they took it in turns to mop him up, cuddle comfort into his burned hand, spoon fresh broth into his open mouth. Bessie sighed as gradually order was restored.

'Ah Billy Boy. If only you'd taken after your father and not his brother.' She lifted her shoulders at the girls. 'Poor mite. *He* died when he was only twelve. Water on the brain. I didn't know him but they told me once 'is 'ead exploded at the end.'

The girls put their hands to their faces in horror. Tilly said, frightened, 'Billy Boy hasn't got water on the brain, has he?' She remembered a boy in school with a big head and could not stop shuddering. 'His head isn't big, Ma. It isn't big at all.'

'Nay.' Bessie shook her head. 'I just meant in 'is ways. Our Billy was born naughty, I reckon. But then boys are, aren't they?' She drew her chair closer to the table in a semblance of cosy domesticity. 'I heard at the mine office today that Jacko Miles 'as been arrested for pilfering. When some of the bodies was brought above ground, he helped load them in the wagon and went through some of the pockets. Terrible thing to do. Terrible. He deserves to be birched. They say the rector did pray for 'im in church! Never 'eard such a thing! Praying for a thief like that!'

Tilly said in a low voice, 'His mother is consumptive, Ma. He stole a few coppers, that was all. Just to buy some food for her.'

'Stealing is stealing, our Tilly. Don't you forget that.'

'No, Ma.'

'Now Alice and me got that job up at the Court with poor old Geoffrey Three Legs, and you'm 'llowed to take Billy Boy to school with you, we're managing, ain't we?'

'Yes, Ma.'

'That's what I did mean. We 'aven't 'ad to do nothing against the law!' She tried to make it funny and obediently the girls laughed.

But she knew that unless something happened very soon, she would be forced to break the law. She had always miscarried on her fourth month and here it was, end of March and nothing to see except a lump the size of a pudding basin under her apron. It would have to be soon else even old Mother Sithian wouldn't do anything about it. Bessie felt herself sliding down into despair, and thinned her lips determinedly. They hadn't had much compensation from poor old Sir Geoffrey but he had given them work and that was important. The compensation could go to Mrs Sithian and welcome. Cheap at the price, after all.

She wasn't very good after. The bleeding wouldn't stop and Mrs Sithian was worried and kept her lying on her brass bed for the rest of the day and that night. Bessie thought she might die and she asked the old lady to send for Alice but she wouldn't do that. 'You'm all right, missis,' she kept saying. 'We don't want no trouble, do we? Not neither of us, I reckon.'

And she had been right, because after the old woman had bound her so tight she could hardly breathe, she had stood up shakily and walked along the cliff top without fainting once. And Alice had met her where the garden ran down to the path and enfolded her in her arms and brought her in. They never talked about it. Alice had told the housekeeper at the Court that her mother was vomiting badly and the housekeeper had nodded, pleased for Bessie Quince. She'd miscarried again like she'd done so often before, so she could keep the job. She was a good worker was Bessie Quince. And life had gone on . . . as it always did if people left you alone.

163

Tilly never told Bessie how difficult it was at school with Billy Boy in tow. If it hadn't been for Jacko Miles it would have been impossible. Before the bell was rung each morning, Jacko would chase Billy Boy around the yard and up the coal pile until they were both red in the face and Billy Boy had screamed every scream out of himself. It meant he would sit in the big room before the screen went across and rock gently on Tilly's lap while Mr Tompkins said prayers and talked to them about God giving them hands to work with and legs to run with and brains to learn with. Mr Tompkins had certainly learned that when the gentle whimper started up from Tilly Quince's knees, it was time to stop talking and go into the first hymn. Billy Boy liked singing. He joined in and made the boys snigger. But that was better than the whimper, which soon became a high-pitched whine.

In spite of Jacko chasing him all over again at playtime it was hard going for Tilly. He would seize her slate pencil and scrawl over her careful numbers and scream an echo to the pencil as it screeched a protest. After playtime, when it was reading, Mr Tompkins made a special nest of cloaks and coats right next to the stove and Billy Boy would often lie there like a large puppy and watch the flames flickering on the coals. The afternoons were the best because after their bread and pilchards, Jacko kept Billy Boy going for almost an hour, roaring like a lion, encouraging him to yell back until the whole yard was in a frenzy of activity. Billy Boy loved that. When the bell clanged in the porch he would make his way inside without Tilly, curl up on the coats and be asleep before the afternoon prayer had finished.

Yes, perhaps they could have managed if no one had interfered. Bessie and Alice thought working at the Court was a sight better than cracking rocks for copper in all winds and weathers; Alice had to avert her eyes when she went past Wheal Three Legs on her way to the Court. She could not bear the thought of working there again, though both she and her mother assumed that as soon as the workings were sealed off properly, there would be new burrows and more work.

But then, when the few remaining farmers and fishermen trickled back from the war that was soon to be called 'Great', silent and staring or drunk and wild, old Geoffrey Three Legs asked for Alice to dress his stump, rub his poor aching back, wheel him into the summer house each afternoon and read to him from *The Times*. Just the obituaries. Sometimes the final casualty lists. That summer of 1919 was long and empty; a waiting time; a no-man's-land of in-between. But Bessie, stunned with grief and powerless, saw what was happening at the Court and knew that a no-man's-land did not go on for long. She went to see the mine captain to find out when the mine would reopen.

He sat at a desk built on its own platform and stared down at her. He was a big man, frizzy grey hair glistening with goose-grease, large features in a large face. Even from far below him she could see the pores in his skin.

He said heavily, 'Not sure, missis. We've sealed off the damaged area. Drained it well. Could be working it now. But we en't.' He wasn't telling her anything she didn't know already. He let a wry smile turn his mouth down very slightly. 'Thought you might be coming to tell me something. Your Alice having the ear of the owner, like.'

She flushed. News, especially that kind of news, travelled fast.

'She do 'elp 'im with 'is leg. No more than that. They don't talk nor nothing.'

He made no comment but the slight smile disappeared.

She said, 'We need to get back to the work we know.'

He sighed and returned to his ledger. 'Aye. Don't we all.' There was an awkward pause and she turned away, defeated. Then he called after her, 'Soon as I know something myself, I'll let you know, missis. Tell your girl that.'

Much later that night she told Alice. The girl sat at the table, bowed with weariness. Tilly ran round, making bread and milk with a spoonful of bee sugar. Mother and daughter ate well enough at the Court but Tilly always had broth or bread and milk for them in the evenings. 'You'll make a good mother, our Tilly,' Bessie often said, and silently prayed it wouldn't be too soon. Jacko Miles was always hanging around her and his sister had only recently died in childbirth, aged thirteen. But now her concern was all for Alice. 'You'm getting more and more tired, my 'ansome. What's he doing to you? You would tell us, wouldn't you? If he tried to take advantage?'

Alice smiled. 'You don't think I'd let 'im get that way, do you, Ma? He's just such a lump to move around. "Put me leg on a stool," he goes. "Push me forward and get that cushion down me back, girl. Hoist me into the bath chair . . . gently . . . gently."' She took old Geoffrey off so well they all laughed and Billy Boy stopped rocking for long enough to shriek with them.

''Course I'd tell you, Ma. It isn't like that. Honest.'

But it was like that. Alice was young and thought the best of everyone, and when he slid his hand up her skirt she still thought it was an accident and didn't mention it to Bessie. And then she had to, because he tore her blouse which she had made from her father's Sunday shirt, and that upset her more than anything. She sobbed bitterly that night and couldn't eat the lettuce Tilly had pulled an hour before, nor drink the tea she had made from the spoonful of leaves Jacko had given her that morning.

Bessie stood above her, fingering the ragged shoulder of the shirt. John had been given the shirt for his confirmation down at Tregeagle Church. So it was nearly thirty years old. He was C of E and though he went with Bessie to the chapel, at heart he had always been C of E.

She said heavily, 'We'll 'ave to leave, my 'ansome. Nothing else to be done.'

'Not both of us, Ma!' Alice covered her mother's hand with her own. 'He'll know why if we both leave at once. We'll 'ave to think of something . . .'

166

Bessie said passionately, 'If only we was let alone! We coulda managed real well if we'd been let alone.'

Billy Boy set up a howl at his mother's voice and she gathered him to her and finished feeding him and then herded him up the ladder in front of her. He was in a paddy by then and tried to kick down on her face. The girls looked at each other. ''E's getting worse,' Alice said dully. 'I went Tregeagle way last week and asked the rector about 'im. An' 'e said that Billy Boy was what they call MD, and that stands for mentally deficient. There's a lot going on about mental things now because of the war. But when it's inherited there's nothing can be done.'

Tilly covered her face with her hands and let out a sound. She was not surprised because Billy Boy was so naughty at school, and if it weren't for Jacko . . . 'It's Ma,' she wept. 'What will Ma do?'

'Ma will be all right. She is so strong . . . stronger than copper. Stronger than steel.' Alice thought back to the bitter winds of last March. 'She might even send him to Pa.'

There was a silence in the kitchen. Outside the open door the evening sun picked out the lettuce bed. It had been cloudy all day; now the sky was streaked with dusky red and the sea glittered beneath it. Beauty and danger. Tilly shivered.

Alice said, 'I reckon I could manage some of that lettuce now, our Tilly. Could you pick me a fresh one? And stop worrying. It were getting Pa's shirt tored . . . that's what done it for me. Getting Pa's shirt tored.'

'I'll mend it,' Tilly said eagerly. She wasn't the best needlewoman in the house by any means, but the thought of sitting outside tomorrow morning before school and stitching her father's confirmation shirt was like a blessing.

Alice made more tea and changed the shirt. She ate the lettuce and shared the bread and cheese cook had given her and when Bessie climbed down the ladder, she smiled at her confidently.

167

'I've thought about it, Ma. I'll say I've got consumption –
that will put the old devil off surely?'

Bessie looked at her, hand to throat. 'It might do. Ah.
But . . . oh, our Alice. I don't like it. Seems like inviting
illness.'

But Alice was laughing. ''Course it dun't, Ma. And tell
you what . . . Pa would laugh his head off. Can't you just
see it?'

The three of them could see it only too well. Bessie
laughed through her tears; Alice laughed as if she hadn't a
care in the world. Tilly smiled and crossed her fingers
behind her back.

Fourteen

1920

They had thought that first winter was hard. The Peace Winter, all the miners called it, but it had brought little peace to Cornwall. At first most small communities stuck together and down Tregeagle way the mine disaster had brought them close on that first Armistice Day, and they helped each other where they could. Mr Tompkins put up with Billy Boy, people put up with Jacko Miles and his pilfering. Miners turned to fishing if only to catch enough pilchards to press for their own families. But then, during that second winter, the hardship began to tear them apart. Many of them moved up-country to the clay pits around St Austell. Some of them were lucky enough to get work with the Great Western Railway Company. Some of them starved. Others, in their bitterness, tried to oust friends and neighbours from hard-won jobs so that they could fill the gap. Bessie and Alice had a hard time of it. It was an awful winter.

It started in September of 1919, when school opened after the harvest, and its difficulty was really down to Billy Boy. He had grown fast that summer, stooking corn with Tilly; in the freedom of the cornfields his gangling awkwardness had not been a nuisance. But he was too big for school and Jacko had left to help his uncle throw out mackerel lines and bring them back in. Tilly had been twelve the previous spring, and had earned another year at school by taking Philip Radjel's place. Philip had died during the Peace Winter. His last wish had been to see Miss

169

Casson by his bedside and she had come, and then sat with him holding his hand until the end. His mother had said she was an angel and Tilly had not even smiled at the thought. Working next to Miss Casson, seeing her cuddling and bandaging the little ones when they fell on the grit of the yard, buttoning and unbuttoning them, holding them when they heaved up the rotten fish they had eaten the day before, and still teaching them to read and write and sing songs . . . She had known that Miss Casson truly was an angel.

But though Mr Tompkins might in other circumstances have allowed that arrangement to continue, by September he had decided that Billy Boy was too big to handle and Tilly had to leave. They all hoped she could find work where Billy Boy could still be with her but there was nothing up at the Court, and when she cut the winter greens at the farm, Billy Boy wandered off and knocked over some of the crates of cabbages and then fell into the River Geagle – and that was the end of that.

After Christmas, when 1919 – 'eat the fat and leave the lean' – turned into 1920 – 'my plate's empty' – Tilly found the only way to get some peace was to walk Billy Boy tired. The slight girl in her shawl and bonnet and the cumbersome eight-year-old, already wearing his dead father's work clothes, became a familiar sight tramping the downs and playing tisk-tasket around the standing stones. Tilly kept singing the songs Miss Casson had taught the children and sometimes Billy Boy would join in. 'Where have you been all the day?' Tilly would trill as the mist swirled around them. And his rough voice would come back to her, 'Billy Boy, Billy Boy.'

She got him to clamber down into the many small coves and explore the shallow caves where their singing boomed and echoed eerily and made them both laugh. 'I've been walking all the day, with my charming Nancy Gray . . .' Billy Boy shrieked with joy at the next line, and eventually learned it and bawled out, 'And me Nancy tickled me fancy . . .'

At least once a week they got as far as Penburra Cove and watched Jacko swim out to the Crab Rocks pulling the baited mackerel line after him, fastening it and swimming back as fast as he could before the cold got him. Once they had arrived just as he went out to unfasten it so that his uncle Philip Miles could pull it back and take off the fish. Billy Boy had wailed unhappily at the sight of the struggling creatures being piled into panniers, and that night he had not slept for crying for them. So they timed their visits for when Jacko set the line; Billy Boy never connected that with the end result, and nobody mentioned it.

A week after her thirteenth birthday, in March, she stood with Philip Miles watching an almost naked Jacko chase Billy Boy up and down the beach, the one boy screaming with delight, the other growling like a rabid dog. Tilly laughed and shook her head as if she were the doting mother of both boys.

Philip Miles, a dour man who had emerged from the Treleg disaster with no visible injuries, yet never laughed and rarely spoke, said suddenly, 'How old was you last birthday then?'

Tilly said, surprised, 'Thirteen, sir.'

'Ah . . . well, you could do worse.' He jerked his head towards the shoreline where Billy Boy was being splashed unmercifully by Jacko. 'Been selling the fish to the railway gangers, makes a change from their salt beef. Soon as I got enough money I'll get me a boat and our Jack will be on it from the start.'

She knew what he meant and felt her face glow like a griddle. Philip Miles did not look at her, but after a while he said, 'He could do worse'n you too, I reckon. Looking after that one . . . full-time job.'

'Ma and Alice . . . they rely on me . . .'

'He won't live for ever. They don't, not that sort.' He heard her quick intake of breath and added, 'You ask the rector if you don't believe me. He's one of the guardians of Wayward House. He do know about simpletons like that one.'

171

He strode off, then, and Jacko picked up the signal immediately and scrambled into his clothes to follow him, yelling farewells at her and then Billy Boy, sending Billy Boy on his way with a jabbing finger.

Billy Boy always slept well after their walks, but when they had been to see Jacko and his uncle he went up the ladder by himself straight after tea and was asleep until ten the next morning. Bessie said, 'I don't know what you do with him, our Tilly, but whatever it is, it makes him happy.' She smiled at her daughter. 'You're a born carer, my girl. Just like your dad.' It was the best compliment in the world and Tilly flushed like a griddle again and smiled.

The winter of 1920 was when Alice started to become ill. The joke about consumption had worked very well. The next time old Sir Geoffrey slid his hand around her waist she had fainted right away and the housekeeper had been summoned; and she in her turn had told Bessie to stop her work that instant and remove her daughter. At first Bessie had thought their lie was backfiring badly; the house-keeper was a Mrs Sims whose favourite phrase was 'Mrs Sims don't stand no nonsense', and apparently fainting in domestics was out-and-out nonsense. Another faint and Alice would be gone; probably Bessie too.

But Mrs Sims had known she would find no one as thorough as Bessie. And Sir Geoffrey had declared that there wasn't a body in Cornwall could dress his stump and rub his back like young Alice Quince. So they had both returned to the Court and Alice had made sure that she never actually collapsed on to the carpet again; she had merely told her employer that she 'felt faint' and he had released her immediately and advised her to sit down.

But then as the winter went on and on into spring, Alice did indeed begin to feel faint. Sometimes she was very hot, sometimes shivering with cold. She did not mention these peculiar symptoms to anyone, and her mother would not have guessed at them had Alice not developed an irritating little cough. Bessie watched her like a hawk, terrified that the plan really had misfired and God was punishing them by making their lie a truth. When she boiled the kerchiefs that winter she examined each one for signs of blood. There was none. And after all, if Alice had worked outside as a balmaid there would have been far more risk of 'going down'. She was in a warm, dry house most of the time; the best possible place, surely?

The rector called. Tilly had done nothing about Philip Miles's suggestion, so he must have said something himself. She had just returned from the afternoon walk – it was almost dark – and there was a lot to do. The fire was the most important so that she could settle Billy Boy next to the range with the pebbles he had collected, and start on making a broth for supper. Visits from clericals meant a tidy house and tea and sitting down politely.

He came from the cliff path, instantly recognizable by the silhouette of his wide-brimmed hat, which he took off as he approached. As if she were a lady.

'Oh sir . . . 'tis you—' She tried to bob a curtsy and keep her apron full of kindling. 'Did you . . . would you care to come inside?'

He said, 'It was your mother I came to see. Tilly, isn't it? I remember you at school. Your work with the children. Highly thought of.'

'Oh. Thank you kindly, sir.' It was freezing in spite of the shelter from the wood shed. The March winds that year were particularly cold. She said, 'Ma and Alice will be another two-three hours I reckon.'

He nodded. 'Foolish of me. I know they work up at the Court. I was on my way to a meeting – came along the cliff path – and thought I would call and see how you are.' He gestured sideways at the rest of the terrace of cottages, all dark and obviously deserted. 'The other tenants have left, I see.'

'Yes.' He was a nice man, kind to Jacko too. 'Ma do say we are ladies of the manor now!' He laughed and she poked her elbow towards the door. 'Come and rest awhile

173

before starting back, sir. Soon as I get the fire going I can make tea. We've got tea. Mrs Sims lets Ma have the scrapings now and then.' She stopped talking, remembering Ma saying fiercely to Alice that a spoonful now and then weren't 'zackly taking bread out of babies' mouths up at the Court.

He smiled, though it was so dark already she could only see his teeth beneath the broad brim of the hat. 'You take the kindling in and get it started. I'll bring some blocks.'

'There's wood a-drying, sir. No need for more till I starts on the broth.'

'You'll need it later. Carry on in, Tilly.'

He picked up one of the old pilchard buckets and began to stack wood methodically, and after a moment's hesitation she went inside, sent Billy Boy into the wash house to scrub his hands and face, and started on the fire. Even Billy Boy was awed by a visit from the rector and she could hear him working the pump handle almost vigorously behind the door.

He said behind her, 'You see to Billy Boy before he floods the wash house completely!' He smiled again. 'Leave the fire to me.'

She obeyed him of course; what else was there to do? When she brought a shiningly scrubbed Billy Boy back into the kitchen he had found the rush lights and lit them and filled a small pannikin with water from the kettle, to boil quickly on the leaping flames. She made tea and brought it to the table. Really it was only dust from the wooden caddies up at the Court but it was brown enough when she poured it, and there was fresh milk, too. He drank appreciatively. 'Forgot it was so far,' he said in between sips.

'You'm best taking the top road going back, sir,' she said, holding Billy Boy's cup for him. ''Tis a mile or so further but the cliff path be dangerous after dark.'

'I noticed one or two places where the edge was crumbling. But I'm on my way to Pendeen Watch. There's a meeting there tonight and I'm doing a sea service tomorrow.'

She was surprised enough to say unguardedly, 'I allus thought they was Methodies at the Watch, sir.'

'They are.' He grinned. 'Most of my flock are Methodists. They like to keep a foot in both camps, Tilly. Just in case our Lord prefers one to the other.'

She loved him then, and remembered him coming to the school and telling Jacko Miles very gently, 'We're all God's children, Jack.' She blurted, 'Did Philip Miles ask you about our Billy Boy there—' She nodded towards the hearth where Billy Boy had settled himself with the day's haul of stones and shells.

He looked at her and perhaps saw a wisdom older than thirteen years. 'He did. But maybe I should wait and talk to your mother another time.'

'She won't let him go, sir. Not none of us. Because we're part of our father, you see.'

The rector was silent for some time, then said quietly, 'That is wonderful, Tilly.' He drank the last of his tea. 'I think I will call to see her, however. It occurs to me that it might be possible to find work for you at Wayward House. Your mother might feel differently, then.'

Tilly's face brightened. It sometimes irked her that she could not contribute to the household expenses. She said, 'Would you like some more tea, sir? I can hottle the pot.'

'No thank you, Tilly. I'll be on my way. Regards to the rest of the family.' He crouched by Billy Boy and picked up one of the shells. 'I like that one, Billy. My mother had a hairbrush backed by shell like that. Mother-of-pearl it's called. Keep it safe, dear boy.'

Billy Boy said, 'Tickled me fancy,' and rocked back with laughter. The rector touched his head, perhaps blessing him, then straightened and went to the door. 'Goodbye, Tilly. God bless and keep you.'

Tilly watched the dark shape of him make its way to the garden gate, and then disappear. Her eyes filled with love for him. He had not called her 'daughter' or 'my girl' – not once. He knew her name, he knew Billy Boy's name. They were proper people to him, not just parishioners. She went back inside to start on the broth. She thought, as they all thought, 'We'll be all right. Pa is watching over us and we'll manage.'

When the letter arrived on Monday morning Tilly was feeding Billy Boy his bread and milk while he tried to snatch the spoon from her. She was saying for the umpteenth time, 'No, Billy Boy. Let Tilly hold it so that it goes in the tunnel and not in the siding!' He laughed and opened his mouth and she shot in another spoonful, with an imitation train whistle that made him splutter helplessly. And there was a hammering at the door and a shout of 'Postman, missis!'

They were both transfixed. Neither of them could remember having a letter before. And of course it was for Ma, so would have to wait until the evening. Tilly weighed it in her hand, examined the handwriting by the open door, held it away from Billy Boy, who would have ripped it to pieces on the spot. Eventually she put it on the mantelpiece and chivvied him into his clothes; but all the way down to the beach where Billy Boy, wanted to hunt for more mother-of-pearl shells, she was thinking about it. Brown ink and proper writing like Mr Tompkins had taught them, thin upwards and strong downwards, all sloping gently towards the right . . . it had to be written by someone important. She told Billy Boy they must make a nice supper for Ma and Alice that night, something special in case the letter brought bad news – which of course letters did. 'Broff,' suggested Billy Boy.

'I'd like something different. We could get a herring or two from Jacko maybe . . . but often they're too tired to eat fish. Shall we walk round to Farmer Zellafield and see if there's any scraps of meat we could put in with the vegetables?' Billy Boy was uncertain. It had been at the Zellafield farm that he had upset all the crates of cabbage. But he followed her eventually, and tried to stay out of sight when she went to the back door. Mrs Zellafield looked over her glasses and saw him instantly. She

176

tightened her mouth and pushed her glasses up her nose to view the other figure standing three granite steps below her. The girl looked up at her and for a moment Mrs Zellafield saw John Quince as he had been before he went down the mines. The dark dreaming eyes, snub nose and wide, well-shaped mouth . . . he had written her a poem once after seeing her work in the hayfields and she old enough to be his mother . . . she remembered a couple of lines from it. Something like 'strong and warm' and then 'food in the barn'. And here was his child while he lay under the earth somewhere.

She said, 'Don't let that lad anywhere near my 'usband! 'E don't forget nothing, does my Zell. And that lad made extra work on a very hot day.'

'He's with me now, Mrs Zellafield. I won't let him do any damage. We was wondering . . . I'd like to tickle up the broth a bit tonight. For Ma and Alice, you know. And we was wondering if you had any leftovers.'

Mrs Zellafield noticed she wasn't asking, just wondering. 'Strong and warm', John Quince had called her. And him about the same age, then, as his girl now. She turned abruptly and went into her kitchen, but she did not close the door, so Tilly stayed where she was and put a hand behind her to grip Billy Boy's canvas smock.

Mrs Zellafield came back with a parcel wrapped in brown paper.

'See what you can do with that,' she ordered. 'I was so sorry to hear about your sister. Wondered if it were the miner's cough.'

'She never went down the mine, Mrs Zellafield.' Tilly cradled the parcel like a baby, her face one big smile. With this she could make enough broth to last the whole week.

'But she worked at the top, didn't she? And the doctor was only saying last week, it's spread through the air. The germs are shot out from one person to the next.' She saw that Tilly's smile was withering and added quickly, 'But don't take no notice of me. Everyone do have coughs at this time of year. Now just get that lad off the farm before my Zell comes home.'

They went, Tilly calling back, 'Thank you, Mrs Zellafield,' until she heard the door close. Then she broke into a run, Billy Boy close behind her. He kept it up all the way home and burst into the kitchen like a cannonball to collapse in front of the empty firebox panting loudly.

'You cain't be that bad,' Tilly congratulated him. 'You ran like a deer ahead of the hounds!' He loved that and clapped his hands.

By the time Bessie and Alice came home everything was ready; Tilly had made a thick stew with Mrs Zellafield's scraps of meat and added four big dumplings as they came through the door. Alice looked better than usual and Bessie was in full voice, telling the two girls that Mrs Sims had taken on another girl to do the rough and promoted Bessie herself to brass and silver. 'Keep my hands out of water for the rest of the winter,' she rejoiced, sniffing appreciatively as she unwound her shawl. 'Now tell us where this meat do come from.' She looked up sharply. 'Nothing Jacko Miles been taking, is it?'

'Oh Ma! Course not. Mrs Zellafield gave it to us this afternoon. Mutton. Scrag end.'

Bessie looked at her daughter through the steam. 'Did you go a-begging, our Tilly? Did you send our Billy?'

'No, Ma! I did not!'

It was true in one way; not in another.

She reached up to the mantelpiece. 'Look. This did come this morning. I thought it must be bad news. And this is a treat. Take our mind off it. And good for Alice.'

That did the trick. Bessie ripped open the letter and read it laboriously while Tilly dished up the stew. Alice joined them from the wash house and Billy Boy banged his spoon on the table and yelled 'Broff!' at the top of his voice.

They sat down and Bessie read again, frowning, then laid the letter down and picked up her spoon. 'This looks good, smells good and I'll be bound it tastes even better!'

178

She put out a hand and ruffled Billy Boy's hair. 'Go on, my boy. See if you can manage by yourself tonight. Never mind the mess, just eat it and enjoy it.' She watched smilingly as Billy Boy tucked in, then waited until Alice and Tilly did the same before starting herself.

Tilly swallowed and said apprehensively, 'Well, Ma. Is it bad news? Has the mine closed for ever?'

Bessie shook her head. 'No, my love. Nothing to do with the mine. It's news from my brother. Your uncle. Uncle Lemuel. You won't remember him, he left the village afore you was born. He always travelled for his work. A thatcher he was – reeds, straw . . . He even roofed a widow's cottage with sods once. Charged her nothing. Kept the rain out even if it did look like a mud hut!' They all laughed, though Billy Boy did not know what she was talking about. She fingered the letter. 'Seems he ended up in one of his own thatched houses, got him a wife.' Her face lengthened sadly. 'Lost her too, it seems. He got my letter telling him about your dad, and a year later his wife died in labour.'

Alice made a sound of distress; Tilly kept her eyes on her mother. There was more to come. Billy Boy slurped some more stew and Tilly spooned him another helping.

Bessie said slowly, 'He says if things are hard here we can go and live with him. Work for me ready to hand.' She smiled. 'Fancy me saying that – the work is stitching kid gloves. Ready to hand! His wife did it and made a tidy sum each week, too. Perhaps you could do the same.'

She waited. There was a long silence. Even Billy Boy stopped eating and rested his spoon on the table, looking at them. Alice said in a small voice, 'We can't leave Pa. Not buried down that mine. We can't do that.'

'And the people up-country won't understand our Billy,' Tilly said, thinking of Jacko Miles.

Billy Boy banged his spoon and set up a caterwauling and for a while they were all busy pacifying him and then finishing their supper and clearing away. Bessie went up the ladder with Billy Boy and settled him into the truckle bed. The girls could hear her singing to him very softly as

179

she moved around the upstairs, folding clothes and tidying his shells into a tin box. And then the singing stopped and her voice dropped as she talked to her dead husband. They busied themselves downstairs to give her some kind of privacy, and at last she came down and they moved their chairs from the table to the hearth and sat watching the last of the fire before bedtime. It was then she said quietly, 'I will say no to our Lem then, my dears. Offer him a home here if needed, perhaps. Send him our love. Leave it at that.' They nodded. She smiled and said, 'We couldn't have gone anyway. He said he could provide a home but no money and we would have to make our own way there. Two hundred miles an' more. Don't know how we were supposed to do that, do you?'

They were so relieved they all laughed.

Fifteen

1922

On 9 March 1922 Tilly Quince was fifteen and working in the kitchen of Wayward House. She had started just over a year ago when Billy Boy had been allocated a bed in the MD ward. Bessie had been appalled, imagining they had left out the 'a' in the middle. 'Our Billy is not mad!' she protested to the reverend, tearful, furious. 'He's slow. That's what he is. Slow. Oftentimes boys are the slow ones in a family – 'specially when they got sisters as bright as 'e's got!'

The reverend had calmed her down. He never told them that he had had quite a fight to find a place for Billy Boy. The matron at the home had received a letter from the medical authorities about certain requirements for children who were mentally defective. They needed more space than normal children. 'Space for having their fits,' she said grimly to the guardians. 'The high-ups en't so keen on metal bedsteads either. Seems like some of them thinks they're provided for the banging of heads!' She had four of these children and she did not want any more. The reverend pointed out that part of the 'arrangement' was that this boy's sister would be working there, and therefore on hand to help.

So Tilly started work on the MD ward. Matron told her she was very welcome indeed because she was used to looking after them sort of creatures. Unfortunately she was also very popular with the four other children on the ward and they appreciated her far more than Billy Boy had ever done. After all, she was his sister and he had long taken her for granted. They thought she was like Miss Casson, an angel. She washed them gently with their own wash cloths, and boiled the cloths after so they were always fresh. She dressed them without once slapping at their hands, and she sang them songs. When Billy Boy shouted raucously, 'And me Nancy tickled me fancy . . .' she asked him to teach the song to the others. They picked it up quicker than he had, and he didn't like that, either. He protested loudly, so loudly that matron declared he would have to go and Tilly must go with him. Then she relented, and after a great deal of discussion with the reverend, Tilly was put to work in the kitchen and Billy Boy began the arduous task of 'learning how to behave himself'.

A system of rewards and punishments was being introduced in hospitals up and down the country and it worked well. It also generated a kind of sullen misery in some of the children, especially Billy Boy, who had known family love and the kind of freedom Tilly had offered over the previous year. But he soon learned that if he was a 'good boy' he could see Tilly at midday and eat his dinner with her. If he wasn't he ate with the other four boys, who smeared their food across their mouths and licked it off. Tilly still fed him herself and pretended the spoon was a train going into the tunnel of his mouth.

The best reward of all happened on Sundays, when Bessie, Alice and Tilly took him for a walk which ended up at the cottage with eggie sandwiches and something special from the garden. Onions were his favourite but he liked radishes too and watercress fresh from the River Geagle. Sometimes, in the season, Jacko Miles brought mackerel in vinegar.

The first time he ran away all the rewards came to an abrupt end. He went a whole month without seeing his sisters or his mother. When the visits were reinstated they were all shocked at his appearance. His eyes were sunk deep into his face and he had lost a great deal of weight.

182

'He needed to,' matron informed them. 'He was very overweight for such a young lad.'

He ran away three times that first year, and then he came to terms with the system and learned to behave himself sufficiently to see Tilly every day for a whole hour and his family every Sunday afternoon. He did not sing and he did not speak very often, but he did exactly what he was told, and Bessie, who had been frantically worried about him, gradually accepted that Wayward House was the best place for him.

Matron wanted to give Tilly the day off for her birthday.

'It's what we generally do, child. You remember making tea when you first came – so that cook could go home for her birthday?'

Tilly nodded. 'But my mother and sister will be working. I wondered . . .' She faltered to a stop. Her wondering was leading to an enormous request.

'Go on, child. What is it you want to say?' Matron had grown fond of this slip of a girl and, like Mrs Zellafield before her, noticed the 'wonder'.

'Well, I wondered whether I could have more time with my brother, matron. I won't let him out of my sight, I promise.'

Matron looked at her and did some wondering herself. How anyone could think that the company of that loutish lad was a birthday treat was beyond her comprehension. But if the girl had gone home for the day Billy Boy would have created havoc all night long.

She nodded. 'Back at six o'clock,' she stipulated. 'And don't stuff him with those blessed herrings – we were up twice last Sunday night with him.'

So Tilly, fifteen and already aware that she and Jacko Miles were going to be together for the rest of their lives, went to the farmyard where Billy Boy was cleaning the cowsheds, curtsied to the farmer and asked whether she could take Billy Boy off for the day. When he heard that this was her birthday treat, the farmer, like matron, thought she must be a bit soft in the head herself. He took away Billy Boy's bucket and pushed him towards his sister, and Billy Boy, bewildered but very willing, took Tilly's hand and they went down the lane towards home.

Tilly took him into the wash house and sponged him down with the water in the copper, still warm from yesterday's wash day. Then she dressed him in a pair of his father's mining overalls and took him down to the beach to look for shells. At midday they went back to the cottage for turnip and onion mash and hot tea and sorted his shells for his collection. And at three o'clock they went to Penburra Cove to meet Jacko Miles and his uncle, Philip Miles.

Tilly timed the meeting so that the mackerel would be safely creeled and the two men either tramping back to Treleg or getting dressed. However, she found them dressed and tending a small fire in the lee of the north tip of the cove. Billy Boy was overjoyed, screeching his usual greeting of 'And me Nancy tickled me fancy' as he ran down the dunes towards them. Jacko waved his scarf and came to meet him; Philip Miles forgot to look taciturn for a moment and made a place near the fire for the new arrivals. Billy Boy took everyone's attention for some time; his face seemed to fill out again, his lifeless eyes sparkled, he cavorted around the fire and wanted Jacko to chase him immediately. To Tilly's amazement it was Philip who stood up, growling like a dog, and started to stalk Billy Boy around the fire. Billy Boy took off, screaming with his strange hoarse laughter, and Philip bellowed over his shoulder – 'Talk to her, our Jack! And put them other fish in the fire!'

Jacko did as he was bid, digging out an old tin from under the flames, opening it up and adding more fish to whatever was inside.

'What is it you have to tell me, Jacko?' Tilly could feel her own spirits rising. She hated not seeing Billy Boy more often; she wanted to wash him and dress him properly and get rid of that beaten look on his face for ever. To see him running free like this was a breath of fresh air for her.

'Must get this tin right under the ashes . . .' Jacko was lifting the embers with his foot, pushing the tin beneath with a stick. She knelt and took the stick from him.

'How long will they take?' Already she was anxious about the time. Six o'clock matron had said, and six o'clock she meant even if it was Tilly's birthday.

'Half-hour. They'll be crispy then. Bill will like that.' He was the only person she knew who shortened the childish Billy Boy to the manly Bill. She would have to stay; she could not deprive 'Bill' of crisp-skinned mackerel.

He sat back, flushed, his damp clothes steaming in the heat of the fire.

'Uncle Philip thought you'd come. Birthday and all. Gutted two extra fish for you.' He smiled at her and her heart turned over. He had always singled her out for his little kindnesses but it had only been in the last year that her heart had started its tricks.

'Fancy him knowing about my birthday.'

'I told him. He said fifteen was a good time to get things straight. You bin working long enough . . . got some money behind you . . . knows your own mind. Sensible woman, he do reckon.'

'And what do you reckon, Jacko Miles?' She was laughing at him in order to stop all the jumping in her chest but the laugh was interrupted by a gigantic hiccup, and then they both laughed.

He said seriously, 'I don't care about any of that. I've knowed since we was little kids that we'd be married and live together till one of us died.'

She didn't laugh or deny it; she realized that she had known it, too. Her face went hot and she just managed to control another hiccup. Right the other side of the cove Billy Boy screeched and they both smiled at each other. Then Jacko leaned forward. He didn't kiss her but he brushed his lips back and forth over hers and kept doing it until she thought she might faint. Then when Billy Boy's screeching grew closer, he said against her mouth, 'We'll have him to live with us, too. He'll be all right along with us.'

That was when she wept. Because he would be more than just all right; Billy Boy would be in heaven.

Philip Miles flopped on to the sand and Billy Boy flopped by him.

'Well? Did you tell her?' he panted. 'What did she say, boy?'

'She din't say nothing.'

'Nothing?' Philip Miles's gaze swivelled on to her face, beetroot red in the firelight. 'Nothing about the boat and the cottage?'

Jacko laughed. 'I forgot to mention about the boat and the cottage,' he said. 'But she'll say yes to that.'

Uncle Philip snorted. 'Listen, my girl. I told you before, young Jack is coming in with me on this boat – got one in me sights so it won't be long. And when he do leave home, I will move in and take care of my sister. So you and he can have my cottage. Give yourselves a couple more years to save up for a new bed and some crocks – mine has seen better days – and you'll be right and tight for the rest of your days. What do you say to that?'

She stared at him incredulously. He was such a dour man; since the mine disaster he had hardly spoken a word until one night when he'd got drunk at the Miner's Lamp and stood on the granite bar shaking his fists at the ceiling and shouting hoarsely that he should a gone with the others and he was living out of his time. And now this . . . giving his cottage to Jacko and to her, Tilly Quince. It was wonderful; it was better than anything she had dreamed of. She had been willing to go hungry with Jacko, had been willing to live with his mother and look after her in between whatever work she could get. And now . . . she said just above a whisper, 'Oh yes. I says yes, sir.' She turned to Jacko and said loudly, 'Jacko, I says yes.'

'I did hear you say yes, Tilly Quince.' His face was split in half with a huge grin. 'And I reckon if you says it again the whole of Penbeagle and Penburra and even Three Legs will 'ear you!'

Philip Miles turned to Billy Boy. 'You 'ear them, my son? You 'ear what they are a-saying?' He leaned forward and tickled Billy Boy behind the ear. 'Come on, stretch that mouth towards my 'and now – let's see a smile!' And Billy Boy did not stop smiling for a very long time.

For some months now, Alice had known something was badly wrong. She had said to her mother that it could not be consumption because there was no blood, not ever, in her rags. 'You would tell me the truth now, our Alice?' Bessie had asked, deeply worried by her daughter's fears. 'You know I would, Ma,' Alice had said. 'I'm so tired, and yesterday Mrs Sims found me asleep on the footstool when she brought in the tea. Sir Geoffrey's foot was in my lap and I had my cheek next to his bunion!' She had laughed, but Bessie had not joined her. Mrs Sims had already told her this tale with great displeasure.

Bessie had said, 'Listen, my maid. If you don't get better soon, we'll see if we can get you up to my brother's in the Cotswolds. Change of air, not so damp . . . could be just the ticket.'

'But if I en't working, Ma . . . how shall I get there?' Gentle Alice had looked terrified at the prospect.

Bessie had bitten her lip thoughtfully. 'I reckon we might persuade Sir Geoffrey to buy you a ticket on the train, my 'ansome. Mrs Sims did tell me that 'e's got shares in that there railway . . . I dun't know what she d'mean by that—' she laughed, 'not plough shares, that's for certain! But it makes 'im powerful with the owners or the directors or someone. We'll see.'

Alice had looked unhappy. 'I don't want to leave you, Ma. And our Tilly too. The three of us, we're so right and tight together.'

'An' Billy Boy. Don't forget our Billy.'

'I never forget Billy, Ma.' The easy tears had flooded Alice's eyes. 'Our precious trust.'

'Let me speak to Mrs Sims, Alice. She's got a good opinion of us as a family. Asking about Billy she were. Said we were an example to others.'

'Oh Ma . . .' Alice had broken down completely. ''Tis you. You are the example and Tilly and me, we just follows on behind.'

Bessie had hugged her favourite and soothed her. And when Tilly got home she left the two girls to make supper and walked down past the empty cottages to the cliff path and the sea and she had talked to John Quince, talked to him straight.

'Tilly's all right,' she said. 'You've kept an eye on Tilly – you always did and you're still doing it. Looks like it will be Jacko Miles for her and that won't be bad because she'll care for his mother like she do our Billy. An' you've looked after Billy too, because he's settled in that Wayward House real well. Now it's Alice's turn. If I can get old Geoffrey Three Legs to pay for a ticket, I can send her up to Lemuel. He's a good man and he'll keep her and give her a bed for a while till she gets better. And I want you to do the rest, John Quince. I want you to make her happy. I know you can do it. So get on and do it!'

She had waited a moment and nothing happened, so she had turned and walked back up to the house. She was almost there when she heard him laugh. She had whipped round quickly and stared back at the sea. It didn't happen again. She had whispered, 'Was that you? Was it you, my darling? Are you here all the time?' She had known nothing would happen, but she had waited a long time. And, growing deep inside her, had been the conviction that John Quince had not gone away.

That Sunday, Tilly had gone for Billy Boy very early and they had spruced him up and wrapped themselves in their shawls, then walked to the River Geagle and into Tregeagle Church for morning service. The reverend had smiled at them from the pulpit and his prosings had lasted no longer than half an hour, so Billy had been able to bear that. 'It wasn't too bad,' Bessie had pronounced as they

188

walked back home along the cliff. Billy Boy had galloped like a pony, slapping his buttock and shouting 'Amen' at the top of his voice. Tilly had loved it; the vestments and the candles and the enormous crucifix towering above them with the figure of Christ drooping from it by all those nails . . . She had gone to church with her father and remembered him bowing his head whenever Jesus's name was spoken . . . She had bowed hers too and Alice had bobbed a curtsy on the way out.

'All that popish stuff,' Bessie had said, not entirely disapprovingly.

Alice had said, 'If I can curtsy to that miserable old man up at the Court, I can certainly curtsy to Jesus.'

Tilly had said nothing, but she smiled. She loved it when Alice spoke up like that. It was like the old days when Alice had been in charge of the little ones at school. She had never been the same since the mine blew up and two of the other balmaidens had blown up with it.

But something *had* happened to make Alice's life better. In October 1921, Sir Geoffrey's godson had come to 'cram' for Oxford. Gilbert Tedenford had brought his own tutor and a box full of books and driven a Ford car which had been shipped in from America. He had been eighteen, a year or so older than Alice; he had spoken with an impeccable accent, but apart from that he could have been Alice's brother. His brown hair and eyes, his height and girth, the length of his fingers, the snubness of his nose . . . they had been the same. Even Mrs Sims had said, 'Remarkable. Quite remarkable. Yet you can still see he is the master and she is the maid. It's the bearing of course.' Mrs Sims had spoken with authority; she was an expert in all matters of class. 'He walks freely, moves his hands. When you're making up the fire tomorrow morning, notice how he helps himself to his breakfast.'

Bessie had noticed. At first she had thought it was because he knew what he wanted and had lifted the salver lids with no fumbling, the napkin held around the handles

189

firmly; but then twice he had changed his mind. And that was what it was. Neither she nor Alice nor Tilly would have dared change their minds. 'He's sure of himself even when he isn't,' she had said later to Mrs Sims. And that lady had nodded.

It had taken Gilbert two weeks to seduce Alice. He had driven her and Bessie home the first evening he arrived, and every evening afterwards while he was there. It had been obvious to Bessie that Alice was smitten, but who wouldn't be? He was good-looking, his bland English features put together like Alice's, so that what could have been unremarkable became Adonis-like. His manners were perfect – he had treated them both as if they were royalty. But girls of sixteen were smitten often by men above their station; they knew their place. And Alice had been sensible; she had already had to deal with old Geoffrey Three Legs, she could deal with this schoolboy. But though Alice was her mother's daughter and had known very well this could go no further, she had been powerless to stop it. Just as Bessie had let her apron fall in front of the fire three years before, so she had let her own plain serge dress be unhooked to fall around her ankles. She had let herself be kissed and adored and kissed again. When Gilbert had asked her if she loved him, she had found herself whispering that she loved him beyond death itself. It had been a strange thing to say, for how could it be so? Yet the words had formed in her mouth and emerged with her breath, and he had known they were true. Gilbert had never met anyone like her; he knew that her class lived by different rules, but it had not occurred to him that they were the rules of survival. Had she been the daughter of a gentleman she could have played a number of roles, and one of them might well have been an honest one. But she would have been in control of the situation in all of them. Alice had no such control; she could be thrown out at any time. She should have put up defences, just as she had done two years before when his godfather had stepped out of line; a faint now would have been the answer. But she had loved him beyond death itself and there were no defences at all.

She had been happy. Her life had become wonderful; when she arrived at the Court each morning Gilbert had already started his studies and she would walk across from the ha-ha and see him behind the enormous sash windows of the library, he one side of the table, his tutor the other. She would not stop, but she would slow down, and as she moved into view he would look up and his nice, ordinary, beautiful face would light up with delight, and his eyes follow her until she rounded the corner by the dairy and went in through the buttery door. Later in the morning he would visit his godfather and read to him from the newspaper and she would massage Sir Geoffrey's thick neck and listen to the full syllables and the slightly clipped consonants dropping from Gilbert's well-shaped lips and marvel that her lips knew his.

When it was time for him to go, he had begged her to come with him. His parents would love her; his little sisters would think she was an angel; as soon as she was eighteen they could marry and he could take on the estate just as his father wished. Before he had met her it had seemed a dreary way to live his life, whereas now it sounded like the Garden of Eden. 'It's called Tedenford, Alice. D'you see? Tedenford.' He had written it down in big letters. 'Can you see that the middle bit says e-d-e-n and the outside bit says T Ford! The Garden of Eden with a Model T in it!' They had laughed like the children they were. And then it had been March and time for him to go, and they had made their promises and wept. The car had spluttered beneath the arch of the stable yard. He would write; he could not live without her. He would talk to his father and come back for her.

It was in April when Alice coughed her first blood. The three women were huddled over the fire talking about the possibility of snow. Bessie said, 'Last time we had snow was when we started up at the Court, our Alice. D'you

191

remember?' Tilly looked into the fire and saw a time before that when the snow had fallen on the sea like a pall for the dead miners. Alice said nothing; she was looking pale and peculiar. And then she gave her ladylike small cough, reached for her rag, and the next minute it was as if all the blood in her body was spouting from her mouth.

Bessie was frantic; she tried to tip Alice back, as if she could tip her blood back to wherever it had come from. Tilly took over and held her sister slightly forward, her spine straight. 'Not much more, my dearest, not much more. Into this rag now – we'll throw that one on the fire – let me wipe you. There, there. Don't cry, my dear. All gone now. Breathe gently . . . easy, easy . . .'

Bessie was sobbing with fear. 'We must get the doctor, Tilly. Can you run over to Tregeagle?'

Tilly did not look at her mother. The cliff path would be muddy and perhaps covered in a treacherous layer of snow by now. It was almost three miles to the church and then along the road to the doctor's house but it was ten on the road . . . 'I'll be as quick as I can, Ma. Will you give her some water in a minute? She might vomit – she must have swallowed some of that blood—' She crossed the ends of her shawl over her bodice and tied them at the back, took her sou'wester from the peg by the door and rammed it on her head.

Her mother, now cradling Alice, looked up and said, 'Oh Tilly.'

And Tilly said, 'Don't be frightened, Ma. It won't happen again.'

She sprinted down past the empty cottages and along the top of the cliff. Truth to tell she had no idea whether it would happen again or not. If it did, Alice would surely die then and there, she could not have much more blood in her to spill. But there was a chance it would not happen again, and if she could persuade the doctor to come then he might save her.

It was a black night. The scuds of sleet were hard and hurt her face; it was almost too cold for them to turn into snow, and at first she pushed her hands up into her shawl. Then she stumbled and fell, helplessly rolling until she managed to free her hands and grab at a rock. After that she ran with her hands in front of her and the brim of her sou'wester pushed back regardless of the weather.

She reached the turning for the church and started down it much too fast, giant-striding with her legs and grabbing the overhanging branches of hazel at the same time. She got to the lychgate and hung over the coffin-rest trying to get her breath. A storm lantern swung in the arched porch, lighting up the sleet as it beat almost sideways from the north-east. That meant the reverend was in the church, maybe praying, maybe setting out the hymn numbers for next Sunday. She pushed herself upright again and ran down the path, stamped her muddy shoes on the mat and pulled open the church door.

A single candle lit the small nave; at the top, next to the candle, the reverend knelt at the altar, head bowed. The draught from the open door guttered the candle flame; he must have felt it too, but he made no movement.

She crept in and let the door close behind her, then slid into the first pew and knelt too. Normally she wasn't very good at praying and often found herself thinking of Jacko Miles and Billy Boy racing along Penburra Cove or Mrs Zellafield, who had twice waylaid her with a few giblets or a piece of mutton wrapped in newspaper and told her to make some strong broth for that sister of hers.

Now she found it very easy to pray, except she was not praying to God.

'Pa,' she breathed. 'Are you there? Can you do anything for our Alice? She feels the same way about young Mr Gilbert as I feel about Jacko. But 'tis easy for me . . . not for her. And now she is coughing blood, it will be harder than ever. Make her better, Pa. Please make her better.' She squeezed her eyes tight shut and stopped breathing in an effort to send the message out into . . . where? Somewhere her father could pick it up of course. Right here, in this church. She imagined it in big burning letters . . .

Make Alice Better . . . They went up towards the darkly arched roof, past the crucifix with its drooping burden, and stopped.

The reverend's voice said, 'Tilly, what are you doing here on a night like this?'

She breathed, then opened her eyes and told him. But she did not stand up or unclench her hands. It might take a while for Pa to read those words.

The rector said, 'Come on. We'll go down to Dr Garrett's together. He'll give us a lift in his trap back to Miners' Cottages. All will be well, Tilly.'

She loved him already, but never more than then. He was the reason Pa had read her words; Dr Garrett would never have come to Alice if it hadn't been for the rector; he certainly would not have taken little Tilly Quince back home in his trap. God had arranged for the rector to be in church that night; Pa had used him to let her know he had seen her message and everything would be all right . . . What had he said? 'All will be well.'

She smiled into the sleet as the doctor's fat pony trotted out on to the Land's End road. All certainly would be well. She was sure of it.

Sixteen

April 1922

Spring came at last that terrible year; and still Alice and Bessie worked at the Court, and still Tilly worked at Wayward House, and still Billy Boy 'behaved himself', because the biggest and best reward ever was coming his way. Tilly had to wait until she was seventeen but then Bessie said she could marry Jacko Miles and take Billy Boy to live at Uncle Philip's cottage right next to the engine house of the old mine. The only difference now was that the three women lived in terror of the future and wondered how long they could go on without being discovered.

Dr Garrett, furious at being called out in such weather conditions, furious that the priest had insisted on taking the girl up into the trap with them – and why was the priest there anyway, none of his business – had pronounced Alice free of consumption. 'Your daughter has a persistent cough, d'you say? Speak up, woman! When did it start?'

The reverend, hanging about near the door, had said sternly, 'I think Miss Quince is well able to speak for herself, sir.' And at the same time Bessie had quavered, 'Prob'ly since the explosion, doctor sir. Soon after then we did notice it.'

'I see.' The doctor had ice in his voice as well as his hair.

Alice said happily, 'I told you, Ma, din't I? I knew it weren't consumption!'

'Then what can it be?' Bessie looked pleadingly at the

doctor. 'There must be something that makes her cough up blood like that, doctor sir.'

'It's the coughing, madam. The girl has broken a blood vessel in her throat. I can prescribe soothing lozenges but it will cure itself in time. I take it you have no money for my bill, let alone medicines on top.'

The priest, bedraggled but dignified, spoke up again. 'I will settle your bill, Garrett. Write the prescription.'

Tilly, standing as close as she could get to the reverend, knew he was making matters worse. The doctor would have been quite happy to take out his ire on the three Quince women; the reverend was making it difficult. But still she loved him for being there.

The doctor ignored the request and started to repack his Gladstone bag. Bessie, seeing the consultation coming to an end, quavered a little louder this time. 'She is so tired lately, sir. And she do feel badly too.'

Garrett looked back at her with overt dislike. 'That's because of the pregnancy, woman. Classic symptoms. Dare say she feels faint often enough too, is that so, girl?' He looked back at Alice. She had fainted.

The reverend gave them two days to talk about it, then arrived at Miners' Cottages on Saturday evening. He brought a tiny nosegay of primroses from his garden. 'They've come out at last.'

Tilly quoted delightedly, 'April brings the primrose sweet, scatters daisies at our feet.'

As usual, he had a special smile for her. 'Well done, Tilly. You minded Miss Casson well.' He took off his hat and sat down in the proffered chair next to the fire. 'Are we to see Billy in church tomorrow?'

There was a silence, then Alice said, 'We didn't think as how you would want us no more, reverend. Not after . . . that.'

His look was so kind Tilly knew she must cry. He said, 'God wants all his children, Alice. Especially now, when you are two souls in one.'

196

'Oh sir . . .' Alice bowed her head.

Bessie stood up and put her arms around her favourite. She came straight to the point. 'We don't know what to do. We've been up to the Court as usual but it cain't go on, sir. And we don't know what to do.'

He said steadily, 'Go on as long as you can, Mrs Quince. As long as Alice is able. Then I can arrange for her to stay in Truro until the baby is born. No one will know.'

'I don't trust the doctor, sir.'

'He will remain silent on the subject, that I can promise you.' The exchange between the men had been terse, to say the least. The doctor had voiced his resentment at being spoken to as if he were 'a common man' and the reverend had said, perhaps irrelevantly, that if any of this got out, there would be no doctor's bills paid – he could guarantee that, as he paid most of the medical bills incurred by the people of his parish.

'Thank you, sir,' Bessie said, pressing Alice's head close before releasing her. 'You will take a cup of tea with us, sir? Tilly, fetch the cups, there's a dear. It will be good to come to church tomorrow. Very good.'

They settled round the table. Alice dried her eyes and lifted her head.

'What will happen afterwards, sir? When the baby is borned?'

'He will be taken into a good family of my own choosing, Miss Quince. Have no fear, I will always watch over him.'

'Oh no, sir!' Alice put her hands to her throat. 'Oh no. I cannot let that happen. Not Gilbert's baby. We will be married one day . . . the baby will not always be unlawful. When Gilbert has finished at university, we will be married. If he knew now that this had happened, he would not go to university. So I cannot tell him. You do understand?'

The reverend was very surprised. 'I thought . . . obviously I thought you had suffered at the hands of Sir Geoffrey. I was going to speak to him as your father would have done. This makes everything different. This young man is his

197

godson I believe? The Tedenford boy? Yes. That makes a great difference.'

'I cannot go to the place in Truro?'

'Yes. Yes, you can go. It means, however, I have no moral ground on which to stand!' He laughed suddenly. 'In fact, I am quite unable to blackmail Sir Geoffrey. Which I suppose is what I intended to do!' He looked at the three faces opposite him, all troubled now. He put a hand across the table to include them all. 'Do not worry, ladies. This is going to be a secret from everyone, it would seem. I do understand that it must be so, Miss Quince. Your motive in standing alone, if only for two or three years, is excellent and I respect you for it. Let me think about it again. I am sure I can find someone who will foster your baby until such time as the young man is able to take on his responsibilities.'

There was really no more to be said on the matter. He asked about the garden and Tilly said she had planted potatoes and hoped to dig them for Easter. And then he took his leave. And they tried to live normal lives.

They had not reckoned on Mrs Sims.

Mrs Sims had grown fond of mother and daughter Quince and though Alice was young and therefore necessarily foolish, she had admired the way she had first of all dealt with Sir Geoffrey and then young Gilbert. She had liked Gilbert, too, and had been sorry for him: banished to the desolate Court in order to study his Latin and Greek. He would end up running the family home, and what good would Latin and Greek do him then? So although she had kept an eye on him, she had blinked occasionally when she knew that he and Alice were running wild in the garden. She had known that he had made a swing from the elm below the ha-ha, and from the attic rooms where she was inspecting the servants' quarters she had been able to see Alice at the end of each parabola and imagine her small screams of delighted terror. But she'd felt it would do the girl good to behave like a child again. She had not been so sure about Gilbert. Indirectly he was her responsibility, and when she had seen him climbing the rope of the swing and shaking the residents of the rookery out of their nests, she had held her breath in case he should fall. They had both been children. If Gilbert had been born eight years sooner he would doubtless have been blown up in one of the trenches. She had watched them with a small smile on her stern face. This surely was why that terrible war had been fought. To give children a chance to play freely.

Circumstances had discovered Mrs Sims's blind spot. Even when she had started to suspect Alice's secret, it was Sir Geoffrey who got the blame. 'He's no better than a goat!' she said indignantly to her friend Mrs Zellafield. 'That poor girl,' mourned Mrs Zellafield, thinking of John Quince, and then of Tilly Quince and her enormous brother who could only be about ten years old.

Mrs Sims said suddenly, 'I'm going to have a word with the reverend. He keeps an eye on the family and he will know what to do.'

So the news of Alice's pregnancy came full circle and the reverend knew the time had come for her to go to Truro.

Bessie spoke to Mrs Sims privately. 'She's been coughing blood this past few weeks and the reverend has found a sanatorium where she can work for her place. Light duties, that's all. Lots of fresh air and special food. She dun't want to let Sir Geoffrey down, ma'am—'

'Let *him* down? Dear Lord above! Nasty old goat – and her with consumption too! I did hear from someone that it might be catching. I just hope it is and he gets it!' She saw Bessie's face and patted her arm. 'Take no notice of me, my dear. You are doing the right thing entirely. Discretion . . . 'tis the better part of valour every time. I will break the news to Sir Geoffrey. You take her home now and spare her all the sad farewells.'

Later that day Mrs Zellafield dropped in to Wayward House with six goose eggs for matron and some scrag end for Tilly. Tilly was ironing ancient towels used to 'mop up' in the MD ward. Mrs Zellafield was incredulous.

199

'Ironing floor cloths?' she asked.

Matron answered her. 'Not quite floor cloths, m'dear. Tilly likes them soft. She spoils those boys.' She smiled as she said it; the boys responded well to Tilly's 'spoiling'.

'I've got some shells for your Billy, child. Will you take me to him?'

'I'll do it, Mrs Zellafield.' Matron was only too pleased to show off the highly polished corridors of Wayward House; it was a credit to her and not many members of the public ever saw the inside of the house. 'He likes sea shells, does he? That's very kind of you.'

'Oh yes!' Tilly beamed her full smile across the kitchen. 'And the mutton as well! Thank you very much.'

Mrs Zellafield had had no intention of breathing a word about Alice Quince but the sole company of the matron of Wayward House as they wound their way through corridors and up stairs, proved too much for her. Matron was a woman who did not feel the need to fill long silences with conversation. Mrs Zellafield was the exact opposite. She waited until they were inside the attic room where the MDs were kept separate from the rest of the school, and then holding her side against an excruciating stitch, she said, 'I'm thankful that Tilly and her brother are safely in your care, matron. If only Alice could have been employed here . . . a nicer girl it would be hard to find. Well brought up. Her father was killed in the mine explosion—'

'Come forward, Billy. This kind lady has brought you a present.'

Billy Boy cowered; he recognized Mrs Zellafield. She leaned forward, although he was taller than she was. 'Look, Billy. Shells. Look.' She pulled the bundle from her voluminous bag. The shells were wrapped in newspaper and she spread it on the floor. Still Billy Boy stayed behind his bed.

'Take no notice, Mrs Zellafield.' Matron turned her back on the boy. 'He will do as you say quite soon. Continue to talk. What were you saying about Alice Quince? The older sister, I gather.'

'Yes indeed.' Mrs Zellafield was thoroughly rattled by now. There was an implicit threat in matron's promise of Billy Boy's obedience. She felt a need to take attention away from the boy. 'Such a pity. Sir Geoffrey should know better, someone so young and inexperienced—'

Matron was suddenly all ears. 'D'you mean to tell me the girl has got herself into trouble?'

'*He* got her into trouble, matron!' Mrs Zellafield was indignant. She glanced over to where Billy Boy crouched, anxious that he should not overhear them. 'Better not say more in front of the boy.'

'They don't understand anything, Mrs Zellafield!' Matron laughed scornfully. 'No brains. We have to wrap the bed frames in old blankets because some of them bang their heads against the iron! Ridiculous! Billy – come here this instant and see what this kind lady has brought for you.' She had forgotten for a moment what a mess this ward was in; bits of old blanket and spare pillows everywhere – Tilly did that to protect the boys when they fell. She'd have to put her right. It looked bad when visitors came in.

'Mrs Sims is very angry with Sir Geoffrey.' Mrs Zellafield was desperate to take matron's mind off poor Billy Quince. 'Very angry indeed. Treating a young girl as if she were a piece of meat!' They were strong words but needs must when the devil was driving.

There came the strangest sound from behind the rag-wrapped bed: like a growl, and like a cry of despair. Mrs Zellafield told her husband much later that it was a wolf-howl, though how she could have known that was a mystery as there were no wolves in Cornwall.

Billy Boy erupted from his hiding place with all his clumsy, unbridled energy suddenly focused. The women were blocking the open doorway and he needed to get through it and down the stairs to Tilly. He put his hands together as if in prayer and charged. Shells scattered everywhere; matron, trying to step forward and catch his flying smock, rolled on them and her legs went up in

201

the air higher than her head. The other boys screamed their delight when she crashed down at Mrs Zellafield's feet. Mrs Zellafield called, 'Billy Boy! 'Tis only me! Come back and see the pretty shells, my 'ansome!' Matron scrabbled at the hem of Mrs Zellafield's black dress and Mrs Zellafield leaned down and slapped her hand away and made for the stairs with more success than matron had had.

'Mrs Zellafield! I have broke my back – I'm sure of it!'

'I'll send help,' Mrs Zellafield said tersely, and began on the first flight of stairs, though much more circumspectly than Billy Boy, who seemed to be taking them six at a time and was already pounding along the middle corridor.

The chase was on and Mrs Zellafield was outclassed. This new Billy Boy was familiar with the layout of the house; he knew exactly where he was going. Mrs Zellafield had no idea. When she screamed advance warning of a runaway, Billy Boy knew that the ground-floor corridor leading to the kitchen would be policed, and with a cunning far beyond his accepted capabilities he got out of a window on to the roof of the corridor and ran along the ridge with no fear and no hesitation. When he reached the kitchen roof, which sloped down to the dairy, he slid down to the guttering, shuffled along it to the drainpipe and slid down that on to the slate floor.

Tilly was still ironing when the back door opened and Billy Boy stood there, dripping sweat and tears. She put the iron back on the range and went to him, arms open. He was a head taller than she was and crouched to put his forehead against hers, which was something he did when he was distressed.

'All right, Billy . . . all right. Tell Tilly. Have you made a mess? Don't worry, dear boy, don't worry. It won't be for much longer. Then we'll sing our songs again and go to the beach every day . . .'

He sobbed, 'Alice.' He took a deep and shuddering breath. 'Alice,' he repeated.

She knew immediately what had happened. Mrs Zellafield . . . how *could* Mrs Zellafield? But she'd said something and Billy Boy now knew about the baby.

Tilly held his head against hers. 'Alice is leaving the Court today, Billy Boy. She is going to stay in a lovely house not far from Truro. And she is going to get better.' Tilly had wanted to tell Billy Boy what was happening after that first visit from the reverend – the primrose visit. Billy Boy understood a great deal and needed to be part of the family all the time, whatever happened to them. Ma kept saying, 'He's only ten, still just a baby.' And that was true most of the time, but not all of it.

His sobs were easing. Through the kitchen door they could hear sounds of running feet. He whispered as clear as could be, 'Where have you been all the day, Billy Boy?' And then he pushed her away, turned and was gone. Out of the door across the yard, past the dairy, towards the woods which clothed the combe. Even as she grabbed her shawl he reached the trees and disappeared.

Tilly turned as Mrs Zellafield burst into the kitchen. The farmer's wife was holding her side again and panting like a dog, mouth open. She came to a halt at the table, leaning on it with one hand, her eyes fixed on Tilly imploringly.

Tilly answered the unspoken question. 'Billy has gone home. And I am going too. I do not know what happened up there, but he needs me.'

Mrs Zellafield gasped, 'It was my fault. I let something slip and he understood – whatever that woman says, he understood!'

Tilly paused. 'Yes, he often understands. Matron will probably withdraw his rewards, and punish him too, for running away. That's the trouble.'

Mrs Zellafield pushed herself upright with superhuman effort. She controlled her breathing, swallowed, took another gulp of air and said, 'Not if I've got anything to do with it, she won't! She's fell down and hurt her back. I will offer to do her job for her until she is better. Rewards will not be withdrawn and punishments will be very carefully thought out.' She looked at Tilly. 'Go on now, my 'ansome. Don't forget the mutton and 'ere's a handful of shells I saved. Look after your Billy tonight and I'll see you both tomorrow morning.'

Tilly lost another few precious seconds simply staring at Mrs Zellafield as if she, too, were an angel. Like Miss Casson. An angel in human form. And then she tucked the newspaper parcel into the waist of her skirt, poured the shells into the pocket and took to her heels.

Billy Boy might not understand simple instructions such as how to eat his broth – it was beyond him to wait until it was cool enough not to burn his mouth but not so cold that it began congealing – but he could pick up undercurrents; not necessarily through actual words, but from voice tones, from a raised hand across the speaker's mouth, the eyebrows drawing together. When his mother and sisters were distressed, he always knew and would wail and cry helplessly. When they were happy he would laugh his harsh hyena laugh and fling his ungainly body about in a crazy dance. And he understood now that Alice was pregnant, unwillingly pregnant by Geoffrey Three Legs. And he remembered the talk of Jacko's thirteen-year-old sister who was unwillingly pregnant by one of the miners four years ago. And who died. And he knew that his daddy was dead and he was the only man in the family.

He ran fast; he had learned how to run fast when Jacko chased him across Penburra Cove, and he ran like that now. He pushed his misshapen head forward, flailed his arms, pumped his legs, filled his lungs with the damp air. His time had come, Billy Boy's day had come. He kept to the woods until he reached the pasture land below the Court and then he slowed and kept to the hedgerow, and there was the ha-ha and above it the long terrace and one of the windows belonged to Sir Geoffrey's room. He kept his eyes on that window and reached the ha-ha just before darkness fell.

*   *   *

Tilly crossed the Land's End road and started down the lane to Miners' Cottages. She understood why Billy Boy had made for the trees and thought she would catch him up somewhere along the lane, but there was no sign of him and when she went indoors she found her mother and Alice cutting up the onions for that night's supper and no sign of Billy Boy. Bessie was aghast.

'Where would he go?' she asked fearfully. 'Poor boy, poor baby, where would he *go*?'

Tilly said, 'He might have gone to you, Ma. He would not know you left early today. He might have gone to the Court.' Bessie was already tying her shawl into place. Tilly frowned. 'Or he might have gone to Penburra. To look for Jacko.'

Alice said sensibly, 'Or he might be on his way back home, keeping to the cover. He'll be frightened that matron will send someone out to catch him.'

'I'll not let him go back there,' Bessie said, tying on her bonnet fiercely. 'He'll not go back there again and that's flat.'

'Mrs Zellafield is going to take on the work while matron is laid up—' Tilly waited for the questions to finish and then told them what Mrs Zellafield had told her. And as she spoke she began to wonder, and she turned to the door. 'Ma, stay here with Alice, please. I'll go up to the Court and if he's not there I'll come home along Penburra. It's getting dark and I know the path well . . . I'll find him, I promise. Please stay here in case he comes back. Please.'

Alice added her persuasion and at last Bessie agreed.

It was almost two miles to the Court and Tilly reached the gates in ten minutes. As she limped up the drive, she called Billy's name now and then. It was dark between the trees but there were no sounds and he would have heard her. She prayed he had not gone to Penburra; he was so clumsy and if he put a foot wrong . . . She reached the grand front door and turned left for the opening into the stable yard and Mrs Sims's quarters just as a horseman came through at a brisk trot and then galloped off down the drive. There were lights everywhere at the back of the house; the stable boy was lighting another storm lantern by the back door; Mrs Sims's downstairs quarters were lit, and the shaven lawns running down to the ha-ha were patterned with window-shaped lights.

She panted, 'What's happened – the horse—'

The stable boy recognized her. 'God save us, miss! What you doin' 'ere? Your family are in enough trouble as it is – dun't need no 'elp from you! That was Jim Thomas a'going for the doctor! Your brother prob'ly dun for our squire and that's a fack!'

She stared at him, but before she could question him again, the kitchen door opened and Mrs Sims herself stood there.

'Is that you, Zacky Stevens? Has Mr Thomas gone for Dr Garrett?'

'He 'as that. And the little Quince girl be 'ere, missis.'

Mrs Sims peered out. 'Alice – is it you? Oh it's Tilly. Have you got Billy with you, child? He can only have been gone half an hour, maybe less.' She saw Tilly already turning away to run back. 'Don't go, my maid. He'll be all right. Just come in a minute so that you can put your mother's mind at rest. Come on, now.'

Tilly would not have gone in except that Mrs Sims had called her 'maid', just as Pa had done. She hesitated, and then knew that she must hear exactly what had happened. The stable boy had said Billy had done for Sir Geoffrey. She turned back and followed Mrs Sims into the scullery, past the maids, and turned left into the housekeeper's downstairs sitting room.

It was furnished with a desk and a lot of chests holding small drawers; it was where Mrs Sims did the household accounts and kept a record of all that happened in the servants' quarters. She ignored the desk and went to the tiny grate where a fire was sending sparks up the chimney. 'Come and warm yourself, child. Tilly, isn't it?' She pulled a chair forward and urged Tilly into it. 'Now, it seems you

206

are looking for your brother, and now we are going to be looking for him, too. We should tell each other what has happened because it might help.' She studied the girl carefully and added, 'If Sir Geoffrey prosecutes – which I don't think he will – we shall have to get our stories straight. Do you understand that?'

Tilly did not wish to waste any more time, so she said briefly, 'The matron of Wayward House had an accident. It might be Billy's fault. Mrs Zellafield was there and she did tell me about it. She says she will make it all right for Billy. But he were main frightened and he ran. I thought he would be home but he weren't.'

'No.' Mrs Sims drew up another chair and sat on its edge. 'He came here, Tilly. He said he was going to kill Sir Geoffrey for what he did to your sister. He attacked him, but he couldn't kill him of course. Then he ran away. Sir Geoffrey began ringing as soon as he saw Billy's face at the window. I went in in time to see your Billy run back out and across to the ha-ha. Sir Geoffrey was on the floor. His wooden leg was on the fire – there were coals all over the hearth and I had to deal with them first of all. During which time Sir Geoffrey told me that Billy had burst in on him, threatened him, picked up his wooden leg which he had unstrapped, belaboured him with it so that he fell from his chair, then hurled the leg into the fire. And left.'

There was something in Mrs Sims's voice which Tilly could not quite identify. It could have been that she was trying not to laugh. But when she spoke next she sounded very serious.

'Tilly, I think you might have trouble. Sir Geoffrey is not badly hurt but he has been made to look . . . foolish. Attacked by a ten-year-old boy. He will not like that. There will be no work for you . . . no place at Wayward House. I would like to talk to your mother, but as you are here perhaps you can pass this on.' She looked at Tilly, who was too bewildered to respond at all and stayed silent. Mrs Sims said, 'Billy will be frightened, child. Perhaps . . .

perhaps you should go to the vicarage and ask for the reverend's help. I understand that in the past he has been very helpful to your family.'

At last Tilly comprehended something and nodded vigorously.

Seventeen

April 1922

Tilly thought her chest must explode before she reached the vicarage that night in early April. There were a few stars but the moon was swallowed in cloud and it was dark as she pounded along the Land's End road. The vicarage had been built in the last century for one of the Bassett family who was a hunting cleric. It was set in the moors, a Victorian Gothic mass, expensive to keep up. The reverend lived in the stable block above his horse. There were no lights to be seen and Tilly did not even clang the bell in the yard. She veered across the road and took to the bracken and the rabbit runs which would eventually lead to the top of Penburra Cove. She reached the cliff path without mishap. She did not worry about rabbit holes and hibernating adders; she knew that Pa would keep her safe.

There was light coming off the sea and her mother was silhouetted against it, unmistakable in her bonnet with her shawl wrapped tightly around her. Billy Boy was by her side, just as familiar, his canvas smock coming to his knees; with no coat, no outdoor clothing of any kind. Tilly could have called. They were both below her on the outcrop of rock that was stuck into the sea like Bessie's darning needle into a sock. The tide was going out. It was from there that Jacko swam out with the mackerel lines. She had called to him often from above and he had heard and turned and waved before diving into the sea. But now she did not call. Now she stood as still as they were standing. They all waited.

There was a little breeze, not a brisk April breeze at all, a zephyr of a breeze that spoke of summer and swimming. It pushed aside some of the cloud and the moon was visible; Tilly looked up at it, and in that instant Billy Boy went into the sea. Or perhaps just went. She looked back and he was no longer standing next to Bessie. Bessie was alone. In the moonlight Tilly could see her holding her shawl around herself very tightly, her face, ashen-white, looking at the sea, looking and looking. Tilly herself looked. There was nothing; not a flailing arm, no splash, just the heavy surge as the tide sucked at the land and retreated.

After a long time, the figure of Bessie moved. It clambered very slowly up the headland and along the cliff path to where Tilly waited on the other side of the cove. Bessie was weeping. Tilly would not have known it if the cloud had eaten the moon again, but it continued to shine and she could see that Bessie's face was wet with tears.

'I knew you was here, our Tilly,' she said hoarsely as she came up the last rise. 'I'm glad you was here. I'm glad we was both here.' She came up close and leaned forward. Tilly put her forehead against her mother's and knew what had happened before a word was spoken.

When the sobbing subsided, Bessie said, 'He told me he had finished off old Three Legs. He understood what that meant. I didn't stop him, Tilly.' Her voice rose with the pain of it all. 'I didn't stop him. I couldn't see him swing, could I?'

Tilly did not tell her that Sir Geoffrey was alive. Billy Boy would not have swung for his death, but he would have been properly hospitalized and they would never have seen him again. She thought of Jacko and the little home they would have made for Billy Boy. Her own tears ran freely with her mother's.

Bessie choked, 'Don't grieve for him, my dear girl. He is with his Pa now. Safe from everything. And happy.'

'Yes.' Tilly could barely speak. ''Tis us now, Ma. We got to live without Billy.'

'Yes . . . yes.'

After a while they enfolded each other and turned into the breeze which was no longer zephyr-like. And as they dropped into Tregeagle they saw a light in the church.

Tilly turned her mother into the tunnel of hazel.

'The reverend is there, Ma. He will make a prayer for Billy. Come on.'

Slowly, like two very old women, they trudged to the lychgate and up to the porch. And back in Miners' Cottages, Alice felt her baby move for the first time. She gave a small cry and put her hands to her abdomen.

Eighteen

April 1922

The reverend had a way of taking everything into his head very quietly, soaking up facts and feelings, never separating them because how could you ever separate facts and feelings? But sorting them out so that instead of a terrifying hailstorm of impossibilities, instead of starting every utterance with 'if only', you could see a tiny shelter from the storm, a way of maybe going forward. Because there was no way back. Either you stayed still and lost everything or you went forward.

By the time they had knelt together in the ancient church and the reverend had prayed for Billy Boy's immortal soul, it had indeed started to rain. Tilly surveyed it from the church porch with deep dismay because her mother was in no state to negotiate the slippery footpath back home. But the reverend said calmly, 'It's good. A proper search for Billy will have to wait. And that gives us time to think. We must let Billy rest with God now while we, as mere mortals, put one foot carefully in front of the other until we reach Miners' Cottages. God will be with us at every step.'

He was right about that, as he had been right about Billy Boy. 'Oh Lord, let the trumpets sound for the return of your child, William. You trusted us with this precious soul and now you have taken him back to glory. Help us to bear the loss, and to know that he and his earthly father are together again.' Tilly knew that the trumpets would indeed sound for her brother and that he would run and shout with happiness as he deciphered their so-familiar tune.

They saw the lights as they climbed that last headland. Alice had put a lantern in both windows and just inside the wood shed, where she was waiting for them. Inside the house, the fire burned in the range and the kettle was singing.

'You didn't find him?' she asked fearfully as she let them in. She turned and tried to bob a curtsy in the direction of the reverend but he took her arm and put her gently into a chair.

'Sit, my child. Your mother and sister found me in the church and told me one part of what has happened to-night. Now you and I will hear it all. You must be strong for the sake of your child.'

Tilly looked towards the corner of the hearth where her mother stood, head bowed, face suddenly twisted with grief. It was where Billy Boy had always sat, sorting his shells.

Tilly said quickly, 'Billy is with Pa now, Alice. He is safe with Pa.'

Alice bowed her head almost on to the table. She said in a low voice, 'They came looking for him two hours since. I think I must have known. Then. The world felt empty.'

The reverend reached for a chair, drew it to the table and sat down. Bessie forced her face straight and began to make tea. She said, 'He found me. Billy found me at Penburra Cove. Tilly said he loved it there, watching Jacko and Philip Miles setting the mackerel lines. So I went there afore it got dark. And I just waited and when it got dark I went up on the headland so he would see me against the night sky and he found me there. He told me he'd killed old Geoffrey Three Legs because he'd hurted our Alice. He knew what it would mean. The judge and the courtroom and then the gibbet. So he was going to find his father himself. He kept calling Pa . . . Pa . . . and climbing down rock by rock till we were right over the sea . . . I went with 'im. I din't try and stop 'im.' She threw that morning's

213

damp tea leaves on to the back of the fire where they spat and sizzled, then she reached for the caddy on the mantel and put some more of Mrs Sims's scrapings into the pot. 'Fetch the cups, our Tilly, there's a good girl.' She set the pot on the hob and turned round. 'I let him go. You saw, din't you, Tilly? I knew you was there. I was that thankful.'

They all looked at Tilly as she set out the cups and poured the tea. She told them what had happened . . . Mrs Zellafield and matron and the shells and Billy Boy's escape over the roof and his goodbye to her. She told them about her own search, Mrs Sims's covert scorn of Sir Geoffrey, the run along the road to the rectory and through the raw moorland to Penburra. And then she said, 'I din't see him go in, no splash, no nothing. The sea gathered him.'

Alice said, 'But he didn't kill no one, our Tilly. He isn't no murderer.'

'No.'

The silence was heavy. Bessie was making a groaning sound. Alice said, 'If only you could 'a got there sooner, Tilly. If only Ma had known Three Legs wasn't hurt, she could 'ave stopped Billy. If only—'

The reverend leaned forward. 'Do you think it would have made things better for Billy?' he asked. 'Geoffrey Bassett is too important. Important men are vain. Billy made him look a fool and he would have paid for that.' He sat back. 'And so would you. You would have been herded into the workhouse and Alice would have been made a scapegoat. Billy would never have survived prison.' His words were brutal but he spoke so gently, so gently. He drew their stories together so that they had a picture of Billy Boy himself doing the one grand thing of his life, making of the whole fiasco a thing of heroic chivalry. 'What did he say to you, Tilly? The first part of his special song?'

'He never said it before, sir. Always the bit about Nancy Gray cos that made him laugh. But this were very solemn. "Where have you been all the day, Billy Boy?", that was how he said it.'

The reverend said, 'It was his hour. Can you understand

that, Bessie? Alice?' He did not ask Tilly; he knew that she understood very well. 'The Bassetts may well twist events to make him out a would-be murderer. Others – like Mrs Sims – may ridicule the whole thing. But we know, you know, that Billy had to do what he did. He loved you that much. You have to go on for his sake. You have to leave here before Sir Geoffrey can wreak his revenge. If you do not, then Billy's magnificent attempt to defend you will have been wasted.'

He looked at Bessie and she said, 'He'll be washed up and there will be no grave for him, no one to claim his poor body.'

The reverend looked surprised. 'I shall be here, Bessie. But it is more likely that the sea will keep him, and if that happens I will make some secret memorial for him. A cross. At the top end of the churchyard. Would that please you?'

'Will it bear 'is name, sir?'

'No. That would risk more talk, more gossip. I will bury his name beneath the cross.'

She nodded dumbly; it was not good enough but she was powerless now.

So he made plans. He would go himself to the Zellafield farm and borrow the spring cart that took vegetables and flowers to Penzance to catch the train to London and Covent Garden. Then he would drive them to Truro where the milk train stopped. They could ride in comfort as far as Plymouth, but then they must leave the train because Sir Geoffrey would know by mid-morning that they had left the cottage, and he would be looking for them at stations on the up-line.

Alice was fearful. 'We don't understand about trains and stations, sir. Would it not be better to take to the road? We're good walkers.'

He nodded. 'Yes. But you will not get far enough soon enough. By mid-morning tomorrow a version of this story will be spreading and three women together will be recognized. How long before the rumours reach the Court

215

and Sir Geoffrey demands your apprehension? Walking is a slow business. By train you can be outside the county by midday.'

Eventually they agreed to it because they did not know what else to do. The reverend disappeared and they began to put their few precious belongings into three sheets, which they knotted around stout sticks from the wood shed and then shouldered experimentally. 'Can you bear the weight, our Alice?' Bessie sank her feelings into concern for her favourite. 'This one might be lighter. Try it.'

It was six o'clock in the morning when they trundled on to the up-platform at Truro. The milk train was already snorting impatiently as the trolleys of churns were pushed towards the double-brake vans at the rear. The three women were numb with cold; primroses and daffodils might be clothing the banks of the lanes, but the damp air was deathly chill and they had been travelling for six hours in the open cart. The reverend had tried to encourage them to walk with him occasionally, but they were exhausted already, and all he could do was to give them his greatcoat to wrap them around into one. He might have smiled at the thought of that, but anxiety permitted no smiles for a long time. He was risking his vocation and his livelihood by helping these three souls; the living of Tregeagle was in the gift of the Bassett family. They owned him just as they owned the mines and miners and . . . these three women. He strode along, splashing through mud and mire, knowing that this was as much part of his ministry as conducting services at Tregeagle. This was living prayer.

The station at Truro was built high up where one of the famous Cornish viaducts bridged the enormous valley. At that time of the morning the town was emerging from the mist, the top of the Victorian cathedral seeming separate from its base. The reverend took Alice's bundle and shouldered it inexpertly as he hurried the women on to the platform and into a carriage. Then he went back to the booking office and bought their tickets. He had not had sufficient funds in the rectory and had committed another unforgivable sin and taken church money from the locked box in the vestry. How the women would fare from Plymouth to Gloucestershire he had no idea, but he believed with complete faith that they were in God's care.

They looked out of the window, afraid of the noise and the steam and the bustle. One by one they came close to the window and tried to curtsy to him. Tilly was the last one. He took her hand so that she could not bob down behind the door as the others had done. He said, 'Listen, Tilly. When you reach Plymouth, wait outside the station and look for wagons supplying the moor villages: places like Tavistock and Okehampton. Ask politely if they will take you up. Then head for Exmoor. Keep clear of the highways. There is plenty of trade between Exmoor and Bristol so there should be wagons. Alice will not be able to walk far. You remember your geography lessons with Mr Tompkins and Miss Casson? The big map of the British Isles on the wall? Picture the map, child. I have your uncle's address and I will write to him. It could be that he will meet you in Bristol.'

A whistle blew, someone was waving a green flag. Tilly said, 'Sir, sir. Can you tell Jacko? Can you tell 'im, I will never forget him. Not never.'

The reverend had not known about Jacko. He stared. Then began to walk alongside the moving carriage.

'I will tell him tomorrow . . . no, today. Tilly, be happy. Always be happy.'

Tilly nodded. 'I will, sir. It must be just as easy to be happy as to be unhappy. Mustn't it?'

He was forced to release her hand. 'I'm sure that is true, Tilly. Good luck! God is with you always.'

He watched the rear vans sway from side to side as the train gathered speed. He wondered what he had done, sending this small vulnerable family into the unknown. Then he turned and went back to the wagon. It had to be back at the Zellafield farm before noon. And then he must write that letter to Lemuel. And then see young Jacko Miles. And then, perhaps tomorrow, he would go into Truro and request a meeting with the bishop. Tell him everything. Then, perhaps, he would resign.

The train stopped at every station for that morning's milk. St Austell and Grampound Road and Doublebois and Par and Liskeard and St Germans . . . they remained jumbled in Tilly's head like an ancient litany. The compartment had doors on either side so that passengers could climb in and out whether the platform was on the left or right. People left the train and went behind hedges and buildings to relieve themselves, but the Quince women were afraid to move. Alice leaned protectively over her stomach, careful not to sigh or groan as the iron tyres rattled over the rail joints creating their own accompanying percussion, ta, ta-ta-ta ta, ta-ta-ta ta. In spite of the rattle and commotion of arriving in Plymouth, she was first out, dragging her bundle, looking for the cloakroom which the reverend had told them would be there. 'This way,' she called like a seasoned traveller. They followed her and marvelled at the ladies' waiting room with its enormous mahogany table and leather chairs and the cubicles leading off . . . chains to pull like at the Court . . . each chain with its white enamelled pull edged with brass . . . the big square hinged lids over each privy . . . and the woman in the long white apron following them in with polish and rag . . . ''Tidn't 'ardly decent,' whispered Bessie.

But it was good to wash themselves and take off their Sunday bonnets to tidy their hair. It woke them up after the long jolting journey; vague stomach aches disappeared, the bottomless misery lifted just a little. They had never been anywhere like this before and in spite of everything they were curious.

It was earlier than the reverend had predicted: the enormous clock suspended from the canopy told them it was ten thirty. At that time Alice was usually folding the newspaper before Tom and Matthew arrived in Sir Geoffrey's room to haul the ungainly figure, minus wooden leg, into his enormous bath. Alice then had half an hour to hang newly laundered clothes in the dressing room, pack away the night liniment, and take the lacquered box containing ointments into the next-door sitting room where she would anoint the stump, strap on the famous third leg and then serve sherry. It was nothing, yet it was poor Geoffrey Three Legs's life. Mrs Sims, in a very good mood after finishing off his sherry one day, had told Alice that on Sundays, when she did not appear, he was as miserable as sin itself. He liked to see her fastening back the curtains, ironing his newspaper, setting out his shaving 'tackle' – he called it this as if he were still a seaman – and folding his clothes. When she had started the job three years ago, he had had bouts of temper brought on by the pain in his leg. She had seen him hurl his food across the room, and once, when she had been greasing his leg, she had hurt him and he had leaned forward and hit her across the head with such force she had landed several feet away. He had shouted at her to go and she had stood up, holding her ear ready to burst into tears and run from him. But she had seen that he was close to weeping himself and been suddenly full of pity. ''Tis all right, sir,' she had said very gently. 'No harm done. I'll be sure to be careful next time.'

He had thought he had her then; he had thought he could use her. A few months later he had torn her shirt trying to have his way. That was the time when she had thought up the idea of fainting, and he had been convinced she was ill and would have to leave. Things had changed then. He never actually respected her – he respected nobody – but he had begun to appreciate her.

She wondered who would oil the wheels of his life now. Mrs Sims was loyal but she had no real fondness for him, none of the staff did. Alice thought sadly how little his money had bought him. If he had reopened the mine or let the ex-miners have their cottages rent-free until they found other work – things he could have done without any trouble to himself – he would have been loved. But he had not done this. He had been convinced the miners had caused the explosion in some way and he had taken an easy revenge. Just as he would if he caught up with the three of them now.

Tilly, fully awake after the session in the ladies' room, was running the length of the platform: past the general waiting room and the door with the brass label announcing 'station master', and another smaller one, 'lamp room', and then the clutter of platform trolleys reassembling after unloading goods of all description. Alice said suddenly, 'We're wasting time and we've got a good start. Let's get out of the station while we can and look for wagons going north and west. Like the reverend said.'

The delay had cost them the easy lifts into Dartmoor. The wagons delivering goods had long gone, the ones collecting milk and vegetables were piled high with no room for passengers, especially three of them with bundles as big as themselves. The station approach was full of traffic, new cars (very rarely seen in the toe of Cornwall) that honked as they rounded the bend, and the road was full of children – urchins. They ran past the newspaper stand, the fruit and flower stall, snatching whatever they could and then disappearing. A policeman appeared ostentatiously, swinging his truncheon at his side, and they melted away, leaving only the comparative quiet as a reminder that they had been there at all. 'Like rats,' Bessie said, while Tilly remembered Billy running along the sand of Penburra Cove, screaming.

The policeman stopped in front of them and they froze.

He said gruffly, 'Where you from then? Mutley?'

The three of them were dumb; they barely understood him.

He repeated his question loudly, though by that time he had taken in the neatness of their clothes, their light brown hair and fair colouring. When they still said nothing, and were so obviously terror-struck, he screwed up his face

220

and added, 'We don't like gyppos here. If you got pegs for sale in them there bundles, I advise you to go back to your caravan and forget it. Got that?'

Bessie and Alice were rigid with shame and outrage, but still wordless. It was left to Tilly to say very clearly, 'We are not gypsies, sir. We are travelling to Gloucestershire to see our uncle, and these bundles are our belongings. Perhaps you could point out the quickest way to reach Exeter.' She had no idea why she named the town on the river, perhaps because it was the only one she could remember from Miss Casson's map.

The policeman was abashed; he suggested the train and then the main road to Exeter where they might well be taken up on some cart or other and then – at last – the turning off the Exeter road that would take them into the foothills of Dartmoor.

'Gypsies!' Bessie mourned. 'We look like gypsies! No one has ever called me that before. A respectable family like ourselves . . .'

'Gypsies are often respectable, Ma,' Tilly assured her mother. 'It could be that they will be travelling our way and will help us.'

Alice said firmly, 'We will use our feet and legs, Tilly. Just keep remembering that map the reverend talked about. And put one foot in front of the other.'

By the time they reached Marsh Mills the sun had broken through the mist. The road began to rise out of the enormous valley and they could look back and see the city held in the palm of the Tamar: the harbour with its many docks and piers, and the houses, terrace after terrace, climbing higher and higher.

'Never seen nothing like it,' Bessie marvelled. 'Your father came when he was a young man but there was no work, and back home he could always get a meal out of the sea.'

Tilly wondered whether there weren't any fish in the sea by the Tamar but she did not ask questions. The road was steep and her shoulder was aching from the weight of her bundle. She looked sideways at Alice, wondering how she was faring. Alice had her free hand on her stomach and a little smile on her face. That meant the baby was moving again; she had told them about the first time and it seemed to please her. Tilly did some sums in her head. They would surely have reached Uncle Lemuel by July. The baby would not be born until September.

Nineteen

The rest of that month tested the three women to their limit. That first night they stopped walking when they came to a milestone which read 'Plymouth ten miles'. Tilly and Bessie could have continued perhaps another five miles but Alice was drooping like a tired horse. On the other side of the hedge was an empty stable, empty that is, of horses; they discovered during the night that it was well used by rats.

Bessie lit a fire on what remained of the cobbles, and boiled water from a nearby ditch in John Quince's spare tea can to make tea. There was bread left and a few crumbs of cheese and they all felt much better for it. Had they known that it would be over a week till they ate bread again, they would have quailed that night beneath the thin sheets which held their bundles. As it was they woke to a glorious morning: thin, piercingly bright sunshine everywhere, rabbits feeding on the dew-soaked grass, a few moor ponies in the distance. Bessie boiled more water and poured it over the dregs of last night's tea, Tilly rolled their belongings into the sheets again and tied them on to the sticks, Alice went behind the ruined stable, but afterwards took huge breaths of air and felt much better; and then they set forth, each of them feeling that they were being led by John and Billy Quince. It was a heady sensation and lasted until after midday.

Alice and Tilly had known from their geography lessons that Dartmoor was an enormous and unfriendly place, but after six hours of walking along the track which was taking them north towards Tavistock and seeing nothing except soaring hills and swooping valleys, they started to appreciate how vast and wild it was. Bessie urged them on repeatedly: 'There must be a farmhouse soon, my maids. There were sheep droppings back there . . . someone has to look after sheep . . . just this one hill . . .' But the summit of that one hill showed them another one beyond, reached by another deep valley. And Alice was dropping with exhaustion.

The second night was spent beneath a tumbledown wall. Bessie had gone ahead and discovered it in yet another valley. It afforded protection against a small but biting wind that sprang up as darkness fell, but why it had been built there was a mystery. Bessie and Tilly found enough dead brushwood to start a small fire, but it did not last long and their empty stomachs and the cold kept them awake most of the night.

They left the track the next day in search of food. There was an overgrown hedge which must have kept cattle in at one time; it was springing with fresh shoots which Tregeagle children had always called bread and cheese. They fed on that most of the morning. In the afternoon they found a stream and spent time gathering dead hawthorn to feed a fire. The next morning, while the dew was still on them, Tilly found mushrooms and they breakfasted royally. Afterwards Alice brought them up. ''Tis only baby sickness,' Bessie soothed. 'There will be nourishment left inside you, don't worry.' But her worried expression did not match the words. She said to Tilly, 'We've got to find shelter and food soon. Do these hills go on for ever?'

Tilly said, 'We must try to find the road again, Ma. We must 'ave turned and twisted all day yesterday. We were walking away from the sunset last night. If we can go north-west we're bound to find a track. Let's walk away from the sun so it's on our backs, then rest awhile.'

They filled John Quince's tea can from the stream and rolled up their belongings again and started off. They had to make diversions to avoid enormous rocks which suddenly reared out of the hills; they found another stream and turned south to drink at it. They had no idea how far they had come; Tilly dreamt that they came upon the milestone again and discovered they were still only ten miles from Plymouth.

Every night Bessie would boil whatever they could find. Dandelion leaves, nettles, a vinegar plant for flavour. Somehow they survived, but they all knew it could not go on much more. Alice's 'baby sickness' was continuous throughout the day and at the end of that terrible week she lay down in the thin afternoon sunshine and slept. Bessie lay by her, Tilly the other side. Before she slept Bessie said, 'We'll make up for it through the night, my maid. Alice dun't seem to get the sickness at night.'

They all woke just after sunset, and while there was enough light in the sky they gathered what firing they could and boiled up that day's gleanings, and then set their course by the north star.

Dawn found Bessie and Tilly trying to shelter Alice with their bodies. She had collapsed after four hours and they had dragged her behind a wind-torn bush out of the April breeze – 'loud and shrill' – and waited for the next day and the sunshine.

So it went on for another two days and two nights. It was Tilly who suggested a few days' respite. 'Let's spend all day looking for firing, Ma.' She indicated Alice still sleeping. 'If we can keep warm and drink your broth for a while, Alice will be strong enough to walk properly again.' She saw her mother's expression and knew that despair was taking over. 'Listen, Ma,' she said urgently. 'Once we've found the road again, we'll be all right. We'll stay right by it and wait. Roads are there for wagons and carts and people. Someone will come by.'

But Bessie had gone past despair and was waiting for resignation. John and Billy Quince were still there but they were waiting for that resignation, ready to take her and

Alice and Tilly away from this dreadful place. Who was she to fight them? But Tilly suddenly took her shoulders and shook her, something she would never have done unless desperate.

'Ma!' she said loudly. 'Alice is having a baby! If we give up we're no better than murderers!'

So Bessie dragged herself to her feet and went to look for brushwood, and almost immediately came upon dried sheep droppings. She stared at them in disbelief; not only would they make a good steady fire but they were proof of habitation. She prised them from the thin grass and took them back to where Tilly had scooped out a small fire pit and edged it with stones.

'No lack of rocks, Ma,' she said. 'We'll heat them throughout today and wrap them for Alice through the night.'

'You're a good little maid, our Tilly,' Bessie said.

They worked nearly all that day gathering fuel for the fire that would save their lives, filling the tea can from a ditch and straining the mud through a corner of one of the precious sheets. There were nettle beds and a drift of cowslips for food; for once, warm and drowsy, Alice kept it down and slept again, a grateful smile lifting her face. As darkness fell Bessie banked the fire with earth and wrapped the hot stones as best she could. They put fresh stones around the red mass of embers and slept until the early hours, when Bessie roused herself in the after-midnight chill and renewed the stones, pushed fresh wood into the embers and slept again.

There was a pale grey slice of sky in the east when an angry shout roused Tilly. She sprang to her feet, not knowing whether to be delighted or terrified.

The voice shouted again then yelled, 'Who's down there trying to set the hills on fire!'

Bessie woke with a start; Alice did not move. The two of them looked up and saw the vague silhouette of a wagon against the sky on the slope above. A loaded wagon.

Tilly was running towards it before her mother could stop her.

'Oh sir – sir—' she panted, falling over invisible tussocks in her hurry to climb out of the valley. 'We're that glad to see you! Where are you going?'

Bessie shrieked behind her, 'Tilly – come here this instant!' And in front of her the driver of the wagon cracked his whip.

'We don't like your sort on the moor. You start a brush fire up here and it will ruin acres of land – you gypsies are the bane of our lives – get away!'

'We're not gypsies!' Tilly stopped short of the wagon and the whip. 'And we know about brush fires. Anyway there's nothing here to ruin! We're walking to Tavistock and we're lost!'

Bessie joined her and put a protective arm around her shoulders.

'She's right, sir. We're country folk. And we're lost—'

The wagoner made a sound of disgust. 'How can you be lost? You keep walking down the road till you come to somewhere. Yelverton it will be.'

'We lost the road, sir.'

'What d'you think this wagon is riding on?' He stared from the woman to the girl. 'No, you ain't gyppos, they know a road when they see one. You're visiting the prison, en't you?' He held up his whip; they could see it plainly now dawn had come. 'Don't say nothing. I'm sorry for you.' He reached behind him. 'Here. Cook this in your fire.' Tilly ran forward and took a turnip the size of a football from him. 'I'm taking this lot into Plymouth for the early train and I shall be bringing milk back. If you're on this track I can take you to Tavistock.'

They tried to thank him but he cracked his whip again and lumbered on. And then they could see, quite plainly now, two iron tyre-tracks in the grass.

They reached Tavistock just ahead of the 'April showers'. Bessie called them Atlantic gales. Weather was different in these high and lonely places and it was easy to understand their barrenness. They were swept and scoured and drowned and baked all year round.

But Tavistock was different. Its tall elegant buildings and cobbled streets were like an oasis of civilization reclaimed from nature. The Quince women had been to Penzance once and had seen the environs of Plymouth station just a few days ago. The platform streets of Market Jew Street in Penzance had entranced the girls and they had scurried up and down the twisted steps from road to pavement thinking that towns must all be like this: man-made games for children. The enormous monument to Davy at the top of the street had slowed them slightly but they knew about him and his lamp; he was a friend.

As for Plymouth, from what they had seen from the train it was just . . . too big. And they had been conscious that they must leave it as quickly as they had come. The Bassett hand hovered over it.

Tavistock was different. Solemn and important; not big, but very conscious of its own dignity. The sheer height of the buildings diminished the women. Their faces constantly turned up to look for the sky between the rooftops, so that they felt as if they were cowering.

The wagoner, kindly enough but silent in the face of what he thought was a prisoner's family, let them down at the point where the grass road became harder and cobbles appeared between the green. Here, in a field, half a dozen step-down traps awaited; their drivers white-coated, horses caparisoned with ribbons, muzzles well into haybags hanging from their harness. Tilly felt better for such a pretty sight; better for the gill measures of milk they had all enjoyed, which had washed down the tough old turnip eaten six hours before but still stuck behind her ribs.

Alice looked desperately for somewhere private where she could bring up that bitter breakfast and pass water. Bessie was suddenly completely disorientated; the sight of the tiny majestic town isolated in these endless hills was so out of place it seemed unreal. She hurried after Alice and the two of them were violently sick. It was the dratted great

228

turnip, of course; she felt no better afterwards, there must be more to come up.

Tilly hung back, watching each milk float collect its three churns and hang them about with the measures. The drivers doffed their hats at the wagoner and stood on the step of the float to balance the weight of the milk, and without a word from them, their ponies would nod their heads until their ribbons flew and then take the weight of the trap very slowly until they were on the cobbles and could work up a trot. Tilly clasped her hands to her chin, smiling her pleasure, and the milkmen, seeing the small pretty girl in her shawl and broken boots, doffed hats to her too, and she curtsied in return. She knew it was because of their special song; she had heard it sung by the cowmen up at the Wayward House.

'The milkman came and the milkman saw
The pretty maid in her lamb's wool shawl.
He did nod and she did bow
And he said, you're a pretty sweet-maid, that I vow.'

And Ma knew it too, because she ran ahead of Alice and grabbed Tilly's hand and jerked her back, as if the little ponies would mow her down.

They walked slowly through the main street, past little gardens, railed in but surrounded by benches so that people could sit and watch the flowers grow. There was a town hall and a row of houses marked by shining brass plates, and more railings enclosing a school, and a church and a chapel and a forge and a hostelry with a big yard for horses and carriages. Even the pump had a low wall built around it, and on the wall was a cluster of shining bright pails. Tilly kept turning and walking backwards and then sideways so that she could see everything.

'Why don't we stay here, Ma? It's pretty and it's safe and we could get work and lodgings.'

'We couldn't get either, Tilly. We're on our own. No one would give us work.'

229

'We were on our own at home. And we had work there.'

'People knew us. Because of your father. They knew we were respectable. Your uncle will do that for us. There's work for all three of us and we don't have to leave his house for it, either.' Bessie took Alice's arm. 'Don't linger too much past the inn, my love.' She felt Alice dragging back. 'What is it, child? Alice? Are you all right? Give me your bundle – Tilly, take your sister's other arm. Come on . . . best foot forward. There's another of they benches under that willow.' Bessie was panting, Alice was almost a dead weight. 'Bit of privacy . . . there's my girl . . . lean against me. That's it.'

'What is it, Alice?' Tilly knelt in front of her sister. The willow fronds swayed in a slight breeze. 'Did you feel faint?' She looked at her mother and saw the terror in her face. They both waited for the cough and the rush of blood. Neither came. The fronds were still; they could not be seen.

Alice said, 'It's nothing. I thought I saw someone . . . something. I was daydreaming.' She closed her eyes and breathed carefully. Then she said, 'Tilly, would you run back and look for me? A motor car was in the yard. Can you see whether it is a Ford car?'

More wild looks passed between Tilly and Bessie. Bessie remembered well the Ford car in which young Gilbert Tedenford had driven her and Alice home when he was at the Court. Could it be . . . could it possibly be . . . that he was here? Could it be that John and Billy Quince were indeed watching over them and had arranged this wonderful coincidence? She held Alice's shoulders and closed her eyes while Tilly gathered her skirt and flew back the way they had come. And Alice too, weary and ill, closed her eyes and thought how her dear love would take them to Uncle Lemuel's in his car, and there would be a secret wedding so that the baby would be lawful, and then a secret waiting until he was of age and could claim his family.

And then Tilly came back, her eyes dark with fear. She

had gone up close to the car and had seen it was one of the Ford cars and had let her hopes ride high. The door to the inn had opened, and she had flung herself down beneath the parapet of the pump when she saw that the two men who emerged were wearing policemen's uniforms. They had been silent as they walked past the car and came towards the pump, then they had paused and one of them had said heavily, 'I don't like this. Hunting women isn't our job. Attempted murder in Cornwall isn't our job, neither. And that reward . . . it's going to be tempting for any Tom, Dick or Harry to take a gun out to shoot a rabbit or two and be looking for something a bit bigger.'

The other one had said, 'Don't worry about it, John. From what I heard from the carrier, those vagrants out on the Tor was aiming to camp outside the prison all summer in the hopes of seeing their brother in one of the prison gangs. Poor devils.'

Tilly gabbled the information and then said, 'I'm so thankful I went back, Alice. Else we wouldn't have known that there was a reward out for us. Even here. We've got to get out of this place.'

Bessie, still standing behind Alice, swallowed fiercely and closed her eyes again. Just for a moment she had imagined that John Quince had deserted her. But he had not. Tilly was right; he was still here, still looking after them.

She said, 'We must go as soon as you feel strong enough, Alice.'

Alice nodded. 'Was the car a Ford car, Tilly?'

Tilly folded her arms around her sister and held her close. 'It was, my dearest. But while the policemen were still talking and I was still hiding, a man and a woman came out and got into the car and drove it away. They were both as old as Mr Tompkins.'

Alice dropped her head on to Tilly's shoulder, gave a short, sharp cough and leaned over suddenly as blood filled her mouth.

*   *   *

They hid among the ornamental willows most of that day. The delicate fronds swept to the ground and sheltered them from prying eyes. But nobody passed that way. Their initial terror gradually subsided as time went on and no one came to arrest them. There were sounds: church bells, street calls, some children playing, perhaps in the school yard. But the small enclosed garden remained magically empty. Bessie tried to make a joke of it. 'Can't mess up a tidy place like this with people!'

Some time in the afternoon, Tilly tied a kerchief over her head, smeared dirt into her face and went to the back of the inn to beg some bread. The pot man looked her over with scorn. 'Want to feed the ducks do 'ee?' he said with heavy sarcasm. But he gave her a basket of leftovers, and as the sun went down they ate it all with enormous relish, and then walked out of the neat little town and into the night on the road to Okehampton. Bessie shouldered two bundles and she and Tilly walked either side of Alice, linking their arms behind her back and beneath her arms. Bessie said they would walk till midnight and then look for a barn. But the toy town that was Tavistock did not herald farmland and farms, and by midnight they were in the same terrain as before, an apparently empty wilderness. They looked now for a sheltering wall or hedge. The cobbles had petered out some time ago and the wheel ruts that marked the track were invisible until either Bessie or Tilly stumbled into one. There was no moon that night but it felt as if it was a long way past midnight when the rain began.

They dragged on, their clothes gradually becoming heavy with water, then Tilly stopped and sniffed the air like a cat.

'Wait, Ma. I can smell smoke.'

They stood, drooping, dripping. Bessie said wearily, 'No one 'd try to light a fire in this weather, our Tilly.'

'Chimney smoke, Ma. Sooty.' Tilly shifted slightly. 'Take Alice, Ma. I'll try to follow my nose!' She tried to laugh too, but sneezed instead.

She went to the edge of the wheel track, blinked the water from her eyes and stared hard into the rain. She had the impression that the land fell from the edge of the road into another of those interminable valleys. The smell was stronger. There were no lights to be seen, but if the valley was curving away it could be that a cottage was tucked almost beneath them.

She called back, 'Stay where you are, Ma. I'm going to take a few steps down but I won't go far—' She stopped there and yelped. Her right leg, lower than her left, was being held. A tight grip but not a cruel one. Not an animal. Maybe one of those constables. Maybe an escaped convict. The yelp turned into a scream.

Bessie was instantly by her side, her stick with its heavy bundle scything the darkness like a Turk's scimitar. It connected with something and there was a shout. Then they were both pushed and shoved on to the track; they fell backwards next to Alice who was sitting or kneeling somehow. Two figures stood above them. There was a dialogue in a language they did not recognize.

Bessie, squirming to her knees, said, 'Romanies!'

'Ah. Romanies,' one of them said. 'You know about Romanies?'

Bessie did not answer. She was crouched above Alice, pulling her up, trying to feel for her heart.

Tilly panted, 'You frit me! Didn't see you! Smelled a fire – a chimney fire!'

'Four chimney fires more like.' One of the men looked around. 'How many are there? You got menfolk with you?'

Again it was Tilly who answered. 'No. We're going to Okehampton. My sister is ill. Can you help us?'

There was another dialogue in the strange language. Tilly got the impression that these men were unwilling to get involved. They had enough problems of their own, she knew that. She also wondered whether they knew about the reward being offered for three vagrant women.

Bessie made a sound of despair. 'I cain't find no heart-beat, Tilly.' She leaned down. 'Alice! Alice, wake up – come back to us, my maid! Come back now – for the baby's sake, my dearest! Come back to your ma!'

A wind blew up from the valley and brought a sudden squall. There was no sound from Alice. Bessie wailed suddenly. The two men began to move away.

Tilly scrambled to her feet and ran after them; she slipped in one of the wheel ruts and would have gone down again if she hadn't grabbed an arm.

'Take us with you,' she gasped. 'There's a reward for us. It will be worth your while. They want us alive, not dead.'

A hand came out of the rain and pulled her upright. She felt fur, smelled blood; rabbits. They had been trapping rabbits.

The man held on to her. 'You know what it's like then, don't you?' He snuffled a watery laugh. 'A reward, eh? No one offers a reward for us. But they kick us out and on. Out and on. We got to keep on the move. You know what it's like now, don't you?'

There was something in his voice; she sensed that he had already heard of the reward. There was nothing to lose.

She hung on to his arm like grim death and said loudly above the sound of the drumming rain, 'Alice is going to die. She's expecting a baby. And someone wants to hurt us.'

'Who?' the other voice said sharply.

'Sir Geoffrey Bassett.' The gypsies knew it all now. What was the point of trying to hide anything? They would all be dead soon. One way or another.

'That bastard Three Legs? Down Land's End? Sent Abel in a convict ship for taking a pheasant!' The other man started forward. 'Come on now, Rufus. Get these women out of the rain.'

Tilly barely remembered the dangerous, sliding journey down the side of the valley and into the gypsy encampment. She knew later that they were taken into 'Rufus's' caravan, their sodden clothes draped between the wheels beneath, rough calico nightshirts pulled over their heads, rabbit stew set before them. Rufus's wife tended Alice.

There was the sharp smell of spirits to revive her and then tallow for her chest. A soothing murmur from Bessie explaining what had happened, and little whimpering sobs from Alice.

There was scarcely room to move in the caravan. The pot-bellied cast-iron stove took up one end, the beautifully covered bed the other. Pots hung from the roof and there was a table where Tilly and Bessie ate their stew. Right next to them was the child-size truckle bed which had been brought in for Alice. They all shared a chamber pot and a big china wash bowl, but there were cups and plates and spoons for everyone, and the candles in their sconces gleamed on the brass kettle and the skillet and innumerable hanging charms. Tilly curled into her chair and slept and Bessie lay on the floor next to Alice and put her head near Alice's feet. She would never have chosen this form of rescue: gypsies were the lowest of the low throughout the countryside. But here was warmth and succour which was denied them from their own. She found herself smiling. 'You're still there then, John Quince. A-trying to show me the other side of the coin!'

It was during the journey to Okehampton that Tilly taught Rufus and his family to sing 'Billy Boy' and told them the story.

Twenty

Alice took a long time to recover. Rufus's wife, Sheba, was also expecting a baby, and tried to get Alice to share the raw rabbit-livers which she ate each night with fresh young dandelion leaves. Alice did her best but often had to creep away and bring them up behind a hedge.

They camped in the lee of ruined Okehampton Castle, which grew out of a mound ringed by a dry moat. It gave Bessie the shivers because she thought it looked like the engine house of Wheal Three Legs gone to rack and ruin. But she would always be grateful to the gypsies for not giving them up. She took over the cooking in the caravan, and besides rabbit stew she used the skillet and made pancakes with the eggs Rufus stole from nearby farms.

'It's no wonder they move you on,' she said to Sheba, knowing she should refuse the eggs, but hoping that Alice would eat some of them.

'Oh 'tis not for stealing the eggs!' Sheba laughed. 'They never know the eggs 'ave been laid – my Rufe do stand there with 'is 'and 'eld out!' She became more serious. 'They move us on because they move us on.'

Bessie did not like to mention the dirt, the rats, the absence of any rent. The gypsies had their point of view and the farmers and villagers had theirs. All Bessie knew was that the gypsies had saved Alice's life and probably hers and Tilly's as well.

Tilly knew a few precious weeks of a different sort of

happiness, something she could not identify. It was as if she were living some of her daydreams; reality seemed a million miles away. She played with the gypsy children, and even when they worked the work was a game. Picking mushrooms and cowslips, gathering wood for the half a dozen stoves, teasing fresh hay from last year's ricks to refill the palliasses . . . none of this was work because it had no background of anxiety. Once Alice was sitting up and helping Bessie with the cooking, Tilly was free to do what the gypsy children did. Bessie grieved that she was running wild, going native, getting completely out of hand; but when she pulled the blossoms from the cowslips and let Alice suck the nectar, when she warmed the mushrooms in fresh cow's milk to make a soup that Alice enjoyed, when she pushed extra soft hay into Alice's mattress and tucked it all in with one of their sheets fresh-laundered and blown dry in the late April breezes, Bessie made herself stop worrying. Tilly was clothed after a fashion, warm at nights, well fed and – importantly – she looked healthier than she ever had.

The other girls of fifteen went with the women into Okehampton and sold pegs, and told fortunes, and threatened ill-luck to housewives who would not cross their palms with silver. But Tilly was small for her age and was good with the little ones and much more useful as a nursemaid. When the sun shone in the afternoons she would make a nest for the little ones in the long grass, snug and out of the wind. They would curl up like kittens and she would tell them stories or sing to them. They loved the story of the high-born lady who fell in love with the gypsy king and left all her luxury to live with him.

'Last night I slept in a goose-feather bed
With the sheet turned down so bravely-O.
And tonight I will sleep in a cold open field,
Along with the raggle taggle gypsies-O.'

They all laughed at the thought of it. Their caravans were

237

warm and cosy and shining with brass and silver. Nothing raggle taggle fitted that.

It was a pastoral idyll and it could not last. By the end of May-month Alice was strong enough to walk down to the White Hart and sip porter from Rufus's tankard. It made her gag, but gave her enough strength to walk back to the encampment, and enough appetite to eat some of her mother's pigeon pie. They ate alone from the little table under the window and watched Tilly join the others for a communal supper around the open fire. There was to be a family meeting during the meal; it was a sign of the gypsies' trust that Tilly was allowed to stay and share their food. Bessie watched her find her place not far from Sheba and sit, stretching dirty bare feet towards the fire, pushing her greasy hair behind her ears. She looked like the others, and Bessie said, 'It won't be long now before we can start our journey again, will it, Alice?'

'Ma, I've told you. I could leave tomorrow if you like. We've got the summer ahead of us, remember.'

'Yes. And we need to be with Lemuel before that baby decides to be borned.' Bessie smiled to take the sting out of her words but she was very serious. They had the whole of June and July for travelling. August was Alice's eighth month and they must be installed in their new home by then.

Tilly herded the little ones to their beds while the adults gathered closer to the fire and decided on the moon times when they would leave and the towns they would 'work' for the next few weeks. Their circle started at Land's End and ended there, too; they went no further north than Okehampton. Their forebears had come from Ireland in open boats over two hundred years before; they camped within reach of prehistoric sites, quoits and standing stones at the tip of Cornwall, King Mark's stone at Fowey, the ancient castles at Lostwithiel and Okehampton. Sheba explained this to Bessie. 'We would go on for your sakes but 'tis our destiny to reach these places at full-moon time.'

Bessie and Alice nodded, accepting that they must go on now without the gypsies. Tilly understood completely. It had snowed on the sea when her father died and later her father had lifted his arms from the sea to gather Billy in without a sound, without a splash. The land and the water and sky told you how to live. The hills of Dartmoor had filled Tilly with life, so that she knew the Cotswold hills would be kind to her. She would miss Sheba and Rufus and the gaggle of children who followed her around the camp and the fields; she would miss the life, the absolute freedom, the assumption that everything the land produced was for every person whether they had worked to produce it or not. She recognized that Romany rules were not for her and that she had been lucky to share them for a while.

Rufus took two of the horses and put Alice and Bessie up on one and Tilly in front of him on the other and they set out at sunrise on the last day of May and rode out of Okehampton and through Sticklepath and South Zeal, Crediton and Bickleigh, skirting Exeter and reaching Tiverton in the late afternoon. They unloaded their bundles and a bag of food near a stream, watered the horses and let them into a field, and ate together for the last time. Alice and Bessie were sad, grateful, reassuring the Romanies that they might meet again in the future. Tilly knew that would never happen, and she felt her heart would break. She knew that the winter months culled the elderly without mercy. Most Romanies had a short lifespan. Rufus might not see his expected baby grow to Tilly's age. She watched him tie the second horse to his, fill his water bottle, check the position of the sun. She must never forget him, the strength of him, the moleskin coat and wide battered hat that kept sun and rain off. She held his boot as he sat astride the horse, bareback, relaxed, the old rope reins loose in his hands. 'When you reach the Maiden Stones, you might hear of someone called Jacko Miles. A fisherman. Tell him about us. Tell him we're making for Dunster and Kilve and Bridgwater. We shall cross the Avon at Pill, over to Shirehampton. Tell him we're well. He will get you mackerel and ray and ling.'

'Jacko Miles? I'll look for him, never fear. And if ever you can get word to us, we'll be pleased to hear it.'

She clung to his ankle for a moment longer, then turned and joined her mother and sister. They gathered her to them. Just for one terrible second, Bessie had thought she might lose her younger daughter. And Tilly had been John Quince's special child.

They missed the warmth and security of the caravan that night and did not sleep. It was dry the next morning but an uncomfortable little wind blew this way and that and seemed to mirror their rootlessness. After the bleakness of the moors, Devon became beautiful with its soft rolling hills and warm red earth. They found a road that led northwards, but then turned determinedly west.

Tilly said, 'We're crossing from one coast to another. That's all right, Ma. It will take us to North Devon and the Bristol Channel and we can follow the sea then.'

Alice shuddered. 'We've had enough of moors,' she said.

Tilly felt sad. 'You din't see the best of it, Alice, only the worst. It were lovely round Okehampton. The grass were polished and you could slide down it. And there were everything you needed there – it's where we picked the mushrooms and the cowslips.'

'I know. I know.' Alice was weeping. 'It's all so foreign and I'm so frightened. What will the baby think? Not knowing anyone . . .'

They comforted her as best they could. Bessie said, 'This is good rich country. Next farmhouse, I'll knock on the door and ask for some shelter.'

'Ma! We've got half a day's walking to do!'

'We didn't sleep, our Tilly. We need to rest up. We've got time.'

But Bessie looked anxiously sideways as she spoke. They had had one night in the open and Alice already looked exhausted.

She got them shelter in a barn that night and the next, but after two weeks on the road they had covered less than forty miles, and that in good weather and ideal conditions. Alice had to put everything out of her head except the necessity of placing one foot in front of the other; she began to look like a zombie. They reached Dunster the first week in June, Watchet three days later. And there they stuck for another four days while Tilly laid one of their sheets between rocks and caught some unwary mackerel. They lived close to the cliff on a shelf of shingle, sheltered from the morning and evening mists by overhanging rocks. They kept a fire going and Bessie rubbed Alice's swollen legs and fed her baked mackerel and told her stories of her own girlhood on Porthcurno beach.

The rain started again in mid-June. Soon they were on the Somerset Levels, between Kilve and Bridgwater, where shelter was scarce. The trees were stunted and grew one way with the prevailing wind. The land was drained by a criss-cross of rhines – small canals – but was still soggy enough to hold their feet firmly when they left the foot-paths. They had to keep walking out of their way to find bridges across the ditches. The rain was warm but incessant. They were back to looking for shelter.

Beneath one of the bridges there was enough dry land for them to find temporary cover. It was full of sedges and teazles and Tilly hammered them down as best she could and made the kind of nest she'd made for the gypsy children in the summer grass. Alice crouched there, barely knowing where she was. Bessie rubbed her legs and then her hands while Tilly tried to pull up the dryer grasses for a fire.

'Won't do no good, my maid,' Bessie said. 'Can you go on a bit further? See if there's anything in sight we could aim for? If we knew there was something out there we'd feel better, I reckon.'

Tilly was gone like a shot. They were practically dragging Alice now and they had turned and twisted so much Tilly had no idea whether they were moving in the right direction. She needed action the way a young animal does. She crossed the bridge at a run and followed the footpath with eyes down, hoping superstitiously that when she lifted them and stopped for breath a farm would have materialized. It had not, but about half a mile away on the edge of yet another dratted rhine was the figure of a boy of about her own age, apparently raking the water.

She approached him carefully; perhaps he had gone mad in this watery land. He looked up and grinned; he had a moon face rather like Billy's and a hat like the one Rufus wore, wide to keep the rain off his shoulders.

'Hello!' she called. 'What are you doing?'

He held up his rake. It was huge. Wooden with teeth six inches apart and an eight-foot-long handle.

'I be dredgin',' he said. 'If we dun't dredge our rhines then our field will be underneath the water by tomorrow. You can 'ave a go, if you like.'

She said, 'I will help you and pleased to. But first, is there somewhere my mother and sister can find shelter? My sister isn't well and needs to rest until the rain stops.'

He put the handle of the rake on one shoulder and tugged at his hat.

'There's the boat house, I s'ppose.' He shook his head. 'Do drip all the time though, en't much shelter to be 'ad there.' He looked at her and saw she was shivering. 'Be thee afraid of ghosts?'

'I don't know.'

'There's an old cottage. Me and my brother used to play there till 'e were drownded in the floods. It's got a roof. And a chimney.'

'That will do fine. Where is it?' She looked all round. The rain did not make for much visibility and there was no sign of any dwelling.

He said, 'Just follow this rhine, next bridge along, and then about a mile, and you'll see it. But you got to come back and give me a hand. You promised.'

'I will. I didn't promise, but I promise now.' She beamed at him. 'Thank you. What's your name?'

'Todd. Ma do call me Toddler. And you're little. Are you called Tiddler?'

'Almost. Tilly. I'm called Tilly. Tilly Quince.' She spoke over her shoulder. She was already on her way back to fetch the others.

They saw no ghosts. The strange thing was, they didn't see Toddler again, either. The walk to the haunted house took them nearly two hours and there was no sign of him then. But when Tilly went back later to help him with his dredging, she could not find him, nor his rake. They were at the house for almost a month and saw no one until the end of their stay. Much later Tilly wondered whether the place had been haunted or was some magical sanctuary for them.

The house was simple enough; built for a farm labourer or perhaps someone who had been in charge of the dredging, because there were four of the enormous wooden rakes which the boy Todd had wielded so expertly still leaning against the privy wall. Downstairs were two small rooms, the one with the grate and the chimney was inhabitable, the other not. Upstairs it was the same, two small rooms, the thick dust on the floorboards pock-marked with water leaks. The house had been used by chickens; their droppings were everywhere and made good fuel for the fire. As the warmth reached her Alice looked at her mother and sister and smiled. 'We'll do fine here,' she whispered confidently. 'This is where we'll stay.'

Bessie nodded. 'Just till the weather be'aves itself,' she agreed. She had managed to send a letter to Lemuel from Minehead asking him whether he could meet them at Gloucester. Alice was nearly seven months gone and the walking was not doing her much good. Bessie still had her wedding ring, which she planned to use for a night's board and lodging once they reached Gloucester. If they had to wait for Lemuel then she would earn money soon enough in the city. She and Tilly had done some milking at a big

243

farm near Kilve Court and had been rewarded with as much milk as they could drink and cheese rinds to last a week if need be. So that first night in the haunted house Bessie had filled John Quince's tea can with milk and they had sat around the fire and toasted the cheese and drunk the milk and dried themselves, and felt an enormous resurgence of their spirits.

When Tilly could not find Toddler she scouted around for a mile or two and eventually found the farm he must have come from. The rain had eased off and someone was calling three or four cows in from the muddy field. Tilly watched and counted them; they were in good condition. She looked down at her feet; the grass was lush.

Chickens were everywhere. A woman came out of the house and scattered corn, then walked over to a barn, opened one of the doors and disappeared inside. The chickens pecked frenetically for some time then started to move into the barn. Tilly moved with them. The woman came out again carrying a milk pail.

"Oo are you?' she said. 'Where did you spring from – bin in the water, 'ave you?'

Tilly bobbed a swift curtsy. 'We got wet in the storm,' she said.

"Ow many of you, for Gawd's sake?'

'My mother and sister. We're walking to Gloucester and we're sheltering back there for the night.'

'Not the waterman's cottage? Tis 'aunted, that place. Three of them there and they was all drownded in the floods two year ago. You want to get out of there!' She began to walk towards the cowshed. Tilly hurried after her. 'Could we sleep in your barn overnight? We'd be no trouble. We could help. My mother and me – we're milkers—'

'Get away, child. We got work to do 'ere and we like it dun the way we like it dun.'

'Todd will vouch for us. He told us where the house was. I came back to help him dredge the ditch but he was gone.'

'Todd?' The woman turned and stared at her.

'He said you called him Toddler. Todd for short.'

The woman dropped the bucket with a frightful clatter; she screamed and put her arm across her face. 'Get out and leave us alone! Go on – get out – we're good-living folk – dun nothing to reproach ourselves with. Just leave us alone – d'you 'ear?' A man came out of the byre and shouted at her and she picked up the bucket and scurried to him.

Tilly was rooted to the ground for a moment. She looked over her shoulder and saw no one else. She picked up her wet skirt and ran for the barn.

The birds made a fuss but she chook-chooked at them and after a while they settled and she found three eggs and pocketed them. Then she began to collect hay; she brought the hem of her skirt to waist level and tied it there then filled it with soft dry stuff from last summer. Somehow she got through the door again and started back. She thought she heard another scream but took no notice; she must after all look an odd figure with her bare legs beneath the enormous stuffed circle of padded skirt.

Bessie laughed and hugged her when she came in. Their sojourn with Rufus had cured her of words like stealing. She showed Tilly her finds from around the tumbledown cottage: a battered saucepan and a skillet, three chipped enamel mugs – 'like the three bears' – best of all a stack of logs behind the cottage, one of them already spitting on the fire. Then she spread the hay for Alice while Tilly boiled the eggs. 'I reckon that woman thought you was a ghost,' she said.

They all laughed.

Twenty-one

They stayed in the haunted house for over three weeks, waiting for Alice to regain some strength. They discovered that the previous owner had grown a little garden and it was yielding summer cabbages and a straggle of hard peas. Tilly went on forages like a young vixen and came back with milk and eggs and pippins. She made traps for the rabbits like Rufus had made, and then wept when Bessie skinned what she had caught and put it into the pot. As July wore on towards August it was hot and they would dabble their feet and legs in the rhine and several times Alice said wistfully, 'This is a good place, I wish we could stay here.'

Bessie greeted remarks like that with unnatural briskness. 'When the hens stop laying or our Tilly gets caught milking one of they cows . . .' or 'when that danged rain starts raining again . . .' But she and Tilly were thriving and though Alice was pale and very thin, she was completely relaxed.

On 21 July the thunderclouds stacked up over the Bristol Channel and the air almost crackled with electricity. At midday Tilly was so uncomfortable she took off her dress and, in her petticoat and bloomers, slid down the bank of the rhine and into the water. Alice, watching from the shade of the house, clapped her hands and then bent right over as if trying to touch her toes and gave a hoarse cry. Bessie came running, and after a bewildered moment Tilly scrambled out of the water and joined her.

Bessie was as white as Alice but her voice was controlled and terse.

'Baby's on the way. Don't be frightened. Go and fill that big old pot with water from the pail, put it on the fire. Then make up Alice's bed and come back and help me to get her inside.' She turned to her favourite. 'It's normal, my lovely. It might get worse afore it gets better, but it will get better, never fear.'

Bessie had heard those words herself many times before; she no longer believed them, but they still helped her and she prayed they would help Alice. She held the thin shoulders tightly as if she could force into them some of her own stolid strength. They were shuddering con-vulsively and Alice suddenly wailed and tried to grip the hard clay of the earth. Bessie whipped up Tilly's discarded dress and draped it over the arched back as if to keep her warm; it was a futile gesture in every way, with the next enormous contraction the dress slid off as Alice keeled over and fell face down.

It was then that the first drops of rain splatted on to the roof.

Somehow they got her into the house and laid her on the hay-filled sheet. She lay curled up on her side; when her mother managed to take her dress from her they could see that all her muscles from neck and shoulders down to calves and feet were cramped rigidly. Her face too was tight, jaws clamped shut so that when she occasionally made a sound it was like a knife in a grinder.

Bessie was suddenly frightened; Alice's body was in one continuous spasm, there were no gaps between the pains, no time for her to take a breath, a sip of water. She was clasping her knees so tightly her thighs were pushed into her stomach. Bessie had been through pregnancies and miscarriages and that dreadful abortion, but this was different. This was not right. And they had no one to help them.

Tilly dragged on her dress; the rain was hitting the roof hard and finding places to get inside. She said, 'I'll go to the farm. They will know about doctors and things. I'll be as quick as I can.'

Bessie sobbed relief and tried to gather the rigid bundle that was Alice into her arms. Alice screamed and the sound came through her nostrils. Tilly ran.

She knew the way so well, it did not matter that the rain drew a veil over the faceless countryside; the first bridge then straight ahead to the next and then round to the west for a mile and there would be the farm with its byre and its barn and its clucking accompaniment of chickens. She ran like the wind, her wet petticoat sticking to her, sawing under her arms, the rain running down her hair and neck and soaking her dress from the outside as well as the inside.

She had run almost two miles before she realized that she must have gone a long way past the farm. Panting with frustration she turned and ran back the way she had come until she reached the bridge. She had passed it again and not seen it. She held on to the stonework of the bridge and hung her head, sobbing now. When she looked up, Todd, the boy with the wooden rake, was coming towards her.

'What's to do now, Miss Tiddler?' he asked. He stood there, uncoordinated, limbs coming from his smock haphazardly, rain dripping from the brim of his hat. 'You found the haunted house, din't you?'

She nodded, speechless. He looked at her. ''Ave you seen a ghost then? Tha's what drove me and my brother away from it. But they won't 'urt you.'

This time she shook her head then summoned breath enough to say, 'We need a doctor, Todd. D'you know a doctor?'

'Everyone on the Levels knows Dr Youde. Good man is the doctor.' He hesitated. 'I cassn't fetch him, Tiddler. But I can send someone else. Will that do?'

She nodded, bent over with a sudden stitch in her side, and when she looked up he had gone; the rain had swallowed him and he had gone. She went back over the bridge and across the field and over that bridge and then

248

stopped as the sounds reached her ears. She bounded forward; Alice must have been able to open her mouth to scream. Surely that was good?

Alice died before the baby was born and Bessie had to wrestle him into this world without his mother's help. They could not weigh him but Bessie reckoned he was over five pounds which was a good weight considering he was at least a month before his time.

She said this some time after she had kissed her favourite and called on God to save her and tried to breathe life into her blood-filled mouth. It was Tilly who cut the cord and washed Geoffrey and wrapped him in her own sheet, and sat by the fire cuddling him and singing to him quietly. He was oblivious to everything except her arms, her sad brown eyes smiling at him, the smell and feel of the rain and the warmth of the fire. When she laid him on her shawl and whispered to him to be a good boy now, he slept contentedly while she pulled her mother gently away from Alice's body and washed her sister.

'The doctor will come soon, Ma. Be brave. He will write a death certificate and then we can think what we have to do next.'

'He wun't come now, Tilly. That was just gone midday you went for him, 'tis dark now, my maid. He dun't think it's worth his while to come to see a couple of gyppos.' She dropped her head and started to keen again and Tilly took her hand and shushed and reminded her that she shouldn't wake Geoffrey.

'Where d'you get that name from? His father's name be Gilbert!' Bessie looked wildly around the room. 'Alice – weren't his father's name Gilbert?' Then she saw the awful mess on the floor that was Alice, and she howled and dropped her head in her hands. Tilly said no more; she fed the fire and leaned over Geoffrey and watched her own tears fall, and was glad of the rain because it was as if heaven itself was weeping for Alice.

*   *   *

249

It must have been past midnight when the rain eased and then stopped; the silence was instant and she realized her mother had stopped wailing some time before. Tilly picked up Geoffrey and put him in Bessie's arms.

'I must go and get milk, Ma. Will you be all right? Can you make something – can we soak a rag or something – like they do for the lambs?'

Bessie said nothing, but she took the baby and stared down at him and saw something there that gave her purpose.

'Ah. Tilly. He do remind me of—'

'Yes, Ma, I know.' She wrapped herself in her mother's shawl. 'Will you be all right?'

Her mother nodded and Tilly slipped out of the door and made her way across the field. The clouds had gone and stars pricked the night sky. She felt she had never seen it before. And she hadn't; not as she saw it now. Before, she had been part of Alice; now she was not. She started to weep.

She was on her way back with her father's tea can full of milk when she heard the muffled plod of horse's hooves and thought with a sinking heart it must be the doctor. They had kept the world at bay for over three weeks and now it was about to force its way on them. Certificates and registry officers and burials . . . How would her mother hold up when Alice was taken from her and put into strange earth?

She gritted her teeth for a moment then hurried towards the sound of those hooves.

'Doctor?' she called. 'I'm Tilly Quince. You were called to my sister, I do believe.'

She never forgot what happened next. A figure slid from the horse and came towards her like a whirlwind. And it was Jacko Miles.

Twenty-two

Jenna drove them to Truro station to catch the six thirty train to Plymouth. The plan was that she should drive on and meet them at Plymouth station and they would all go by car along the A38 towards Exeter and wait for heaven to send them a sign when they should turn off.

When this was mooted – after she had come back from Tregeagle and Charles and John had left and, finally, Laura had emerged from the shed – Jenna had declared that the whole thing was 'a load of crap'. Caroline asked crisply whether she had any other suggestions. 'They need not be better. But if we had a few alternatives on the table it would enable us to—'

'The whole idea is crap!' Jenna insisted. 'The idea of returning Billy Boy's tin to the churchyard was so that we would have closure.' She spread her hands. 'I come home two hours later and discover we have reopening!'

Caroline repeated levelly, 'What other suggestions do you . . . suggest?'

'I thought we had all come to the same conclusion.' Jenna's voice rose a notch. 'Laura's had enough. Look at her. Sorry, Laura, but you're just not with it. I think we should call it a day. You and I will go back to work, Mum. Laura will resume normal service. We'll get together at Christmas – perhaps a nice hotel somewhere – and compare notes.'

'How can you talk like that?' Caroline looked at her daughter incredulously. 'We came down here for your sake

251

– you were in a car crash with your husband and he was killed and you were traumatized! And you're talking as if you've got over a nasty cold!'

Laura had been sitting staring at nothing. She said now very clearly, 'Please stop talking like this. It's horrible.'

The other two subsided like pricked balloons. Jenna said, 'Sorry, Laura.' Caroline followed suit. Then added, 'Do you want to be alone again, darling? You know we will understand completely.'

Laura blinked and looked at her properly. 'I can't stay here on my own now, Caro. Jen was quite right when she talked of a reopening. That is exactly what has happened.'

'I was sort of joking, Laura.' Jenna spoke in a small voice. 'What has happened . . . exactly?'

'You were here. You heard. Your uncle . . . sorry, I suppose your cousin once removed . . . is that the relation-ship? Anyway, Geoffrey – who changed his name to Miller so that he would sound like a proper brother to your mother – lied to me all our married life. I don't know him any more. I have to do what Charles Cledra calls reconstructing. Who knows, perhaps I'll be able to do that if I find out where he was born . . . Yes, that would be a good starting place.' She looked very directly at Jenna. 'That is what has happened . . . *exactly.*'

Jenna responded instantly. 'Then of course we will try to follow their journey. I simply had not registered . . . What a fool.' She drew a breath and stood up. 'I've become completely self-centred . . . me and my precious grief.' She laughed derisively. 'So pleased with myself for reaching this particular plateau, I didn't realize you were hanging on by a thread!' She went automatically to the kettle. 'Funnily enough, I thought it would be Mum who would be thrown by this latest bit of the puzzle.' She tried a grin in her mother's direction. 'You know how she is about her precious big brother. I thought when it turned out he wasn't her brother at all, she'd probably throw a wobbly. Sorry, Mum.'

Caroline threw her a wry smile in return. They were both

shocked when Laura said, 'Good news for Caro. Except that he is now dead, of course.'

There was a small silence while they both stared at her. Then Jenna said, 'What do you mean, Laura? How could it be good news?'

There was a pause then Caroline turned to her daughter. 'Sorry, love. All the things you've thought about me were spot on. I didn't really love your dad because I was in love with someone else. Someone I couldn't have. My brother, actually.' She gave another smile. 'We're finding out a lot about ourselves as well as the Quinces, aren't we? That's why we have to go on looking. Just for a while.'

'But – but—' Jenna looked wildly from one to the other. 'For God's sake, Mum! Laura is here – she is listening to what you are saying!'

'I told her about it some time ago. I didn't think it worried her at the time. Obviously I was wrong.' Caroline's eyes filled suddenly. 'Laura, I wish I'd kept my mouth shut.'

Laura looked at her with a curious detachment; she made no attempt to reassure her, and it was Jenna who passed her mother a piece of kitchen roll to dry her tears with. Laura stood up and went to the kettle and began to make tea.

'Yes, I can understand that.' She put the teapot on the table and looked at both the others in turn. 'I apologize for my attitude. I know that all this probably proves Geoff loved me, and you see that as the only thing that matters. But I don't. I need to understand why he kept so much to himself all those years. Charles Cledra thought that to try to retrace the journey the Quince women made back in 1922 would be one way for me to reconstruct everything.'

'Then . . . OK.' Jenna poured the tea. She said, 'Do you know something else that's interesting? We've been together here since June and in all that time we have never been honest with one another. And now . . . we are. That's got to be good, hasn't it?'

Caroline touched her daughter's wrist and noticed how thin it was.

'Of course it's good,' she said.

She wished she could tell them about John; about the singing happiness that lifted her soul in spite of so many things. For the moment, just this precious moment, the difference in their ages had been put aside. He had held her, kissed her eyes and her nose and then her mouth, and she had kissed him back. She knew – of course she knew – that marriage was out of the question. He deserved children; he would be a wonderful father. But in spite of that, she was still cocooned by his love. It was the most enormous relief to know that she hadn't been in love with Geoff. She had loved him to the exclusion of all other men, but she had not been in love with him. And Steve . . . he had swept her off her feet and she had been so glad to be swept because she had thought it would 'cure' her of Geoff, for ever. But then he had left her, and Geoff had been reinstated. Until now. At least, whatever came of it, she knew what it was to love a man; to be absolutely certain that he was right for her and she was for him. This precious space in time when she and John Canniston had met . . . this was where love was.

She smiled at the other two. The journey was a chance to hang on to this moment. She and John Canniston would not see each other. John was going to look for information about her father, and she was going to look for Alice. They were linked by their separate missions. They need not think of the inevitable ending.

So the decision was made; they were going to tread in the Quince footsteps. The actual details were very much more difficult. They knew from John that the journey had started very early in the morning on the train from Truro. But the Quinces had left the train at Plymouth. Perhaps because of lack of money for tickets, perhaps – as John said – because Sir Geoffrey Bassett's power would have extended throughout the Great Western Railway. Whatever the reason, they had planned to walk from Plymouth to

Gloucester and their route would probably have depended on whether they could get lifts, lodging, food . . . in fact on a number of complete imponderables. It was not only the imponderables that frustrated Jenna; it was her mother's and aunt's acceptance of them.

'We know it's all a bit up in the air—' Caroline dropped her voice, hoping to sound reassuring and instead made Jenna feel she was being condescended to. Jenna only just stopped herself from exploding.

'A bit up in the air?' she repeated incredulously. 'It's ridiculous, Mum! You would be the first to see that, normally! There were roads and tracks eighty years ago that have now disappeared! We could try a dozen alternatives and find no clues whatever. I mean, how do you expect clues to have survived eighty years of wind and weather, anyway? Are we looking for the embers of a fire they might have made? A strand of cotton from a dress? For Pete's *sake*, Mum!'

Laura, whose sense of purpose was carrying her through the void somehow, said, 'I suggest we take the first turning off the A38 that seems to lead up into the hills. They would have made for Tavistock first of all, then dropped down to Okehampton. We might find nothing. We might get all the way to Childswickham and find nothing, but nothing can often mean something, too.'

They looked at her and she spread her hands. 'It could mean that they hadn't gone the way we went. Or that they had found work and stayed put somewhere for a couple of months. We could look at parish records in other churches. Alice's death might show up that way.' She shook her head. 'Don't keep seeing the hopelessness of it all, Jen. There could be someone sitting in a pub somewhere whose mother told them about the three women who worked at Downalong Farm for a couple of months.'

Jenna opened her eyes wide. 'Where's Downalong Farm?'

Caroline answered. 'It's imaginary, darling. Laura is showing us the possibilities here. They're just as likely as the impossibilities.'

'OK, OK. I give in.' Jenna smiled at them both. 'I have to say the whole thing seems completely phoney to me. But I'll go along with whatever you decide. Will that do?'

Laura managed a smile in return. She said, 'It will do very well. On the understanding that when it gets too much for you, you will let us drive you to the nearest station and you will go back to London and your job.'

Jenna tried to laugh and couldn't manage it. She said in a shaky voice, 'You . . . *women!*' And then they fetched the train timetable, made packing lists, and decided to get the car checked at the garage in St Just.

Ever since Charles Cledra had told them that Geoffrey was not Tilly's son, Laura had felt cold. She had not been able to control her shivers when she sat in the shed and listened to Charles, and though she had washed out Caroline's hairspray that afternoon in very hot water, her scalp had still felt icy to the touch. In the days that followed, while they made vague plans then discarded them, she had remained in a world of her own. The rain went on falling steadily and felt as cold as snow when she went to the garage to take the car to St Just. The other two did not offer to come with her; she knew they wanted to discuss her change . . . Personality change? Character change? She had been a support to both of them for so long that they simply could not take her abrupt withdrawal. If it hadn't been happening to her she would doubtless have found it just as unacceptable. She was no longer connected to them. The close link offered through her marriage to Geoff had slipped sideways. She did not know her real mother-in-law, she certainly did not have a sister-in-law, nor a niece by marriage. An aunt, a cousin, a second cousin . . . what did that mean? She spoke aloud in the car, 'Not a lot.' Then she thought how strange it was that Charles Cledra had had a wife who had died. About the same time as Geoff had died. Apart from causing him to chew the inside of his face, it hadn't seemed to make much difference to him. She turned right on to the Land's End road and switched the heater full on. She knew she was being unfair. Charles was still probably reconstructing his life. The Quinces might well be part of that reconstruction. Perhaps that's what archivists did the whole time: reconstruction work.

The other two waved her off fruitlessly from the porch then retired to the kitchen. Jenna said, 'She didn't even see us. What on earth's the matter with her? I can understand it up to a point. But then . . . surely she doesn't think Geoff could have been in love with you?'

'Of course not. It's simply . . . her whole world has been turned upside down.'

'So has yours. You seem to be enjoying it.'

Caroline laughed. 'It's a relief in a way. Perhaps Geoff and I were too close. Perhaps I have felt . . . I don't know.'

'Pervy?' Jenna shook her head at her mother's shocked expression. 'Come on, all this feeling – misplaced feeling – knowing you, you felt pervy. It was incestuous for goodness' sake! That's how you would see it!'

Caroline continued to look shocked for another five seconds and then started to laugh. 'Oh Jen. You're coming back to us. I've missed you.'

Jenna smiled but said, 'Has it been that bad? As bad as Laura is now?'

'Yes. Very much like Laura is now. Laura used to know that Geoff was still with her. Now she is not sure. And you . . . have you discovered that Jeremy will always be part of you?'

'I think that's what it is.' She remembered swimming out beyond the surf and seeing Jeremy next to her. She said, 'Actually, though, it might be more than that. I think John Canniston saw him once.' She told her mother what had happened and then said quietly, 'I should tell you something else, Mum. He's in love with you. We had quite a talk that afternoon.'

Caroline drew a quick breath, then said just as quietly, 'What did you say to him?'

'I choked him off.' She held up a placating hand. 'None

257

of my business. I know that. And I'm sorry now. D'you want to talk about it?'

'No. But if I do, I will talk to you. Is that OK?'

'Of course.' Jenna folded an Ordnance Survey map and put it into a clear wallet with three others. She said, 'That's why your world has not turned upside down, isn't it? That's why you know you were never really in love with Uncle Geoff.'

Caroline closed the zip on a holdall and stood it next to the suitcases in the hall. 'Could be,' she replied non-committally.

'Right.' Jenna tucked the wallet into her handbag. 'Shall I make some sandwiches for our lunch?'

'That would be excellent.'

'What would you like?'

'Surprise me. And try to surprise Laura too!' Caroline continued along the hall and started upstairs. 'I'm going to clean the bathroom.'

They reached Plymouth in time for breakfast, which they ate in the coffee shop at the station. Jenna had left the car in the station car park and met them on the concourse. Then they stood outside and stared along the approach road. Traffic was already thickening and it was very difficult to imagine Tilly, Alice and Bessie standing here, not knowing which way to go, frightened and bewildered. Laura at last seemed focused but the pain on her face was awful.

Jenna said, 'What we've got to remember is – the station layout will have altered a lot in the past eighty years. This is not what they would have seen.'

Caroline said, 'There's just a chance that John's grandfather went with them as far as Plymouth. He was going to investigate that.'

'It's not likely, Mum, is it? He took them to Truro in a horse and cart. He had to return that at some point. Anyway, I thought you said the rector was looking for information about your father?'

258

'He is. But he's going through the old story too. His grandmother, Helen Casson, kept diaries and he has them up in the attic at the rectory.'

Laura said suddenly, 'If only I had answered the door, all those times he tried to call on me. I might have been more . . . prepared.'

'I doubt that.' Caroline took her arm. 'Come on. Let's get the car and find our way out to the Exeter road again. Looking round the station was a bit pointless.'

Surprisingly, both Laura and Jenna shook their heads. Jenna laughed and Laura smiled.

'We know for sure they were here. And we're trying to follow them. So we had to come here.' Jenna looked at Laura. 'Right?'

And Laura said humorously, 'Right.'

They trooped across the approach road to the car park and Jenna drove gingerly up the steep twist of dual carriageway to the sign that took them up to the enormous intersection of Marsh Mills. 'Thank God for the motor car,' she muttered as she got into the proper lane. 'Imagine doing all this on foot.'

It was still raining as they joined the A38 again. They were silent, staring at signposts . . . Lee Mills . . . Ivybridge. Then Laura suddenly said, 'Here, Jen. Take the next exit. We need to get up on the moor.'

'Really?' Jenna indicated and gave her aunt a quick sideways glance.

They turned off and almost immediately there was another turning, also to the left, with a red bar across the signpost.

'I know it's a dead end, but take this one, Jen!' Laura leaned forward. 'This would have been the old original road. If they came this way, this is the road they would have taken.'

Caroline and Jenna exchanged glances; Laura's contribution to this latest enterprise had been dogged, silently stubborn. Suddenly there was a positive note of enthusiasm in her voice. But the road was, after all, signed as a dead end.

Jenna slowed right down as the hawthorn hedges, red with haws, crowded in on them. 'Hope we don't meet a tractor . . . or even a bike,' she murmured. 'Watch that rabbit!' warned Caroline at the same time. They all laughed, even Laura.

They bumped on, apparently going back the way they had come, but climbing all the time. The road widened slightly and became stonier, then began to curve towards the right. 'It's what Geoff called a staircase road,' Laura said, with a hint of excitement in her voice. 'It loops upwards so that the gradient is shallower.'

'Like the Corniche in France.' Jenna nodded. 'Jem and I were on a coach trip last year . . .' Her voice died slightly, then picked up. 'He called it looping the loop.'

As she spoke the hedges came to a sudden end and the moorland opened around them; it was like entering a different country. Even the misty drizzle stopped. They were above the low cloud. They could see sky and land but no discernible horizon. Jenna stopped the car and pulled on the handbrake.

'My God,' she said. 'We're in some enchanted place!'

Caroline and Laura stared. Caroline said, 'Is this the dead end?'

Jenna said, 'Well, we've run out of road, that's for sure.'

Laura sat back and unclipped her seat belt. 'Let's get out and have a look round.' She suited action to word and stood holding the roof of the car and staring around her. Ragged scarf-ends of mist curled around her legs; she walked forward and turned to look at Caroline as she emerged from the car. 'We're not out of road, not really. There are tracks – maybe it's a footpath – going straight up over this hill, but look, there's fresh gravel here. It turns left again and goes downhill.'

Jenna joined them, and it was she who saw the hand-painted arrow, close to the ground and almost invisible in the mist. It said 'Venables Farm' and pointed along the freshly gravelled way. 'It's a drive. Leading to a house.'

Jenna sounded disappointed. 'That's why the road is still there, I suppose.'

They stood looking at the arrow as if they expected it to reveal something else. Then they walked back to the car and stared along the footpath at the folding hills of Dartmoor. Laura said in a low voice, 'Imagine being on the run . . . it was April wasn't it? April can be such a cold month.'

'The cruellest month,' Jenna quoted just as quietly.

Caroline walked a few yards along the old road. 'It seems to go on for ever,' she said. 'Bracken and clumps of blackberry bushes and then – the sheer rollingness of it all!'

The other two laughed at her description. She gave a small exclamation and went to a clump of bracken.

'Come and look at this – Laura, have you got your glasses? My God, it's an old milestone.' She turned to Jenna. 'What does it say, Jenna? I can't see it properly.'

Jenna crouched and traced the indentations with her forefinger. 'Plymouth ten miles,' she said slowly.

They stood for a moment. Laura said, 'This is where they were. I know it.' She half turned. 'That farm . . . Venables Farm. They could have stayed there on that first night.'

Jenna said, 'They arrived in Plymouth at . . . what? Say ten thirty. They probably walked for six hours. They would have done more than ten miles.'

'They had to find their way.' Caroline protested. 'And they would have had to rest. Alice was pregnant. And they were shocked.'

'True.' Jenna nodded. She straightened and made for the gravel drive. 'Come on. Let's go and ask questions.' She locked the car and strode off and the other two followed more slowly.

The drive turned downhill and the farmhouse nestled into the side of the hill. It was swathed in mist as they came upon it, and beneath it was solid cloud, but it probably had a perfect view of the Plymouth sprawl below and the sea beyond that. Jenna waited for them at the gate; inside the house a dog was barking crazily. They approached the front door with caution.

The doorbell was large and shining brass, its pull-rope very white. Jenna pulled it; it sounded like a fire bell.

They waited; the dog was now the other side of the door, scrabbling at it and still barking.

'No one in.' Jenna turned away just as someone called from the side of the house. They all spun around. A very blonde head appeared through a loggia.

'I'm gardening.' The head was followed by a body dressed in jeans and a green canvas apron. They all belonged to a woman probably Caroline's age. Her hair was in a long plait and her jeans were badly ripped but there were diamonds in her small ears and gardening gloves on her hands. She was very attractive.

'Don't want to go inside and spread mud. How can I help you?' She was also very charming.

Caroline glanced at the other two and then answered. 'We're on a sort of mission. Or perhaps a pilgrimage.' She smiled in case she sounded pious, and the other woman smiled back but said, 'I don't actually go to church.'

Caroline was startled, but Jenna laughed. 'We're not some kind of door-to-door missionaries. Honestly. The thing is my great-grandmother and her two daughters walked from Plymouth to the Cotswolds back in 1922. We were hoping to retrace their route. We're pretty certain they took the sharp left turn from the main road – it could have been the road to Tavistock in those days. And we wondered whether they might have called here for shelter or water.'

The woman said humorously, 'In 1922 I wasn't actually born.'

Laura took over. 'Of course you weren't. Neither were we. And the people who could have helped us with this are dead. Sorry to bother you. It was a long shot. We wondered whether any of the people who owned this farm might have handed down a story about three women arriving on their doorstep.'

The woman said, 'Actually, my husband might have been able to help you, he's so interested in the property. But he's in London this week. We bought the farm two years ago from people called Warren. It had been a working farm but when they bought it they did bed and breakfast for walkers. They bought it from a cousin of old Jack Venables, who inherited it in the early eighties. We've kept the name.'

Caroline smiled again. 'Well, never mind. We're pretty certain they stood at that old milestone opposite your drive. They probably went on to the next farm.' She turned the smile on Jenna. 'My daughter said they would have walked more than ten miles from Plymouth in six hours. Of course they were used to walking – they walked every-where.'

The woman said slowly, 'When we came there was a building just beyond the milestone on the other side of a hedge. It was a complete wreck. I think it had been a stable. They could have slept there.'

'In the open?' Caroline looked startled.

'What time of year was it?'

'April.'

'Hmmm.' The woman made up her mind suddenly, and held out a hand. 'My name is Kate Lansdown. Look, I need a cup of tea. Come in and have a look at the map of the moor and have one with me. My husband found this enormous map in a shop in Truro and has hung it in the kitchen. Supposed to be from Victoria's reign. It will give you some idea of what they were taking on. The moor is a country on its own.' She led them around the side of the house as she spoke, and paused under a large porch to take off her shoes. The back of the house looked on to a steep slope of moorland which had been skilfully land-scaped to make an attractive garden.

Laura exclaimed with pleasure. Jenna laughed. 'My aunt is a gardener, too. I'm Jenna Adams, by the way. This is my mother and aunt.' Caroline introduced herself and Laura followed suit. Kate Lansdown nodded as she opened the back door on to an enormous farmhouse kitchen.

'A family of three women, looking for a family of three women. Interesting.'

They trooped in and took the proffered chairs around the table. Kate Lansdown went to the Aga and shifted the kettle into position, fetched mugs and milk. 'I do the occasional column for the *Western Post*. I could put something in about this pilgrimage. You might get information that way.'

Laura said quickly, 'No. No, that wouldn't do at all. This is a very private search.'

'Search?' Kate paused as she poured the tea. 'Not so much a pilgrimage as a search? May I ask what you are looking for?'

Jenna put a warning hand on Laura's knee beneath the table and smiled brilliantly across it. 'We won't know until we find it.' She stood up. 'So let's have a look at that map over there and see where Bessie might have gone.'

There was much scraping of chairs, and exclamations at the map. Kate Lansdown accepted the rebuff and came behind them to point out the site of the farm, which ran from the Tavistock road, and the myriad lines of footpaths wandering apparently aimlessly over the bulk of the moor. 'These would have been used by shepherds. There were a great many sheep on Dartmoor at one time and then it became overgrazed. But you can still see the remains of sheltering stone walls and the occasional drinking trough. Here are the tors . . . the prison is here now . . . this is Okehampton Castle . . .'

'The Quinces must have followed the road. Where did they lose time? If they got work it must have been in Tavistock.'

Kate nodded. 'You may be right. Apparently the Venables family let the farm run right down. They couldn't have offered any help. And these places—' she tapped the map – 'they were probably all gone by the twenties.'

They sat back down and sipped their tea. Caroline said,

264

'They could so easily have got lost. If they wandered from the road they had no landmarks to guide them. And Alice . . .'

'Let's get back to where the road peters out,' Jenna said, suddenly brisk. 'We could walk for a couple of hours . . . see what sort of landscape they were dealing with.'

She bustled them out, thanking Kate profusely on the way.

Kate said, 'It's been interesting. Keep me posted. And I wouldn't spend too much time on the moor just now with this low cloud. If I were you I'd drive straight to Tavistock and see if I could pick up the scent there.'

They waved and went back down the drive to the car. Once out of earshot Caroline said, 'What's the matter with you, Jen? She was just being helpful.'

Laura laughed. 'The way you gripped my knee – did you think I was going to tell her everything?'

'I wasn't sure, knowing you. Seriously, Mum, she was a journalist. And we don't know what we're going to find. Bessie and Alice and Tilly . . . they deserve their privacy.'

'So this trip isn't such a load of crap after all?' Caroline asked, smiling.

Jenna drove back the way they had come. She said, 'I hope we can get a decent hotel in Tavistock.' She glanced sideways at the others. 'Sorry, my dears. It did sound pretty hopeless when we were at home talking about it. But there's something about Dartmoor. Up there . . . I could sense danger.'

Twenty-three

October 1999

They were all charmed by Tavistock. Laura thought it was 'elegant', Jenna called it 'solid' and Caroline said – as Caroline would – that it was the neatest, tidiest town she'd seen. The other two laughed at that, and Jenna suddenly hugged Laura's arm, thankful beyond words that she had emerged from her zombie state and rejoined the human race as represented by her family.

She said, 'This was definitely the right thing to do. Even if we don't pick up a whisper of what happened to our three relatives, it was still the right thing to do. Solidarity and all that.' Her mother raised her brows at her and Jenna added, 'Yes, OK. I know I was the one who called it a load of old cobblers—'

'Not quite the word you used, Jen,' Caroline inserted smoothly.

'But since we stood by that dratted milestone,' Jenna continued unabashed, 'I've got into the swing of it.'

'You said you felt danger, Jen,' Laura reminded her.

'Perhaps it was anticipation,' Jenna said.

Caroline said, 'Actually, I feel it too, whatever it is. I think Venables Farm was still of this world . . . somehow.' She laughed. 'And the moor . . . well, we know the moor is dangerous. Rather *Wuthering Heights*. But this place . . . it's so pretty and precise. But as we drove through, I felt it. No, it's not anticipation for me. It's definitely danger. I think Bessie brought her girls here. And something happened.'

The other two stared at her, a little shocked because her

266

words were so out of character. Jenna expected her aunt to 'work on several levels' as she would put it. But for a long time now, and in spite of things that Jeremy had said, she had thought of her mother as basically cold, and unlikely to be in touch with her deeper and more intuitive feelings.

Caroline laughed apologetically. 'I know. I sound like Gypsy Rose Lee, don't I? But haven't you noticed that when a – a room – or a house – or something—' she waved her hands helplessly – 'when everything is too neat and tidy, it often means there are nasty secrets beneath?'

And suddenly Jenna started to laugh.

They had arrived as the daylight was fading. Then they had gone to the touristy-looking pub just away from the centre of town and next to a pretty willow-fringed duck pond. Caroline had manoeuvred the car to the back, although there was a lot of room at the front of the building. 'Don't want cars messing up such an attractive frontage,' she commented, following the parking signs carefully. 'Just look at that well! And the pails along the parapet wall! It could have come out of a nursery rhyme book.'

'They were trying to keep the wildness of the moor right away,' Laura speculated, peering through the windows at the few nasturtiums left in the window boxes – and carefully barbered so that they trailed rather than straggled. She thought of the flowers at home subjected to the Atlantic winds and withering so fast and wondered whether she could live there again. Alone. And then she thought of Charles Cledra and his restructuring.

Jenna said, 'It's all for the tourists, Mum. In Bessie's day it would have been just a working pump, not a bucket in sight, let alone that dinky parapet. You can see it's just been built.'

The inside of the pub was low-ceilinged, oak-beamed and unevenly floored. The season was over so there were plenty of rooms; they opted for a family one. Laura was not certain about it but the other two were adamant that they

267

should stick together. 'It's part of the exercise,' Jenna said. 'It's en suite, so no problem there.' Laura smiled.

'Dining room and visitors' lounge down the back stairs and to the right,' said the motherly-looking woman who took them up and explained the tea-making facilities and the workings of the television, and gave them a folder which told them about meal times.

Laura thanked her and said, 'We've only booked for one night but it may be that we would like a second. It depends if we find . . . anything.'

Caroline said, 'We're hoping to discover whether my mother came this way . . .' She hesitated then added, 'It was a long time ago.'

'I've lived in Tavistock all my life,' the woman told them. 'When was it?'

'Well, it was 1922, actually. So, long before your time.' Caroline smiled ruefully. 'It's all a bit of a shot in the dark.'

The woman lifted her shoulders. 'You never know. Not many strangers came through then – especially a woman on her own.'

Caroline said, 'Oh, she wasn't alone. She was with her mother and sister. They were trying to get to Okehampton, probably. They could have asked around for lifts.' She shook her head. 'We don't know.'

The woman said encouragingly. 'There were lots of wagons going and coming from the town, then. I'll ask my parents tomorrow. Dad was one of the milkmen – I expect you've heard of them.' She smiled when they shook their heads. 'They used to wait on the other side of town for the milk wagon to bring the churns up from Plymouth. And they'd have their horses and floats all flying with ribbons and they'd jingle themselves into town and round the streets . . . Must a bin quite a sight.' She nodded. 'I'll ask Dad. And I'm Margaret, by the way. I'll be back on duty tomorrow at midday.'

*   *   *

They settled themselves in and watched the news on television and then went down for dinner. The strange exhilaration of the day began to fade, leaving them tense and on the edge of boredom; it was only nine o'clock. 'We should have brought our knitting,' Caroline mourned. And Jenna sighed at this further proof of what she termed her mother's new parochialism.

Laura decided on a very hot bath. 'I shall then indulge in the ultimate luxury,' she announced, 'and watch the television from the comfort of my bed!'

Caroline sat at the small table, switched on the lamp and began to pore over her notes again. Jenna scrabbled in her bag for her mobile, to see whether there were any messages. There was one. She pressed a key and incredibly John Canniston's voice came through.

'Jenna. This is John Canniston. Can you telephone me? My mobile number is . . .' He recited a long list of numbers. She found a pen and paper and replayed the message so that she could take it down.

Caroline looked up. 'Who is it?' she asked.

'Not sure. I've got a number. I'll try it.' She punched in the eleven digits and said over the ringing sound, 'Damn. Not a good signal in here. I'll go into the corridor, Mum. Won't be long.'

Her caution was justified. John answered the call and immediately said, 'Is your mother within hearing distance – or Laura?'

She said, 'I'm in the corridor of a pub in Tavistock. Laura's in the bath and Mum's in the bedroom. I told her I couldn't get a signal in there. What's happened?'

'I'm not absolutely sure of my facts yet. But there's another secret – mystery – call it what you like – about Caro's father – your grandfather. I don't know whether I should go on with this, Jenna. It seemed to me, back in Treleg, that Laura was near breaking point. And Caro . . . was . . . OK.' He paused, then said, 'Are you still there?'

She said, 'Yes.' She was thinking how right he was; her

mother had been 'OK'. And of course it was because of this blasted vicar.

He said, 'Listen. Can I just check I've got your grandfather's forename right? What did your grandmother call him?'

Jenna almost laughed. 'Bertie,' she said flatly.

'Yes. That's right then. He was definitely Caro's father. But the wedding certificate is dated a year after Caro's christening. That took place in 1946 – and the marriage in 1947.'

Jenna blinked and looked over the landing banisters. The foyer below was deserted and no one was at the desk so Margaret had gone home.

'Really? How amazing. I mean . . . Nanna. How did she allow that to happen, for goodness' sake?' She gave a little laugh. 'There's more to her than meets the eye. But if you're worried about Mum's reaction, don't be.'

'It's more than that, Jenna. I've been working through parish records – obviously as a first enquiry that is easier for me. Caro's christening lists her father all right. But no mother . . . well, actually, it says "mother unknown". And whatever sort of disgrace it might have been just after the war, I cannot see your grandmother allowing that to be recorded in church. The one certain fact we have about Tilly Quince is that she was courageous.'

Jenna frowned. He was right, of course. He was always right, damn him. And the way he spoke of 'Tilly Quince' . . . as if he knew her.

She said slowly, 'Am I right in thinking that parish records and civil records go hand in hand?'

'Certainly that applies at weddings. But christenings are not legal contracts. Caro's christening could have taken place at any time. However, her date of birth is recorded as that year: 1946.' He paused, then said, 'You understand the – the possibilities here, Jenna? It's more than likely that Tilly was not your grandmother. I haven't gone any further and wonder whether I should. I think it might break Caro's heart to discover that Tilly was not her mother.'

Below her, the door opened and noise from the lounge bar poured into the foyer. Two men appeared and one of them said loudly, 'Those bloody cans have been on that parapet, ready for use, for over a hundred years. If someone's knocked them off then I'm going to put them back and you're going to help me!' The outside door opened and they both went outside and Jenna thought with half her mind that the well had been there when Bessie brought her girls to Tavistock; it hadn't been built for tourists. This was how it had been. And again she sensed danger.

She said, 'I don't know . . . I don't know what to say. It – it's incredible. It's impossible. Nanna and Mum . . . they were so close.'

He said, suddenly decisive, 'I'm dropping it, Jenna. I can't do that to Caro.'

'She should be given the choice, John.'

'She still does have a choice. She could find out by herself. And that would be easy enough – a proper enquiry in London – I expect you can do it on the internet these days.' He sounded so strong now. 'At the moment she has no doubt at all about her mother. I came to Cheltenham to investigate her father, not her mother. I'll continue to do that.' He gave a small unamused laugh. 'Thanks, Jenna. I've been all at sea about this. Talking to you has made it clear. There is no way we can do this to your mother.'

There was a pause. Jenna felt as if he had stirred the contents of her head into some kind of broth. Nanna had been famous for her broth . . . *you put anything in the vegetable basket into a pot and boil it for two hours or more* . . . Jenna leaned on the landing banisters, unable to stand straight any more. Below her the men came back into the foyer and she heard one of them say, 'That was a good job jobbed' . . . then they disappeared into the lounge bar again.

John's voice said, 'Jenna? Are you still there?'

She said quietly, 'What about me? What if I . . . need to know who I am?'

271

He said instantly, warmly, 'Oh Jen . . . I shouldn't have told you! Oh dear girl, your grandmother will always be just that . . . your grandmother. Trust me, Jen, we are all connected. She is still there and will always be there.'

She said nothing, unexpectedly choked by his words. There was a long silence. Then at last she said in a stifled voice, 'Thank you for not gilding the lily.'

'What do you mean?'

'That was . . . right. She will always be my grandmother and my mother's mother too. If you'd added anything else it would have spoilt it.'

'I . . . OK.' His voice was now terribly uncertain.

She said, 'The only thing is . . . John, this is totally selfish. But I need to know now. I need to know where we all come from. God . . . this is how Laura is feeling about Geoff. But Mum . . . I'm not sure. I'm not sure whether, for her, ignorance may well be bliss. I just don't know.' She realized that she was near tears.

He said slowly, 'How about this. Let me do it properly. Registrars . . . London if necessary . . . then we can make a proper decision about whether or not to tell Caro.' He waited, then said, 'Jenna? Are you all right?'

'Yes. It's just that it sort of came to me then . . . she has always seemed more than strong – tough. And she's not. She's so vulnerable. Almost fragile.'

He said simply, 'Yes.'

'Do you mind – have you got time to go on with this?'

And he said again, 'Yes.'

Unexpectedly they all slept very well that night. Laura, soothed by her bath, did not make use of the en suite until the grey light filtering through the curtains woke her at seven thirty. The other two slept on until she emerged, dressed and ready for breakfast. Caroline was almost bewildered.

'Haven't slept so well for ages,' she marvelled, looking at her watch on the dressing table. Jenna said nothing; she had been completely exhausted after John Canniston's phone call, and had felt terrible fabricating a story about a client for the benefit of her mother. Caro had been concerned.

'Are they really going to keep your job open, Jen?'

'I think so. But that doesn't matter, Mum. I'd get another job. I could work for Beddoes, perhaps? It might be fun to work together – what do you think?'

Caroline thought it was the best thing Jenna had ever said to her and she smiled almost mistily. 'It would be marvellous, my love. It would be such . . . such . . . *fun*!'

'It would, wouldn't it?'

In view of that and the awfulness of not knowing where either of them came from, it was a miracle that she had simply collapsed into unconsciousness as soon as she got into bed. Laura passed her a cup of tea.

'You still look tired, Jen. Drink this and have a shower. We're seeing that nice Margaret later. Who knows, we might find another small piece of the jigsaw.'

Jenna took the cup and heard herself say, 'It shouldn't matter, Laura. The three of us, we're all right. We – dammit, we love each other. And we're connected by that. Surely that is enough?'

Laura smiled, 'Of course. That is paramount. And it's wonderful to hear you say so, darling. I know that this quest, or whatever we like to call it, seems ridiculous to you. Yet you've come along anyway. And I'm so grateful—'

Jenna said vehemently through the steam from her tea, 'No! I was a fool! It's not ridiculous – never was and never will be. It's important. It's a way we can honour those other three women.' Caroline and Laura looked at her with raised brows and she added defiantly, 'I mean it!'

And they laughed and said almost in unison, 'We can see that!'

But Margaret could not really help them. 'It's just too long ago,' she said. 'Dad can remember the old collections and deliveries. He can even remember some of the songs they used to sing. But he can't recall three women being on the milk wagon.'

'Can you remember any of the songs?' Caroline asked. 'Was one of them "Billy Boy"?' She sang a few bars and Margaret nodded her head, then shook it.

'They had their own songs, you see. Mostly to do with milkmaids and such. There was one . . .' She leaned over the desk and sang a few bars. 'See? It doesn't ring a bell with you, does it?'

'Ah well.' Laura lifted her shoulders. 'We won't book another night then. We'll press on to Okehampton and make some enquiries there.'

'Could be they never got off the moor,' Margaret said pessimistically. 'It's a dangerous place now, but then . . .' She raised her eyes.

They smiled. 'It's all right, Margaret. We know they got off the moor and reached their destination.' Caroline glanced at the other two. 'Shall we have lunch here first?'

They nodded back at her. Jenna felt dreary. John was going through official channels and would come up with concrete answers. Here they were going on 'feelings'. It was all so insubstantial.

She said, 'D'you mind if I peel off and go for a bit of a walk? We can't discount them having been here, and just in case, I'd like to walk where they walked.' She could see they were both touched, and added firmly, 'You never know, they might have dropped a handkerchief or something!'

Caroline laughed and tucked her arm into Laura's. 'Let's go to the police station. They may well have records of vagrants passing through – I don't think they would have been welcome in this neat little town!'

'And so much more practical than looking for lost handkerchiefs,' Laura said, thinking that Caroline was joking.

Jenna made a face in their general direction and zipped her jacket as she went into the courtyard. It seemed to be getting colder every day now. She found herself thankful that the Quince women had undertaken this journey at the beginning of the summer.

She wandered over to the duck pond first of all and parted the fronds of willow that hung everywhere like some gently shifting curtain. There were one or two benches arranged at the water's edge, perhaps for children to feed ducks from. She smiled at herself. As if Bessie would have found time to sit and feed ducks.

She moved away from the pond and took to the road again. Caroline would drive this way when they left the pub to go to Okehampton, dropping down the other side of the hills where there were farms and streams, and it was civilized. The road was like a shelf, with a precipitous slope one side, and she went to the edge to look over into the deep valley. The view was beautiful, delightful with its swooping grassland, the gorse still out here and there, the sun already at its zenith. She climbed down off the road and found a grassy clump to sit on. She did not want to think about what John might find in Cheltenham, but she knew that if she did not give herself time to accept some of the things he had said, she would surely develop an enormous headache. So she sat with the countryside all around her and tried to be calm. There was nothing she could do. It may well be that this second mystery would have to stay that way for ever. But then . . . perhaps not. She did not know. And Jenna hated uncertainty. Even with the terrible uncertainty of grief she had grasped at the difficult straw of being able to find Jeremy again. And when she had released that straw, it was because she was so certain that Jeremy was still inside her head. Not a ghost, but the reality of herself. And now, here she was again, literally cast adrift. And trying to pretend that her mother would be all right if she never knew . . . And of course if she married John Canniston she *would* be all right.

Far below her the road twisted in an enormous curve to negotiate that steep drop, and there was a wonderful space next to a stream draining from the top of the hill. Even as she looked, an awful old motorized caravan, belching exhaust, came around the bend and drew up on to the grass by the stream. There was a loud bang and then the clattering engine was switched off and there was peace again.

Jenna discovered she was sitting up very straight, considering the possibility of her mother marrying the rector. She had not liked the thought of John Canniston falling head over heels in love with her mother. She had been jealous. Not only because of her dead father, but . . . something else. Petty jealousy. That's all it could have been. And then she had convinced herself that Caroline did not reciprocate John Canniston's ardour and everything had been all right again. But there had been times when she had wondered about her mother. The 'good works' for instance. What were they all about? And anyway wouldn't marriage be the answer? Jenna did a Charles Cledra and gnawed at the inside of her lip. She recognized that she still wasn't keen on the idea. But if Caroline . . . felt . . . something special for this strange man, then surely, surely, it would be good? How on earth was Caroline going to react if . . . it was still *if* . . . she discovered that Tilly was not her mother? She really must not find out. Somehow she must never ever know. Particularly as it was John Canniston who was doing the investigating. She might turn against him.

Jenna felt her head buzzing again and tried to relax against the side of the bank. And then the most amazing thing happened.

Far below her, people had spilled out of the converted bus or whatever it was. Someone had gone to the stream with a bucket and filled it with water. Some kind of paraffin stove was lit and a kettle placed on it – Jenna could smell the distinctive oily aroma from up here. A woman on her own tended the little stove and assembled cups and spoons and teabags. Jenna squinted: the weak October sun glinted on silver teaspoons. And even as she noted that they were 'travellers' of the most unpopular kind, the woman started to sing.

'Where have you been all the day, Billy Boy, Billy Boy?'
Jenna stood up. Thinly the voice came from the deep
valley. 'Where have you been all the day, my Billy Boy?'
Jenna began to giant-stride down the steep slope.

The police station was empty except for the uniformed
man behind the desk. There were flowers on the window
ledge and a row of chairs along the wall. 'It reminds me of
the centre,' Laura commented.

'And the archive office in Truro,' Caroline agreed. The
policeman looked up from what appeared to be a ledger
and asked if he could help them.

Caroline went to the desk. She was wearing a saxe-blue
cashmere sweater over jeans and her hair was thick and
heavy as it swung just under her chin. She had a sense of
being in the right place at the right time. She was with
Laura and Jenna, supporting them; it was a good feeling.
The thought of John was still in her head and it was
enough for now. It gave her a kind of sublime confidence.

She smiled. 'We wondered whether you could help us –
not strictly speaking with a police matter, though it may
have been . . . we're not sure.'

The policeman smiled back; he was having to write up
the week's reports because the computer had crashed. This
looked a more interesting job.

'Can you give me some details? Unfortunately our computer isn't working, but if I can help in any way it would be
a pleasure.' Which it certainly would be after listening
earlier to Thomas Leggit rambling on about sheep rustling
over Princetown way. Sheep rustling indeed.

Caroline told the story. Three women, walking from
Land's End to the Cotswold hills eighty years ago.

'Eighty years?' The policeman looked disappointed.
'That's a bit too far back, madam. And unless we were
called in for some reason . . .' He looked up into Caroline's
face and said, 'I'll ask my sergeant if you like, though he
doesn't always take kindly . . .' He picked up the phone
then replaced it. 'While I make a few enquiries, you could

277

try our Miss Marjoribanks. She taught at the school and enjoys a bit of a chat about the old days. She likes to think of herself as an unofficial archivist. I could telephone her, see if she's got half an hour.'

Caroline glanced back at Laura, who nodded vigorously. The policeman began to leaf through a directory.

Miss Marjoribanks lived in a cottage on the way out of the compact little town. It was on the old road across the tops which had led, at one time, down to Plymouth. The original cobbles could be seen here and there, grassed over and gravelled in parts. Furze Cottage was still thatched, though no longer with furze. The reeded eaves came low over the bedroom windows, protective like a duvet

Miss Marjoribanks answered the door, almost twinkling with delight. She was short and shaped like a cottage loaf, her white hair falling out of a top-knot balanced on top of her head.

'When Bobby told me you were looking for your relatives, I was interested immediately. My father was a preacher and knew so many stories . . . My goodness, I could write a book with what he told me except it's what they call classified information!' She was laughing as she led the way into a tiny room overlooking the moor. 'I've already put the kettle on. Sit down and tell me everything and I'll see if it fits in with anything I know. Will that do?'

Caroline looked doubtful but Laura nodded. 'It will do very well, Miss Marjoribanks. We're really grateful you are giving us your time like this.'

'Oh my dear, it's such a pleasure. And please call me Marcie. Everyone does and I like it.'

They all nodded and smiled at each other and Caroline took up the story again. It sounded thinner and thinner each time they told it. Three women passing through this townlet . . . What was so surprising about that – was it simply the fact that they were on foot?

Marcie asked, 'How long did they stay?'

'We don't know,' Caroline said, biting her lip.

'Did they perhaps go into the inn for refreshment?'

'We asked there. Nobody knew.'

'Ah . . . well now. That is a bit difficult.' Marcie stood up and went to the range to make tea. 'They must have simply walked through, I'm afraid. If they'd enquired for work or bought food, I think I'd have heard something from my dear father.' She poured and handed cups around. 'He would have worried about them, d'you see? He cared about people. Three women on their own . . . he would have worried about them.'

Caroline visibly drooped. Laura sipped her tea appreciatively and shook her head. 'Never mind, Marcie. No need for you to worry. We might never actually trace them, but this is much more than a search. It's a kind of pilgrimage. They were walking from Cornwall to the Cotswolds. An amazing thing to do.'

Marcie said, 'And you're doing the same?'

'We've got a car.' Laura smiled.

'All the same . . .' Marcie passed a plate of biscuits. 'It's a lovely thing to do. Just wish I could have helped to make it more . . . you know, solid!' She laughed. 'They probably came past this cottage, you know. The milkmen used to wait in their jingles for the wagon with the churns to arrive from Plymouth.' She nodded at the window. 'Over there on the moor they waited. Every morning, Sundays too.'

'We've heard about them.' Caroline roused herself. 'My mother would have enjoyed all that. She loved . . . occasions. Christmas and Whit-walks. She told marvellous stories about those times. She was . . . very special.'

Marcie said, 'She would have liked my father then. He was good with stories.'

The ringing of the telephone startled them all. Marcie put down her cup and reached up to the mantelpiece where it sat next to the clock.

'Bobby, you again? What now?' She listened then said, 'She's right here. The blue jumper. Yes. All right. Here she is.'

She passed the receiver to Caroline, who listened,

279

blinked, listened again, then said, 'How – how *awful*! As if they were criminals!' She waited, then nodded, then said, 'I should think not indeed!' She listened again. 'Yes. One can understand their resolve not to become involved . . . yes, quite. But that's it? No more trace of the women?' She visibly swallowed. 'Thank you. Thank you very much indeed. Yes, of course I will.' She handed back the receiver and said, 'He wanted to send good wishes to you, Laura. And to Miss . . . Marcie.'

'He's a good lad. They all are. I can never remember their names so I call them all Bobby. They don't mind.'

'He said that his sergeant had found a – a directive – dating from that time. The early twenties. It was from the Cornish police. Sir Geoffrey Bassett of Tregeagle had ordered the immediate arrest of three women from the Land's End area believed to be on the run. It was in connection with an attack on Bassett's person.' She swallowed hard. 'Apparently it could have been construed as what he called . . . DOA. That meant dead or alive.' There was a cry of protest from Laura and a gasp from Marcie. Caroline said quickly, 'The Devonshire Police refused to take it on or make it public. They were afraid that farmers out rabbit shooting might take a potshot at innocent travellers.'

There was a silence then Marcie breathed deeply. 'That's why my father did not know about it. It is certainly something he would have preached against.' She stood up and made for the teapot. 'Do you think these three were the women you are tracing? Were they your family, my dears?'

'No way of knowing for sure,' Caroline replied. 'Your Bobby emphasized that. But I'm sure he thought they were the same three women. And I think so too.'

Laura shook her head at the teapot. 'Not for me, Marcie. I think we should be going to find Jen.'

Caroline stood up. Marcie said, 'Now listen. They must have been all right. There'd certainly be reports of injuries or deaths.'

'Yes. You're right.' Laura looked across at Caroline.

'Whatever it was . . . must have happened in another county.' She shook Miss Marjoribanks by the hand and thanked her.

'I've done nothing, my dear, nothing.'

'You've eliminated some possibilities, given us tea, reassurance, made us feel our trip isn't a complete waste of time.'

'Never! Never a waste of time to know and understand what has gone before! Otherwise how can we learn a thing?'

She stood at the door beneath that heavy thatch and waved them goodbye. Caroline and Laura hurried back into the town and almost immediately saw Jenna. She was running towards them as if there wasn't a minute to spare. Caroline started to make a joke about catching a train.

Jenna gasped, 'We have to leave! I've been talking to some travellers down in the valley – they reckon they are proper Romanies – not sure about that – but they know about Billy! I heard them singing the song and I went down and they told me the story!' She stopped and held her side, breathing heavily.

Caroline said, 'What story?'

'About Billy Boy killing old Three Legs and then being taken into the sea by a white horse!' She pushed herself upright. 'Apparently all Romanies know the story – it's a kind of legend with them! Isn't that just wonderful? Billy Boy is a legend – our uncle, Mum. He's a legend.'

Caroline said, 'Good Lord. Perhaps that's how Bill Legge knew about it. He heard it from the gypsies?'

Laura smiled. 'At last. A breakthrough. We now know they were here and somehow they contacted the gypsies. Perhaps they knew there was a price on their heads and they joined some group—'

'A price on their heads?' Jenna looked even more frantic.

Laura explained and calmed Jenna's horror. 'They might not have known, Jen. The important thing is they got through – never lose sight of that. It is the one sure thing in all this.'

Caroline nodded. 'Darling, you're in a bit of a state. This is all good news, surely? Let's go and have lunch, then we can drive down to Okehampton, get a room there and have a look around.'

Jenna swallowed and took a deep breath, then let it go. 'You're right, of course. I had some crazy idea of catching up with that dreadful old bus and asking more questions. But . . . yes, you're right.' She produced a smile with obvious effort. 'All that rushing down into the valley and back up again has given me an appetite!' They strode down the street like soldiers.

Caroline said, 'The three musketeers!' and laughed. She felt on top of the world.

Twenty-four

October 1999

They reached Okehampton at three o'clock and booked three rooms at the White Hart because there were no family rooms and they simply could not decide which way to make a split between double and single. They had a walk around before early darkness fell. The grey day had become greyer still and there was a chill in the air that was pure winter. Laura thought sadly that normally she would be stacking logs close to the house, hanging strings of onions in the kitchen, storing potatoes and carrots and apples, and, when the weather permitted, putting the garden to bed for the winter. She longed to put the clock back to the time when she still believed that Geoff and she had shared . . . everything. She had to go on with this ridiculous search now because she had to *know*. But she was frightened to death of what they would discover. That last night at home she had dreamed that the reason Geoff had been so understanding about her inability to have children was because he already had a child. And that child was Caroline. She had woken from this nightmare at the moment of discovery and had tried to calm her thumping heart. She had been drenched in sweat. Because if Geoff had fathered Caroline who had been her mother? She had made a sound then and covered her face with her hands and Caroline had appeared in the doorway and asked what was the matter.

Laura dismissed the hateful memory of that now and made some comment about the old church in the middle of the road and the fairy lights even now coming to life.

'It's like a picture postcard,' Caroline agreed. 'Look at that row of shops!'

Jenna said almost ruefully, 'Oh Mum, you're so easily pleased with everything lately!' And Caroline smiled, knowing that to be true, and not understanding it herself because, after all, the future held no John Canniston and the present held no John Canniston. Yet he was here with her. That time in the kitchen at Widdowe's Cottage had spread its warmth everywhere. She held it in her heart and felt pure joy.

Jenna watched her and knew that the aura of happiness that seemed to light up her mother must be because of John Canniston. Which made it terribly fragile; she herself had asked John to go on with his enquiries. They already knew that Tilly was not Geoff's mother; now it seemed she might not be Caroline's either. Which meant that neither Caroline nor Jenna belonged to the Quince family.

Jenna shut her eyes tightly and leaned on Laura, feeling again as if there were a wooden spoon inside her head stirring up her brains.

Laura said, 'Are you all right, Jen?'

'Feel a bit funny,' Jenna managed.

'Yes. I do too. Everything is so unreal.'

Caroline said, 'Let's go back and have a cup of tea and talk to the landlord.'

Pleasant and helpful he might be but he could not help them with any information about the Quinces or the gypsies. But he did say that later that evening if they went into the snug they might be lucky and meet up with Old Robbie, who had farmed north of the castle all his life, and his father before him.

'Apparently his father hated the gypsies. It was before all the rules and regulations. They could camp on any common land. Took what they wanted, poached . . . you've

284

probably heard it all before. Robbie comes in most nights. He's well into his eighties so he might remember something.'

They did not feel hopeful. Only Caroline did justice to her dinner. Jenna said she didn't really like steak. 'Why on earth did you order it then?' her mother asked.

'I've only just gone off it. I think I might be a vegetarian, really.'

Caroline stared at her in amazement, then turned to Laura. 'What's your excuse?'

'Not really hungry.'

Caroline sighed and finished her coffee, then went through the lounge and peered into the tiny snug. Sure enough, there was a man in the corner who could have been over a hundred, so bent and gnarled was he, rather like the ash sticks resting against his chair. She had heard of owners looking like their dogs, but . . . ash sticks? She smiled and went over and introduced herself.

'I'm staying here with my daughter and sister-in-law. We're trying to find some information about my mother's family. Three of them came this way back in the summer of 1922. They could have been with the gypsies. The landlord told us that your father had dealings with the gypsies and you might be able to help us. May we come and have a chat about those times?'

The old man peered up at her; he now looked exactly like a tortoise.

'Can if you wants. No one's interested any more in them days. Be nice to remember 'em again. Better world then. Freedom – no one knows the meaning of the word now. Free to roam wherever you do want to. Especially children. I well remember sliding down castle slope on a piece of board, laughing my head off even though I fell each time—'

'Hang on, let me fetch the others,' Caroline said hastily. 'They will want to hear all this.'

So the four of them sat around the table and Old Robbie talked. He was seven in 1922 so his memories were gilded;

summers were long, winters were short and sharp, the moor was an enormous playground, Christmas involved sledges and bells and moleskin trousers for church. There were wassailers and cinnamon sticks and sledges and bells, lots of bells . . . Jenna said, 'Were the gypsies around at Christmas?' and he stopped in his tracks.

Laura said gently, 'They would have been in their winter quarters. There used to be an old quarry towards St Just where they congregated during the winter. December to the beginning of March, then off they went again.'

Old Robbie said, 'They often uses quarries, shelters them like. Mucky 'erberts they are.'

Jenna nodded. 'The ones I saw at Tavistock were like that. But maybe they were better in your day. I've heard that the old horse-drawn caravans were really beautiful inside.'

'They were that. All a-dangling with charms, nice copper kettle on the stove, little truckles for the kiddies. And underneath the floor was the pots and pans – they clanked and banged all the way . . . all the way . . . clanking and banging.'

Laura leaned forward. Her white hair was on end as usual, her eyes the deepest violet. She said in the same quiet voice she had used before, 'Robbie, when you were a boy – really young – did you play with the gypsies?'

'Father told us not to. He said gypsies stole children away. And he could've bin right. But . . . there was a girl. She wasn't one of them. She told stories. It was summer and she made dens for us in the tall grass and put her shawl over us and told us stories. I don't remember the stories, nor her name but . . .' he stared at Jenna – 'she looked like you. A bit.'

They were riveted. Laura said, 'Was one of the stories about a boy called Billy who went into the sea?'

But Robbie's memory was dredged clean and he looked into her violet eyes and said, 'Where have you been all my life?'

They stared at him, telling themselves he had meant

something else; then he chuckled deeply and they sat back, Laura flushing, Jenna laughing, Caroline looking disappointed.

'We'd better go,' she said. 'I think we've come to the end of the trail somehow.'

They bought Robbie a glass of stout and wished him goodnight and Jenna was already out of the door when he said, 'There was another girl, you know. Came in here for her porter. Always sickly and coughing up blood. Miner's cough she said. More like consumption, I reckon.'

Caroline said in a low voice, 'Alice.'

'That was it. Alice. Rufus Daley took 'em over to Tiverton. They was going to follow the Somerset coast up to Bristol.'

There was another startled silence. Jenna pushed herself back into the snug. 'Rufus Daley?' she asked.

'Who's that then?' Robbie looked up. 'I knew someone of that name. Might have been the same person.'

Jenna shook her head and went out again and Caroline and Laura followed. They crowded into Laura's room and sat on the bed.

'So the trail does not end here.' Caroline sat sideways so that she could see the other two. 'One of the gypsies took them to Tiverton and they went on into Somerset. And Alice was still with them. She *must* have made it all the way to the Cotswolds.'

'But . . . coughing blood . . . poor soul.'

Jenna said, 'They were living healthily enough. Out in the open. That was the treatment in those days. Maybe it worked for her, too.'

'Maybe.'

They all had their special images of the Quince women and there was silence while they incorporated a new Alice into the picture: Alice, coughing blood.

'We'll see whether Jenna's travellers arrive tomorrow and have a word with them, then we'll go on to . . . to . . . I'm not sure.' Caroline looked at the others.

'Dunster?' said Jenna.

Laura recalled the old map in Kate Lansdown's house. 'Dunster, Kilve, then the Levels around Bridgwater Bay.'

After breakfast they walked down to the ruined castle and sure enough, tucked into the trees was the decrepit motor home; paraffin smell seeped through the damp leaf mould all around it.

'It's not as picturesque as the horse-drawn caravans,' Laura said trying to smile. 'But needs must when the devil drives. Times change after all.'

They got nothing from the woman who answered their knock; she obviously regretted talking so freely to Jenna the day before and was determined not to go any further. She denied all knowledge of Rufus Daley or any other Daley, and kept reiterating that they hadn't broken any laws and would be on the move before sunset. 'We're late this year. Won't be back before Christmas at this rate.'

'So you're doing the same circuit as Rufus Daley and his family?' Jenna persisted.

'Told you. Don't know no Daleys. Now leave us alone!' And she retreated into the bus and slammed the door.

They waited no longer but returned to the White Hart, paid their bill and left well before midday. They were tired. Jenna had spent a fruitless hour last night trying to telephone John Canniston, and Laura had slipped into the nightmare again and when she woke out of it had been too frightened to sleep again. Only Caroline was still ebullient.

They reached Dunster in time for a restorative lunch at Reeves Restaurant. No one there knew a thing about the three women who had walked that way eighty years ago. But there had been another enquiry.

Laura and Caroline were incredulous; Jenna kept very quiet. She was pretty sure the enquirer couldn't have been John Canniston, but supposing it had? Caroline glanced at her, expecting her to bulldoze in with a string of questions, and when she simply sat there looking at her vegetarian lunch, Caroline said to the girl who was serving them, 'Somebody enquiring about the Quince family? Are you sure?'

The girl shrugged. 'No names were ever mentioned. Three women was what he said. Or so my gran told me.' She grinned. 'I think my gran fancied him. She said he was her age – seventeen at the time or thereabouts – thick curly hair and rode a black horse. She reckons he'd stole it! Anyway she never forgot him. He was asking about three women. Walking.'

'Your gran – could we talk to her?'

'I doubt it. Unless you manage to find a medium or some such.' The girl laughed. 'This all happened when she was a girl – about eighty year ago I reckon.'

Jenna relaxed and picked up a fork to tackle her cauliflower bake. She waited until the girl was out of earshot then said, 'It was Jacko Miles. I thought at first she was talking about last week or something!' She gave a little laugh. 'We know that Nanna married Jacko when they were eighteen but we never wondered how he got from Treleg up to the Cotswolds. Now we do. He chased after them. On a stolen horse!' She laughed again and after a moment while they assimilated this latest small nugget of information, the other two joined her. There was a kind of blessed relief that Jacko had gone after Tilly; it became more of a romantic fairy tale and less of a nightmare. Laura said, 'Well, I think he must have drawn a blank here, just as we have.'

Jenna nodded. 'Let's get on while we've got the light.'

Caroline nodded, too. 'I agree. Let's head for Kilve and then the flat country between there and Bridgwater.'

They drove along the coast, marvelling at the scenery, knowing it would not have changed very much since the three women had struggled across it. Laura felt almost guilty for riding through it in such comfort.

They approached Kilve about three o'clock. Grey cloud was producing an unpleasant drizzle. They pulled into a farmyard without much hope and found the farmer's wife in the kitchen of a sizeable farmhouse.

She opened the door wide. 'You're lost, aren't you.' It wasn't even a question. 'I'm making tea for the milkers in the shed.' She jerked her head in the direction of a barn on the other side of the yard. 'Come on in and have one and I'll try to put you straight. Got a map?'

She bustled around while Laura and Caroline tentatively took seats at the big table. Jenna stood behind her mother and tried to explain about their quest, but the woman just nodded, put three full mugs of tea into a washing-up bowl and left them to it while she went, head-down to protect the mugs, across the yard to the barn.

Jenna said, 'This is no good, Mum. They wouldn't have come to a big prosperous farm like this.'

'They might have done. And anyway we can find out about routes across the Levels towards Bridgwater. Sit down and help me open up this map.'

The woman came back in. She dried her face on a roller towel behind the door and smiled at them. 'Sorry about that. Got to look after the workers. We'll have ours now.' She set out four more mugs and poured tea. 'Everyone gets lost across these moors – the lanes run alongside the rhines and one rhine looks the same as the next. Your best bet would be to get back on the A39 – you want Bridgwater, I take it?'

Caroline said, 'Yes. But we're trying to follow in the footsteps of our family. It's a sort of pilgrimage.' She flashed the woman a smile. 'We're fairly sure they came through Kilve and we think they would have avoided any highways.'

'When did they go through?'

Caroline laughed. 'Eighty years ago. In the summer of 1922. You wouldn't remember them. They wouldn't have come knocking like we did. Unless it was to beg for food and water.'

The woman laughed too. 'I'm thankful you didn't think I was that old!' She sipped her tea. 'Actually they could have knocked like you did. We used to put a sign outside asking for help with the milking at times. There were bad floods in 1920. A lot of lives were lost round here and we were short of labour for two or three years after.' She sighed. 'But I wouldn't know about that.' She looked at their map. 'If I were you, I'd keep as close to the coast as you can get. That would be the way they'd navigate, wouldn't it? Follow the sea down to Bridgwater then right along the Bay – Burnham and Berrow and Brean.' She leaned close to Caroline. 'Look, if you cross the river here, you're on the Levels. Keep going to the west – the lanes twist and turn terrible but you'll probably smell the sea!' She straightened. 'If your family were heading up-country, they'd be likely to do the same thing.'

They sat around the table talking about it, and then the men came in from milking and they made very grateful farewells.

Jenna knew she was beginning to go downhill; there was no longer any real reason for this pilgrimage or whatever it was. It paled into insignificance against the news that John Canniston had delivered two nights before. She said, 'Shall we bother? It's almost dark, it's raining and it's so hit and miss.'

Laura agreed. 'Let's find a pub somewhere and have another night's sleep.'

But Caroline was suddenly determined. 'We'll just have a quick look at the terrain. Prepare ourselves for tomorrow. We've got another hour of light—' She ignored the protests from the others. After all, she was behind the wheel. 'I promise we won't stay long – look, there's a pub over there – I can even read the sign. The Boat House. We'll come back there.'

The other two agreed unwillingly and Caroline took the next left turn and almost immediately crossed the first of many rhines in this watery landscape. Within ten minutes they were lost. They were incredulous; all landmarks seemed to have been swallowed up, there was no longer any sign of the Boat House, the hedges that had bordered the road had gone, and there was not a house or a building of any kind in sight. The fact that the cloud was sitting firmly on top of them like the lid of saucepan meant they had no way of deciding where the west was. Jenna insisted loudly on turning back. Caroline crossed another wide ditch and stopped the car. 'I suppose I could turn here,' she said, wishing very much she had driven to the pub immediately. 'I don't fancy it on this narrow road but I can't see any intersections, can you?' Nobody replied and she added, 'And I certainly can't smell the sea, either.'

Jenna said, 'We passed something. Could have been a farm. Don't turn yet, Mum. Stay put. I'll run back and have a closer look. Won't be a minute.' She got out and then came back. 'Put your hazard warning lights on.'

'There's not likely to be anything else coming this way.'

'No, but I don't want to lose you.'

Caroline wailed, 'Oh my God!' But Jenna had already gone and was doing a swift jog back the way they had come.

She crossed the little humpbacked bridge and ran on for about a quarter of a mile, then paused and looked over the ditch. She still could not see the house but a shape that might have been a gate post showed slightly greyer against the grey of approaching darkness. She frowned and peered, and then saw with a start that it was a man. He was standing very still, apparently staring in her direction.

She collected herself and called to him. 'Excuse me. We're lost. Can you direct us back to the old Bridgwater road?'

He began to walk towards her. She got a grip on herself; he was shambling and she could outrun him any time. In any case the ditch was between them. He was carrying something. A rake? He reached the opposite bank and looked across it. For a moment he stared at her, frowning. Then he spoke and his accent was so thick she hardly understood him.

'Thought you was summun else. Thought you was Miss Tiddler.'

Her heart leapt into her throat because she heard 'Miss Tilly'.

'I am, in a way,' she said, just as hoarsely.

There was a pause, then he seemed to accept that.

'You back to look at the place? An' you'm lost again? Remember what I tole you? Follow this rhine, next bridge along, and then about a mile. There be a cross but it's growed into the grass now. It's next to the house. You'll have to look.'

She had to force her voice to work. 'Who made the cross?'

He shrugged. 'The woman? Or was it your man? The one what rode the black mare. Who else woulda dug 'er into the earth?'

Jenna was rigid. She was not surprised when he turned and walked into the grey evening. She was almost certain who he was but she called after him nevertheless. 'Are you Billy? Are you Billy Quince?' But he was already gone.

She was weeping when she got back into the car, so thankful to see that her mother had turned it somehow, terrified that Laura and Caroline, too, might be dead and gone with Tilly and Bessie and Alice. It was wonderful to be gathered into her mother's arms; to have Laura fuss around her from the back seat, finding barley sugars and tissues. She told them what had happened, incoherently at first and then more clearly, and then very clearly and with emphasis as she apprehended their shocked disbelief.

'It was Billy, I tell you! It must have been! He thought I was Tilly – he called me Miss Tilly!' She started to weep again. These people – Tilly and Bessie and Alice – might not even be her family but Billy had still thought they were.

'He knew we were looking for Alice – he *knew*! He told me where to look. A wooden cross. He said someone on a black horse had made the wooden cross.'

Laura and Caroline exchanged glances. Laura said

slowly, 'Wasn't that what the girl said in Dunster? Jacko Miles stole a horse and came looking for Tilly?'

'Not quite,' Caroline tried to sound casual, and failed. 'This cannot be happening.'

'It is – it is happening!'

'Look, we can't go hunting for wooden crosses now,' Laura pushed herself back into the car seat. 'It's dark. Let's get back on the old road and see if we can get rooms at that pub. We'll come here tomorrow—'

'We'll never remember where this is!' wailed Jenna.

'We must make a note of the turnings we take now and just reverse them.' Laura scrabbled in her bag. 'I'll do it.' She extracted a pen. 'Good job you managed that three-point turn, Caro. Come on, let's go.'

And this time the return to the Bridgwater road was straightforward, and the pub could offer a family room with a king-sized bed. They shared it and, wrapped in each other's arms, they slept the night through.

The church bell woke Laura first, tolling monotonously for the early Mass. She lay very still and thought of John Canniston opening up one of his three churches for the day's services. She deliberately reminded herself that he had been in Cheltenham for some ecumenical conference and had intended to make some enquiries about Caroline's father in that time. She shivered slightly at the thought, but it no longer gave her the horrors as it had done after her nightmares. It had to be put to the back of her mind now.

She eased herself sideways out of bed and went into the bathroom. When she emerged, Jenna had made tea and the church bell had stopped. They got ready and went straight to the car park. There was no sense of urgency but nothing else was important. Caroline drove again and Laura fished out the notepad she had used the evening before and gave the directions in a clear, level voice. It was nine thirty when they reached the humpbacked bridge. Caroline did a three-point turn and parked as close to the bank of the rhine as she dared. They got out and stood for a moment looking around them. Jenna was visibly shivering.

'I jogged back. About a quarter of a mile. D'you want to take the car?'

'I don't think so. We're trying to replicate what they did back then.' Caroline glanced up at the sky; the cloud was still there. 'I wonder if it was as murky for them as it is for us?'

Laura said, 'It was summer, remember.'

Jenna swallowed audibly. 'Billy did not ask where you were. I think he met Tilly. Just Tilly. Perhaps there was a thunderstorm or something and she left Bessie and Alice sheltering and went on by herself to look for a farm.'

They began to walk, looking for another bridge over the endless rhine. They were almost ready to give up when they came upon it. 'Next bridge along, and then about a mile,' Jenna recited a little more steadily. Then said, 'He was carrying a rake. A very long rake with wooden tines.'

Nobody commented on this. The field was squelchy, and moving across it needed concentration. There were no hedges, just the criss-cross pattern of drains. At each drain they found a way over; sometimes a stone-built bridge, more often two planks only just clear of the water. They walked for an hour and there was no sign of habitation. Then Jenna spotted the ruined cottage.

'It's just the sort of place they needed,' she said joyfully. 'Come on, this must be it.'

The small building was derelict and mournful. Inside there was a grate full of wood ash and two iron saucepans in the hearth. The stairs led to two tiny rooms beneath a slateless roof. 'Poor things,' Laura murmured.

'Probably better than some of the places they found,' Caroline said rallyingly. She looked round and realized Jenna had gone outside. 'Jen seems to have forgotten that she thought this whole thing was a load of crap!' She grinned at Laura but got no response. 'Darling, are you all right?'

'I don't know.' Laura stared around the bleak kitchen. 'I hoped that this journey would provide some kind of answer for me. How could I have been so stupid?'

'You're not stupid, Laura. It will provide an answer. Not a solution, but certainly an answer of sorts.'

'I'm going to have to do what Charles is doing. Reconstruct. I thought I'd done all that.' She looked unutterably weary and Caroline put an arm around her.

'Do you wish we'd never started any of this?' she asked.

'No. I simply wish that Geoff had told me about it. That's all.'

'Maybe it wasn't his secret. And if Tilly asked him to keep it . . . he could do nothing else, could he? She was his mother to all intents and purposes, after all.'

Laura shuddered convulsively, but at that moment Jenna called from outside.

'I've found it! I've found the cross!'

It had been laid flat on the ground and a rock put on it so that it would not blow away. Grass and weeds covered it completely and Jenna was scraping them away. Caroline knelt and helped her to roll away the rock. And there it was; two spars, cross-lashed with twine and inscribed, probably with a hot poker:

Alice May Quince 1905–1922 RIP

Laura stared at it then went back into the kitchen and stared at the floor. 'You were born here, then, Geoff. Alice gave you life, then died and Tilly took you on. And then what?' She waited. Nothing happened. Her whisper became fiercer. 'Come on, Geoff! If Billy can talk to Jenna, you can talk to me. What happened next?'

Behind her Caroline said gently, 'They lived happily . . . not quite for evermore but a good long time. And when Tilly's Jacko died she married my father and Geoff married you. It's as simple as that, Laura.' She waited and then added, 'And Billy did not appear to Jenna, darling. She is very vulnerable, we both know that. When she told us he was carrying a wooden rake, I knew instantly it was not Billy. It was someone who is employed to keep the drains free. He would know the area thoroughly. Probably discovered the cross himself.' She walked over and took Laura's hand. 'Let's go home. We can be back at Widdowe's Cottage in three hours. Let's go back now and leave poor Alice in peace.'

Twenty-five

1922–45

Jacko dug the grave.

Tilly went back to the farmhouse, sneaked into the barn and stole some milk. The rain had eased by that time and the farm was exactly where it had been the day before. She looked for Todd, but by then it was well past midnight and the countryside lay soggy, warm and completely empty. Bessie sat with the new baby, empty-eyed. Jacko Miles brought in two pieces of wood and some twine and Bessie cross-lashed them together as she had seen John Quince do many a time, and then heated the stair rod they had used for a poker and burned Alice's name into the wood.

By four o'clock, as the sky lightened, everything was ready. They wrapped Alice's body in the three sheets which had come with them all the way and lowered her gently into the grave. Tilly recited as much of the funeral service as she could remember. Bessie gradually straightened her back and stood, suddenly tall against the dawn.

They ate, then; eggs from the day before, milk to drink. Then Bessie began the tedious task of feeding the baby and Jacko drew Tilly outside.

'I'll go for a trap,' he said. 'You must be ready by the small bridge over the drain where Todd was waiting last night, when he told me where to find you. We'll make for Bridgwater and leave the trap. Get a train. I've got money. And there'll be more.'

Tilly assumed he had stolen money, just as he had stolen

the black horse and was about to steal a trap, too. But he added sombrely, 'Ma and Uncle Philip be dead, Tilly. I sold up. Nothing for us back in Cornwall while old Three Legs is alive.' She made a sound of distress and he held her shoulder for a moment. 'You're my family now, my maid. You and your ma and that babby. And me. We'll be all right.'

And they were. Lemuel was a slow, gentle man, overwhelmed at first by the influx of four extra bodies into his narrow life. The cottage could barely hold them, but the weather was perfect in the rolling Cotswold hills that summer and until Jacko could make himself a little box room beneath the thatch he slept under the stars rolled in a horse blanket, which appeared, like so many things, out of the blue. When planks also began to appear, one at a time, planed and seasoned properly, needing only a little work with a saw to make them fit over the ceiling joists, Lemuel protested.

'Word do get about, my son,' he said to Jacko as he passed one of them up through the trap door. 'I don't want no trouble coming 'ere. Not with my sister and her girl and the babby. You'm going to be the closest thing I got to a son-in-law one of these days, young Jacko. I want to be proud of you!'

Jacko looked over his shoulder; two more boards would have been very nice but most of the roof space was floored now.

He smiled down at the leathery face of the man he was starting to call Uncle Lem. 'Who owns your cottage, Uncle?'

'George Cooper. The fellow what runs the sawmill – you knows that already.' Lemuel looked up, aghast. 'You didn't get these from 'im, did you?'

'I thought he would appreciate the improvements to his property, Uncle Lem. Perhaps I could talk to him? Tell him what I done and why I done it—'

Lemuel was even more aghast. 'Dun't you do no such

thing, my lad! We'd all be out on our ear'oles and no mistake!'

'Oh. All right, Uncle Lem. An' I won't do it no more. And I'll find a way to pay him back so he won't ever know.'

'You'd best 'prentice for me, Jacko. You might be able to do up a few of his cottages for nothing. That would help.'

But Jacko had other ideas. He made himself useful around the sawmill, clearing up and stacking logs and carrying the sawn wood to the trailers, which were pulled by two enormous shire horses down to the canal at Sharpness or to the railway goods yard at Gloucester for transport all over the country. He busied himself for nearly three weeks before it got to the ears of the owner, George Cooper. Then it was only because Jacko fell off one of the woodpiles and cut his head open and had to be packed off home for Bessie to doctor him.

'What was he doing – bit old for playing isn't he?' Mr Cooper asked, looking at the fleeing boy, braces only just holding his trousers up. 'Making a nuisance of himself – you'll have to watch out there, Ted.'

Ted Jenkins was the foreman and on good terms with Mr Cooper. He laughed. 'He's been useful, sir. Ready for any job around the place. They must be crowded up at Withy Cottage. Glad to get him out of it each day, I suppose.'

When Jacko appeared next, Cooper was waiting for him and took him into the shed which served as an office. At the end of their talk Jacko said, 'I've worked on boats, sir. I'd rather be a carpenter than a fisherman or a thatcher.'

'And why's that, lad?'

'Keeps you out of the wind and rain, sir.'

George Cooper laughed and took him on at the sawmills with the warning, 'If you take any more wood without permission, you'll be out of here before you can say Jacko Miles. Understood?'

Jacko swallowed and said, 'Understood, sir. Thank you, sir.'

*   *   *

On Tilly's eighteenth birthday they were married. It was three years since Alice had died giving birth to Geoffrey, and no one in Childswickham knew that she had ever existed. Bessie had decreed that it should be so; even Lemuel accepted that Geoffrey was her child. Bessie no longer trusted those in power in the land and she was certain that Geoffrey would be taken from them if the truth ever got out. But then the unexpected happened.

Bessie took to glove-stitching like a duck to water; it was a pleasure to her to do work that allowed her to stay in the house. The gloves arrived, the best kid leather cut to shape, short gloves and long ones, big ones and small ones, but all ladies' gloves and needing the finest stitching. Bessie kept her needles sharp, crushing the old gas mantles for cleaning powder and pushing the needles into the big bar of carbolic soap at night. She worked right next to the window in the cottage kitchen, and when the light was good she could stitch a dozen pairs of gloves a day.

The finished gloves were collected on a Saturday night and new cutouts left. Mr Oates came on his bicycle, basket on the front and back, panniers over the back wheel. He invariably accepted a glass of cider from Lemuel, and dearly enjoyed a jaw with Bessie while Tilly put Geoffrey to bed and sang him to sleep. The sheer domesticity in the cottage attracted him greatly. He told Bessie of his lonely terraced house down in Cheltenham Spa and how much it needed a woman's hand. Soon after Tilly and Jacko were married he asked Bessie if she would consider 'getting hitched' again.

She was suddenly coy. 'Who to?' she asked him.

'Well, me, good lady. Jimmy Oates himself. He's got money of his own, so he has. No mortgage on the house, all mine, all mine. And it could be yours too. No more gloves to sew. Little tea parties . . . the ladies of Cheltenham enjoy their little tea parties . . .' He was, as Bessie put it, full of it. But she knew that her eyes would go eventually, and dear Lem had fallen off a roof last week, which for a thatcher was the beginning of the end. Then they would have to rely on Tilly and Jacko. And what about Geoff?

Jimmy Oates was doubtful. 'Always wanted a son, I did. But I ain't sure, good lady. I ain't sure. Not so young as I was and he's used to the fields and so on. I ain't at all sure.'

Bessie talked to the others and put her case. Jacko looked astonished. 'It was always understood that me and Tilly would see to Geoff,' he said. 'We was going to look after Bill, and when we couldn't do that it was as if Alice wanted us to have Geoff.'

Bessie wept, then. Though she did not want anyone to know about Alice – because there was no birth certificate for Geoff and no death certificate for Alice and only that deep hole and the wooden cross above it, flat to the ground – nevertheless Alice had been her favourite. She had lost a husband, four babies, and two grown children, and now this young lad who had swung the school gate open for Tilly and played chase with her dear Billy Boy . . . here he was giving her a chance for another life.

She said, 'Tilly's a lucky girl, Jacko.'

He said, 'My Uncle Philip thought I was the lucky one, Bessie. He'd seen a bit of Tilly and knew I would be all right there. I wish my Ma an' him could see us now. The happiest pair in the whole of England, I reckon.'

Dear Lem looked on, uncomprehending. He wondered why they were all crying and all smiling and all at the same time. He got up and made a big pot of tea. The very next day when it was a Sunday and he should have known better, he went to replace some trusses of straw on the farmhouse a few yards down the lane. The others were all at church – Jacko unwillingly – the farmer and his wife had been up early for milking and were taking a nap. They heard nothing. At one o'clock Tilly ran over to tell Lemuel the potatoes were done. She found him at the foot of his ladder, his eyes wide with surprise. He had been dead for some time. The farmer refused to believe it and six months later was still saying, 'But we din't 'ear nothing. And we was right underneath him and his bluggy ladders!'

The whole village grieved for Lemuel; he was quiet and gentle and kind in all his ways and the words 'he'll be sorely missed hereabouts though he were a foreigner' were heard often. But his death removed the last obstacle for Bessie. She married Jimmy Oates and her matron of honour – 'matron!' she scoffed – was her younger daughter, Tilly.

It was a different marriage but a good one. Jimmy would never untie her apron strings and whisk her into the wash house. But he brought her flowers on saints' days, provided money for food on the table and firing in the coal cellar, and once a month, sometimes twice, was allowed to 'do what he liked'. There was no fear of unwanted pregnancies any more; he was fairly decorous and in a curious way Bessie quite enjoyed his lovemaking. It made her feel special. She was to go on feeling special until she was into her eighties.

It was Jacko who decided they would announce that they had adopted Geoff.

'No need to do nothing official. We'll just let it be known. That will cut the connection with old Three Legs for good an' all,' he told Tilly. 'Them as gets to know – the men at Cooper's and the women in the village – they will understand we are doing it to free Bessie and Jimmy Oates. There will be no questions asked. He will be Geoffrey Miles and that will be that.'

'What if we has some babies ourselves, Jacko?' asked Tilly, her face as red as a boiled lobster.

'I reckon he'll help us to look after them.' Jacko's grin nearly split his face in half.

There were no babies. They never spoke of it. They had Geoff, and as he grew up he seemed closer to them than any children of their own could possibly have been. He was clever, too. Top of the class at school, scholarship to the grammar school, always reading, always finding out about things. Not that they could afford to let him take up the scholarship; that went without saying. But everyone was proud of him.

He had no regrets about what his schoolteacher mourned was a lost chance. He loved the outdoors as much as Tilly did. They would ramble the Cotswolds in all weathers and all seasons. Tilly still enjoyed feeding her family from gleanings from the land, besides growing vegetables in the long narrow garden of the cottage. Jimmy Oates would bring her the occasional package of sewing to be done and she took on alterations for George Cooper's wife and then his daughters. They were relatively well off: when Ted Jenkins retired, Jacko took his place as foreman and talked of buying a car. Both Tilly and Geoff laughed at him. But three times he visited a motor salesroom in Stonehouse and took one out for the day to 'see how she runs'. Geoff and Tilly would sit together on the back seat holding hands nervously while Jacko honked their way down to Cheltenham to visit Bessie and Jimmy Oates. When the owner of the salesroom got wise to him, Jacko transferred his 'custom' to Stroud for a while. Then he bought a Norton motorcycle and a sidecar, and that fulfilled all his ambitions for speed and daring.

Tilly had known since the Penburra beach days that life with Jacko Miles would have a dangerous edge to it which might – or might not – be fun. Her month-long stay on Dartmoor with the gypsies had blurred the limits of right and wrong which most people from Treleg defined so rigidly. Jacko's petty thieving could always be defended, and the thefts of the black horse and then the trap – even of the floorboards – were part of the terrible fight for survival that summer of 1922.

But the business with the cars . . . she could see it was funny. Jacko laughed uproariously and so did Geoff. And so did she. But underneath the laughter she knew very well that Jacko had cheated. She laughed louder. And that night when he started to kiss her she clung to him fiercely and returned the kisses with a passion which surprised him. Afterwards, they lay in the little room under the eaves, still entwined, and he teased her about it.

'Life in the old dog yet,' he murmured, nibbling her ear.

She played along and said in Mrs Cooper's hoity-toity voice, 'To whom do you refer, pray?'

'Well, me of course.' He deliberately spoke in a broad Gloucestershire accent. 'You'm still in your twenties and I be an old man of thirty-one! You better be careful not to wear me out!'

She did something she had never done before and he gasped and clutched her and laughed as they started all over again. And she responded fiercely and prayed that this time . . . surely this time . . . there would be a baby.

'I love you, Jacko Miles,' she whispered. 'I love you for everything you are, but most of all, your kindness and your loyalty.' And she remembered him on that horse in that marshy field. He had come to save them. And to claim her. And he had been willing to give Billy Boy a home. And he loved Geoff as much as she did.

But he had no children of his own. And . . . somehow . . . because of Alice . . . she had a son. They had been married for eleven years and she had never missed a month. They did not talk about it, but Bessie had no such inhibitions. 'Your father only had to look at me,' she said when Tilly became twenty-one. 'You're lucky,' she added quickly. She had meant it, because with Geoff six years old Tilly could have had another three young 'uns hanging on to her apron strings. Withy Cottage could have been a slum instead of a pastoral idyll. By the time Tilly was coming to the end of her twenties Bessie spoke of it no more. When they visited her in the borrowed car, she would get out Jimmy's old tiddly-winks board and they would catapult the little wooden counters all over the place and Geoff would laugh delightedly whether he won or lost. Once she said, as if asking for reassurance, 'We're a right tight little family, aren't we?' And Jimmy and Jacko answered in unison, 'That we are, Bessie!' then laughed as delightedly as Geoff did and said no more.

But around the time of the Munich Agreement, when the world was gathering itself for war, and Tilly was thirty-one and helping to get in the hay for the next-door farm, Jacko strayed.

She knew it that night when, aching and sun-burned, she wanted simply to sleep. There was something about his lovemaking that night; something almost desperate. She tasted tears on his face when he kissed her and afterwards he did not go to sleep for a long time. He held her on his shoulder and told her how much he loved her. She turned her head into his neck.

'It's all right, Jacko. It's all right. I will always love you.' She stroked his rough Cornish hair and whispered, 'Go to sleep, my handsome. Tomorrow everything will be all right.'

And it was for a time. And then Jacko strayed again. And once more. And then he left Cooper's sawmills and joined the Army. And got himself killed.

Geoff was eighteen then. It was at the time when Britain stood alone; Dunkirk had happened and somehow that terrifying defeat had been turned into a victory. No one sang about hanging out washing on the Siegfried Line any more; the Maginot Line had gone, France had gone, but the little ships had crossed the Channel and brought back our boys and Britain had survived. If that wasn't a victory, what was! And then the whole country had to wait to see what old Adolf would do. Geoff was called up and because he was midway through a seven-year apprenticeship as a motor mechanic he was sent to an airfield in Norfolk and given a crash course in aircraft maintenance. Tilly prayed so hard she sometimes felt as if her brain would burst through its skull; she stayed with Bessie and Jimmy until the Battle of Britain started and then the three of them went back to Withy Cottage for a time.

It was there, in 1942, when America came into the war and everyone began to hope for the best again, that George Cooper came to see Tilly. Jimmy smoked a peculiarly smelly tobacco and the house was full of its fumes, so George and Tilly took a walk up to the churchyard and stared down at Lemuel's headstone.

'Perhaps you could have a few words added, Mrs Miles,' George suggested tentatively. 'Just a reminder close at hand that your husband lived and worked here for almost twenty years.' He glanced sideways and saw that she was dry-eyed. 'There will be somewhere over there, I don't doubt. And his name will go on the honours board inside the church but I thought . . . they were very close, him and Lemuel, weren't they? Like son and father.'

''Tis a good idea, Mr Cooper.' Tilly nodded. 'He would like it. Yes, he would like that. He thought a lot of Uncle Lemuel. I'll see to it.'

'No, dear lady. Let me do that. Write me some words, whatever you think fit, and I will arrange it. And there is another thing. His pension. It will be sent to you at the end of each month.'

She was surprised. 'He never said nothing about a pension, sir. You've 'ad men there for almost fifty year. He was with you less than twenty.'

'It will be graded accordingly. And sent by post in case you would prefer to be discreet. And one last thing.' She waited, wide-eyed now. 'I intended to hand over the deeds of Withy Cottage to your uncle. He kept it in good repair for me and his rent was never late. The same can be said for you and your husband. I will therefore enclose the deeds with the first pension payment.' He held up his hand. 'I don't need thanks, Mrs Miles. And I hope you will continue to do sewing for my wife and daughters. In the circumstances.'

He escorted her back home and put his head around the door to tip his hat at Bessie. Thankfully, Jimmy had gone to sleep in his chair and Bessie had knocked out his pipe into the grate. Tilly sat close to her mother and told her about the pension and the cottage. But did not mention the 'circumstances', whatever they might be.

Twenty-six

Geoff survived and was demobbed quickly, because he had been accepted at St Paul's training college in Cheltenham for their special two-year teacher's training course, known as the emergency ex-Forces training.

He spent a wonderful summer with Tilly, walking and talking about the past and the present and the future. They had told him very briefly about Alice and Gilbert Tedenford years ago, making it sound like a fairy story. Now he wanted to know more about it. He asked questions about Jacko and his uncle, Philip Miles, and about his other uncle, Billy Quince and his grandfather John Quince.

He said, 'Ma – I should call you Mother now, shouldn't I? Or Tilly. Such a pretty name. I'm glad Grandma never shortened it to Mattie!' They both laughed. 'Please don't worry about any of this. I understand why you haven't talked about it to anyone else. While there was any possibility of anyone taking me away from you and your Jacko, it was necessary to keep it in the dark. And now . . . well, it was a dreadful time as far as I can make out. Let it sink gradually out of sight. It will go no further than me. I promise you that, dear . . . Tilly. You have survived. That is the important thing. You and Grandma . . . you won through!' He made a joke of it, leaping about in the corn stubble waving his hands dramatically.

She laughed again, then sobered. 'We would have died without Jacko, you know, Geoff. Did I tell you about the black horse?'

'You did.' He was silent for a long time then said, 'You got through that, too, Tilly. No Jacko for the last five years. You got through them.'

'I'll never forget him. He brought . . . adventure.'

'He was an adventurer all right.'

He thought she did not understand the full implication of that word. But she said, very quietly, 'Mr Cooper gave me the cottage. And a pension. He's a good man, I know that, but he also asked me to keep working for his wife and daughters.'

Geoff said, 'D'you mean that he knew – Mr Cooper knew – about Dad? Oh Tilly . . . I'm sorry.'

'Does everyone know?'

'Course not. Dad told me. Before he was sent to France. Just in case there was any trouble.'

'In case one of the girls became pregnant?' There was bitterness in her voice.

'I don't know, Tilly. But he didn't want you left destitute. Tilly, he *loved* you.'

'Yes. Yes, he did. And she didn't get pregnant, did she?' She managed a smile up at him.

He smiled back. 'Are you thinking what I'm thinking?'

'What are you thinking?'

'They've got a phrase for it in the Forces, Tilly. I reckon Dad fired blanks!'

She was a moment understanding what he meant, then she put a hand to her mouth and looked at him over her fingers. 'That – that's awful, Geoff!'

'Isn't it just?' And they both dissolved into laughter.

He lived with Bessie and Jimmy in the week and came home at weekends. He loved everything about the course – the hard work, the teaching practices, the lectures, the essays, the other students – even Jim's evil-smelling pipe every evening did not worry him. He would sit upstairs in their freezing parlour, spread his papers over the plush tablecloth and work until Bessie called him down for cocoa and a snack: sometimes chitterlings, sometimes brains on toast, sometimes some of the brawn that she made from sheeps' heads. Jimmy grumbled that he was 'spoiled rotten' and he would grin and agree wholeheartedly.

Then, one night in the first term of his second year, when he was deep into a book about education and play, Bessie laboured up the stairs and opened the door a crack. She wore a sort of doily on her head, held in place by a wide black ribbon tied tightly under her chin, which hid the fact that she had two or three chins which wobbled with a life of their own if not constrained. The doily came round the door and she said in a stage whisper, 'Can I interrupt, my handsome? I wasn't going to say nothing but Jimmy tells me you've got a right to know. An' by the time you has your supper I shall be nodding off.'

He looked at her over imaginary glasses and spoke in his cartoon teacher's voice. 'I hope this isn't another excuse to get out of physical training classes, my girl.'

She crouched over her apron and held on to the door-knob. 'I shall wet myself if you go on like that, our Geoff.' She straightened and came into the room. 'No, this is serious. Can you spare a minute or two?' He nodded and she pulled out another chair, very careful not to move any of the papers lying close to the table-edge. She took a portentous breath and said, 'You know that Mrs Abelforth who comes for whist on a Sunday night and has a daughter who lost her husband back at Arnhem?'

Geoff nodded, his heart sinking. Bessie had tried to bring the two of them together.

'Well. She's got a job as a nanny with a chap who lost his wife. Mrs Abelforth is hoping they might hit it off. But we shall see. This chap was at Arnhem too. Mavis says he's in a bad way. Has the consumption.' Geoff knew the daughter was Mavis. He felt great sympathy for her. Bessie was filling in details now; big house round by Pittville Park. Baby about six months old. No mother but Mavis said she thought she might have been French. Geoff wondered where he came into all this. Was he supposed to rescue Mavis from a fate worse than death?

310

Bessie paused then said, 'Tilly said as how you was very interested in your mother. Alice.' Her voice lingered over the name and she looked across at the unlit gas fire for a moment. He made a sound of assent and wondered what was going on behind that round face, those brown button eyes.

Bessie said, 'Well, something you might not know about her . . . she really loved your father. And . . . we think – we think he loved her. But then, there's this baby.' Her eyes refocused on him. 'Sounds like this chap – the one what Mavis is working for – sounds like he is your dad. I was all for saying nothing, doing nothing. But Jimmy says you might want to meet him.' She looked into her grandson's eyes and saw Alice, and unaccustomed tears flooded her eyes. She said quickly, 'He calls himself Bertie Miller. But Mavis has seen photographs. Beautiful house and gardens. He says they handed the place over to other relatives fifteen years ago when he first went abroad. But . . . it was Tedenford. And 'is name was Gilbert. Which would shorten itself to Bertie. I think this man be Alice's Gilbert. Your father. Gilbert Tedenford.'

Geoff stared at her, watched as the tears poured down her face, then gathered her into his shoulder. He saw the doily slip down on to her lace collar and felt her throat and multiple chins shaking against his neck.

When she spluttered into hiccuping childish sobs, he said, 'Are you sure? Why would he come to Cheltenham? It's all a bit coincidental, surely?'

'I don't know – I can't question Mrs Abelforth. She's a fly one, she might begin to wonder . . . but . . .' She looked at him, and for a second he saw her as she must have looked to John Quince, beautiful and sparky and not in the least like Uncle Lemuel. Then the tears came again. 'I did wonder whether he had come here to try to find Alice.'

'Oh Grandma. He wouldn't know about anything – how could he?'

'Well, Mrs Sims knew. Mrs Zellafield, too. Old Three Legs is his godfather, remember. If 'e went back after he finished with university – he said he would and Alice was always certain . . .'

These were names Geoff had heard as bit players in the drama that had surrounded his Uncle Billy's death and his real mother's pregnancy.

He said, 'But they wouldn't have known about Uncle Lemuel and Childswickham.'

'They might. I made no secret of it. And they might have mentioned it to him. If he was frantic. And if he promised never to let a breath of it get to old Three Legs.'

'But then – supposing he had gone looking for Alice after he finished at university. Three . . . four years later, perhaps? That would have made it 1926. He would have driven to the Cotswolds and there we would have been. Presumably he was called up in 1939. So he had thirteen years to find me, Grandma. Thirteen years.'

She said in a low voice, 'Supposing he managed to follow our trail just past Kilve Court? Tilly and me, we did some milking there. We might've said we was going across the Levels. Supposing 'e found her grave and the cross I made to mark it?'

He swept the papers aside and reached over to take her hands in his.

'Listen. We don't do anything about this. It's gone. I've no curiosity about him at all. Jacko was my dad and always will be. And I know that your Alice was my mother but Tilly brought me up. I love Tilly as my precious Ma. And that is that, Grandma.' He squeezed her hands. 'Gilbert Tedenford found someone else, Gran. Had a baby with her. He's all right – certainly won't want to be landed with a grown-up son!'

She stared at him for a long time. Her hands twitched inside his several times but she did not pull away. At last she nodded. Then she stood up and left him in peace.

But peace eluded him after that. He talked to Tilly about it and though she understood she still said, 'Poor Gilbert. Poor, poor Gilbert.'

Geoff was indignant. 'He seduced Alice, for goodness' sake! All right, it seems he did love her but if he didn't try to contact her between 1922 and 1926—'

'He could have done, Geoff. You're just guessing he left her alone for four years. He may have written every day, for all we know.'

'And never will know. Let sleeping dogs lie. That's my feeling.'

She glanced at him almost humorously. 'Can you do that, Geoff?'

'Yes,' he said curtly.

'Where does he live?'

'One of those big places in Pittville Park.'

'And how do you know that, my son?' She was laughing now, and he shook his head wryly.

'Gran said. Then I met Mavis when I was taking a walk in the park.' He, too, laughed. 'I guessed if she was a nurse-maid she would be wheeling out the baby.' He stopped laughing. 'There's another thing. The baby.'

Tilly said softly, 'Yes. The baby. Perhaps her mother died – like Alice – and he thought at least he could make some amends. Poor Gilbert.'

'Poor Gilbert be buggered!' he said. And that shocked her into complete and disapproving silence.

Bessie felt a curious mixture of nostalgia and curiosity about this latest 'turnip', as poor old Jimmy called it. And it was Jimmy's advice that won in the end. 'It's a fair old turnip for the books but let it go, my old dearie,' he said. 'I've noticed it makes you cry so don't go into it. Just let it be.' And that was Bessie's philosophy, always had been. But she couldn't stop wondering why Gilbert Tedenford was in Cheltenham, why he no longer had an estate, what he had said or done to Three Legs, and how he had come by this baby girl of his.

Mrs Abelforth brought Mavis with her to the next evening of whist. It seemed that Mr Abelforth had a touch of gout in his left foot and was only too pleased to have the house to himself. 'I've left him a thermos of cocoa and some sangwidges. Jones let me have some leftover bread and I warmed it in a hot tea towel and it's like new.'

Bessie sat Mavis near the fire and kept a hand on her shoulder. She thought of how it had been after John Quince had died; how they had banded together to make the best of it all. She wished that Geoff could open his mind to starting his own family. He would need someone to look after a house for him, cook supper and warm his slippers. She sighed heavily. Mavis was a good girl, a really good girl.

They played four hands before supper and Mavis and Jimmy lost heavily. Mrs Abelforth said, 'One way and another, Mavis, things are not going well for you, are they?'

Mavis shook her head and smiled bravely at Bessie. 'I've lost my job, Mrs Oates,' she said. 'Baby Caroline do cry something dreadful and I gave her a tiny little tap on the wrist. Mr Miller, he won't have it. He was nice enough about it, took the blame on 'isself he did. Practically agreed with me that Baby Caroline was better for me being a bit strict with her, but said that he couldn't bear it. So he would give me a really good reference . . . Well, as you know I only went there to try to take myself out of myself. And it suited me not to work out my notice. I wasn't really cut out for nannying and perhaps it's as well Stan and me never . . . you know. I don't think I care for babies much.'

Mrs Abelforth patted the back of her daughter's hand. 'It would be different with your own, Mave. There's plenty of time yet.'

Bessie nodded. 'You'll meet someone nice, my dear. Look how lucky I was with my Jimmy.'

Jimmy looked down coyly.

Geoff borrowed a motorcycle and sidecar that weekend and took Bessie with him to see Tilly. He remembered Jacko and his 'outfit', as he had always called the old Norton motorcycle. The hills were silver with frost, every twig rimed, a plantation of firs outlined like Christmas trees. Tilly hugged them both so tightly Bessie swore she was being strangled. Geoff thought that her slight figure was now thin. He had applied for a job at the local school and knew he would get it. But that was still two terms ahead and she needed company; she needed to cook and clean for someone other than herself.

She had made rabbit stew and they ate it at midday. Geoff spoke of his final teaching practice, which would either win or lose him the job at the local school. Bessie was still full of the news about Gilbert. Tilly kept glancing at Geoff, and he knew she needed to talk it over with him again. She couldn't take it in; she was still keen for him to meet his so-called father. After they had washed the plates and put them away he suggested a walk.

'Grandma needs a little sleep by the fire. Can we go up to the beacon before dark and look at the view?'

So they took the footpath at the back of Withy Cottage and hiked up to the five-barred gate and then across the field and up to the top. Neither of them spoke about Gilbert Tedenford while they walked. Geoff identified landmarks, trees and houses and field patterns. Tilly told him that one of the Cooper girls was getting married after Christmas, and he wondered which one. 'Evelyn. 'Tis Evelyn Cooper,' Tilly said.

'I meant something else,' Geoff said.

'Yes.' She smiled at him. 'Well . . . only one more to go.' Then she laughed. 'Unless Jacko strayed with both of them!'

Geoff said solemnly, 'Still only one to go, Tilly!'

She said, 'D'you think he'd mind? Us laughing about him, I mean. Shouldn't we take it all a bit more seriously?'

'Not if we want to go on loving him. And we do, don't we?'

They reached the top and marvelled as they always did at the view around them. And then she said, 'Geoff. I feel so sorry for Gilbert. Searching for Alice all these years. Finding some kind of consolation with another girl and then losing her, too.'

'I knew that was what you would say. Grandma felt the same when she heard, too. But Tilly, we agreed that it's all past. If he is my father, I really don't want to know him. Jacko was a great father for a boy – a boy himself really. In spite of what you call his straying, I still love him. And so do you. Don't take it any further. Please.'

Her silence told him so much. He said, 'Listen. In another six months I'll be back home, Tilly. We'll pick up where we left off. Life will be full and good again. I promise.'

She glanced at him, smiling. 'Dear Geoff. You know the decision is yours.'

And so it was left.

That Christmas they were all at the small terraced house in Cheltenham. It was a quiet time; Jacko was gone but Geoff was still safe. They were good at counting their blessings. They walked in Montpelier Gardens and down the Promenade to window-shop. On Boxing Day they congregated outside the Queen's Hotel while the Cotswold Hunt assembled and the stirrup cup went the rounds. Geoff had given Tilly a narrow fur tippet and matching hat for Christmas. She had lowered her skirt to the fashionable New Look length; and with her bits of fur she looked old-fashioned, almost Victorian.

She felt someone watching her from the other side of the milling horses. She thought at first it was a woman holding a child high to one of the riders. The child was beautiful, russet hair beneath turquoise blue bonnet; mittened hands flung high with sudden joy. So small, probably just twelve months, difficult to say. She disappeared from view and Tilly, smiling, looked for her lower down between horse-legs. And met a pair of brown eyes looking straight at her. The eyes belonged to a man; she knew instantly who it was and who the child was, too. She felt her own eyes widen as she saw the awareness in his, then a kind of fear, then the hope. She shook her head at him and turned to Geoff.

'Let's go.' She pushed her hand into his arm and pulled urgently. 'Quickly – come on – into the hotel—'

316

But that would have brought them face to face so she walked straight ahead towards the Rotunda and into Armless Row. Geoff repeated, 'What – what is it?'

She couldn't tell him. Seeing Gilbert Tedenford like that, knowing that for a moment he had thought she was Alice, was terrible. She had never knowingly hurt a living soul. She felt she had stabbed him and twisted the knife.

They didn't see him then but he must have somehow followed them, and the next day a letter was lying on the hall floor addressed to Miss Mathilda Quince. And she knew it was from Gilbert. It said simply:

Dear Tilly, I thought you were Alice. Will you come to visit me? I need to see you more than anything. I have a daughter and she has no mother. Alice should have been her mother. I know Alice and my baby are dead. I am not mad, Tilly. But I am ill in other ways. Please come.
Gilbert Miller

Tilly showed it to the others as they ate sausages for breakfast. She said, 'Geoff, I am sorry, but I have to go. Because of Alice.'

Bessie looked at Geoff. Jimmy said, 'What's wrong with that anyway? He might be going to leave her something.'

Geoff said, 'We take nothing from him. Remember that, Tilly. We have everything we need. We take nothing from him.'

'I was thinking we might give him something, my son,' Tilly said very quietly. 'You are right, we have everything. We could spare . . . something.'

Geoff looked down at his plate.

She went to see him that afternoon. The woman who had lifted the child up to see the horses answered the door. She was not surprised to see Tilly.

'He's expecting you,' she said. 'He's resting in the sitting room.' She led the way through a wide hall, past a curving

317

staircase. 'I'm helping out with Caroline but I'm the house-keeper and she's a baby. She needs twenty-four-hour care.' She tapped on a door, opened it a crack and looked in. 'Go on in, my dear. I'll bring tea.' And she stood aside.

Gilbert was sitting in a deep armchair by the open fire. Through long windows she saw a garden, a frost-crisp lawn, a stand of silver birch, sweeping borders of shrubs. She looked back at the man. She could see now that he was indeed ill. Her mother had said years before that he and Alice looked like brother and sister and she saw now that he had Alice's brown eyes and silky hair that flopped over one eye. Alice's face had been hollowed out by the dreaded consumption and so was his. Her hands had been almost transparent and the one he extended to Tilly now was the same.

She came forward and took it and let him draw her round his chair to another one. He said, 'Tilly, I'm sorry. Oh God, I'm so sorry. I'm not surprised you ran from me. I was unfaithful to Alice. I was in France. No excuse. I have hated myself ever since. When I heard that she . . . her name was Solange . . . had been killed I tried to pretend that the baby was Alice's. But . . . then I saw you.'

She sat down abruptly. He went on talking as if he would never stop. About his family and their rejection of him when they found out about Alice. And his search . . . his stupid pointless search. 'I packed in the university . . . everything went. I tried to find Alice's mother. Nothing. I'd heard about the attack on my godfather. It was Alice's brother. I got some of the story from the housekeeper. She told me that Alice was pregnant. They all thought it was Sir Geoffrey. I knew of course. I was nineteen and half crazy. I drove all the roads I could find between Cornwall and Gloucester. There was a boy near Bridgwater. He took me to some tumbledown house then disappeared.'

Tilly looked at her hands. She knew it must have been Todd. She heard a strange sound and looked up. Gilbert was weeping. She did what Alice would have done. She crouched by him and wrapped her arms around him.

318

She tried to imagine him finding the cross . . . probably only a year after Bessie had burned Alice's name on it. Nineteen years old . . . She put her cheek against that silky hair, so like Alice's, and wept with him.

She had loved Caroline when she had seen her between the horses of the Cotswold Hunt. When Mrs Pettifer, the housekeeper, brought her in after tea, Tilly held out her arms and the child went straight to her. It was the happiest day of her life. Later, when Geoff arrived with the motorbike and sidecar, Gilbert couldn't take his eyes off him and announced that it was the happiest day of his life since he had left Alice. Geoff was completely disarmed. He watched them both with a rueful smile, held Caroline high while the child screeched with joy, and then cradled her securely in his elbow. Later, he said to his grandmother, 'I know when I'm beaten. It was like being caught in a rip tide. You can't stand against that kind of joy.'

It was accepted immediately that Tilly would move to Cheltenham, live in the Pittville Park house and bring up the baby, and to keep things decent, Geoff moved in too. He said to Bessie, 'I have to keep an eye on everything now, Grandma. And anyway, it's only right.'

Tilly was instantly at home. She looked after the family as if she had done it all her life. She chatted to Mrs Pettifer, took over some of the cooking, wheeled Caroline in her high Silver Cross pram to see her Grandma Bessie, and met Geoff from college just as twilight became darkness.

She and Gilbert were married after Geoff qualified as a teacher. Gilbert lived long enough to celebrate Caroline's second birthday. Then the three of them, Caroline, Geoff and Tilly, went back to Withy Cottage, from where Geoff could walk to school and back; where everybody knew them and turned a blind eye to the fact that Tilly had remarried and then had come home with a two-year-old infant and no more money than she'd had before. They knew she had lived well; good luck to her, most of them said. Geoff

319

looked after her and her baby just as she had looked after him. If she had married for money it had certainly all gone.

In fact there had not been much; the house was heavily mortgaged and what was left Tilly made sure was tied up safely to pay for Caroline's education. Geoffrey Miles changed his name to Geoffrey Miller, and newcomers to the village seemed to think he was Caroline's father.

And then he brought Laura home.

Twenty-seven

It was wonderful to be home and in her own room alone; for Laura all other feelings were submerged in sheer relief. There had been times during the last four days when she had forgotten her underlying pain and positively enjoyed the sense of solidarity, of being one unit in a whole of three, of replicating what Bessie and Tilly and Alice had done. And there had been a sense of purpose too; she could not imagine how it would help her to know where Alice had died but she had kept a kind of faith that something would be shown to her. But on the way home she had wondered what it had all been about. Why on earth had they all put themselves through that emotional mincing machine? Where had it got them? The three of them had stood by the two spars marking that grave, and stared down at the soggy turf and concocted their own scenarios of what had happened. She herself had tried to believe that this was the place where Geoff had been born; but it need not have been so. He could have been born in a gypsy caravan or on a beach at Minehead, or maybe at Lynmouth. She would never really know; not for certain. She had continued to stare down at the cross and willed herself to have some kind of vision like Jenna had had. To find acceptance the way Caroline had so obviously done. Nothing happened. Absolutely nothing. Except that she had desperately wanted all this to end so that she could go home.

They had arrived back at the Boat House to pick up the

rest of their things and discovered that the clocks had gone back in the early hours; summer time was at an end. So when they got home and Laura went upstairs at eight o'clock it was actually seven o'clock and if she didn't sleep, a wakeful twelve hours lay ahead. She was certain she would not sleep. She was frightened of having that nightmare again.

As soon as they got in, Jenna went outside into the garden with her mobile telephone. Caroline said she would make coffee but Laura declined and went straight upstairs. The kettle was boiling anyway, so Caroline put cocoa into a jug and made some of that instead. Then she took it into the parlour with a tin of biscuits, switched on the fire and got out the knitting bags. It was only natural to feel anti-climactic; a little bit of ordinary domesticity would help to bring them down again. She heard Laura in the bathroom, then above her in her bedroom; surely she would come downstairs just to say goodnight? Caroline made herself knit three rows of a navy blue square, then poured herself some cocoa and sipped at it. She had got used to them being together; that was the trouble. How on earth would she manage back home at work?

She stood up and went to the window. Because of the lost hour the garden was in complete darkness and there was not even a silhouette to show where Jenna might be. Caroline went into the hall and picked up the phone and dialled the rectory. She counted twenty-one rings and put the phone down as Jenna came in through the kitchen.

'I was ringing John Canniston,' she said. 'He must still be at that conference whatever it was. And no answerphone. He's very behind the times.'

'One of the nicer things about him,' commented Jenna. She looked around. 'Where's Laura?'

Caroline sighed. 'I think she must have gone to bed.' She led the way into the parlour and poured another cup of cocoa and passed it to Jenna. 'This whole thing is not helping her after all, Jen.'

Jenna took the mug and sat down, sighing too. 'Look at you. Cocoa. Knitting. My God, Mum, you have changed. Completely.'

'The sad thing is . . .' Caroline knitted half a row then looked up. 'I think she'll be better without us. Perhaps it really is time for us to go, Jen.'

'Don't be daft. You remember what she said before. She couldn't live here alone again.'

Caroline pursed her lips. 'Maybe the last few days have changed her mind.'

'Mum, it's Sunday. We left here on Thursday. We've had three nights away, that's all.'

'I suppose so. Yes, of course. It seems much longer than that.' Caroline turned her needles. 'What can we do, Jen?'

Jenna twisted her face consideringly. She had already told John Canniston what she intended to do.

'I go. You stay. You pick up where you left off. Wednesdays – maybe Fridays too – at the CF place. Church on Sundays. Knitting, gardening, sketching. Chatting with John and Charles.' She held up her hand at her mother's automatic protest. 'You will have to be a sleeping partner at Beddoes for a while.' She tried for a silly laugh. 'Put Beddoes to bed for a while!'

'You sound as if you've got it all mapped out,' Caroline said, surprised.

'Not really. I've taken advice on the matter.' Jenna gave a rueful grin. 'I think it might have come straight from up there.' She jabbed at the ceiling with her forefinger. 'And I don't mean Laura!'

Caroline knitted silently. She thought Jenna was talking about Jeremy.

Jenna drank some of her cocoa and closed her eyes. 'John says that I'll be all right now. He says I've unlocked the door.' She opened her eyes and looked at her mother, who had stopped knitting and was now staring at her in astonishment. 'No, I don't quite know what he means, either. He seems to think that a lot of people under stress slam a door shut on themselves and won't open it to

323

anyone or to any new ideas!' She laughed. 'He says that's how he knew you and he were all right. Because you always told him exactly what you were thinking.'

Caroline said, 'When did you talk to John?'

'Just now. In the garden. On my mobile.'

'How would he have your mobile number?'

'Oh – I gave it to him back at the Harvest Festival – he said he wanted to be able to get in touch with any family details.'

'Where is he?'

'Not sure. He pulled into a garage so that he could pick up his phone.'

Caroline blinked hard. 'It's Sunday. I thought he'd come home for the services today.'

'Ah. He's got a new curate. A woman. He went to see her four or five weeks ago.'

Caroline said numbly, 'I remember. Truro, 24 September.'

'He said I opened the door – just a crack – when I bawled him out that time he thought I was drowning myself down in Treleg Cove. And since then, things have happened, and apparently I've taken the door off its hinges.'

Caroline still looked stunned. 'What things? What things have happened?'

'Well. We've done our pilgrimage. And he's found out that you are a year older than you thought you were and technically you were born out of wedlock!' She managed a smile. 'Nanna legalized the whole thing just about in time, I gather.' She began to tell her mother all the small pieces of information that John Canniston had made into a whole. All except the first suspicion he had had: that Gilbert Tedenford's second child was not Tilly's.

'Apparently poor Gilbert knew he wasn't going to last long – TB, same as Alice. So he settled somewhere in the Cotswolds – hills, fresh air, all that stuff. And he met Tilly. I bet you anything he thought she was Alice. And Tilly – Nanna – fell for him just as Alice had done. And the next thing they knew, you were on the way!'

Her mother was staring at her in sheer disbelief. Jenna said, 'All right, so I'm making a story out of it. What else can we do, Mum? We've got all these little bits of information – we have to *assemble* them somehow. And you have to admit it makes sense.'

Caroline said, 'Our name was Miller. Nothing like Tedenford.'

'I just told you. He was disinherited, chucked out . . . he took another family name. Don't you think it's wonderful, Mum?' For a moment Jenna sounded pleading. 'It sort of completes the whole circle. The love story that could not happen for Alice happened for Tilly.' She added quietly, 'It could happen for you. It could happen for me.'

'What are you *talking* about? My mother would never – I could never really believe that she married again, anyway! All her memories were of Jacko. Geoff's too. I was envious of Geoff for having such a character for a father. I didn't know that Geoff was adopted by Tilly and Jacko until John Canniston told me. I thought they'd been in their teens when they had him. Compared with Jacko Miles, *my* father seemed . . . a nonentity.'

'Oh Mum . . .' Jenna put down her cup and reached for her mother's hands. 'So much went on. So much happened in those years. I wanted John to tell you what he'd discovered, but he insisted it should be me. The thing is . . . we knew that Alice was Geoff's mother but we didn't ask questions about his father, did we? John told us about Gilbert Tedenford before we went on our pilgrimage but I still didn't think Gilbert was an important character. And the fact that Billy had tried to kill Geoffrey Three Legs, and then Bessie called Alice's baby Geoffrey . . . well, it still made you wonder whether the old squire himself – had actually raped Alice. But Geoff must have had to produce some kind of certificate when he was conscripted, and he was never officially adopted. He told the authorities what he knew. Tilly and Jacko had done their best and he had a pretty good picture of how it had all happened. And John has done some jolly good detective work in between attending the ecumenical conference! He thinks – John thinks – that Tilly held out against marriage – she had some pretty peculiar principles if you remember – and when Gilbert knew he was going to die, she agreed to it and it was then they registered your birth. And they were happy . . . that's the important thing. He'd gone crazy looking for Alice, blaming everyone for her death, giving away huge chunks of money to the miners at Treleg, getting drunk . . . His family had to protect the estate and they gave it all over to a cousin in Wales. But Gilbert found a kind of redemption during the war. He was at Arnhem. Decorated for bravery, apparently. And then he found Tilly. Don't you think that's marvellous? You and Uncle Geoff were brother and sister, just as you thought.'

Caroline was some time assimilating this. She stared into Jenna's brown eyes and watched them slowly fill with tears. And she pulled her close and murmured maternal incoherences and Jenna wept just as incoherently and knew exactly what John Canniston had meant about opening doors. With the rush of tears Jeremy floated out and then the ardent young Gilbert Tedenford floated in, and then the middle-aged Gilbert Miller floated out, passing Jeremy on the way as he came back in. It was absurd, ludicrous, but that's how it was. She felt awash with all the passionate lovers in her family history.

'We've got to tell Laura,' she sobbed. 'She needs to know everything. She must not feel she is being left in the dark again.'

Caroline suddenly wanted to forget this whole thing; just go to bed and wake up and perhaps see John. Or perhaps not.

She said, 'Darling, it's past midnight and she was totally exhausted.'

'We haven't changed this clock. It's only just gone eleven o'clock, Mum. She's probably thrown out by the hour and can't sleep anyway.' Jenna retrieved her wool and wound it carefully. 'We have to tell her, Mum. No more secrets.'

Caroline sighed. 'All right. Must admit I think we've all

had enough. But I know you're right. I'll make some more cocoa. You go and fetch her down.' She paused. 'Is this going to make everything worse for her, Jen?'

'I don't know. But even if it makes it worse, she still has to know.'

Jenna made for the hall and the stairs and Caroline carried the tray back into the kitchen. She stood there looking at the black window which reflected everything back to her: the cooker, the big table, the ladder-back chairs and herself. She was standing there, in Laura's kitchen, alone. She had lost her mother, husband and brother and for a time Jenna had turned against her. But she had always had Laura. And now she was frightened she might be losing Laura too. The reflected Caroline was a usurper; the kitchen was not her kitchen, everything belonged to Laura and Laura would want it back. Because . . . something was wrong. She had listened to Jenna, and to what John had discovered, but there was still something wrong.

She squeezed her eyes tightly and turned her back on the window and tried, almost physically, to recapture – hold on to – the wonderful sense of well-being she'd had since that night not very long ago in this very kitchen. All she could recapture was the memory of explaining to John that he must look for someone else; someone who would be young enough to give him children.

Jenna clattered in. 'She's coming down. She looks a bit like a zombie.' She filled the kettle at the sink and glanced over her shoulder. 'So do you, actually. I'm sorry about this, but if we leave it till tomorrow she will feel totally left out and that's so wrong, Mum. We're the outsiders. She's the one, always has been, who belongs here.'

This was so close to Caroline's own thoughts that she began to shake. Jenna was shocked.

'What is it? Sit down – just sit – I'll see to the bloody cocoa for God's sake! Are you ill? Has John Canniston phoned?'

Caroline shook her head to both questions and tried to

smile. 'Goose walked over my grave,' she said shakily. 'It's that extra hour you keep talking about – can't keep up with it!'

Laura came in, then, and though she did indeed look like a zombie she was immediately concerned for Caroline.

'You should have said your mother was ill, Jen. I wouldn't have stopped to go to the bathroom and everything. Let me do that . . . Cocoa, good. Maybe an aspirin. It's been so stressful it feels as if we were away a week instead of just three nights!' She bustled about, appearing to be the old Laura again, full of remedies and reassurances. Caroline let it all happen; she let Jenna tell Laura about Gilbert Tedenford loving two women, and him fathering Geoff and then Caroline. She let Laura pour cocoa and realized it was her fourth cup that evening. She swallowed two aspirin and felt her muscles start to relax.

When she climbed into bed clutching a hot-water bottle she wondered why on earth she had gone to pieces like that; what could be the matter with her? Jenna was right; the ending of the Quince story was . . . just right. A completed circle. Alice's death and the terrible journey from Cornwall to Gloucestershire were justified. There was no way she, Caroline, could ever link up with John Canniston; she had never let it become even a possibility. And right at the beginning, when she had heard of him from Jenna, she had wondered whether he might mean some kind of new life for her daughter.

She curled herself around the hot-water bottle and closed her eyes.

Jenna, in the small room next door, lay on her back and stared into the darkness and tried to believe what John Canniston had told her about his suspicion that Caroline might not be Tilly's child. She had to be: because if she, Jenna, was no kin at all of the Quinces why on earth – or indeed in heaven – would Billy Boy have come to her on those Levels and told her where Alice was buried?

In the room across the landing Laura, too, thought of Billy Boy. Everything still seemed pretty pointless; the way

328

Geoff's family had strived and struggled and fought and never quite got there . . . her own childlessness . . . Geoff not really sharing himself with her as she had with him. Now there was this latest revelation that Geoff had shared a father with Caroline. But there was one small chink of light. Billy Boy. She had no doubt that he had come to Jenna on those watery Levels. There had to be something in that. She sighed, leaned over and switched off her bedside lamp. If only he would come to her . . . let her in. Make her part of Geoff again.

Twenty-eight

It took a week for Jenna to sort out her return to London. She was surprised to discover that in spite of the terrible grief which she had thought had rendered her completely useless all through the summer, she had sorted out her affairs almost as objectively as she had so often sorted out the affairs of her clients. The mortgage had been insured and the flat just off the Edgware Road was now hers. She said soberly to her mother and aunt, 'If I sold it I would be a rich woman. But for now I'm going to live in it. I promise I won't be morbid about it. I think it will give me comfort now.' She looked across the table and smiled slightly. 'I think I'm the only one of us who got something out of our pilgrimage . . . because in the end that's what it was, wasn't it?' They both nodded but were silent. Jenna shook her head gently. 'I was the one who said the whole idea was crap. But then . . . well, I'm just thankful that though Tilly wasn't Uncle Geoff's mother, he's still my uncle and you're still my aunt.' She covered the back of Laura's hand with hers and added uncharacteristically, 'My very special aunt.'

Laura smiled briefly but managed to say humorously, 'Thank God. You're unpredictable and often quite rude but I'm really glad you're still my niece by marriage.' She paused. 'I've got Geoff to thank for that, at any rate.'

Nobody commented on that last remark. Jenna transferred her hand to her mother's. 'You'll stay on a bit? Resume normal service next week? I don't know how

Oxfam and the Centrifugal Force lot have coped without you for a whole fortnight!'

Caroline, too, tried to rise to the occasion. 'Nor me. But they must have done.' She sandwiched Jenna's hand with hers and said, 'The pilgrimage was good on a lot of levels. The bottom line was that we all had a break. This past week I've really enjoyed working on those drawings again. Thank you both for drying out Geoff's sketch book for me – I'd never have had the heart to layer each page with blotting paper like that. It worked splendidly.'

Jenna glanced at Laura and said, 'A pleasure. We mean that.' She cleared her throat. 'I notice you've started something quite different. Two people. A couple. Are they anyone we know?'

Caroline stood up and began to move crockery to the sink. 'No. Not really. I saw them in Truro when I was gazing out of the window of the archive place. They reminded me of you and Jeremy. And then of Laura and Geoff . . . Tilly and her Jacko. Maybe of Bessie and John Quince too.' She gave a small self-deprecating laugh. 'Maybe they were representing every young couple in love. I'm not sure. I might know when I've finished the painting.'

'Oh Mum.'

'I know. Silly. I've become very sentimental in my old age!'

Jenna said vigorously, 'Old age be buggered! It's since living here with Laura in Widdowe's Cottage. Since knowing about our heritage!' She turned to Laura. 'Isn't it, darling? Tell her!'

Laura looked across at Caroline, smiled slightly in assent and stood up. 'D'you mind if I go for a walk? Everything seems to have dried out nicely. I'd like to look at Penburra Cove.'

'D'you want us to come?' Caroline said swiftly, and Jenna stood up, but Laura shook her head very definitely and went into the hall for her coat, then drifted back through the kitchen, into the garden and down to the cliff path.

Jenna said, 'Penburra. Wasn't that where Billy was

supposed to have gone into the water with the white horses?'

'I think so.' Caroline peered after Laura's diminishing form. It was a grey, still day but it was November and mists could come off the sea without much warning. 'I wish Charles would come and see her. We've been back for a week. And in a way he instigated the pilgrimage – at least he was the one who persuaded her to do it.'

'Ring him. He might not know we're back.'

'John would have told him.'

'How would John know we're back? Have you rung him?'

'No.' Caroline made a wry face. 'But you did. The night we arrived home, don't you remember?' She had got over what she called her 'funny turn'. It had been a bit of an anticlimax, that was all . . . coming home after finding Alice's grave and practically living through what the other Quince women had suffered.

Jenna shrugged. 'I could have been anywhere. He was so full of his news I didn't have a chance to say where we were. I used my mobile, remember.'

Caroline looked at her for a moment then said, 'I'll ring Charles. It's Saturday and he might like a walk to Penburra Cove.'

It took Laura longer than expected to reach the cove. In spite of the good weather, the cliff path was still muddy from heavy rain the previous Sunday and some of the precipitous slopes had been very difficult to negotiate; she had had to concentrate on each foothold. She hadn't wanted that. She had wanted to stride out, just get from the cottage to the cove without thinking. She was reminded of the awful day she had gone to Tregeagle Church to look at the place where the Reverend Carridon had planted the tin box in memory of Billy Quince. She had had to face up to the fact then that everything that was happening – unfolding – whatever you liked to call it – was emphasizing her role as an outsider. She heard back from Caroline, from Jenna, from Charles, from John; nothing happened directly to her at all. And it just underlined the fact that if Geoff had wanted her to be included in the momentous happenings of his life, he would have told her.

She reached the river, saw the stepping stones were covered, and waded through, careless of her walking shoes and thick wool socks. When she reached the top of the small combe she suddenly realized there was no way she could cross the Geagle and she would have to walk down to the church, right along one bank to the bridge on the Land's End road, then right along the other bank, passing the rectory as she went. She almost wept with frustration, then saw it as yet another example of the way she was excluded, and tightened her muscles stubbornly as she tramped across the heather and turned left at the church footpath.

So it was midday as she climbed the headland and looked down into the cove and then across to the other headland where the rocks dropped more gradually into the sea. She stood there, conscious of her wet, sore feet and her overheated body beneath the waxed cotton jacket. Below her the sea breathed gently as the tide crept over a ridge of pebbles and on to the white sand. Rearing up from the cliff was the bracken: ochre red at this time of year, crowding to the horizon, apparently endless. She knew that the Land's End road was probably less than a mile away but the feeling of isolation was doubtless as intense as it had been when Billy Boy had come here in the cold spring of 1922. She stayed where she was for a long time, waiting for . . . something.

Nothing happened except she became more and more uncomfortable. She moved at last, and began to walk and clamber down on to the beach. She tramped across it on to the rocky headland the other side, slipping and sliding on the seaweed as she scrambled up to where she imagined Billy Boy might have stood and watched the white horses creaming in and . . . maybe . . . jumped into their midst. And given birth to a legend.

She stood very still, eyes half closed. Someone must have been with him in order to bring back the story.

Someone . . . maybe on the other headland where she had stood herself . . . had seen Billy Boy go into the sea and had taken the story back to Tregeagle or Treleg or Wayward House.

She sat down on an outcrop and without thinking began to unlace her shoes, push them off and peel away the heavily wet socks. Then she stood up and unzipped her jacket and let it fall behind her. And then she began to clamber cautiously down the rocks towards the sea. She thought she heard a shout but she was thinking too hard to pay attention . . . The water was quite shallow where it met the rock; the seabed was visible even on a grey day like this one. Why hadn't he waded back to the beach? Had the tide been much further in? Would that have made any difference? The water lapped over her ankles and soothed her feet. She bent to roll up her trousers. It was then that she heard it and stopped where she was, doubled up as if she might be going to dive into the water. Any movement might have interfered with whatever line of communication she had found. She felt her ears tingle with the effort of listening. And then it came again.

'Where have you been all the day, my Billy Boy?' Hoarse but roughly clear; the second line of the folk song. And it was not coming from the sea, as she had first thought, it was coming from the opposite headland.

She waited for the delighted reply to that question . . . waited to hear that Billy Boy had been walking all the day . . . but another voice crashed over any reply.

'Laura! Don't do it! Laura!'

She peered under her arm at the curve of the cove and saw Charles Cledra floundering through the sand towards her. He had ruined the song but she had heard it . . . she had actually heard it! She straightened, laughing.

'Charles – I'm *listening*! Didn't you hear it – the song?'

He arrived at the base of the headland and hung on to a rock, gulping air. "Course I heard it. It's Bill Legge – up there – he's staying with me while he gets over some virus he's got.'

334

She looked at him and then at the other Bill standing up there, silhouetted against the grey sky, and knew instantly that Caroline had telephoned Charles; this was no coincidence at all. She began to laugh. Nothing was spoiled. Bill Legge continued to sing hoarsely that he had been walking with Nancy Gray; Charles stood below her gradually regaining his breath. The world turned and she was part of it.

She said, 'Oh Charles, did you think I was going to drown myself? I took my shoes off because they're soaking wet. And I'm hot in this waxy thing.' She stopped laughing. 'Dear Charles, were you going to rescue me? But there's no need – the water is shallow here. I've got a feeling that this was not the place where Billy Quince jumped into the sea. Look – I can paddle back to the shore.' And she stepped off the rock and disappeared into the sea.

Twenty-nine

November 1999

By the time they got back to Charles's car, which was parked among the ferns just off the Land's End road, they were all exhausted. Bill Legge took the lead because he had brought Charles through the bracken in the first place, and it was as if he had been following some unmarked path through the scratchy undergrowth. It was well marked now because Charles had been in a hurry and had smashed the ferns down unceremoniously. Even so it was heavy going and the numerous rabbit holes did not make it easier.

'All we want now is to turn an ankle or two,' Charles panted as he negotiated himself and Laura around a mini-warren. Ahead of them Bill Legge let out a shout of laughter and flapped Laura's coat above him like a banner. Charles had kept his on; he was much wetter than she was and squelched at every step.

For the fifth, sixth, seventh time, she said, 'Charles, I'm really sorry.'

And he replied similarly, 'What were you thinking of, woman?'

And she became slightly tart and said, 'Well obviously, as I've already told you a dozen times, I didn't think it was more than knee-deep.'

'But you must know – every idiot knows – that light is refracted through water in such a way that—'

'Charles, if you tell me that again I think I shall hit you!'

Bill gave another shout of laughter and whirled Laura's jacket again.

Charles said, 'Sorry. I was anxious. Dammit, I was terrified.'

'But you must have realized I wasn't trying to drown myself, so therefore I was going to swim out.'

He said, 'No, Laura. I did not know either of those things. And as I cannot swim and have an aversion to the water, the prospects were not good.'

She stopped walking and stumbling and looked at him.

'But you came in to save me.'

'And – also obviously – it was you who saved me.'

'Yes, but the intention was there.' She gave him that look again; realization was dawning at last. She said, 'Oh Charles.'

He managed a rueful smile. 'Didn't think I had it in me, actually. You know, leading the sort of life . . . bit of a recluse till John Canniston came and got me interested in . . . some things.'

'I know what you mean. I was the same. More reclusive, I suppose. You had a job and I . . . Anyway, all's well that ends well.'

'Or, perhaps, begins again.'

She looked at him a third time. Bill Legge moved out of earshot but they could hear him humming a tune.

She said, 'Charles, you have made a life as a widower. I thought I had, too. But it seems a bit of a sham now. I've got to start all over again.'

'That's what *I* said, Laura. And I know what you mean and how you feel because my reconstruction seems a bit pointless now. But today . . . I did something that had nothing to do with construction. Caro rang me and said you were in Penburra Cove looking for Billy and I was frightened. I've got Bill staying for a few days and he knows the terrain. We came here and he found his way across this featureless bracken and there you were, no shoes or jacket, about to go into the sea like Billy did.'

'I told you—'

'Yes, but you hadn't told me, then. And I came in after you. Dear girl, I know you better than you know yourself.

337

Better than I know my own self. You are impulsive. And, it seems, so am I. We don't have to begin again together if that is too much for you. But we could begin on parallel lines. Like rail tracks. And if we ever thought of anything else, we could find some points and change over . . .' He laughed ruefully. 'That metaphor isn't working, Laura. But you know what I mean.'

Her eyes were filling, yet she was still looking, and smiling too. 'I think I do. And I wouldn't have wanted anyone else to pull me out of the sea—' He tried to correct her and she held up a hand. 'You rescued me, Charles. You rescued me, I promise you that.'

'Bill Legge had something to do with it, too.' His smile was broad now. He knew he had talked her round.

She nodded. 'This is where they were, Charles. The Quinces. This is the real place of pilgrimage.' She reached and took his hand. 'Charles, I have to say this. Perhaps it is a little too impulsive. But although the parallel railway lines sound very sensible and comforting and . . . oh lots of things . . . I think I would prefer to be on the same track as you. On the same train. Actually in the same compartment.'

He made a sound which may well have been a sob, then he gathered them together inexpertly and hugged her. The smell of wet wool and seaweed was overpowering. She said into his ear, 'We're like two grizzly bears locked in combat!' They both started to laugh and could not stop. Ahead of them Bill Legge burst out with 'And me Nancy tickled me fancy. Oh my charming Billy Boy.'

Caroline said, 'This week has been strange, Jen, hasn't it? Those few days away must have exhausted us. We've sat around doing nothing yet acting as if we've sorted it all out.'

Jenna was still looking down the garden and imagining Laura walking that so-familiar cliff path. She said over her shoulder, 'We found out a lot, Mum. It was a pretty emotional time. We're bound to feel exhausted.' She

338

chuckled. 'Anyway, we haven't done nothing. You've knitted at least a dozen more squares and worked every day on your sketches.'

'Yes. But that was in an effort to – to – settle again. Laura and I haven't been to the centre or shopped or anything. Those few days were so disturbing—'

'Change that to devastating, Mum. Starting with the moor, which seemed almost to breathe at us, and ending with Billy telling us where to find Alice's grave. And that cross, Mum. Oh, that cross.'

'Yes.' Caroline cradled her empty cup and thought back. 'Yes. Devastating is the word.' She thought of the most devastating thing of all and took a breath. 'About that boy who directed you to the grave, Jen. Surely it was someone who worked on the Levels? When you said he had a rake I thought it might be one of the farmer's lads keeping those drainage ditches free of weed or something.'

'Mum, I can't explain – I don't really want to try in case I get doubts. It wasn't Billy. Yet it was.' Jenna turned to look at her mother and felt her eyes fill. 'And he came to help us. That's all. End of story.' She put a hand on her mother's shoulder. 'I'm all right, honestly. Otherwise I wouldn't be going back to the office . . . I wouldn't be any good to them.' She moved on to the sink. 'I'm glad you're staying on for a while. You're good for Laura.'

Caroline said, surprised. 'I'm not so sure about that now, Jen.'

'You fit in here. You've got her going to church and to that drop-in place in Penzance.'

'Perhaps they don't need us any more. There's been no call from them since we got back.'

'You could ring them, Mum.' Jenna ran water into a bowl and began to wash up. 'Try John again, why don't you?'

Caroline said nothing and Jenna flashed her a smile. 'I see. That would be forward, would it?' She shook her head at her mother. 'He'll ring when he's got something to tell us. Anyway, he doesn't know we're home yet. But that's OK, he's got my mobile number.' She said quickly, 'I'll just check my phone.' She scrubbed her hands dry and pulled it out of her pocket. 'Oh . . . for goodness' sake! It's out of juice. I haven't charged it since we got home last Sunday. Damn!'

Caroline said neutrally, 'He could have used the land-line. The only calls we've had have been from the railway enquiries place at Penzance, and your firm, and that friend who is keeping an eye on the flat.'

'Like I said, he thinks we're still on the road. He probably thought we would go on to the Cotswolds and look around there. Maybe we should have done.'

'Darling, we'd had enough. Especially Laura.'

Jenna nodded. 'Mum, you don't think Laura was – is – desperate? This Penburra thing . . . she said something to me about feeling like an outsider—'

Caroline shook her head very definitely. 'Laura wanted to be by herself. It was as simple as that. Anyway none of us are in the least bit suicidal. If you remember, John thought you were going to drown yourself that day.'

'Yes. Funny that.' Jenna looked musingly at Geoff's sketch book and then took a breath and stared across the table at her mother. 'Listen, Mum. I thought John Canniston was a jumped-up pious prig at first. Took himself far too seriously. But then . . . I watched you. And through you I learned he was . . . OK.' She shrugged. 'Maybe I got over that thing I had about Dad. I'm not sure. It could have been Billy Boy—' She snuffled a little laugh. 'But I think it was down to John himself. And you. And now that damned picture.'

Caroline held up a hand. 'You don't have to say any more, darling. I do understand completely. If you can see a way to be happy again—'

Jenna made a scornful gesture. 'That's just it. Don't you see? I've managed to stop thinking incessantly about me, me, me all the time. I've had to learn all over again to see the sky and the sea and the bloody, bloody flowers that keep on bloody blooming. And, most importantly, to see *you*! Mum, he loves you. And you love him and age makes no difference—' she laughed – 'even though it seems you're a year older than you thought – that's down to Nanna of course!' She sat down abruptly. 'You've met each other before you're dead, that's the main thing. Get on the telephone, Mum. Go and see him. Please.'

Caroline stared at her daughter as if she had never seen her before. She started to stammer questions at her, then stopped. Jenna said a challenging 'Well?' and Caroline eventually said, 'I should have trusted him.' And then she shook her head as if to clear it and said, 'You never showed the least bit of interest in him.'

Jenna ignored both remarks and pointed to the hall and the telephone. 'I'm going to finish my packing, put my mobile on charge and clean my room. The Paddington train leaves early tomorrow and I don't want to have to be hoovering while you're still asleep.'

Caroline watched her go upstairs and then telephoned the rectory. There was still no one at home and still no answerphone, so she cancelled the call and stood in the hall listening to Jenna actually singing above the note of the vacuum cleaner. Then she made up her mind; the only place he might be was in Penzance at the Centrifugal Force . . . Wayward House.

She shouted up the stairs against the roar of the vacuum cleaner.

'You won't want the car will you, Jen? No reply from the rectory but I have to do a bit of shopping in Penzance. Won't be long.'

She grabbed the keys and her shoulder bag and was gone. She was vaguely aware of Jen shouting back at her, but the vacuum was not switched off so it could not have been important. She backed the car out of the garage. She had to sort this out; it was suddenly urgent.

She parked at the top of Market Jew Street and stuck an hour-long parking ticket in the windscreen; that was all it would take. She crossed the Causeway and took the steep hill with its platform pavement and steps down to the road.

341

The stone figure of Davy stared down over the view of Mount's Bay but she did not pause as usual, it was Saturday and she needed to watch where she was going through the horde of shoppers. She reached the double-fronted building and glanced through the window of the shop in case John was unloading any donations from his parishioners. The shop was not crowded; there was no sign of John but a grey-haired woman stood out from the customers. She wore black trousers and a blue blouse topped by a dog collar. Caroline hesitated, and then opened the door and went in.

There was a little pause while a transaction took place and a customer left. The woman looked up and smiled her willingness to help.

Caroline said, 'You must be the new curate at Tregeagle? I thought I'd say hello.' She stood there awkwardly, wondering what else to say.

The woman held out a very slender hand. 'How nice. I'm Margaret Pemberton, known as Maggie, and yes, I am the new curate.' Her smile grew into a grin. 'Hello!'

'Caroline McEvoy. I'm staying with my sister-in-law at Treleg.' Caroline felt a sudden thankfulness that she could still call Laura her sister-in-law.

Margaret Pemberton shook hands with renewed vigour. 'John was telling me about you. You both help next door I believe?' Caroline nodded. 'He's rather good at getting volunteers, isn't he? Nobody told me that my job description included serving in a shop but apparently if it's not actually in the description as such, then it jolly well should be!'

They both laughed together. Caroline stopped feeling cautious, and knew instantly that she liked this woman and that she would be a good right hand for John. And that was important.

She said, 'Actually I can't raise John on the telephone and wondered whether he might be around here. I haven't been to the centre for two weeks now and could do a day – two or three I expect – next week.'

'You will definitely be popular. They're very short-handed.' Margaret came from behind the counter. 'As a matter of fact, I was just going through to check that the soup is heating. John is supposed to be in charge this morning but he starts talking to some of the men and forgets about the lunch or teas or whatever.' She led the way outside. 'I expect you know that about him anyway. I've only actually been working with him for a couple of weeks!'

Caroline said nothing and followed her into Wayward House and down the long passageway. Sure enough an enormous saucepan was on the cooker and something was bubbling much too noisily inside it. Margaret grabbed a wooden spoon and began stirring and adjusting the heat at the same time.

Caroline said, 'I see what you mean. Is it ruined? Let me.' She took the spoon and carefully explored the base of the pan. 'Slightly caught,' she commented grimly. 'Honestly, you'd think he could keep an eye on a boiling pot now and then, wouldn't you?'

She glanced at Margaret and saw that she was trying not to laugh. She smiled herself and shook her head. 'Sorry. I gather you two are running the show between you so I shouldn't criticize!' She kept stirring as she pulled the trolley towards her and reached for soup bowls. 'You carry on – may I call you Maggie?'

'You certainly may. And thanks. When we close for lunch I'll pop back in and give you a hand with washing up.' She paused on her way back out. 'John always calls you Caro. Would that be all right?'

'Of course.'

Margaret went back down the passage and paused by the door of the communal room before going out of the front door again. Three seconds later a very contrite-looking John Canniston arrived in the kitchen.

'Caro, it's so lovely to see you – when did you get back?'

Caroline looked up momentarily from the soup. He looked the same and yet not the same. Her heart – or

343

where it should be – made itself known. Her voice held a slight tremor. 'A week ago tomorrow.' She studied the surface of the soup which was no longer bubbling and smelled . . . all right. She said, 'Another five minutes and this would have had to go down the sink. It's happened before, hasn't it? Maggie was expecting exactly what we found when we got here.' She had to toughen her voice to get rid of the tremor but hadn't meant to sound like a carping headmistress.

He practically hung his head. 'Yes. But not all of it had to be thrown away. Maggie skimmed off at least two or three pints. And we weren't overcrowded anyway . . . I'm sorry, Caro. There's a new chap and he started talking and I didn't want to cut him short and . . .' He lifted his head. 'Oh Caro. I can't believe you're here again. I thought perhaps something awful had happened and you'd gone straight back to Cheltenham and work and . . . oh my love.'

He removed the spoon from her hand, laid it carefully on an empty plate and took her into his arms. Her heart finally gave up and melted and she put her own arms around his waist and felt too many bones.

'Are you eating properly?' she whispered into his ear. 'Wayward House isn't really your brief, John. You could be writing your sermon and looking out on the estuary and—'

'I love you, Caro. I know what you said about having children and I've taken the time to think about it very carefully. But it makes no difference because we have simply *got* to seize the moment, my love. It's our moment and it would be so bloody ungrateful to turn it away.'

She pressed her forehead into his shoulder. 'How would I fit into – into – your life, John? I'm involved in buying and selling in a commercial world, my dear.'

He tried to lean back to see her face but she dared not look up at him. He said, 'Darling girl. You work with people and I work with people. I find it easy to love them and you don't. But you don't let soup burn and I do. We really are perfectly matched!'

She snuffled a small laugh and reached blindly for the

wooden spoon again, and he released her and dried her eyes for her while she stirred. She laughed again. 'Isn't it silly – the few days we were away I was so happy . . . so happy just knowing that you loved me and I loved you. And then . . . you telephoned Jenna at some point, did she tell you about finding Alice's grave on the Somerset Levels?'

'She telephoned me, actually. I was on my way home from the conference. She was so enthusiastic about it all. And I thought you were all on your way to Gloucestershire to follow through with Geoff's childhood and Tilly's marriage to Alice's Gilbert.'

'Laura wanted to come home. And you were dealing with that end. Thank you for that, John.' She switched off the hob and glanced at him. 'Should we – or maybe just me – go back to that time? There's something about my birth that doesn't quite add up.' She smiled. 'I don't mean that I was born in 1946 and not 1947 as I was always told! It's Tilly. My mother. If she and Gilbert had an affair and she became pregnant, why didn't they marry immediately? Why wait until I was almost two years old? It's not like my ma. She was fearless. Knowing her, she probably thought she was having me for Alice or something equally quixotic!'

John shrugged and poured the soup into a tureen on the trolley. 'Let's serve this and wash up. Denise is coming in to do the teas so we'll be able to go back and tell Laura and Jenna that we're going to be married. The future is what matters now, Caro.'

'Yes,' she said. Then again, 'Yes! You're right!' She followed him into the big communal room and was delighted when Shanks called out, 'The cucumber lady! Nice to see you again!'

She smiled as she served the soup. She was happy; she had never been happy like this before. It had never occurred to her that she might make a very good clerical wife. It wasn't quite such a crazy idea after all . . .

Denise appeared at three o'clock and John went next door to ask Margaret Pemberton whether she would drive his car back to the rectory, then they both hurried up to the car park. Sure enough, after two and a half hours, the traffic warden was showing a great interest in Laura's car.

She started to run towards him, stumbled and would have fallen if John hadn't clutched her arm. He held her against him as if she were drunk, his jacket open to show his dog collar. 'Steady on, darling. Sometimes you forget your foot isn't really your foot!' He looked up smilingly. 'Has my wife forgotten her disabled parking card again, officer?'

Caroline looked at him, wide-eyed and speechless. John swept on. 'My fault. We've been working at Wayward House,' he explained. 'Always takes longer than it should.'

'Oh well. In that case . . .' The warden looked from John's collar to Caroline's foot, moving aside with a smile while Caroline unlocked the driver's door. John grabbed her again and almost carried her around to the passenger side. He opened up and settled her in with exaggerated care then went round to the driver's side and got in. 'Thank you, officer,' he called through the window as he started the car and used far too much accelerator to edge out of the park. Caroline held on to the glove compartment, watching pop-eyed until they were halfway down Market Jew Street, and then collapsed back into her seat and put a hand over her mouth to stop herself laughing.

'You lied. You should be defrocked,' she crowed.

John was shocked at himself. 'Why did I do that? There was no need. We could have paid up and borne it! It just seemed so . . . right. As if we'd come in a full circle!'

'Your wife!' she said as they swung across the roundabout and took the road to St Buryan. 'You said I was your wife!'

'That was merely anticipating the fact,' he said on much firmer ground.

'And you said I had a prosthetic foot!'

'I said nothing of the sort. I sort of implied something was wrong with your foot!'

She said with a touch of admiration, 'You did it so much better than I did.'

They were passing a reservoir and there was a lay-by. He pulled into it.

'D'you know, Caro. I think it was another way of telling you how much I love you. Does that make sense? I wanted to rescue you – be your champion—'

'Oh John . . .'

They stared across the enormous expanse of water, metallic-grey beneath the November sky. And then they started to laugh.

Thirty

Jenna greeted them with a kind of fond exasperation.

'I suppose you didn't hear me when I shouted good luck down the stairs.' She rolled her eyes at John. 'She called to me that she was going to do some shopping. As if I didn't know!'

They both laughed as if it were a huge joke, then they took it in turns to hug her, and still laughing they collapsed into chairs and started to tell her some story about only just avoiding a parking ticket.

Her mother gasped, 'I put a ticket on Laura's car for an hour and of course it had gone over that and the warden was wandering round looking at it as if he expected it to blow up. And do you know what John said?'

The story fell on stony ground; the point was lost not only because Jenna knew nothing of her mother's fictional prosthetic, but also because she needed to tell them about Laura and Charles.

'Yes, extremely funny,' she said. 'But I have to mention that Laura has telephoned from Penzance, where she is drying out in Charles's flat.'

'Drying out?' Caroline stopped giggling foolishly. 'You mean, she actually . . . No, she wouldn't do that.'

John said, 'Do what?'

Jenna said almost brutally, 'Drown herself. Just like you thought I was doing last month. Remember?'

John stammered, 'Yes. But Laura? I know she was terribly depressed, imagining her husband had shut her out of his family and . . . so on. But surely not to the extent of wanting to drown herself?'

'That's the irony of it. She'd taken off her shoes and socks and jacket and thought the sea was about knee-deep, stepped into it and disappeared. Charles thought that she was going to drown and he went in after her. He didn't have time to take off his jacket and boots – anyway he can't swim, so Laura had to rescue him, instead of the other way round. I gather they're both fairly damp. Not only that but Charles is looking after someone from Wayward House – letting him stay a few nights and trying to feed him up – and *he* thinks it's the biggest joke in the world.' She smiled at their faces. 'If we rate jokes from one to ten I reckon theirs is one and three-quarters and yours is a rather poor four or five!'

Caroline said, stunned, 'When is she coming home?'

'That's it. Not tonight it seems.' Jenna pursed her lips with Victorian disapproval. 'Apparently the chap from Wayward House is going back tonight and Charles is doing a sleep-over there. Laura is going to stay in his flat and listen to all the tapes this chap has made and Charles has collated. She's got this thing about Billy Boy.' She abandoned her significant voice. 'I didn't quite get it all but this chap is her connection with Billy. I think she said his name was Bill too . . . anyway, she wants to immerse herself in what Charles has been doing.' She glanced at John. 'I think you're right and she feels excluded in some way from what happened back there in the Cotswolds and on those benighted Levels. She went to Penburra to . . . maybe to contact Billy. Who knows?' She made an apologetic face at John. 'We can't talk about it too much in case it goes right away but last weekend was very special, John.' She shrugged. 'She wants some of it. That's all.'

Quite suddenly he put an arm around her shoulders and hugged her to him.

'That's as far as you can get to talking about spirituality, Jenna. But that's OK. It's far enough.' He released her. 'I gather you're OK with us too?' He touched Caroline's shoulder gently. 'When I asked her, your mother assured me you're not going to forbid the banns or do anything even slightly disapproving.'

Jenna looked almost sheepish. 'If this is confession time . . . I think I might have been plain and simply jealous.' She waited while her mother protested, then said, 'Our journey was so necessary last weekend . . . maybe we're still on it, I'm not sure. It kind of released us—'

'Opened doors,' John said, nodding.

'I want to go into the future now, whatever happens,' Jenna went on. 'I want you to do the same, Mum. And perhaps Laura and Charles Cledra . . . I'm not sure.'

'That's the second time you've not been sure.' Caroline was smiling, very bright-eyed. She sat down rather abruptly. 'I can't believe you're going back to London tomorrow. Let me come with you, Jen. Just for a few days until you start work again.'

'It's a tempting offer, I have to say. But no. Thanks, Mum, we've been together now since it happened. Five months almost. There will be bits of Jeremy in the flat. I need to . . . deal with them on my own.' She did not wait for a reply. 'Nobody has put the kettle on – I suppose I'll have to do it myself. What do you want, tea or coffee?'

Laura had long ago got used to being in a house by herself. Perhaps it was having so much company over the past few months, but now the prospect of living in Widdowe's Cottage on her own was frightening. Geoff would not be there any longer; the potting shed would no longer be filled with his presence. She had worked hard on the building itself and this winter had intended to use any fine weather to go on with the work of pointing around the granite blocks of the cottage walls. The cottage had belonged to Geoff's family and therefore to Geoff – that was why she had kept it in such good repair. But Geoff . . . had gone. Inexplicably, imperceptibly, he had left her during the last few weeks. That time she had followed Jenna's directions and gone to Tregeagle to see where Billy

Boy's secret memorial had been hidden . . . and then returned to hear that Geoff had not been Tilly's son at all . . . he had been the illegitimate child of Alice . . . unknown Alice . . . that was when Geoff had started to slip away.

And now it seemed John Canniston, who was the grandson of the Reverend Carridon so beloved by Tilly, had found out that Tilly had married Gilbert Tedenford and had Caroline. It was neat; it was pat; it was totally reassuring for Caroline and Jenna. They were all interlocked almost incestuously. She wondered what that felt like.

After Charles and Bill Legge had left the flat she took time to wander around it, looking through windows, picking up books and ornaments and examining them thoroughly. Charles had shown her around cursorily, 'Here's the bathroom and the laundry room – you'll need both, probably. Help yourself to anything in the kitchen . . . fridge, larder, freezer and so on. Clean sheets for Bill's bed. My pyjamas will be huge on you but there are three pairs in the airing cupboard.'

'Charles, it's all marvellous. Just like you. Organized. And so clean.' She looked at him solemnly. 'Actually I don't think we could live together because I'm not organized in quite this way. I mean, I've got herbs drying and bunches of onions—'

'I love your kitchen. But if that's just an excuse . . . well, we need not live in the same dwelling. I suppose. Though I had been looking forward to it.'

'A bit premature?'

He gnawed the lining of his cheek. 'Perhaps. But maybe not. We don't know how much future there is really, do we?'

'Oh Charles . . .'

He said hastily, 'We'll keep our separate abodes.' He stood in the middle of his immaculate kitchen; he was no longer dripping seawater but his clothes hung heavily on him and he looked bereft. She felt her heart go out to him; she wanted to look after him.

He said, 'We'll see, shall we? But we'll see each other

351

every day, won't we? We could make a sort of programme – an agenda. A walk and a meal together each day as a sort of foundation . . .' He stopped because she was laughing.

'It's all right,' Laura spluttered. 'Just that Caro encouraged me into making a timetable of – of various activities we could engage in – trying to make some kind of pattern for dear Jenna.' She stopped laughing and gave him a wonderful smile. 'I love timetables and planning things. We're going to get on so well, Charles.'

He smiled back. Then said, 'Laura, if you're going to put your gear through the washing machine and tumble dryer, could mine go in with it?'

He looked surprised when she laughed again and then hugged him.

'It will be my pleasure.'

She waited until they had gone because she wanted to have a bath first of all. Now, warm and cosy in Charles's pyjamas, the washing machine humming in the background, the washing-up from their meal done and the clean crockery put away, she took the time to wander around the flat and wonder about his neighbours below before she settled down to listen to what she now called 'the Cledra tapes'.

The flat was one of four in a two-storey mansion which had belonged to the Bolitho family. It was set slightly askew in a garden full of shrubs and gravelled walkways. Paper-dry hydrangeas still holding their blue and pink colour made arbours among the escallonia and hebes. Because he was on the top floor Charles could see Newlyn; invisible but probably well known, Mousehole was around the corner and then Lamorna. She stood there for some time trying to see the promenade and the clustered masts of the fishing boats as Charles must see them. He had bought this place when he had started his own personal reconstruction. She thought wryly that she had gone back; he had gone forward. She wondered whether he was strong enough to take her with him. Time would tell. Meanwhile she did not mind being here on her own. There were other people below her and alongside. She had never needed people before; things were different now.

The washing machine had stopped humming and she went into the laundry room and transferred some of the load into the dryer. Charles's jacket and heavy pullover she put on hangers above a radiator. Then, at last, she started playing the Cledra tapes.

Two hours later, she surfaced, pressed the rewind button and sat back, gazing through the window at the view and not seeing it. Charles had made a commentary around Bill Legge's songs and stories; where he had heard them, who had been telling them, his own theories about their sources. On their own they would have been an interesting collection; with Charles's investigative approach they were fascinating, and bore out so many of the conclusions the three women had come to on their 'pilgrimage'. Billy Boy's story was somehow linked with the terrible mine disaster of 1918 as well as the attack on Sir Geoffrey. In one version he had mounted a white horse and ridden into the sea and could still be seen occasionally, riding on the crests of waves. In another his own father had risen from the seabed and held out his arms and Billy Boy had gone into them. Wayward House inmates had described his escape as 'flying'. It seemed he had floored the old matron, then climbed through a window and flown over the rooftops down into the courtyard where his sister was waiting for him. In all the versions he was not really dead at all; he appeared all over the place. On railway journeys between Penzance and Plymouth he could be seen clearing up the mess in the buffet car. He was very good at directing travellers. 'Change at Truro for the Falmouth line,' he would say. 'Make your way to the front of the coach at Redruth. Liskeard for Looe. Par for Newquay. Plymouth for Gunnislake.'

Then there was the Romany tradition. They had kept the songs. 'Last night I slept in a goose-feather bed', 'The milkman saw the pretty maid', 'The caravan has windows too and a chimney of tin where the smoke comes through'.

And what amounted to Billy Boy's signature tune: 'Where have you been all the day?'

Their one story echoed the train travellers'. It was that Billy Boy lurked around the Somerset Levels just after the big flood. He carried a rake and had been seen trying to clear some of the weed from the drainage ditches. Charles's dry comment here was, 'There is no foundation for this particular sighting. It is not on the route taken by the Romanies of that time.'

Laura put the tape back in its box and sat for some time letting her thoughts wash in and out of her head. Then she picked up the telephone and dialled Wayward House.

'Charles, it's me. Laura.'

'Laura. My dearest. Has anything happened – are you all right?'

'Yes, I am. Are you?'

'I was in bed, darling.'

'Bed?' She glanced at the clock. It was midnight. She was full of apologies.

He said, 'Dear, dear girl. As long as you are all right, I'm delighted to hear your voice. Is there a reason – there doesn't have to be—'

'Yes there is. That last bit of the tape. You say there's no foundation for the story of Billy being sighted on the Somerset Levels. But he is there, Charles. Jenna saw him. We were lost and he came and told Jenna the way we had to go and where Alice was buried.'

He was silent for some time then he said, 'How do you know that, my love? How did Jenna know that?'

'She did. It's one of those things that you either know or you don't know. And she knew. And we've always been close so I know she is right. Oh Charles.'

He said, 'Has the tape helped at all?'

'I don't know.' She discovered she was chewing her own cheek. She said, 'Listen, Charles. How about if we lived at Widdowe's Cottage in the summer and came here for the winter? Together.'

She could hear him smiling; it was impossible but it was so.

He said, 'That would be wonderful Laura. Oh I do love you. But you must get some sleep, sweetheart. I'll be with you in time for breakfast, I promise.'

Jenna went to bed early, not only because she had a long journey tomorrow but because, as she said, 'I never liked gooseberries. Green and hairy and sour.'

After a bath and shampoo she dried her hair, then sat by the dark window in one of Laura's thick dressing-gowns and stared down the garden to where she knew the sea was sighing and heaving its shoulders as it came close to the cliff. It would be high tide at midnight, and as it began the six-hour ebb she would sleep. That gave her two hours to write up what had happened in five months. Last Christmas she had been given a desk diary; a page for each day. She got it out now and opened it anywhere. The two pages were both empty. She flipped through until she found something. Friday, 19 February. It had been foggy that day, apparently. She had met Jeremy for lunch: fish soup and rolls; he had eaten four. She read it again and again. Fog, fish and four rolls. Nothing about being happy . . . that was taken for granted. She scooped up the pages and saw similar entries . . . they had gone to Ham Common on a Sunday in March. The 14th: it had been a glorious day. Then on the 23rd they had both had a day off and went to Richmond. Another warm and sunny day . . . March was good. She had forgotten. Spring had come early. And then had died.

The 24th of May of course had been wet, but they had skidded on an oil patch.

She closed the book quickly and sat with the palm of her hand on the cover, breathing fast. Then she swallowed and opened up again. August. September. October. Nothing. She turned to 1 November and wrote carefully, 'We returned from our journey last night.' Then she closed the book again, stared out of the window and let the tears pour unheeded down her face.

Caroline and John spent a long time clearing up the dishes, tidying the kitchen. John said, 'We're playing at house, Caro. Aren't we?'

'Yes.' She smiled at him. 'Will you stay the night? I'm not sure how you feel about it, but if principles are at stake you can sleep in Laura's room. She won't mind.'

'I couldn't do that, my love. Laura's room is Laura's room. I'll take her car, though – don't fancy walking to Tregeagle.' He smiled back at her. 'D'you realize it's 6 November, and everyone's having bonfire parties?'

She was surprised and disappointed. 'We could have had one in the garden and baked some potatoes.'

'We'll do it next year. There's a sort of hole in the rocks, I think it's a mine adit. It's safe – been blocked for years now. But it would be the ideal place for a bonfire.'

They wandered into the parlour talking about other bonfire nights. She picked up her knitting and settled herself in her chair. He watched her as he stood by the door, one hand on the jamb, the other in his jacket pocket. She was talking about Tilly; Tilly had made pasties for bonfire nights, proper Cornish pasties with lots of swede and onion. 'Geoff and Laura would arrive with a couple of kids from the school . . . the bonfire would be ready, of course. We would have worked on it for days before. Tilly would buy loads of sparklers, they were her favourites. Geoff and Laura would bring Catherine wheels and Roman candles and we'd plan it all out together.' She stopped knitting and looked up at John. 'The schoolchildren all thought that Geoff was my father. I knew he wasn't, of course. But Laura never seemed to mind. I don't think he realized . . .'

John said, 'Teachers – good ones – have hundreds of children in their time. Did you ever read *Goodbye, Mr Chips*? Right at the end he remembers all the boys he has ever taught and knows that children belong to everyone who loves them. That's what the story of Billy Quince teaches us, too.'

'Are you reassuring me again, John?' She went back to her knitting, smiling reminiscently. 'You're right, of course. Geoff had a family. But Laura . . .'

'Laura identified with Tilly, perhaps?'

She looked up. 'What do you mean?'

He pushed himself upright and put his other hand in his other pocket. 'Nothing specific. Tilly was a long time childless. Perhaps Laura always thought there would be a baby . . . later on.'

She continued to look at him, knitting forgotten. 'Perhaps,' she said.

'Darling, this is wonderful stuff but I think I should go. May I have the keys of Laura's car – d'you think she will mind?'

Caroline said slowly, 'I don't know any more. Laura has changed. We've all changed.'

He nodded, then laughed and said, 'Actually, I still have the keys from earlier. And I'm sure she wouldn't—'

'John, is there something else? You've found out something else, haven't you?'

'What on earth makes you say that – what else could there be?'

She got up and began to move towards him and for an instant he half turned to escape, then realized how ridiculous that was and took his hands from his pockets to embrace her. She dropped her knitting to the floor and put out her own hands. 'Darling, I know you. You had such difficulty hiding the fact that you were the reverend's grandson. You stayed away from us for weeks. I didn't know why – I was very anxious. And now . . . don't you dare disappear again. I don't think I could bear it!' She forced a laugh as she took his hands and swung them back and forth, as if jollying him along.

He pulled her to him and kissed her, and the kiss flowered into something else so that she hung on to his shoulders for support. And then he held her close and whispered into her hair, 'I promise I will stay with you always, Caro. Always.' And he kissed her again.

357

She drew away so that she could see him properly. His dark eyes and hair were . . . gypsy-like. A name came into her head. Rufus. And then was gone.

She whispered, 'Poor Tilly. Poor, poor Tilly.'

He whispered back, 'You know she was happy, my dearest. She was so loved. Bessie and John. Alice and Billy Boy. Jacko. And then your father.' He pushed her hair from her eyes. 'It seems to me she had a great gift. Forgiveness. She was what they term now non-judgemental.'

'Except to herself.' Caroline held him with her look. 'She could not have made a baby with the man who was Alice's man. She could never have lived with that.'

'She did it for Alice, perhaps.'

'John, tell me. Don't make me feel like Laura. Shut out.' Her voice was very steady.

'Laura feels more than shut out. She feels an outsider.'

She leaned further from him and studied him carefully. Then she said, 'Do you love me, John Canniston?'

'You know I do.'

'Then how could I ever be an outsider? Unless . . . unless I felt you were hiding something from me.'

'I think you know it already, Caro. You're . . . what's the word . . . you are prescient. Very prescient. Your dear Tilly – your life-mother – probably never consummated her second marriage. I would think she agreed to marry Gilbert Miller for your sake, my darling. I don't doubt she loved him – and not only for Alice's sake. But she was always in love with her Jacko, wasn't she?'

Caroline said softly, 'She rarely spoke of my father. And often – oh often – of Jacko.'

Then she said, 'Do you know my mother's name?'

'Solange Bertrand. Nothing else. But it's not difficult to fill in the gap.'

'No. I hope she knew that she could trust my father with her baby.'

'It's more than likely.'

'Yes.' She gave a sharp sigh. 'Strange. I feel more of a Quince than ever. And after Jen's experience in Somerset, well, she must be a Quince.' She put up her hands and cupped John's face. 'They were a funny lot down here, weren't they?'

'Pretty marvellous too. And still are. See what I mean, Caro?'

'What?'

'People. They're very easy to love.'

She laughed and wept at the same time.

Thirty-one

It was Sunday. Caroline said, 'They come round so quickly these days.' And Laura replied, 'I like them. We know exactly what we're going to do, and now that Maggie takes evensong John doesn't have to rush off straight after tea.' She began to clear the breakfast things and peered down the garden. 'There's still some snow about. But the road will be clear.'

It had snowed the day before, tiny gritty flakes that refused to settle on level surfaces but had piled up under the cabbages and the kerbstones and had clung to the hedge at the bottom of the garden. Laura had fought her way down to the old schoolhouse with her tape recorder. Etta Tompkins had been there with her husband, who was painting the cloakroom; under the layers of old paint Dennis Tompkins had found the remains of a painted fruit – which just might have been a quince. Etta had telephoned Laura excitedly, and Laura had telephoned the artist who lived there every winter and who had invited them both to tea and a chat. 'Bring a tape recorder,' he had suggested. 'We might need to refer to our conversation later.' He had met Charles twice now. Charles had fired him with enthusiasm for the early days before the school was closed and he had come up with all kinds of thoughts and ideas. But this was the first 'hard evidence' of the Quinces attending the school.

Caroline had not joined them. 'I don't want to know any more,' she said. 'After all, I'm nothing to do with the

360

Quince family.' She hadn't sounded regretful. In fact she was probably thankful not to have to turn out in the blowing snow.

So Laura had gone alone, and though nothing had come of it, it was possible that the little orange-yellow blob on the wall of the cloakroom was a quince. Roland, the artist, had sorted all the papers from that time and it seemed that Sir Geoffrey Bassett had donated fifty wax crayons at the beginning of 1913. The quince, if that was what it was, was definitely waxy. Charles would be delighted. When he came to lunch she would tell him about it, play the tape and they would make notes for his 'Quince reconstruction'. She had smiled at the thought. Perhaps, before the early darkness fell, they would walk over to the old schoolhouse and he could chat to Roland and ask his permission to take a photo of the quince. Her smile widened. All the years she had lived here alone and never really got to know anyone. And now, because of Charles, things were opening and widening all the time.

She would never forget that first breakfast she and Charles had eaten together on 7 November, when, after telling her about his night at Wayward House, he had suddenly said, out of the blue, 'Your husband actually gave you such a gift, Laura.' He had paused, gathering himself, looking at his toast and leaving it on his plate for the moment. 'John thinks that it's best if Caro and Jenna don't know about it, but I explained to him that you deserved to know.' And then he had told her about Solange and her baby. And suddenly she had understood why Geoff had never spoken of his parentage, why he had preferred to consign the past to the past. She had thought that this was 'the gift'. But then Charles had covered her hand with his and added, 'It makes you the last member of the Quince family, my love.'

It hadn't mattered. And yet it had. Where Caroline and Jenna were concerned, it freed her. Caroline was still her sister-in-law and Jenna was still her niece, but she herself, Laura Miller, was now no more of an outsider than they were.

She said now, 'Come on, Caro. Stop dreaming, otherwise we'll be late.'

Caroline looked up and smiled blindly. 'I can't help it. You know what it's like to be in love, but it's all strange to me.' She got up and fetched the vegetable basket. 'And now . . . this stuff with Jen. I'm really glad Maggie opted out of lunch today, Laura. I can read Jen's letter to Charles and John.'

'Not all of it!' Laura laughed and passed the vegetable knife over. Suddenly she remembered the first time she and Geoff had met . . . in the reception class at Cotswold Primary. She had almost gasped. And his professional expression of gratitude for her help had slipped; he had looked uncertain for a moment, and then he had smiled a genuine welcome. It had been wonderful – and the same feelings were now wonderful for Caroline. But Laura was so content with what she and Charles had found together that she was glad that time was over.

They got the car out between them, Laura opening and closing the garage doors, Caroline reversing confidently on to the road. Penburra Church was no match for Tregeagle but it had central heating and chairs rather than pews, and Etta was there in her mortar board, and a doughty woman called Queenie Maybrick was fussing up at the altar, light-ing candles and whipping a duster over the sconces. They took their places and bowed their heads, and when they raised them John was emerging from the vestry saying good morning and shaking hands all round, with his eyes on Caroline the whole time. Laura whispered, 'If he keeps this up he's going to go base over apex one of these days!' And Caroline just managed to stifle her giggles.

They did not linger after the service; they'd left a leg of New Zealand lamb in a low oven and there were potatoes to roast and mint sauce to remove from the freezer. Everything was ready by one o'clock when Charles and John arrived together; this was the third time they had come for Sunday lunch – twice before they'd come with

Margaret Pemberton, the curate – so the pattern was well established. Charles picked John up and they also brought wine and cheese – and last time a bowl of fruit. This time it was chocolates. There were exclamations all round. 'You must let me do lunch next Sunday. Boxing Day!' Charles discovered, looking at his neatly kept pocket diary. 'Will Jenna be here?'

Caroline fetched Jenna's letter and read most of it aloud. She left out the opening which was 'Dearest elderly virgins – well, for many a long year'. Also the conclusion, 'Sleep soundly and chastely. At least until next spring.'

'She can't make it for Christmas.' Caroline looked up, obviously not too disappointed. 'The strangest thing has happened. When I telephoned old Mr Beddoes to tell him that I could no longer do any work for the auctioneers, he mentioned that his son was doing an extended place-ment with an insurance firm in London – something to do with negotiating. Naturally I imagined he was still at university so I gave him Jenna's telephone number in case he needed a contact at any time – I never thought for a moment that he would use it, of course. But he did. And Jenna suggested he should have a day at her office . . . sort of observing.' She went back to the letter and read on.

'Old man Beddoes – William to you, Mum – has asked me to have Christmas week with the family in Stroud. So Alan and I will drive down on Christmas Eve. We'll probably go to Childswickham Church on Christmas Day – I quite fancy that. We'll certainly go and look at the cottage. Maybe Cooper's wood yard too. But then I wondered whether we could come to you for the millennium fireworks. Alan would like to go to St Ives, actually. Could you manage it? Please be honest about it. If it's too much for Widdowe's Cottage we could probably book a hotel in Penzance and get together for the evening.'

Caroline looked up again and beamed at the two men; Laura had read the letter the day before. John beamed back. 'Would this – Alan – prefer to sleep at the rectory? I'd be delighted.'

'I haven't got the faintest.' Caroline turned her beaming smile on Laura. 'She goes on to warn us that there's no romance in the air and we are not to cook anything up otherwise she won't be able to come. Alan is younger than her—' She glanced at the letter, flipped over a page and read aloud:

'He's practically a schoolboy so there's nothing between us. I boss him about terribly. He actually said to me the other day that he was sorry for Jeremy! I thought for a second I might cry or shout at him or even hit him. I didn't do anything. He's a kid and doesn't know what he's saying. But he's a whizz on the computer and in case you still care, Mum – and you should do with all those shares still in the company – he'll do Beddoes no end of good. I'm looking forward to seeing the family mansion in Stroud. Sounds like something out of Dickens.'

She folded the pages carefully and put them in the envelope. 'What do you think?' she asked.

Laura expected Charles to ask 'About what?' Instead he had a very quick and thoughtful chew and then said, 'I think that by the time Jenna has educated this young man, he will be in love with her, if he's not already, and there's a likelihood that she will be in love with him.'

John said, 'It's too soon. But it could happen. It would be . . . different, of course.' He poured red wine into the tall glasses and picked up the carving knife and fork. 'Don't look too far ahead, Caro. She has a – a companion with whom she feels easy. Apparently. For the moment that is sufficient, don't you agree?'

They all agreed. And while John carved and Caroline

364

brought hot plates to the table, they began to plan for the millennium eve.

Laura speared roast potatoes into a vegetable dish and let the general bonhomie seep into her soul. At one time she had wondered whether Charles was replacing Geoff; now she knew that Charles had given Geoff back to her.

Caroline passed the sauce, made from mint so carefully picked and frozen back in the summer, and thought of her life-mother – John had given Tilly that wonderful name – and the physical journey she had made almost eighty years ago. And then of the journey, much less physical, that she and Laura and Jenna had made since last summer.

Charles said suddenly, 'It crossed my mind that we might make a trip to Tedenford in the New Year. It's National Trust now, and apparently the grounds are amazing.'

Caroline said, 'I'd love that. Perhaps Jenna would come too. Maybe Alan Beddoes . . . if he was interested.'

John said, 'He had better be. Otherwise I rather think Jenna might succumb to temptation and actually hit him!'

They laughed together, as they so often did, then Laura told Charles about Roland and about Dennis Tompkins and his discovery of the crayoned quince on the wall of the schoolhouse.

Caroline stood up to pour more gravy and exclaimed, 'It's snowing again! Oh look, everyone. It's snowing on the sea!'

They crowded to the kitchen window and stared down the garden at the sea, grey in the winter afternoon. Then without a word they filed out into the garden and stood for a few moments letting the snow settle in the folds of their clothes.

They had no idea why they did it.

MPG 4